THE COMING CHAOS

THE ELDER STONES SAGA BOOK 4

D.K. HOLMBERG

ASH
PUBLISHING

HAERN

As Haern struggled to make out where he was, he couldn't help but stare into the distance, his eyes losing focus, straining to enhance his eyesight. Every so often, he thought he caught sight of movement, but he wasn't entirely certain what he was seeing. It was difficult to determine whether there actually was anything out on the road with them, especially with the darkness and the shadows swirling everywhere.

"What is it?" Elise asked.

Haern glanced over at the younger woman. In the days since they had escaped the temple, he and Elise had grown closer. She had come with him because he offered an element of protection, and because he had vowed to ensure their safety as they headed north to Asador, but in that time, something more seemed to be developing between the two of them.

Partly it was because she was like no one he had ever met. She was strong—she had to be strong considering everything she'd been through—but there was something very caring about her as well. Her eyes were deep blue, nothing like the green eyes of people from Elaeavn. Her brown hair hung in a braid, but each night, she paused to comb it out before braiding it once more. He turned away, flushing at the thought.

"I don't know what's out there. I think I See something, but…"

She took his hand. Hers was smooth and small whereas his was callused and the place where the metal had punctured his hand still rough. The skin had healed, absorbing whatever the Forgers had done to him, trapping their metal beneath his skin the same way Lucy had metal trapped beneath hers. When Elise squeezed his hand, he felt that metal there and couldn't help but wonder whether he would find a way to remove it, or if he would always suffer from the effect.

"If there's something out there, you can go investigate."

"I don't like leaving all of you," he said, glancing back to the rest of the women. They weren't all women. Some of them were girls, and many of them were incredibly young. None had wanted to return home, which had surprised Haern. Shouldn't they want to return to their families? After everything they had suffered through, he was surprised they had chosen instead to travel with him.

"You're not leaving us." She paused, biting her lip. "Are you?"

Haern shook his head, smiling at her. "You know that I won't."

"Most of the time," she said.

Haern glanced back at the collection of women. There was a small fire crackling, giving off light against the darkness, bright enough that he worried others might be drawn to it. Maybe that was why there was movement out in the night.

They needed the comfort of the fire, though. Without it, he had recognized the growing uncertainty from all the women, and he sensed their desire for normalcy, whatever that might be.

"You should go," she said. "If there is something out there, we're going to want to know, and seeing as how you might be the only one who can do anything about it, we need you to go."

"You're getting more skilled with the sword," he said, glancing down at her waist and the sword she now carried. It was a short weapon, barely longer than his forearm, but it was easier for her to manipulate. It was the right length of blade for someone like Elise, and though it wasn't made of lorcith—they were too far from Elaeavn for him to have access to that metal—it was quality steel. The the design of the blade wasn't nearly as efficient as it would be had his father been the one to forge it, but it was still a nice blade. Sharp, too.

"I'm not as talented as Jayna," she said.

Haern glanced over to where Jayna sat near the fire. She was tall, nearly as tall as him, and had dark skin and dark hair. There was something about Jayna he suspected made her faster. Maybe it was a gift similar to his Great Watcher–given abilities, though she never spoke of it. It wasn't necessary for him to push when it came to it, either, so he didn't.

"I don't know how much longer I will be as talented as

Jayna," Haern said, chuckling. "She picks things up incredibly quickly."

"She has a good mind for it," Elise agreed.

"It's more than that."

"Probably, but you won't ever have to worry about someone like her."

Haern turned to Elise, frowning.

Elise smiled at him. There was something disarming about the way she smiled, and he found himself smiling back. "You don't need to worry about someone like her because you can fly."

"I'm pretty sure I've shown you that it's not flying."

"It might as well be."

He turned and looked out into the distance, staring into the darkness. Every so often there came some swirling of movement, enough that he knew he needed to investigate, even if it meant leaving Elise and the others here.

"I won't be gone long."

She nodded, backing toward the fire, leaving him.

As he often did, he wished he could bring Elise with him. If he were stronger, maybe he could. Then again, it wasn't so much that he lacked strength with lorcith—not anymore. It was more a matter of worrying for her safety if he encountered something.

Ever since the Forgers had pierced his hands with their strange metal bars designed to confine him, his connection to the metal—and others like it—had intensified. It had changed him, much the way the metal that had been implanted in Lucy had changed her.

Eventually he would need to return to Elaeavn, if only

so he could begin to better understand the nature of the change. For now, he was an escort, providing whatever protection he could. With his newfound connection to the metal, he was able to offer far more protection than he ever had been able to before. Now he actually felt useful.

Haern reached into his pocket, pulling out a handful of lorcith coins. He *pushed* one forward and used that to help him shoot into the night, disappearing into the air and the darkness. Wind whistled around him, and he hung suspended, looking around as he often did, searching for signs of any movement. He could hold himself in a position like this for nearly an hour, and the more he did it, the easier it became. Eventually, he suspected he would be able to remain suspended in the air for as long as he wanted. That was the goal, anyway. The more he worked with it, the more he practiced, the better equipped he was to use this ability if it became necessary.

He saw nothing.

That wasn't true. In the distance, the campfire glowed with a soft light. A dozen or so women sat around it, all of them huddled close. It wasn't so much for warmth—the night wasn't all that cool—but more for the comfort of being near the others. Most of the women he'd rescued had experienced something terrible, and had Haern not come along, they would have been used in far worse ways than he could imagine.

Thankfully there were some like Elise and Jayna, women who were coming out of their shells, finding some confidence—and leadership.

They would need that, as eventually Haern would have to leave them and return to Elaeavn. His search wasn't over. He might have found where his father had been held captive, but he still wasn't done with the Forgers. He didn't know what it would take for him to be done—only that he was determined to see them finished.

There was nothing else moving against the night.

He dropped the coin, sending it across the ground, and then *pushed* off on it, using that connection to allow him to travel farther away from the campsite. Each time he *pushed*, he traveled farther, moving from place to place, *pushing* and *pulling* on the lorcith coins in order to fly. And he didn't know what else to call it other than flying. In that regard, Elise was probably right. It didn't feel like anything else.

The farther he got, the more he worried he wouldn't be able to find them again, and yet there remained the steady connection to lorcith, the calling of the metal that seemed to beckon him. Part of that stemmed from the fact he had left a knife with the women, something of his own he had forged for him to track.

He followed the strange sense. The longer he followed, the more certain he became that there was something out there, but what was it?

Nothing moved that he could track easily.

Haern decided to make a circle, spiraling outward from where the women were camped. If he could focus on that, he thought he could trace his way around, eventually coming back toward where he had seen something.

It took a combination of *pushing* and *pulling*, something that had become almost second nature to him. It no longer required as much focus as it once had, and the longer he did it, the easier it became for him to add additional coins to the mixture. The more coins he used, the easier it was for him to sail faster. He had to split his focus, to divert his attention between each item of lorcith, but doing so had become easier the longer he attempted it.

At times like this, he had begun to think he might actually learn how his father had managed to use the power he had all these years. Perhaps he too could be effective with metal.

As he was *pushing*, he felt lorcith.

It was coming at him.

Great Watcher!

Haern *pushed*, flipping in the air as he shot higher and higher, and redirected himself, using a combination of coins in order to do so, twisting as he went, focusing on where the lorcith had come from.

He *pulled* on that connection, drawing whatever it was toward him, before realizing his mistake.

It was a weapon.

It was nothing like he'd ever experienced before. A solid sphere with spikes of lorcith came streaking toward him.

How was he able to determine that?

Was it only his eyesight, or was it his attention to lorcith? These days, Haern was unable to tell which of his senses he used. They tended to mingle, his connection to lorcith mixing with his Great Watcher–given ability of Sight. The combination made it so that lorcith not only had a pull on him, an attachment he was able to draw upon, but it also practically seemed to glow.

Haern *pushed* off.

As he did, the sphere began to change.

It was exploding.

Small points were shooting outward, something like nails.

He *pushed* against those nails, keeping them from hitting him as he focused on the lorcith coin on the ground. Without the practice he'd had over the last few weeks, one of those spikes might have pierced him.

As it was, they missed.

That still didn't explain who had sent the sphere toward him.

Whoever it was knew he was here.

Did they know about the women?

Haern used a combination of the coins, *pushing* and *pulling* as he traveled, streaking toward the camp. He wasn't about to leave them. He was determined to reach them ready for a fight. He unsheathed his sword in the air, holding on to his connection to it, and when he dropped to the ground in the middle of the clearing where they'd camped for the night, he held out the sword, turning in place.

Elise saw him and reached for her sword. Three others jumped to their feet, including Jayna. Of the women who'd been working with him, training with the sword, only Jayna and Elise might be safe in a fight. The others had good intentions, but he didn't know if they'd be useful against a skilled swordsman.

"What was it?" Elise asked.

"A weapon," Haern said. He stared out into the darkness, looking for signs of movement. It couldn't have been chance that he had detected the sense of movement and then the strange lorcith sphere had been shot at him. The timing was far too suspect to be chance.

"What sort of weapon?"

"One that I've never seen before."

"Where was it?"

"In the sky. Coming at me."

"It was *what*?"

He flicked his gaze over to her. "Someone shot a lorcith sphere at me. There was metal implanted within it meant to explode, but I managed to escape."

"And you've never seen anything like it before?"

Haern shook his head, turning his attention back out to the night. His father had made hundreds of things out of lorcith, and Haern had been a part of many of them, but he had never encountered anything like what had been shot at him.

Were it not made entirely of lorcith, he would've thought it was a Forger weapon, but they used different metals.

He squeezed his hand, feeling the creak of the strange metal beneath the skin. It throbbed softly, a dull sort of ache he was always aware of, and more so when he squeezed his hand like this.

No. It couldn't have been the Forgers. This was someone else, but who?

Haern *pushed* off on a coin, hovering in the air, staying above the campfire, but not so high that he couldn't land quickly. He spun in place, looking out for any signs of movement.

What would his father have done?

He knew the answer to that. He was doing what his

father would have done. Rsiran would have wanted to protect others, as he had done all these years, leaving Elaeavn, his home and his people, chasing down the Forgers in order to ensure their safety. And he *had* ensured their safety all this time. Without Rsiran, the Forgers would have posed much more of a threat long ago. As it was, they'd had decades of peace.

Despite everything his father had done and everything his father was, Haern had to be more. That might be the hardest thing for him to fully grasp.

How could he be *more* than his father?

He didn't have any of his father's unique abilities. He had a common talent. Enhanced eyesight was far too ordinary a gift from the Great Watcher, nothing like Sliding in its usefulness. The only thing Haern had that he considered useful was his connection to lorcith, and he'd never viewed it as all that helpful until he had started training with Galen. That training had helped him find a benefit to it that hadn't realized before. Now that he had the Forger implants, his connection to the metal was even different than it had been during his training.

What he needed was daylight.

Even with his enhanced eyesight, he couldn't see all that well out into the darkness. There could be dozens of people out there hiding, and if there were, he wouldn't be able to find them easily.

It was going to be a long night. He wasn't about to move or do anything until he knew the women were safe. With that kind of weapon out there, the possibility of a strange attack, he wasn't going to rest.

A voice called out of the darkness.

Haern lowered himself, dropping down next to Elise. She looked over at him, worry etching the corners of her eyes, and he smiled, trying to appear as reassuring as he could.

"I'll make sure they can't harm anyone here," Haern said.

"That's not what I'm concerned about," she said.

"What is it?"

"It's you," she said.

Haern smiled at her. "You don't have to be concerned about me. I'm fine."

"*Are* you fine? You seem somewhat obsessed with this."

Haern smiled to himself. Wasn't that what his mother had always said about his father? Could he have come so far that he had become the man he had barely known?

"I just want to ensure that we get to Asador safely."

"We will. With you traveling with us, I have faith that we will."

Haern wished he had the same faith, but he had already seen too much. Even in the few weeks since they had left Dreshen, the journey hadn't been completely uneventful. They'd come across a wagon train of merchants, and though the merchants should've posed no threat to them, when they were moving onward, three of them had tried to attack. Haern had left three dead bodies in their way.

Elise had watched him, a hint of sadness in her eyes he hadn't fully understood. It had taken him a few days to grasp why she might have been troubled—it was the fact he had killed on their behalf.

"I see the way you look at things these days," she said.

"How do I look at things?"

"As if there's darkness in everything."

"That's not how I look at it," he said, turning away and staring out into the night.

"You do. And given what we've encountered, I don't think anyone blames you. These women appreciate that you have stayed with us, Haern. They know you have fought for them. Killed for them."

"I have," Haern said.

"But has it been necessary?"

Haern turned to Elise, studying her for a moment. "If I hadn't done that, they would have—"

"Done nothing," she said. "We had the numbers, and we had just as many swords as they did. We might not have as much experience with them as you, but I still think a dozen women armed with swords would have been more than a match for three merchants who decided to cause us trouble. Eventually, you're going to leave us, and when you do, we need to know we can defend ourselves."

"Which is why I continue to work with as many as I can."

"Haern…" She took a step forward, reaching for his hand and squeezing it. As she did, the strange throbbing intensified. Would it ever stop? "I just don't want you to lose yourself in helping us find ourselves."

"I don't think I will."

"I don't want you to have to think about it. I want you to know it won't happen."

Haern smiled at her. "I'm not sure that can be the case."

She sighed. "Is this what it's going to be like for us?"

"What do you mean?"

"When we get to Asador. Is this what we have to look forward to?" Elise turned and looked behind her, her gaze drifting across the collection of women. One hand touched the hilt of the sword she wore. "Are we always going to have to fear for our safety, worrying about how we will protect ourselves against another attack?"

Haern shook his head. "I don't think it's going to be like that for you."

"Then why is it like that for you?"

Haern sighed. "It's all I know."

"Fighting like this is all that you know?"

"Not like this, but preparing. My whole life, I grew up hearing about the Forgers, men and women of incredible power, their magic meant to harm my people. My father chased them, leaving us alone, disappearing for weeks and sometimes months at a time, coming back only for a little while before he would venture out again, prepared to fight once more."

"And so this *is* normal for you."

"I don't know if it's normal or not, but it's how I know to keep those I care about safe."

"How come he didn't take anyone else with him?"

"I think he tried, but when he did, others got hurt. He was determined not to let that happen again, and so as much as he might want help, he thought he was doing others a favor by excluding them."

At least, that was what he could come up with. Haern wondered what he would have learned had he been able to work with his father sooner. How skilled could he have been had he begun to understand his abilities and the connection to them before now?

Maybe his father would have been able to help him learn how to connect to the metal and use that connection in a more effective way than he had discovered on his own. Then again, it was just as possible that his father wouldn't have been able to teach him anything. Haern used his connection differently than his father did. There was nothing wrong with that, especially as it was all he knew. Now that he had increased connection to lorcith, Haern wondered if he would have been able to learn from his father.

And now he never could.

It was times like these, times when he thought about what could have been and what should've been, that he felt the sadness and sorrow of that loss.

"My parents wanted me to be a seamstress," Elise said.

Haern looked over, smiling. "I never knew that."

She shrugged. "It wasn't something that I wanted. I never enjoyed trying to thread the needle, and I hated poking my finger." She held her hands up, tapping her fingers together. "The only problem was that it was something my parents knew. They thought by teaching me that skill, they could make me more than they were."

"Why? What were they?"

"My father was a farmer. My mother worked the farm with him, though she also collected honey."

"It seems like a nice life."

"It was a nice life, but at the same time, I was like anyone else. I think I wanted to know if there was more for me in the world."

"How so?"

"I went in search of something else. That's when I was taken."

"What sort of something else did you go in search of?"

Elise turned away.

"What was it?" Haern asked, smiling. Whatever it was had left her somewhat embarrassed, and that aroused his curiosity.

"I wanted to sing," she said.

"Would you sing for me now?"

"I don't think I can. I don't have any accompaniment, and I don't know that I want you to hear me sing."

"Why not? I bet you have a lovely voice."

Shook her head. "I don't want you to laugh at me."

"I'd never laugh at you."

She looked up, and she stepped away from him, out into the darkness. As she did, she sang softly, her voice gentle and sweet, carrying a soft and happy tune. It was a song he didn't know, but he found himself humming along with her. When it was done, she stood in silence for a while.

"That was... beautiful," he said.

"You're just saying that."

Haern moved to stand next to her, shoulder to shoulder, and, taking a chance, he slipped his arm around her waist. She tensed for only a moment before sinking against him. "It was beautiful. Much like you."

She rested her head on his shoulder. "What's going to happen?"

"I don't know. If there's another attack out here

tonight, I'll stop it, but I'd like to know who it is and what weapon was attacking us."

Elise lifted her head off his shoulder, looking over at him. "That's not what I mean. What's going to happen to us when we get to Asador?"

"I intend to get help for you. That's where the Binders —the real Binders—will be found."

And he had every intention of getting them to the real Binders, to a place of safety. Once he did, he wouldn't have to worry about others harming them. They would be safe, far from the Forgers and their grasp, and he could alert Carth or one of her people about what he'd witnessed. She would need to know that others pretended to be with the Binders. He had to believe she would deal with that quickly.

"That's not what I mean. What's going to happen to us?"

Haern licked his lips, swallowing. "I don't know."

Elise studied his face for a few moments before resting her head on his shoulder. Together, they stared out into the night.

2

HAERN

MORNING CAME QUICKLY, AND HAERN WAS EXHAUSTED from staying awake, but overnight there had been no other sign of movement or of whatever attacker he'd encountered. As the sun crept above the horizon, the young women all awoke, stirring and yawning, some stretching, and they quickly began to go through the motions of breaking down the camp for the night. There was no sense of organization. Each morning, someone would take the turn of burying the coals, something Haern thought was necessary, though he couldn't quite remember why he would believe it to be so. Dried meat and stale bread were passed around, everyone getting something to eat, but not nearly enough to fill their rumbling stomachs. They had plenty of water, and the streams in this part of the world were plentiful enough that he didn't have to worry about when they would find another, so they drank freely. If only they had more food.

Unfortunately, villages were few and far between along the way, so they were forced to depend on the food they'd brought out of the city. It wasn't much, not enough for them to dispense openly, but it was enough for them to share.

By the time they reached another village, Haern wondered if they would even have enough money to purchase food. He hated the idea of stealing, but he would do so if it came down to it.

Elise sat up, rubbing sleep from her eyes. She had rested on his shoulder after they had taken a seat, and he hadn't wanted to move her. She looked up at him, the rising sunlight glittering off her blue eyes, reminding him of the ocean that crashed along the shores of Elaeavn, a sight he hadn't seen nearly as often as he probably should have.

"I take it there weren't any more attacks?" she said.

Haern shook his head. "No other attacks."

"Did you sleep?"

He met her gaze. For a moment, he thought about claiming he'd rested, but she would likely see through him. She usually did.

"No. I thought it best if I stayed awake."

"What did you expect to see?"

Haern shrugged. "I don't know if I could've seen anything, but I focused on the sense of the metal."

"And you haven't detected anything?"

"Nothing more than what's with us."

Elise had some understanding of Haern and his connection to the metal, and she glanced down at his sword before her gaze drifted to her own. "One of these days, I'd like a sword like yours."

"Are you sure? Mine's a little heavy for someone as weak as you."

She shoved him on the shoulder as she sat up. "I'm surprised with your bony arms you're even able to carry it."

Haern glanced down at his arms. He wasn't nearly as strong as he would be if he had worked at the forge his entire life like his father or grandfather, but the time he had spent there had bulked him up, giving him strength most others didn't have.

"I'm sorry I disappoint you."

She shrugged. "I don't mind bony arms."

"I don't have to use my arms with the sword, anyway," Haern said. "I just use my connection to the metal."

"That's not something you can teach us."

"Unfortunately not."

"I think you want to hide that from us, anyway. You think to use your own special abilities to cheat us out of techniques you don't want to teach."

"That's definitely it," Haern said.

"Haern?"

Haern looked up and saw Erica, a younger girl with a mess of brown hair that seemed to get more and more tangled with each passing day. She was smart and knew this area better than some; she claimed she'd studied maps when she was younger.

"What is it?"

"We're running out of food."

Haern glanced back toward the other girls. How could they be running out of food so soon? He'd thought they had another couple of days, maybe more than that, before that would become an issue.

"What happened to our rations?" Elise asked, getting to her feet.

Erica blinked, glancing over to Elise before turning her attention to Haern. He didn't want the women looking to him for support. He'd rather they looked to others like Elise or Jayna or the other older women. Too many of the younger ones turned to him, their eyes practically begging him to take on a role he didn't want.

"We've been rationing, but I think someone's been sneaking a little bit more than their share."

Haern glanced over to Elise. That had been their concern. With as many women as they had here, they ran the risk of someone deciding they didn't want to cut back on their portion.

"Some of the girls are quite young," Elise said. "They don't understand why they're being asked to ration. We can't get too angry."

"We aren't going to have enough food for much longer," Erica said.

Elise glanced over to Haern. "Then we have to find a place where we can stop and get more."

"That's just it, we're several days away from the next village, and another week or more from the next city, not to mention how far we have to go before we even reach—"

Elise touched her gently on the arm, trying to soothe her. "We are going to be okay," she whispered.

Erica nodded, and she turned away. "I know, it's just that we're hungry. We're tired, and quite a few of us are scared." She twisted her hair in one hand, forming a bit of a knot with it. As she did, she glanced from Haern to Elise. "Can we get going?"

Haern nodded. "I didn't realize you were waiting on me."

"Not on you, but... well, on the two of you."

Haern shared a look with Elise. They would have to be careful or they would start rumors, if they hadn't already. How many times had they slipped off into the night, if only to talk? He wouldn't be surprised if their sneaking off had raised a different sort of question that he should've anticipated, and yet he had been thankful just to have time with Elise, time where they could sit and talk and get to know each other better.

"The two of us are ready to go," Haern said.

In the daylight, everything around them was a little different. They had made their way through a flowing grassy plain and moved into an area dotted with clumps of trees. Every so often, Haern would use his connection to lorcith to hover in the air and get a better view of where they were and what was around them. Each time he did, he was able to see everything all around quite a bit better, but he still only knew they were heading north, making their way toward Asador, though there wasn't a particular road they followed.

"What is it?" Elise asked.

"Where did our attacker come from?"

"I don't know."

"I don't like the fact that there was something here," he said.

And the fact of it was that there was lorcith here.

Because of that, he should be able to find it. In the darkness, he'd wanted only to ensure the safety of the others, but once he'd made certain they were safe, he should have gone in search of lorcith. If they had a weapon like that, chances were good they had more than one.

"Head north. I'm going to meet up with you in a little bit," Haern said.

"Are you sure?"

"Keep on guard. Be ready for whatever might come."

"Aren't we always?"

Haern smiled. These days, they had been better and better about staying on edge. It was their way of protecting themselves. By maintaining their alertness, they were going to be able to defend themselves more effectively.

Elise took his hand, squeezing it.

Haern *pushed* off using a pair of coins, taking to the sky. Once airborne, he focused on the sense of lorcith.

This was something he should have done the night before, and he chided himself for not having done so before now. There was the sense of lorcith that he carried with him. It was more than just the sword, and the knives, and the coins; it was the sense of lorcith from down near the camp. There were knives there that he had forged.

What he was searching for was nothing like that. He wanted to find the sense of lorcith that had come at him, threatening him, and as he focused on it, he found it.

The sense was far too close to the campsite.

Haern lowered himself carefully, prepared to *push* off

on lorcith if some other attacker came, or if the sphere exploded, sending more nails at him.

Only... he didn't feel there were more attackers here.

There was the sense of metal, but there wasn't anything else mixed within it as there had been before. It was smooth.

Haern dropped to the ground in knee-high grasses. He approached carefully, slowly, using his connection to lorcith to follow the sphere, and when he got close to it, he crouched down in the grasses, reaching for it. He held his hand above the surface of the sphere, focusing on the lorcith within it. As far as he could tell, the lorcith was pure, not an alloy, and it was almost a perfect sphere.

Haern lifted it. Small holes within it revealed where the nails—or whatever they were—had been. There was nothing left, so whatever they had triggered and fired at him was gone.

Interesting.

He stuffed it into his pocket and looked around. He wanted to find the nails to better understand how he'd been attacked, another example of what they had used, but he didn't see any here.

Launching himself once again, Haern hovered, though this time he stayed closer to the ground. As he did, twisting in place, he focused on lorcith. There were faint connections to the metal all around him, dozens and dozens of them, none of them very significant, and all of them spread out in a circle around where he had found the sphere.

Haern dropped near a particularly large cluster of them and found three of the nails. Picking them out of the grass, he held them up to the light. They were sharp, shaped like needles that reminded him of Galen's darts, and he frowned to himself.

Could these be poisoned?

He didn't like the idea of that, but it had some merit. It wouldn't surprise him to learn that someone else would have poisoned a weapon like this, especially a weapon designed to explode and rain down nails.

He would have to be careful. He decided to keep these three, but he wrapped them in a strip of cloth before stuffing them into his pocket. It wouldn't do for him to accidentally stab and poison himself. When he returned to Elaeavn, he could ask Galen to help him determine whether or not they were poisoned.

Now that he had found the weapon and the nails it had shot, were there others like it?

Haern *pushed* off, hovering high in the sky as he looked for the sense of lorcith in other places. He stretched beyond where he had been, beyond the campsite, and swept outward in a ring much like he had the night before. In the daylight, he could make out much more detail. A rolling hillside made it difficult to see beyond from the ground, and he headed that direction, worried some hidden attacker might think about harming the women when they made their way past.

He found nothing. No signs of movement. Nothing at all.

According to Erica, there were no villages nearby, so there shouldn't have been anyone sneaking about like this.

And yet, he *had* seen movement, hadn't he?

Perhaps whoever had been out here could Slide.

That would be a useful ability right about now. If Haern could Slide, he could transport all of them to Asador, avoiding the dangers inherent in going by ground.

As he made steady circles of the ground below, he didn't come across anything more that was suspicious. If there was another attacker down there, he didn't see them.

Floating in place, Haern focused on the lorcith from the women and started toward it. On a whim, he *pushed* higher and higher. From this vantage, he couldn't see much other than the changing landscape far below. Colors blurred together, greens and browns and occasionally strips of blue representing streams or rivers. From this high, he was unable to see any sign of a city, though he wondered if he might be able to if he *pushed* higher.

Haern tried *pushing* off, but there seemed to be a limit to how high he could suspend himself above the ground, as if something *pushed* against him, keeping him from going too high.

Then again, the more he worked with his connection, the better able he was to do this. With each day, each passing attempt, he was able to go higher. Eventually, Haern wondered if he might be able to shoot straight up and then arc down great distances all in a single jump.

At last, Haern descended.

As he did, he realized something was wrong.

Lorcith, and lots of it.

It wasn't near the caravan, which he found reassuring,

but at the same time, there was a sudden appearance of a half dozen different items of lorcith.

How many of them would be like the sphere?

Haern had to know.

He unsheathed his sword, knowing it was foolish to go alone. He didn't think it was Forgers. Forgers would have a different metal.

Haern dropped down into a small copse of trees. It was near enough to where he'd detected the lorcith that he thought he'd be able to determine where he was picking up on it, but he didn't see anyone.

This was the right spot. He was certain of it. The longer he stood here, the more certain he was, and the more he could feel the sense of lorcith around him.

Why should that be?

There wasn't any place to hide.

Unless they were lying flat and hiding within the grasses. Even if they did that, he thought that he should be able to find them.

Lorcith. That was what he had to focus on.

It was located no more than a dozen paces from him, close enough he should be able to see something from it. Could he pick up on the shape of the lorcith from here?

With his newfound attachment to the metal, he should be able to do so.

He didn't *pull* on it. He didn't want whoever might be out here to be aware of him, but he held on to a connection to it, trying to wrap his awareness around the metal. It was a strange thing, almost as if he caressed it, holding on to it in a way that would allow him to better understand who and what was out there and how they were using their connection to the metal. As he stayed in place, he couldn't tell what it was.

Until he knew, he remained motionless. He was hesitant to go anywhere else, but he also didn't want to risk someone realizing he was here. They were far enough away from the rest of his people that he wasn't worried they would come across them easily. Haern remained hidden in the trees, his sword near enough that he could grab it and be prepared for an attack if it came down to it.

Strangely, there was no sign of movement.

As he sat there, he focused, wondering if perhaps he was making a mistake. Had the lorcith been there before? He thought it hadn't, but maybe in his search he'd missed something.

No—if it was here, it was because the lorcith had suddenly appeared, not because it had been here before.

Finally, Haern moved forward. If there was someone here, he had to figure out why.

Making his way forward, he gripped the sword tightly.

There was nothing.

He *pushed* softly on the lorcith, barely more than a gentle touch, intending nothing more than to try to alert anyone who might be out there that he had a connection to the metal. There had to be others who had a similar connection. If they were here, he would find them.

Nothing.

This was odd. Not only did he not see anyone, but there was the fact this was pure lorcith.

Haern stepped out of the trees into the open, hating how vulnerable it made him.

Nothing.

He *pushed* on the lorcith.

As he did, it exploded.

Almost too late, Haern *pushed*.

He did so with more strength than he had used before, forcing it away from him, trying to create a barrier all around him to defend against whatever he'd just triggered.

Unless he hadn't triggered it at all. It was possible the lorcith was waiting for him to approach.

Shards of metal came streaking toward him, reminding him of the sphere and the nails he had managed to avoid the night before.

He wanted to shoot himself into the sky, but it took every bit of his connection to lorcith to ensure he wasn't hit by one of these nails.

The strange assault continued.

Haern used every ounce of focus to resist the attack, *pushing* outward with everything he had. The sense of lorcith curved away from him, and he managed to bottle up the explosion.

He held on to the sense of lorcith and waited for another onslaught.

It never came.

As he stood there, leaning forward and panting to catch his breath, a sound echoed toward him.

A scream.

3

HAERN

HAERN LAUNCHED HIMSELF INTO THE AIR, FOCUSING ON the sound, but more than that, focusing on his connection to lorcith. He was tired after barely managing to hold off the explosion, but the women needed him.

He wasn't able to *push* off nearly as fast as usual. When it came down to using lorcith, he had to hope there wasn't another similar attack. If there was, he'd probably be useless.

As he made his way there, another scream echoed.

He swore softly to himself, hoping he wasn't too late. He wasn't going to let something happen to Elise. He wasn't going to let something happen to any of them.

When he dropped to the ground, there was nothing.

Elise turned toward him. "What happened?" Haern asked, looking around.

"Marcy tripped. She hurt her leg."

Haern breathed out a sigh. That was it? And here he had envisioned something far deadlier than someone tripping along the road.

Then again, a fall could be just as dangerous. Someone stumbling might mean the others would have to carry them, and already they were slower than he liked.

"How is she?"

"She'll probably be fine."

Haern slipped the sword back into his sheath, feeling foolish for having unsheathed in the first place. He looked around for signs of anything he should have been focused on before, but there was nothing.

The women had reached a narrow stream, and Marcy had slipped while stepping across. When she landed on the other side, she twisted her leg.

The bone had buckled, and she wouldn't be walking on it for a while. Two of the other women were already splinting the wound. What he wouldn't give for Darren right now. The Healer would take care of this and get Marcy back on her feet.

Haern would end up carrying her. It wasn't that he minded, but it would prevent him from scouting.

"What happened?" Elise asked.

Haern shook his head. "I don't really know."

She glanced at his sword. "You came back here, sweat dripping from your brow as if you had been in a fight."

"It felt as if I'd been in a fight, but…"

He pulled the sphere out of his pocket, handing it over to her.

"What is this?"

"This is what attacked me last night. And then again today."

"Today?" She looked up from her study of the sphere,

her brow wrinkled in a deep frown. "You found someone?"

"That's just it. There wasn't anyone out there. I was attacked, but I don't know how or why."

He told her about what he had detected before taking the sphere back from her, stuffing it into his pocket. It was something that would warrant more investigation, but now wasn't the time.

Besides, what was there for him to investigate? He could tell it was made entirely of lorcith, even the nails. Someone must have triggered it, but when he'd been attacked today, it didn't seem as if anything had. It was as if the spheres had attacked on their own, without anyone setting them off.

"Do you think you somehow drew the lorcith to you?"

Haern shook his head. "I don't think I could have. I wasn't really drawing on a connection to lorcith."

"From what I understand, you *push* and *pull* on it. Wouldn't that *pull* on something?"

Haern paused. It was possible. That didn't explain the speres sudden appearance, though.

"I want to keep moving as quickly as we can," Haern said.

"We're going to have to take our time with Marcy."

"I could carry her. I could get her to the next village—"

"I don't think anyone would like it if you abandoned us like that," Elise said.

"I wouldn't be abandoning anyone. I would just be carrying her as quickly as I could on to the next village." Haern wasn't sure where the next village would be found. When he'd been hovering high in the sky, there had been no sense of another village, no sense of anyone else out there. How long would they have to travel to find it? Erica seemed to think there would be a city in a couple days, but Haern would have expected to have come across evidence of that by now.

He didn't want to leave them, and they needed his protection.

If there were more weapons like that out there, he might be the only defense they had. Swords wouldn't do any good against them.

Haern moved off to the side, staring into the distance. He focused on lorcith, straining to detect other hints of metal like the last, but there were none.

Breathing out heavily, he waited for the women to be ready. Some of them made a litter out of branches and a blanket, and they used that to drag Marcy.

Elise joined him. "I'm not so sure how that will go for her," Haern said.

"It's better than trying to carry her."

Haern glanced over to Elise. "I could carry her."

"And how much does that take out of you?" She smiled. "We can do this, Haern. Besides, this gives some of them a sense of pride. Think about all they had to do to put this together. The fact that they were able to do it by themselves is impressive. Let them have it."

Haern shrugged. "I wasn't going to take it from them."

"It's going to slow us down, isn't it?" Elise asked.

"It will."

"How much?"

"I don't know."

"I know you wanted us to move quickly."

"I wanted to move quickly mostly so we could get you and everyone else to safety as soon as possible," he said.

"We're doing our best," she said.

"I know."

"You aren't going to leave us?"

Haern looked over at her. "I've already told you I'm not going to," he said.

"It's just that when we get to Asador, I know what you intend to do."

"Do you?" Haern smiled as he looked at Elise. "Seeing as how I don't even know what I'm going to do when I get Asador, I'm not sure you can know, either."

"You feel like you need to get back to your home."

"There's quite a bit going on."

"And this all has to do with the Forgers?"

Haern had told her as much about the Forgers as he could, but it was one thing for her to hear of his experiences and another for her to experience things herself. Her contact with the Forgers was limited to the city.

"They're after a dangerous sort of power, and somehow I'm caught up in trying to stop it."

"What if I wanted to help?"

Haern looked back at the line of women. "They're going to need your help."

"They will, but eventually we're going to reach the Binders. When we do…"

It all came back to that. When they reached the Binders, and Carth and her people, Haern wasn't sure what was going to happen. He thrilled at the idea that Elise would come with him, that she would be able to travel with them and help him, and yet, what he had done and what he needed to do was dangerous.

"When we do, we'll figure it out," Haern said.

Elise watched him with an expression that suggested she didn't believe him. Haern wasn't sure he believed himself.

The day went slowly. They made very poor time, having to stop periodically to give Marcy a chance to rest. Her leg throbbed, and Haern tried to think of the various compounds he'd learned of from Galen. Poisoning might be Galen's expertise, but he had been a healer first.

As they walked, Haern searched for something that could be used to help alleviate Marcy's pain. When he found it, it was in a thicket of reeds near another stream.

He plucked a few needles from the narvel plants, a strange thorny bush he'd seen when working with Galen. Galen had used it to incapacitate, but in lower doses, it made for an effective mild sedative.

He bent off one of the barbs, dipping his finger in the thick syrup that appeared before rubbing it on Marcy's lips.

As he watched, Marcy's breathing started to ease. She stopped writhing, and Haern nodded with a certain satisfaction. It had worked.

Now, he just had to be certain he didn't overdo it. He wasn't sure he had any way to reverse it if she suddenly stopped breathing.

Thankfully, that didn't happen.

Haern plucked a few more branches, wrapping them in cloth before attaching them to the makeshift litter.

After resting for little longer, they began to make their

way. They were able to go a little faster now that Marcy wasn't suffering with every bump, and while he wasn't the one to pick up the pace, the others hurried more than before.

"How did you learn to do that?" Erica asked.

"Someone who worked with me knew about various herbal treatments."

"You were a healer?" She glanced over to Marcy.

Haern shook his head. "He was, but not me."

How much better would it be if he were a healer? At least then, he wouldn't feel so helpless when it came to injuries like Marcy's. He didn't like being helpless, and Haern certainly didn't like to watch people who were counting on him suffer.

As they went, Haern searched for the strange sense of lorcith. His strength began to return, and he started to think that perhaps he might be able to withstand another similar attack. Though if one came, would he be able to protect everyone here?

He had to figure out who had been responsible for the attack, and why. Once he understood that, he could ensure another didn't come.

Unfortunately, he couldn't leave these women alone.

And so they walked.

"What are you looking for?" Erica asked at one point in the middle of the day.

Haern glanced over to Elise, wondering how much he should share with the others. If he revealed that he was worried about an attack, would it alarm the others?

"Haern saw something," Elise said.

"Something dangerous?"

"Something."

He didn't like keeping the details of the attack to himself any more than he suspected Elise did, but at the same time, there was no point in worrying the others when there was little they could do anyway. It was probably better for them to think they were hurrying because they were short on food.

"I saw evidence of someone having come through here," Haern said. That was near enough the truth that he wasn't really lying to the other woman.

"What kind of someone?" Erica asked.

Haern glanced to Elise. How much was he supposed to share? He looked to her for guidance, figuring she was better connected in that regard to the other women. If anyone should get to choose how much he revealed about the possible attack, it should be her.

"Are either of you going to share?" Erica asked.

Haern breathed out in a heavy sigh, looking around. "Someone who seems to know what kind of potential I have."

Erica's jaw clenched for a moment. "Are we under attack?"

"Not that we can tell," Haern said.

"But it's possible."

He nodded. There was no sense in lying to her about that.

"Whatever is out there is something I can't determine," Haern said. "When we were camped last night, I went and looked, and came across this." He pulled the sphere from his pocket, handing it over to her. She looked at it, twisting it in her hand for a moment before handing it back to him.

She glanced over at Elise. "Do you recognize it?"

Elise shook her head.

There was something about the way Erica asked the question that left him wondering if perhaps he was missing something.

"What is it?"

"It's probably nothing, but…"

Haern paused, glancing over at her. Erica wasn't the person he would've expected to have known anything about the sphere, but then, he hadn't expected any of the women to have seen it.

"Anything you might know would be helpful," he said.

"I don't really know what it could be," Erica said.

Haern glanced over to Elise before reaching into his pocket and pulling out the strip of cloth he had used to bind up the nails. He unfolded it, holding it outward and showing it to her. "These were within it."

Erica studied it, something in the way she looked at it suggesting she had seen it before.

"Where's home for you?" he asked Erica.

She tore her gaze away from the nails, meeting his eyes. "Why?"

"I'm just realizing that I don't know much about anyone here."

Elise patted him on the arm. "I think they would say the same about you, Haern."

He smiled. That was true enough, and as difficult as it could be, he thought it was time that changed. They needed to get a better sense of each other, if only so that it was easier for all of them to trust one another. It wasn't just about him trusting them; it was about them trusting him, too.

"Why don't we take a break?"

Elise eyed him for a moment. "Are you sure?"

"I think we need to."

"What are you going to do?"

Haern let out a heavy sigh. "I think we need to have a conversation."

As far as he could tell, it was long past the time that they should have done it. He should have recognized that sooner. There was a need for them to sit and communicate, to share, to gain trust. Waiting until now had only made that more difficult.

And they had become reliant upon him, something he didn't want. It was part of the reason he'd been working with them, trying to get them to be self-sufficient. Eventually they would reach Asador, and they would reach Carth or her people. Once there, they would be offered an opportunity to join the Binders. Having seen the Binders and what they were capable of, he thought there was value in the independent streak he saw in these women.

They found a place to stop, a clearing near a small stream where they were able to tamp down the grasses. It was late in the day, and it was time for them to take a break, anyway. They had been going for a while, and many of the women had grown tired. Haern also needed a rest.

When everyone had settled, Haern glanced around. "We've been traveling together for a while now, and I think you deserve the opportunity to get to know me a little bit better."

The women all looked up at him expectantly. Even Elise looked over at him, and she knew him better than any of them.

"I've told many of you that my home is in Elaeavn, a place along the coast, but it's a place that doesn't welcome outsiders. All my life, I've lived knowing about the dangers of the Forgers, people like the man I fought."

He squeezed his hands, feeling the strange metal beneath his skin. It gave him a hint of alertness. Haern tried not to think about why that would be, wanting to ignore the fact that whatever the Forgers had done to him seemed to have made him more powerful. It was different than what had happened to Lucy.

"The people of my homeland have always viewed outsiders with a certain suspicion."

"Why are you telling us this?" one of the women asked. It was one of the younger girls, by the name of Stacy. She had bright red hair and pale blue eyes, and she always seemed to look scared. Despite that, Haern had come to know that Stacy was one of the stronger of the women traveling with them.

"I guess it's so you can begin to understand me. You travel with me, and you're trusting me. I just want you to know that trust is not misplaced."

It was more than that, though. He thought it was long past time that he began to understand more about the women. Not only did they need to know him, he needed to have a better sense of who they were and the kind of things that were important to them. He was bringing them away from their homes, taking them to some strange city, and in doing so, he gave them the promise of something more. But there were times when Haern didn't know if it was the right strategy or not.

"Do all the people in your homeland have the ability to use metal like you do?" This came from Lacey, a smallish girl, probably no more than ten or eleven years old, with long blonde hair she tied up with a ribbon.

Haern shook his head, smiling. "No. Some have different abilities."

"What sort of abilities?"

"Well, when I was growing up, I didn't think much of them, but the more I've learned about them, the more I begin to recognize the sort of things my people are able to do are really quite fantastic. Not only do we have the ability to See with enhanced eyesight—that's my other ability, and the one that had always been the strongest— but some have the ability to Read."

"As in books?"

Haern smiled, turning to Jayna. "No. As in other people's minds."

That set off a murmuring, everyone surprised at the idea that anyone would be able to Read, and yet for Haern, it was a strange thing to consider they couldn't. He had known Readers his entire life and thus knew how to defend himself against them, but if they continued to encounter Forgers, the women would need to learn how to shield their minds, too.

"I know it seems hard to believe, but it is fairly common in my homeland. There are other abilities in my land, too."

"Like how you use metal?"

"Something like that. Some people have enhanced hearing, and some can travel from place to place without walking. Others have different abilities."

"All like *them*?"

Haern nodded slowly. "My father always thought the Forgers were trying to figure out how to copy the abilities of my people."

"Why just your people?" This came from Jayna, who stood at the edge of the circle of women, watching Haern. "Why wouldn't they try to chase other abilities?"

Haern shrugged. "I suspect they are. I don't know all that many other abilities. The person we're going to try to find has different abilities, and hopefully we can see if there are ways she can help, but…"

He didn't know what way Carth would be able to help, if she was even willing to do so. He had to think, given what these women had gone through, that she would grant some sort of aid. He didn't want to think about the possibility that Carth would exclude them. His entire plan was to get the women to Asador, get them to Carth and a sense of safety.

Would they share anything about themselves?

He didn't know if revealing his abilities would convince anyone to share, but he needn't have worried.

Francine spoke up. She was an older woman, with deeply tanned skin that was so dark as to be nearly brown, and hair that reminded him of Rayen's and Carth's.

"I come from a small village in the south. It is not coastal, not like Haern's, but it was comfortable. We farmed and had a simple life. A good life. We were happy. Growing up, I thought I would be a farmer like my parents, or perhaps I would find some other way to serve the village, and as I grew, I decided it was a place of safety. There were times when I wished I had abilities, especially after we were attacked."

Haern frowned. "You were attacked?"

She nodded. "I wasn't there, and only saw the aftereffects. The village was destroyed. None survived it."

Haern wondered if she had been subjected to an attack by the Forgers, but destroying villages didn't strike him as something they often did. They wanted power, but in his experience, they didn't get it by destroying others.

"We had something similar happen," one of the other girls said. Palanza had olive skin, deep brown hair, and matching eyes. "I was out working in the field when the attack came. When I got back, everything was gone."

Several of the others nodded, and Haern frowned as he looked around them. How many had experienced an attack like that?

"How did you end up together?" Haern asked.

"Chance," Lacey said.

"Luck," Francine added, looking around. "If I hadn't found them, we wouldn't have been safe."

There was a murmuring of agreement, and Haern frowned to himself. Whatever they had experienced was awful, but he had to wonder what had triggered the attacks. If it was Forgers, then they had changed the nature of what they were doing. If it was something else, then what?

"I thought we were never going to find safety," one of the women said. "And then…"

They all turned to Haern, watching him.

He was going to keep them safe. He had to. Not only because they looked at him like that, but because of what they had experienced.

How could he do anything else?

4

LUCY

THE SHORES OVERLOOKING THE VILLAGE HAD CHANGED quite a bit in the time they had occupied this space, and the longer she was here, the more Lucy recognized their influence. The women had begun to make the abandoned village their own, using elements Lucy had Slid here, things like paint and construction supplies.

Waves washed along the shore. Lucy had always found the water to be comforting, yet today, something felt off.

In the time she'd been here, trying to understand her purpose and role, she still struggled with understanding just what she needed to do.

Some of that had to do with what was expected of her, but some of it had to do with the nature of power itself.

That was something Ras was trying to teach her. The more she worked with him, the more certain she was that there were aspects she had yet to understand.

She looked around the rocky shoreline. She never came here with Carth, always wanting to keep this place to herself. She didn't fear that Carth would somehow

THE COMING CHAOS | 45

abuse these women, but rather that something would change if she allowed others access. The isolation was protection, almost as much as anything else.

There was another advantage, and it was one Lucy was struggling with. Most of these women didn't realize she had begun to work with the C'than. She had to reveal that eventually, and had to help them understand that her work with the C'than was different than what others had done to them.

It would be difficult for them to grasp, and yet she felt it necessary.

She breathed in the salty air. And Slid.

When she did, she emerged within the village.

There was a sense of activity, of purpose, and her time here had told her that the women who ran the village were skilled at doing so. The longer she spent here, the more certain she was that they no longer even needed her presence. And yet, there was something about coming here, about knowing they still welcomed her, that was reassuring. She wasn't quite able to put it into words.

"You've returned."

She turned around, looking to Eve. The tall, slender woman had her hands on her hips, and a hint of irritation washed across her face.

"I have. Are you disappointed?"

"You've been gone too long this time."

Lucy looked away. She had long ago realized she wouldn't be able to satisfy Eve. The woman had a hard edge to her, but she was growing in skill with her connection to lorcith. At this point, she was able to maneuver it, much like Haern could. With her augmentation, Lucy had the hope that eventually Eve would be able to do even more, but it would take time and practice.

Thankfully, in this place they had nothing but time.

"I didn't think you cared."

Eve pressed her lips together, which surprisingly made her seem almost as if she smiled. "It's not so much that I care. The others do. They're concerned about you."

"Just the others?"

Lucy was determined to try to get Eve out of her shell, but she'd failed up to this point. The only thing she'd managed to do with Eve was to help her realize she had power she wasn't aware of. She wondered if it was possible to reach her even more.

"Why would I care?"

"I thought you might want to continue to work with lorcith. I thought maybe I could help with that."

"If you say so. I just don't know."

Lucy frowned and looked away. There was activity along the street in the village, and the longer she looked, the more certain she was that some of the people were beginning to use their abilities. It was difficult for her to know just what they were able to do. Most of the abilities others possessed were hard to recognize. Some might be Readers. Some might be Sighted, and some might be Listeners. Any of those traits would be difficult for her to determine without getting to better understand their abilities. And there were other gifts they might possess.

"Have any others begun to demonstrate their talents?"

"Some have," Eve said, standing next to her, now with her arms crossed over her chest. "Take Rebecca there. She's starting to hear voices. We thought she was crazy at first, but then we remembered what you said about people from your home."

"Reading," Lucy said, looking at Rebecca. She had curly brown hair, and she was short—much shorter than those from Elaeavn. Her pale green eyes would have marked her as only weakly capable within Elaeavn, and yet the ability given to her had changed things for her.

Reading.

How many others would have something like that?

She had no idea, and she wasn't sure it mattered. At this point, all that counted was that they work through each of the women, trying to understand what might've changed for them, to see if there was anything they might be able to do.

And if so, she wanted to work with them.

If only she had more time.

That seemed to be the curse of everything. With everything she experienced, Lucy continued to feel as if she didn't have nearly enough time for all she wanted to do. She wanted to try to help everyone, to work with them, to offer any sort of assistance she could, and yet she was pulled by the C'than.

Now that she had begun to understand a little more about herself, there was another purpose for her. It was one Carth had initially set her on, and one Ras agreed with.

She needed to help uncover whether there were others who had been infiltrated, others of the C'than who had abandoned the ancient ideals.

Balance.

Lucy had begun to find that balance within herself, and now she had to find it within the C'than.

"You can call it Reading, but like I said, we thought she was crazy. Then she started to point out what other people were thinking. We stopped thinking she'd lost her mindn at that point."

"It's difficult to Read with much control when you're first learning it," she said.

"We're having a hard time keeping her from digging into our minds."

Lucy smiled to herself. It was another thing she would have to teach. They needed to understand how to place mental barriers.

Perhaps she should have taken Carth up on her offer, rather than trying to keep these women separate. The Binders had some way of protecting their thoughts and might have been able to offer the women that protection.

It was even possible that Carth and the Binders had some herbal method of guarding their minds.

"I can work with you on that," she said.

"Can you?" It was the first time Eve seemed genuinely interested in what Lucy offered.

"We have ways of protecting our minds. For now, you might find it easiest just to keep the more useless infor- mation at the forefront of your mind."

"Great. We have to think about gardening and sewing."

"Is that what you think is useless?"

"It is from my days back in my homeland."

Lucy turned toward Eve. She was determined to get a better sense of what the other woman had gone through, and this was the first time she had offered anything that might be of value.

"What more did you experience there?"

"I don't think we need to go into that," she said.

"Why not? If it will help you—"

"I don't have any intention of talking about that with you." Eve started away, and Lucy trailed after her. When she reached Rebecca, the other woman nodded. "Lucy tells us that she can help you control this."

Rebecca glanced at Eve for a moment. "Why are you thinking about tomatoes?"

Eve threw her hands up, looking over at Lucy. "We need to fix this now."

"I will do my best," she said.

And yet, she couldn't help but smile. If Eve was thinking about tomatoes, that told Lucy that she could learn.

Then again, Lucy had always known that. Eve was a quick study, and her stubbornness made her even stronger. It was a trait Lucy knew would be valuable, especially if it came to actually needing to use her abilities.

If it were up to her, she would protect these women from needing to do so. Lucy would defend them, protect them, offering them whatever she could to ensure they didn't have to fight the Ai'thol.

They were capable, and with everything they'd gone through and every ability she'd discovered among them, she couldn't help but feel as if they might be the exact thing they required in order to truly defeat the Ai'thol.

It was ironic that it might be the C'than who gave them what they needed.

"How long are you going to be here?" Rebecca asked.

"As long as I need to," Lucy said.

"Are you sure?"

The other woman studied her, and she smiled. There was a sense of Rebecca trying to dig into her mind, fumbling for her thoughts.

"Why can't I reach your mind?"

Lucy smiled at her. "Many people in my homeland have this ability."

"They can read thoughts?"

"Exactly. Because of that, I know how to defend myself."

It was easier now than it had been even when she had been in Elaeavn. She had been a reasonable Reader then, but if it wasn't until she had left that she had become something more.

Even now, Lucy wasn't sure that anyone would be able to Read her. There were plenty of capable people within Elaeavn. She thought of Cael Elvraeth, rumored to be one of the strongest Readers, and yet even she would have a hard time digging into Lucy's mind.

Rebecca frowned. It looked more like a pout. "What use is it to have an ability that's so easy to defeat?"

"It depends on the person using it. I suspect if you have more time with it, you'll begin to master it in a way that will allow you to dig into thoughts that would otherwise be forbidden to you."

"Such as yours?"

Lucy shrugged. "It's possible you might eventually be

able to reach my mind, but I wonder if perhaps my own augmentation will protect me."

It was something she should test. She didn't necessarily want anyone digging through her thoughts, but if someone did, it might as well be one of the women she'd rescued.

And if that happened, it would be better if she admitted to her involvement with the C'than before they managed to discover it on their own.

She didn't want that surprise.

"How many others have discovered this ability?" she asked, looking from Rebecca to Eve.

"Only one other," Rebecca said.

Eve frowned. "We don't even know if that's what she can do," she said, waving her hand. She turned her attention toward the end of the village, and Lucy stared. There was an older woman sitting on a ledge, her legs dangling.

Lucy Slid, emerging next to her.

She was thin, and Olivia hadn't fully recovered following her captivity. She didn't know if the other woman would eventually gain back the weight she'd lost in captivity or whether this was a new normal for her.

"Olivia?" Lucy asked, taking a seat next to her.

The other woman stared out at the ocean. "I lived my whole life wanting to know what it was like to see the water like this."

"It can be soothing, can't it?"

The other woman shook her head slightly. "I don't find it soothing at all. I find it chaotic."

"Why chaotic?" Lucy tried to Read her, but something prevented it. It was probably the same thing that would keep her from effectively Reading everyone within the village. They had some protections that were offered by the augmentations.

"The way the waves work at the shore. There's a certain chaos to it. It's not peaceful at all."

Lucy looked out, watching, but from here, the way the waves swept into the shore, the whitecaps, had always seemed peaceful to her. She wasn't sure why it wouldn't be that way to the other woman, and yet, she couldn't help but wonder if perhaps there was something more that troubled Olivia.

"Rebecca tells me you might have begun to develop some talents."

"It's too much," Olivia said.

"You can learn to control it."

Olivia's eyes were red. Lucy hadn't realized there was wetness around them, and she cursed herself. She should've paid more attention, should have recognized that the other woman was suffering.

And how could she not? Having something like this thrust upon her would be hard. Lucy remembered how difficult it had been for her when she had first had the augmentation placed, the way it had strained her ability to control it, the overwhelming nature of all the thoughts around her.

"There's just so much."

"What do you detect?"

"Sadness. Fear. Anger."

Lucy frowned. "Emotion?"

Olivia turned away, staring at the water. "There are times when I wish it could be taken away from me."

Lucy sighed. "I can work with the others. I'm going to help them learn how to protect their minds." Even doing that, she wasn't sure it would protect against emotions. Plenty of people in Elaeavn could Read—it was one of the more common abilities—but what Olivia described was something else. Feeling everyone else's emotions constantly would be a terrible thing. She could easily understand how it would cause someone to suffer.

"Can you close it off?"

"I've tried, but everything continues to come to me. It fills my mind. That's why I've come out here."

"Does the ocean help?"

"The chaos helps."

"When I first had my augmentation placed, all the thoughts that slammed into me were too much. I learned to control it eventually, but..." Even now, it was still difficult for Lucy to hold on to that control. She could shut out most of those voices, but it presented a challenge nonetheless. There were times when she couldn't. When she was in busier cities, places where people didn't know how to shield their minds, there was a sense of pressure, an overwhelming sensation of a dozen different voices all crying out for her attention. She was able to mute them a bit, but she still detected them.

"I can help," she said.

"Are you sure?"

Lucy nodded quickly. "It takes time, but I can help you with this." The anguish she saw on Olivia's face was heartbreaking.

These women had gone through so much, and many of them were just now beginning to come into their abilities, learning that something new was offered to them, and she wanted to help them so they didn't have to go through it alone.

When she had dealt with the augmentation and the voices she'd detected, she hadn't done so alone.

There had been Daniel Elvraeth and Carth and Rayen, along with the Binders and, if she was honest, the Ai'thol. The Architect had helped her as much as anyone. Lucy hated admitting that, but because of him, she had gained an understanding of and a control over her abilities she wouldn't have had otherwise.

"If the ocean helps, you should stay near it."

"I don't like coming out here," she said.

"Because you fear the waves?"

"I can't swim."

Lucy smiled. "I can't swim all that well, either."

"I thought you grew up near the water?"

"I did. But even in my homeland, not everybody gets into the water."

Those who lived closer to the shore would spend some time in the sea, but Lucy had been drawn to the forest, and the power that was there. Even now, though she loved looking out over the water and thought she might be able to find answers if she stared long enough, she didn't love the idea of swimming.

"Sometimes I wonder if it might be better if I left," Olivia said.

"Where would you go?"

"Anywhere but here. Maybe someplace where the voices didn't intrude."

"I don't know where you can go that they wouldn't," she said.

"Somewhere else," Olivia said.

Lucy took the other woman's hand, squeezing it reassuringly, and yet she didn't know that she was offering her anything. She understood the terror she would be going through, and just how horrible it must feel. It was so familiar to her, and though she didn't know if she could offer her any sort of reassurance, she wanted to—and needed to.

"Why don't you focus on what you can think of?" she said.

"Such as what?"

"Focus on my mind."

"I don't detect anything from you."

"Nothing?"

The other woman stared for a moment, and again Lucy felt the pressure, but it was vague and faint.

"There is something, but I don't really know what it is."

"Maybe because I'm shielded." Could she open her mind a little bit? Carth had a way of doing that, and Lucy couldn't help but think that if she could do the same thing, it would be valuable. But how was she to do that?

She tried to release her thoughts, opening up as much as she could, but even that didn't seem to make a difference.

There had to be another way. Somehow, she would help Olivia find a sense of peace. As she turned, she realized it wasn't just Olivia whom she had to help find that peace. It was everybody in the village.

The challenge was going to be in figuring out what it would take to help them. Somehow, she would have to figure out a way to budget her time. But then, that had been a challenge all along. She had known she needed to serve both the C'than and to help these women.

And beyond that, she had to figure out what else they needed to do in order to stop Olandar Fahr and the rest of the Ai'thol. The more she worked on the Ai'thol, the more certain she was that there had to be something they could do.

"How long are you staying?" Olivia asked.

She hadn't planned on staying for very long, but she needed to be here.

"As long as you need."

Olivia looked over at her, and the relief in her eyes was reason enough for Lucy to remain.

5

LUCY

METAL SWIRLED AROUND EVE, THE LUMPS OF LORCITH small but tightly controlled by the other woman. Lucy was impressed. Eve was beginning to show even more control than what she had seen from Haern the last time she'd been around him.

"I can use the metal, but I don't have any idea what else I can do." Eve let the metal fall from the sky, dropping to the ground, and she crossed her arms over her chest.

"There are other things you can do with it," she said.

"I'm sure there are, but anything I try to do doesn't seem to make a difference," Eve said.

Lorcith had never been Lucy's strength. She understood how it was used and that it carried with it some potential, but anything more was beyond her.

"I know the metal can be useful, but I don't have much experience with how to use it. You're going to have to be creative."

Eve grunted. "Creative? Like you're creative with…" She shook her head, turning away.

"No. What was it?"

"Nothing," she said.

Lucy studied her and decided not to push.

She had been here for a few days, and the longer she was here, the more she felt there was something she needed to improve. Many of the women were learning aspects of their abilities, and yet the more Lucy worked with them, the more she felt that she wasn't the best teacher for them.

As strange as it sounded, it might be easier if they went to Elaeavn, where there were others with similar abilities. But she didn't think any of the women would allow her to bring them there.

Even the women who had come from Elaeavn—the Lost—didn't want to return. There was a part of Lucy that wished they would, and yet she also understood why they wouldn't want to go back. There was something different about them.

More than that, there was a danger in returning to Elaeavn. They had been augmented. That meant they were Ai'thol—Forgers, according to the people of Elaeavn.

And there were plenty of people within the city who had enough experience with the Ai'thol to fear what that meant.

It would be a hard thing to explain, and even knowing they'd been abducted, forced to take these augmentations, Lucy wasn't sure that anyone would be willing to understand anything more.

It was better if they stayed together.

Still, she couldn't shake the feeling that she wasn't

helping them nearly as much as they needed. There were those like Eve, who wanted to better understand her abilities, to know what it meant for her to have control over lorcith. Lucy didn't know whether there was anything she could offer her. She understood how lorcith could be controlled, but using it was one thing, and knowing a way to help the other woman learn to master it was something else entirely.

And it wasn't as if Eve was a blacksmith. Or even a miner. If she were either of those, then having a connection to lorcith would be more valuable. The only possibility was finding Haern. If she could do that, she might be able to see if he knew of any ways that lorcith might benefit Eve.

"Just keep working," she said. She turned away from the other woman, heading deeper into the village. Several of the homes were newly painted, the colors intentionally drab so that they would blend into the hillside. It was a clever plan, much like how Elaeavn had been designed, though Elaeavn had never been as masked as the founders of the city had wanted it to be.

She found a group of women and stopped. Marcy was talking softly, explaining something to one of them. They were starting to work together, trying to teach each other how to use their abilities.

The more they worked together, the stronger they became and the easier it would be for them to master those talents.

Marcy noticed her watching and nodded to her, and Lucy turned away. She wasn't going to intervene, and it was easier if she let the other woman take the lead.

As she started through the village, something echoed in her mind.

Lucy tensed. She paused, looking around.

It was like a shout.

The clarity of it was alarming, and as often as she had worked with others, she understood the nature of that call, though she hadn't expected to hear it here. Within the village, most of the women were protected from her Reading them easily, the nature of the augmentation making it so that any ability she had was limited. It wasn't eliminated altogether, but it certainly was diminished. And yet, she heard it clearly in her head.

Who was it from?

The answer didn't come.

More than that, she wanted to know if it would recur, and yet it didn't.

She frowned, looking around. Was there anyone in the village who needed her help? The first person who came to mind was Olivia, but the other woman was sitting on the edge of the rock, looking out over the ocean once again. Likely focusing on the chaos she detected out there.

It wasn't Olivia.

It came again.

This time it was clear, the voice cutting through.

A summons: *come.*

She recognized the voice, though she was surprised that she would detect it at all.

Carth didn't usually reach out to her in that way.

She focused on the thoughts, reaching through that connection, and Slid.

She emerged within Asador. It was a small tavern, and there was music near one wall. A pair of provocatively dressed women were making their way around the inside of the tavern, barely glancing in her direction when she suddenly appeared. The rest of the tavern was mostly empty.

A darkened shadow in one corner caught her attention.

"This is how you call me now?"

The shadows began to separate, and Carth leaned forward. "If you won't tell me where you are, it's the only way I can reach you."

"You know I can't."

"I know that you won't, but can't is a different story altogether."

Lucy watched the other woman. She had dark hair, and a scratch along one cheek suggested she'd been in a battle recently, though what sort of fighting had Carth been doing?

"What's happening?" Lucy asked.

"Can't I ask you to come just to visit?"

She started to smile. "Seeing as how you have never done that before, I don't think you would."

Carth motioned to the chair, and Lucy pulled it out. She perched on the front of the chair, nervous that it was a little more rickety than what she was comfortable with. Carth leaned back, resting her head against the wall, an uneaten plate of food in front of her.

"Where have you been?" Carth asked.

"You know where I've been."

"I know you've been working with Ras, but I also

know you have your other assignment you've given yourself."

"And I'm not going to share with you where it is."

"Do you really fear I might abuse them?"

"No."

"Then why not share with me?"

"Because they don't know about the C'than yet."

"You're going to have to share with them eventually."

Eventually. That was the fear Lucy had, and yet she didn't know how to approach the subject in a way that wouldn't lead to fear and anger. They deserved honesty from her, and yet until they began to master their abilities, Lucy didn't know that there was any need for it.

"You need to be spending time with Ras," Carth said.

"I have been spending time with Ras."

"Not the last few days."

"Are you keeping such close tabs on me?"

"As much as I need."

"Listen, if we're going to work together, then you're going to have to trust that I know what I need to do. Much like I'm going to trust you know what you need to do."

Carth started to smile. "That's what I've been waiting for."

"What is?"

Carth got to her feet and motioned to her. "Come on."

"Where?"

"It's time for us to go hunting again."

Lucy frowned. "I'm not sure now is the best time for me to go hunting."

"Your friends will be fine without you for a little while, and besides, this won't take very long."

Lucy had enough experience with Carth to know that such promises were rarely accurate.

Still, when Carth opened her mind to her, a vision flooding her head, she focused on it and recognized where the other woman wanted to take her.

She Slid, emerging in a grassy plain, a large town rising in front of them. A low stone wall surrounded it, and a hardpacked road led toward it. Smoke from dozens of chimneys drifted toward the sky. The air smelled of grain and grass, a pleasantly earthy odor, and yet there was no one around.

"Why here? Is there an Elder Stone here?"

She used her ability to Read, searching to see if she could uncover anything that might explain why Carth had brought her here, but the more she focused, the less obvious it was. There was no sense of Ai'thol within the hundreds of minds she was able to touch. It was nothing more than the typical day-to-day activity.

She looked over to Carth. "This isn't an Ai'thol stronghold."

"It's not. At least, not yet."

"You think it might become one?"

"Knowing what we do about Olandar Fahr, how he continues to move and to try to gain strength, I wouldn't put it past him to attempt something like that, but no."

"Then what?"

Carth looked over to her, meeting her eyes. Shadows seemed to swirl around them, though this close to Carth, she was able to See through them. "What do you remember of the man who captured you?"

Lucy trembled involuntarily. "Enough."

"I'm sure you remember enough, but do you know where he operated out of?"

"I don't."

"No. No one does. There have been rumors of him, and yet all of them are fleeting. He's like a ghost. A specter. And regardless of anything else, he manages to appear and then disappear, leaving no trace."

"He can Slide," Lucy said.

The Architect had been the one who had helped her learn about her abilities, the more she turned her own talents inward, focusing on what she had experienced, the more certain she was that he hadn't been the enemy she'd believed him to be. That didn't change the fact that he had used her, only that he hadn't used her in the way she had thought.

"Have you found him?"

"I've heard rumors," Carth said.

"Rumors?"

"For us to track down Olandar Fahr, we're going to have to chase rumors, and I think the rumors we need to pursue are ones that will help us understand where he might be hiding."

"You want to go after the Architect."

"If anyone would know where to find him, it would be the Architect. And once we find him, then you can Read him, and we can finally get ahead of Olandar Fahr."

"I'm not sure that's going to work the way you believe."

"Why not?"

"Because he's clever." He was more than just clever. He was nearly as calculating as Olandar Fahr. It was possible that he was *equally* calculating, and yet, Lucy did know the two men had worked together.

How much of what had happened was because of the Architect and how much was because of Olandar Fahr?

As she dug into her mind, thinking through her memories, the glimpses she could pull up from her time with the Architect, she still didn't know.

The more she thought about it, the more certain she was that the answers were there, buried within her mind. As Ras had suggested, the fact that she had been around the Architect for as long as she had with her abilities developing suggested she should have some way of Reading him. He might have been able to protect his mind to a certain extent, but her powers had grown each day, and he didn't have the same protections as the women augmented by the C'than would have.

And if she could Read something from him, then she had to figure out what it was.

"He's clever, but he's not Olandar Fahr. And if we can uncover anything about him, then we can use it and we can dig through his mind," Carth said.

There was real venom in her voice, which left Lucy worried.

She didn't want to go after Olandar Fahr with anger. He had done much to harm people, and yet he was not actively attacking them now.

Then again, he was planning. Whatever else was taking place, he was looking for some new edge, some way to gain the power of the Elder Stones, and the longer she searched, the more certain she was that she had to better understand what he was looking for.

More than that, she had to understand why he was searching for that power.

Until she uncovered that, she wasn't sure that they would succeed.

"What's this really about?"

Carth turned her attention toward the village. "We've been chasing him for so long, and we've gotten close, but never close enough."

"You want to capture him."

"I want this game to end."

"What if it's not a game?"

Carth swung her gaze toward her, meeting her eyes. "When it comes to Olandar Fahr, it's always a game."

She started toward the village, and Lucy followed. When they passed through the gate, the sense of the village began to overwhelm her. She focused on the thoughts all around her, searching for answers. There had to be something here, but what?

"Why do you think we would find anything about the Architect here?"

"He came through here."

"He's not here any longer?"

"I told you he doesn't leave much of a trace."

"You mean he doesn't have much of a physical trace. That's why you wanted me."

"I want to know if you could uncover anything that would reveal whether he has been here. Some of these people would've seen something, but they may not be aware of it."

"What you're talking about involves me digging deeply into their minds."

"You don't think that you can do that?"

"I don't know that I should."

"I'm not asking you to find something you can use to blackmail them. All I'm asking is that you uncover anything that might help us track down the Architect."

Lucy studied Carth. This was a side of her she hadn't seen before.

"What happened?"

"I lost half my fleet."

"What?"

Carth clenched her jaw. For a moment, she said nothing. "Half my fleet is gone. They were sailing south, and word of them disappeared. Others went after them and found nothing but debris. Wreckage. No sign of them."

"Have you experienced anything like that with the Ai'thol before?"

"Why?"

"It just seems a strange approach for them."

"The Ai'thol are destructive."

"I'm not disputing that." Lucy had seen enough to know just how destructive the Ai'thol could be, and yet what she had seen didn't suggest that they would destroy without any real purpose. "Were they searching for anything in particular?"

"My fleet would have appeared no different than merchants. Most of them *were* only merchants. Only a few of them were truly members of the Binders, and for them to be targeted means that somebody knew who they were and what they were doing out there."

"And you think this was Olandar Fahr."

"I think it could be no one else. We've continued to unsettle his plans, and the more we do so, the angrier he gets."

"How many were lost?"

"Does it matter?"

"It matters."

"I lost fifty ships. Probably a thousand people all told."

Lucy's breath caught. "That many?"

"It might be more," Carth said. She started off into the city, and Lucy was left looking after her, staring at the other woman's back. She worried that Carth might be looking at things the wrong way. Moving with vengeance in her heart would be dangerous. Carth had always been rational, almost to a fault, and the sudden change—Lucy was unsettled by it.

"Are you sure you're thinking clearly?"

"Entirely clearly."

"I'm just saying—"

"I know what you're saying, Lucy Elvraeth. And I know what I'm asking of you. I'm not asking you to reveal the location of your women, but I am asking you to participate in this with me. Help me find the Architect. Then I can find Olandar Fahr, and we can finally finish this."

Lucy breathed out. She didn't like this side of Carth, but she also recognized she wasn't going to be able to say or do much that would sway her.

And perhaps she didn't need to sway Carth. The other woman needed her support. She needed a friend.

And Lucy thought she could help her find the Architect.

If he had been here, then there would have to have been some movement through the town. There would have to be some memory.

Unless he had somehow used his ability to eliminate any memory of him. He was incredibly powerful. He could have used his ability to Push to hide the fact that he'd come through here.

Was there any way to search through what people had seen, straining for an image of something?

She began to focus on their minds, thinking about what she was looking for. There had to be an element of the Push that she could follow. She had found it within her own mind, so she thought she could trace through it and find out whether any of these others had been Pushed the same way.

As she searched, she found nothing.

She had to keep looking. There must be something in their minds to reveal what had happened.

She continued to search, probing through everyone's mind. She heard the story of the town. It was strange to have such an awareness, almost as if she had been here and lived with these people.

The memories were one-sided, though. She understood the stories of the town, but they would have no memory of her.

It left her empty.

Was she leaving a mark anywhere?

Certainly not in Elaeavn—not anymore. Her time there had been short-lived, and even when she had been there, she wasn't sure that she had left much of a mark on the city. No one would remember her the way they remembered Rsiran, and they certainly wouldn't remember her within the palace. She had been a budding caretaker, nothing more. She couldn't help but think that she needed to do more.

Even in the village, she had gathered the women together but struggled to provide them with safety. They needed her help, but the more she tried, the more she felt as if she were failing.

Lucy frowned.

Those weren't her thoughts.

She had helped those women.

And she had made a mark in Elaeavn. She had made friends with Haern. There were others that she knew.

"He's here," she whispered.

"What?"

Lucy looked up, searching around the town. The touch on her mind had been soft, subtle… and it had been familiar.

Familiar enough that she'd almost not recognized what was taking place. And even now that she understood what it was, she couldn't tell which of her thoughts were hers.

She would have to turn her focus inward, to Read herself the same way she had when working with Ras. And yet, as she focused, she couldn't help but feel as if there was something more there.

"I think the Architect is here."

"How do you know?"

"Because he's Pushing on me."

6

LUCY

CARTH GUIDED HER ALONG THE SIDE STREETS, ONE HAND near the hilt of her blade. The other reached outward, shadows stretching from her, sweeping across the ground. Had Lucy not been so focused on them, she wasn't sure she would have been able to make them out. As it was, she could see the way the shadows stretched outward, pooling and then disappearing.

The power Carth summoned was impressive.

"Do you feel anything?" she asked.

"I'm not influenced by Readers the same as others," Carth said.

"How?"

"I've often wondered about that." She looked in either direction along the street and motioned for Lucy to follow. "I think it's tied to the nature of my abilities. I have both the shadows and flame, and the combination offers a certain protection."

"How?"

"I'm not entirely sure how, only the combination seems to burn off anyone's attempt to touch my mind."

It was an interesting way of phrasing it. Burning it off.

Would there be any way for Lucy to use that?

Not without having an ability with the flame.

What she wouldn't give for something more than what she already had, and yet, what she had was powerful.

"I don't know where he is, only that I can feel his touch on my mind," she said.

"How close does he have to be to do that?"

Lucy shrugged. "I don't know. Somewhere within the town. And he would have to know we were here."

"There are some who can detect a Slide," Carth said.

"It's rare."

Carth looked over. "We're talking about the Ai'thol, so if there's any ability that exists, they would have worked with it, honing it, trying to master it so they can use it."

Lucy frowned. She should've thought about that before. It was possible the Ai'thol would have known they had arrived, and any surprise they had was gone.

"If he knows we're here, then what do you propose?"

"We continue to search for him."

"I need to keep him out of my mind."

"You've learned much in the time since he captured you, Lucy Elvraeth. Use everything you know."

She focused on her own mind, thinking about what she had experienced. She allowed herself to think superficial thoughts—sounds and foods and the people she saw around her. Anything that would keep her from allowing the Architect to dig too deeply into her mind. She wanted some way of barricading him, preventing him from knowing anything more.

She would have to find a different solution. It was more than just erecting a barrier. It was some way of refusing him access to her mind.

How was he able to do that, anyway?

With her augmentation, being able to reach into her mind should be difficult, if not impossible. And yet the Architect seemed to slide into her mind.

Sliding.

That had to be it, didn't it?

He was gifted with Sliding. She'd seen it herself, and he was also a gifted Reader. She didn't know what other abilities he had, other than that he could Push, but that Pushing came from his ability to Read.

She was gifted with Sliding as well. She'd learned how to focus on someone else's mind, using that to help her Slide. Could she pull someone else's thoughts into her mind and use that to protect against the Architect?

Doing so might create a different sort of shielding.

Lucy tried to slam barriers into her mind.

He was digging thoughts out from her head.

It would be dangerous to stay here.

She looked over at Carth, and the other woman had shadows swirling around her. Somehow she was protected from his influence, and Lucy would give anything for the same sort of defense, and yet here she was, trying to find a way to do it on her own.

But she'd already failed when it came to him before, and she would fail again. The Architect was far more skilled a Reader than she was.

Get out of my mind.

She could've sworn there was laughter.

"Carth?"

"What is it?"

"His attempt is getting stronger."

"You think he's closer?"

"He has to be."

Carth glanced at her before nodding. They looked around the town, and she continued to sneak along the streets, with Lucy following her. As they went, Lucy tried to think only superficial thoughts, and yet she was failing. Everything she was doing was not going to be enough.

Each time she began to have those negative thoughts, she forced them away, knowing they weren't hers. Her time with Ras had taught her that…

That was what he was after.

He wanted her to dig into her thoughts, to come up with names and people and places.

Clever.

If that was what he wanted, she was going to try a different approach.

She focused on what she had seen of the Ai'thol. The images of their defeat. Their destruction. The people of Elaeavn cutting them down. She brought those all to the forefront of her mind, flickering through them. She didn't even care that most of those images brought forth other people. She tried to pull up Carth, Rsiran, Galen. All people who had opposed Olandar Fahr over the years, and all people who had enough power to be dangerous to him.

Would it work?

Lucy didn't know, and perhaps it didn't even matter. All that mattered was that she was trying to give the Architect a different type of thought.

What she really needed was to find a way to Read him.

If she could figure out where he was, then she might be able to track that, and use that connection to see if there was anything in his mind.

For him to Read her, he had to be near, which meant there had to be something for her to latch on to.

She paused in the middle of the street. There were a few others out, but they ignored her, moving past her. They were dressed differently than Lucy, their clothes thinner and silkier, her heavy woolen cloak more appropriate for the colder north. Most of them looked to be craftsmen or bakers or farmers. They seemed unmindful of the fact that there was an outsider in the middle of their town, but they still gave her a wide berth.

Carth continued down the street, shadows pooling away from her.

Lucy ignored that.

She tried to ignore everything. The only thing she wanted to focus on was the sense within her mind, the power she could feel, the voice trying to reach into her head and draw out her memories.

Not just draw them out, but influence them.

The Architect wanted to force her into thinking a specific way. She would refuse.

And in doing so, she would find her way back.

She closed her eyes, thinking about those images, and decided that wasn't quite right. What she needed was to latch on to what he wanted.

In doing so, she might be able to figure out where he was.

And once she determined that, she might be able to find out how to stop him.

She closed her eyes again, focusing on everything all around her. She could feel the power pushing on her. It might only be in her mind, and yet she couldn't help but think it was something else.

She listened, Reading herself.

It was a lesson she'd been taught with the C'than. Let the Architect know that she worked with the C'than. Let him know that she had trained with Ras. Let him know that she worked with Carth.

And she felt it.

There was an influence there within her. It was subtle, and as she focused on it, she realized where she could move to peel away. She could feel the way the influence was pressing in upon her mind, trying to trap her.

Removing it required her to look beyond what he was trying to push into her mind. It required her to look beyond that blockage, deep within herself.

It was something Ras wanted her to do anyway. This felt like the wrong time and the wrong way, but perhaps that was what she needed.

She looked beyond that influence.

As she did, she found memories.

She ignored them. That was what the Architect wanted. All she wanted to do was to search for those answers.

When she found them, she latched on to that influence. It was deep within her mind. The Architect was working far more skillfully than she would've expected. There was still much she could learn from him.

It was difficult for her to acknowledge that, and yet, feeling the subtle touch on her mind, she knew he might have been able to teach her quite a bit about her abilities. If only she had stayed with him, she would have been much more powerful…

She smiled to herself.

Using that connection, she tracked it back.

He wasn't as close as she had thought.

But he *was* within the town.

She Slid to Carth and then Slid again, following the connection within her mind.

They emerged outside a small home, smoke drifting up from the chimney. A thatched roof hung out over the street, shadows swirling around it. It seemed ready-made for someone like Carth. The door was slightly ajar, and there were two windows cut into the side of the wall, the glass open, letting a cool breeze blow through.

Lucy approached slowly, tentatively, and Carth stretched out her arm, motioning to her. Shadows drifted away from her, and the other woman unsheathed her sword, stepping forward.

Lucy continued to focus on the connection, the thoughts, wondering whether the Architect was still there or had already left. It was difficult to know. With his power, it was possible that he had already abandoned this place.

When Carth stepped inside, the shadows thickened, becoming something tangible, and Lucy followed her.

When she did, she knew they were already too late.

"He's gone," Carth said.

"He is."

"Are you sure he was here?"

Lucy searched through her mind, peeling away the thoughts. Could he have influenced her in such a way to make her believe he had been here? It was possible, but now that she knew how to Read herself, she didn't think so.

"I think he actually was here, and I think he was surprised we found him."

"Is there anything else you can uncover from him?"

"No." It would take time, and the more she thought about it, the more uncertain she was that she would even find anything. But then, she thought that she needed to. It was critical for what they were doing. If she could uncover what the Architect wanted from her, and what he was doing in this town, then maybe they could learn what Olandar Fahr had planned.

Perhaps it was nothing more than trying to take over this town, but perhaps there was some other purpose.

"Then it's time for us to go," Carth said.

"You don't want to look around here any longer?"

"I don't know that I will find anything else here."

Lucy sighed and stretched out her awareness, but there were too many different voices in her mind, too many different thoughts. As she searched, she couldn't help but feel as if they were close to an answer, but still so far away.

"How did you learn the Architect was here?"

"Rumors come together in a certain pattern," Carth said.

"And you use those rumors to help you find him?"

"I used those rumors to help bring things together. I still think there's more we can uncover."

"How?"

"Because the rumors I heard weren't the only rumors about him."

And if there were other rumors, then maybe they *would* be able to find the Architect.

It was something Lucy hadn't considered before, but now that she was here with Carth, now that she had come so close to the Architect, she wanted to find him and to know just what he'd been doing.

She felt that was important. She didn't know what she would do when she captured him, or whether there would be any way for her to get revenge, and she didn't even know if that was what she wanted. He needed to be captured. The more she thought about it, the more she realized Carth knew Lucy wanted it.

"You planned for this."

"I didn't plan for anything."

"You planned for me to want to capture him."

"You've been focused on your training. You should be. And yet, as I have talked with Ras, I can't help but think you need to be focusing on other things as well."

"Such as capturing the Architect."

"We need to get to him."

"We don't need to. You *want* to."

"In order to find Olandar Fahr, we need the Architect."

Lucy looked around the small room. There was nothing here that would be useful in finding the Architect. There were no items of any value. He had food and other typical items scattered around here.

How was it possible for her to know that?

The only way would be if she'd Read something about him.

And if she'd managed to do that, then she'd gotten deeper into his mind than she'd realized.

She smiled to herself. She swept her gaze over everything in the room again and looked up at Carth. "I need to return to the C'than stronghold."

"Why?"

"I need time to think."

Carth nodded and glided toward Lucy on the shadows. Lucy took her arm, and they Slid.

7

DANIEL

Wind whistled around the courtyard, and Daniel stood with his cloak wrapped around him, waiting for Rayen. Shadows swirled around her as she approached, a dangerous grace to the way she walked. Her dark eyes sparkled, the shadows within them seeming to glow.

"What's taking you so long?" he asked.

"Not all of us can travel the way you do."

Daniel grinned. "I doubt I can travel any differently than you."

Shadows swirled around her for a moment. "I doubt I'll ever be able to travel via the same method."

"You don't know."

"I don't have your heritage."

They had been through this before, but now that she'd held one of the crystals, there was no telling what was going to change for her. Perhaps nothing, but if history told him anything, it was that everyone who held one of the sacred crystals transformed in some way. In the case of Rayen, it would be different than anything seen in Elaeavn.

It wasn't all that different for him. Ever since he'd been to the chamber of shadows, he had viewed them differently. Not only could he see the darkness swirling around Rayen, but it was almost as if he could feel it, as if it were something alive, and he struggled to understand what that meant for him.

"Are you ready to do this or not?" Daniel wanted to get it over with while the others were waiting. This plan had a time limit to it, and it required him getting to see his father in his room.

Rayen looked around the courtyard. They were in the middle section of Elaeavn, between what had once been known as Upper Town and Lower Town. A statue remained of one of the architects who created the city, though it was about the only thing that was original for this courtyard. Most of the buildings surrounding it had been rebuilt following the attack two decades ago, and though the artisans who had been responsible for helping rebuild them were as skilled as any within Elaeavn, they didn't have the same delicate touch as those first builders had. There was simply something about the way the founders of Elaeavn had designed the city that practically drew the stonework out.

"Are you sure you want me to go with you?"

The last time he'd come to the palace, Rayen had avoided coming with him, but then again, he had chosen to go without her. "You have no interest in going to the palace?"

"I'll admit that I'm curious, but I wanted to make sure you're comfortable with it."

Daniel shook his head. "It's long past time I confront my father about this."

"And you need me there for support?"

"Not necessarily for support, but I think that will disarm him a little bit." That was the other part of the plan.

Rayen frowned at him. "I'm not sure I want to be used in such a way."

"What way do you want to be used?"

She rounded on him, shadows swirling around her.

Daniel smiled, raising his hands. "I don't know if I meant it quite like that. Then again, I can't deny that I get a kick out of seeing you like this."

"If you're not careful, you will definitely get a kick."

"Are you going to come with me, or are you going to try to get out of it again?"

"Do you think you can taunt me into cooperating?"

"Yes."

She studied him for a moment before laughing. "I can see why she likes you."

"Who?"

"Carth. There aren't many she willingly games with as often as she does with you. She sees something in you, though I wonder what that is."

Daniel shrugged. "If you were a better gamer, you wouldn't have to wonder."

Rayen glared at him. "I suspect I would defeat you at Tsatsun within a few moves."

Daniel had played with Carth quite a bit, but he had never played with Rayen. He was curious how skilled she would be at that game, and suspected she was much more skilled than most. Carth favored Rayen, even though Rayen believed otherwise. From what little he knew of Carth, she only played Tsatsun with people she felt had real potential. It had to be more than simply Rayen's connection to the shadows.

"I don't know. Carth said you played like a child when I played her last time. She said it was nice to play with someone more mature with their moves."

Rayen glared at him for a moment. "Perhaps I will let you confront your father on your own."

"That's probably for the best. I'm not sure you could handle the palace."

With that, she stuck her hand out, waiting for him. Daniel took it and Slid.

The Slide took him to the courtyard outside of the palace. The wind didn't whistle around here as much as it did lower in the city, though the massive walls surrounding the palace protected them. A flat expanse of grass grew all around, and the fading daylight cast shadows all over, though no more than what Rayen would normally control.

"Why here?" she whispered.

Daniel nodded to the palace. "You see the bars over the windows?"

She nodded.

"Those bars are made of heartstone. For those with my ability, it is incredibly difficult for us to make our way past those bars."

"The metal prevents you from traveling beyond it?"

"Not everyone. Lareth can Slide beyond the bars, and from what he has told others, the Forgers—the Ai'thol—who have mastered a level of control over their abilities also can do so, but most of us cannot."

Rayen turned to him, still holding on to his hand. "Have you tried since you were exposed to the shadows?"

Daniel shook his head. "I'm not sure it makes a difference. They are different abilities."

"Different, and yet I suspect they're complementary in some ways."

"Has your holding the crystal made a difference for you?"

Rayen's jaw clenched for a moment. "Not yet. I still question what will become of me with this change."

"It's nothing to fear."

"Says the man who has not yet held one of the crystals."

Daniel grunted. "It's not for lack of trying."

"Why?"

"Why what?"

"Why haven't the crystals allowed you to hold one?"

Daniel shook his head. "No one really knows. Those who study the crystals, including the caretakers, have never come up with a good explanation as to why certain people are allowed to hold one of the crystals and others are not."

"Caretakers?"

Daniel nodded, smiling to himself. "The men and women in charge of the library. They study the history of Elaeavn. Because of them, we have a better understanding as to the nature of our people."

"Apparently not."

Daniel shrugged. "Not as good as we would like. We still don't know quite a few things."

"Such as?"

"Such as the forest. You've seen the trees there. They hold significance to our people, and yet, there were years when no one knew anything about them. It was almost as if they were intended to be forgotten." He frowned. His words felt too much like what their people had called those who were exiled from the city.

That couldn't be a coincidence, could it?

"What is it?"

Daniel shook his head. "Only something for me to think about. Anyway, the Elder Trees were a part of our past, much like the forest was a part of our past. Over time, we moved away from the forest and began to build the city. There aren't many records. The city is hundreds and hundreds of years old, and the palace was the crowning achievement, built near the very end."

"Which means your people once lived in the trees until they could move into the palace?"

Daniel shrugged. "Lucy might know more about it than I do."

"Why?"

"She was studying to be a caretaker."

Rayen started to laugh. "Lucy?"

"Why?"

"I just don't see it."

"Because she's changed. If you'd known Lucy when she was still here, you would understand."

"Is this something she wanted?"

"I don't know. It's something she was willing to do."

"That's not the same, Daniel Elvraeth, and you know it."

Daniel sighed. He did know that, and there wasn't much that could be done about it. "None of it matters now. She's a different person."

As much as he might have changed in the days since leaving the city, Lucy had changed even more. It was more than just the implant. It was her whole demeanor. He still found her incredibly alluring, but now there was something almost ethereal about her, as if she were some higher being that he was lucky to be around.

"What matters is how you react to her."

"She's already made it quite clear how I can react to her."

"You're still interested in her?"

It had been a while since he'd even thought about how he felt toward Lucy. He wasn't sure, which surprised him given how much he had been drawn to her when he was younger. And not even that much younger. It had been at a time when he was still trying to understand his abilities and what they meant, but it was also a time when he'd been convinced of what he would do and how he would serve in Elaeavn.

Could he really have wanted to sit on the Council?

After everything he'd seen, everything he had done, he couldn't imagine staying in the city and trying to rule. There was so much more that needed to be done. It was hard for him to comprehend that their people preferred to keep themselves separate from the rest of the world as they did. There was no purpose in that.

"Daniel?"

He shook his head, glancing over to her. "What is it?"

"Do you know this man?"

He turned to see two of the tchalit making their way toward them. When he'd been here before, he had hurried into the palace without waiting. Standing here in the courtyard like this left him open to questions.

One of the tchalit coming was a man he recognized. It had been a while since he'd seen him.

"Gabe," he said, nodding to him.

The other man frowned, studying Daniel for a moment. "Daniel Elvraeth?"

"Come on, Gabe. You had to know it was me."

"I saw darkness, and shapes, but…"

Daniel glanced over to Rayen, who smiled at him. "It's been a while."

"I hear you've been out of the city."

"I have been."

"Chasing rumors that Lareth brings back."

Daniel grunted. Quite a few in the city—and among the tchalit—felt the way Gabe did. They didn't view Rsiran in the most flattering light. Rather, they believed him responsible for maintaining the war, isolating Elaeavn, and though he might have been to blame for that, he was equally responsible for offering a level of protection.

"Something like that. I should thank you. Your training has saved me more than once."

Gabe chuckled. "My training saved you."

"You don't have to say it like that."

"I mean no disrespect, Daniel Elvraeth. It's just I find it

difficult to believe you've faced anything of consequence."

Rayen started to laugh, and Daniel shot her a hard glare that she ignored.

"You'd be surprised what I've encountered."

"Truly? So the stories that Lareth brings back—"

"Are generally true."

Gabe shared a glance with the other tchalit. "Is there any reason you've come to the palace this evening?"

"To visit with my father."

"I'm afraid I have instructions to keep everyone from bothering him."

"Including his son?"

"Including you."

Daniel smirked. "Gabe, you know I can just Slide."

"I seem to recall that ability of yours was limited."

"Limited, but that doesn't mean I can't sneak around behind you."

"I'm sorry, Daniel, but I have my instructions."

He was surprised that Gabe would try to keep him from the palace, but even more surprised that his father would do so. Then again, after the way he'd left things with his father, Daniel shouldn't be all that surprised.

"I'm going to go see him."

"You understand that as one of the tchalit, it's my role to protect the integrity of the palace."

"And you understand that as one of the Elvraeth, I have every right to enter the palace."

"Not any longer."

Had his father gone so far as to attempt to refuse his entry?

It would take him disowning him, but after what

Daniel had done, it was possible that his father had done so.

How dare he? After everything his father had done, he would now take this step? Daniel wasn't about to allow him to get away with that.

"If you need to stop me, go ahead and stop me."

Gabe shared a glance with the other tchalit once again.

Together, the two men unsheathed, and they stood in their ready position.

Daniel could simply Slide past them. Once he got to the palace doors, he would be able to get into the palace, and then he could Slide again, but he would run the risk of the tchalit chasing him through the palace. There was another reason for him to consider simply confronting them now. A part of him—a large part, he realized—was curious how he would fare against Gabe. The last time he and Gabe had sparred, he'd been quickly defeated. Would the same fate befall him now?

The real challenge was that it wasn't only Gabe now. There was another of the tchalit. When facing off against Gabe, he was outclassed. With two of the tchalit…

"Would you like me to assist?" Rayen asked.

He flicked his gaze over to her. The fact that she asked rather than intervening on his behalf made him like her even more. "Let me see how I do first."

With that, he Slid.

He emerged behind Gabe, swinging his sword. The other man was quick, turning as if he anticipated where Daniel was going to Slide, and Daniel reacted, darting off to the side, ducking beneath the other tchalit, and twisting his sword around.

He had to be careful. He didn't want to hurt either of them, only disarm them.

He didn't have the same sense from either of those men. They seemed to be fighting to win. Winning meant Daniel didn't survive.

He Slid, emerging briefly on the other side of Gabe before Sliding once more.

The other man likely was a Seer; if so, he would be able to anticipate every move Daniel made. The one advantage he had was that he was able to Slide, something that obscured those who could See.

Doing it enough times would obfuscate anything his opponent might be able to observe. More than that, doing it enough times would make it difficult for them to fight him.

In the time since he'd faced Gabe, not only had he been working with Rayen, among others, rapidly improving his swordsmanship, but he'd also grown far more talented with his ability to Slide.

He didn't need to prove to Gabe that he was the better swordsman. Daniel didn't even know if that would be the case. The other man had trained his entire life to develop his skill. Daniel had only been really working over the last year or so. But he did want to end the fight as quickly as possible.

Another Slide and he emerged next to the second tchalit. He kicked, sending the man staggering, and emerged where the man stumbled, slamming the hilt of the sword down the back of his head. Gabe was there, twisting toward Daniel, and he blocked, parrying a couple of thrusts before feinting an attack and ducking back.

Daniel twisted off in a Slide, rotating as he emerged, but Gabe managed to meet his sword with his own. They attacked one after another, a flowing movement. He couldn't help but be amazed at how effective the other man was at combating him even though he wasn't able to Slide.

It was time to end this. Facing only one of the tchalit was far easier than dealing with two. Daniel performed a flurry of Slides, each of them dizzying, darting from one side to the other of Gabe before he emerged, sweeping his sword around and stopping just short of the other man's throat.

Gabe held his hands up. "You *have* been training."

"I have. Drop it."

"We were instructed not to let you in."

"I believe it."

"I would like to spar with you again."

"Just spar?"

"I had no interest in actually attacking you."

"And yet you did."

"As I was required to do."

Gabe dropped his sword, and Daniel slammed him on the temple with the hilt of his sword. The other man crumpled.

Sheathing his blade, he turned to Rayen. She was watching him, an amused expression on her face. "You were slow."

"Slow? They barely got their swords up."

"Seeing as how I have yet to be defeated by you, I would say that you were slow."

Daniel chuckled. She was far superior to him in sword

skill. "That would be the only way you'd beat me. Maybe when you lose playing your childlike game of Tsatsun, you could spar with me to make yourself feel better."

He started off before giving her a chance to react, suppressing a smile as he did.

When they entered the palace, he paused for a moment. He had the sense he always did when coming to the palace. There was the overwhelming feeling of being in a place he'd known his whole life, mixed with an appreciation for the way the palace had been built, and then there was the overall impression of age, a mixture of power that represented everything their people had experienced.

"It's an impressive building," Rayen said.

"Most of the time," he said.

"Why your hesitation?"

"I just want a moment to gather myself."

"Are you afraid of confronting him?"

Was it fear? Daniel didn't think so, but there was a time when he would have believed that to be the case. His father had always intimidated him, testing him constantly, making him prove himself over and again.

Through it all, Daniel had never been sure if he had earned his father's trust. That was what he had been angling for his whole life. He had wanted to serve on the Council, and he had believed he had to justify himself, which meant he constantly had to push.

"It's not fear—at least I don't think it is. It's more a sense of resignation." When Rayen suggested he do this, he had agreed, but now it was upon him, he wasn't sure this was the right tactic to take.

He had to push that thought away. He knew it was the right strategy. If they didn't do this, his father would continue to cause harm.

"Why?" she asked.

"When I was growing up, he was this impressive man. The ideal of what I should live up to. It wasn't until I left the city that I saw him for what he really was." And even then, Daniel had tried to reject it. It was hard for him to believe his father could've been responsible for allowing the attack on the forest, and yet… he had been.

"Every child must grow up and see their parents for what they are. When you're young, you view your parents as heroic, even if they are not. When you grow, you start to rebel, and it's only upon looking back that you can judge them in the proper context."

"You sound as if you have some experience."

"I went through many of the same things as you did, Daniel Elvraeth."

Rayen was reserved about her past, and he had come to expect that she would dole out what she wanted on her own terms. He respected that, knowing he couldn't push or he would probably drive her away rather than drawing her closer. Instead, he smiled at her.

"Are you ready to go and meet with my father?"

With a nod, they started off through the palace. Daniel hurried up the stairs, wandering through the halls, and found himself before his old door, staring at it. He paused for a moment before knocking. When his father's voice sounded from the other side of the door, Daniel pushed it open.

Two tchalit met him, grabbing him.

8

DANIEL

DANIEL TRIED TO JERK FREE, BUT THEY WERE STRONG. HE glanced over to Rayen, and she frowned at him, shadows swirling around her. He shook his head. Let his father see he could handle this.

Daniel Slid backward, barely a step, but the two men who'd been holding on to his arms were pulled with him. When he emerged, he twisted, slamming them together and then Sliding again. He dragged them down the hall like that, Sliding again and again, each time forcing them against each other. They bounced along the walls before finally releasing his arm and sinking to the ground.

Sliding back to where Rayen stood, he entered his father's room. "That's quite the greeting, Father."

His father sat in a chair near the crackling hearth. A book lay open on his lap, and he looked up, almost lazily, as Daniel entered. "You aren't allowed here any longer."

"Because you decided to exile me? You know that punishment is forbidden."

"*I* have chosen to exile you. Not the Council."

"That changes nothing for who I am."

"It changes everything."

Daniel nodded to Rayen and she followed him in. Closing the door behind him, he said, "Can you seal off the room?"

She cocked her head to the side, frowning for a moment. "Are you sure?"

"Most definitely."

Shadows twined around the perimeter of the room. He didn't know if his father could even See them the way Daniel could.

"You've betrayed our people."

"That's why you came here?"

"I didn't say anything when I saw you in the dining hall, but it's time for your reign to end."

"I think not."

"Cael Elvraeth knows what you did."

"It's a good thing Cael Elvraeth doesn't lead my family."

"She leads the Council."

"For now. Do you actually believe she will continue to do so indefinitely?"

Daniel had heard this line of thinking from his father for most of his life. "I do. Partly because she has outmaneuvered you all these years. The great Malin Elvraeth, who thought all this time that he was manipulating others to do his will. Through it all, Cael Elvraeth was the one doing the manipulating."

He watched his father's face as he said it. It was the

one thing he could say that would enrage his father the most. In this case, Daniel *wanted* to enrage him. He wanted that anger, if only so that he would react predictably. He knew his father could be difficult to gauge, and he was determined not to be outplayed. If nothing else, his time with Carth had taught him that lesson.

"Do you think I don't know what you're doing?"

Daniel smiled, taking a seat across from his father. "And what, exactly, am I doing, Father?"

"You think to manipulate me."

"Says the master of manipulation."

"You say that as if I should feel ashamed."

"I say it as if you should recognize that you have used people along the way."

"I have done nothing but attempt to strengthen Elaeavn."

Daniel sat back, watching his father. He glanced over briefly at Rayen. "Father, let me introduce you to Rayen."

Rayen bowed her head slightly. "Malin Elvraeth. It is a pleasure to make your acquaintance."

His father didn't even look in her direction. "What are you doing here?"

"Clearly I'm acting quite rudely. Oh, wait, that appears to be you."

"I'm not the one who attacked two tchalit, including one who trained you all these years when you were young."

"The same tchalit who were instructed to prevent my access to the palace. Access that my birthright grants me."

"I have revoked your birthright."

"As I've told you, you can no longer do that."

"As you've seen, I can. You will find there are a great many things I am capable of doing, Daniel."

He regarded his father for a long moment before smiling. "You know, there was a time when I feared you."

"You still should."

"I thought you a man worthy of fear. Then again, I also thought you a man worthy of respect. You claim that you have acted in order to strengthen Elaeavn, and yet by trying to exclude those who live in the forest, you weaken it." Daniel leaned forward, resting his elbows on his knees as he glared at his father. "I'm well aware of the deal you made with the C'than." He watched his father as he said it, noting the corners of his eyes twitched slightly. "Yes. I'm also familiar with the C'than. There are a great many things I have learned."

"You know nothing."

"Let me tell you what I uncovered. You plotted with Alera, thinking you could remove Lareth from the city and make yourself stronger. You gave no thought to the fact that, in doing so, you actually weakened the city. In fact, your action very nearly gave the Ai'thol the power they were seeking."

No look of recognition flashed across his father's eyes.

"What's that, Father? You don't know the Ai'thol? Let me explain what they are. You may know part of the Ai'thol as a different name. Lareth has pursued them his entire life."

"Forgers," his father spat.

"Not just the Forgers. The Hjan before them. I'm sure there have been other names, and other atrocities that they have committed. Through it all, they have sought to gain power. There was one thing they weren't able to reach, even when Lareth hadn't fully come into his powers. And you, the great protector of Elaeavn, very nearly overturned that."

"You think that it matters?"

Daniel sat back, smiling to himself. "It matters. It also matters that I found a way to stop it. They no longer draw upon the power of the sacred crystals, trying to drain the energy of the Elder Trees. We have that power back, though I don't know how much longer we will be able to maintain it."

He sat for a moment in silence, glaring at his father. The other man said nothing.

"You're not even going to deny it?"

"What's there to deny? I acted in a way I believed would protect the city."

"Only you knew it would not."

"The Council sees it differently."

"Do they? I would suggest Cael Elvraeth would say otherwise."

"Cael Elvraeth. Have you decided to throw your lot in with her? Perhaps she will adopt you the same way she adopted Galen."

Daniel grinned. "It would be an honor if she did."

It was another statement he made to irritate his father. At this point, he was determined to keep saying whatever he could to agitate him even more.

"The Council has already voted on this issue, if it

matters to you at all. Seeing as how you have abandoned the city over the last few months—"

"I've abandoned nothing. I have done far more than you to protect the city. And now I'm here to finish the job."

"Finish what?"

"That's why I came, Father."

"To do what, Daniel? Do you think you're ready to sit upon the Council? Do you think the family would even support you? Let me tell you the answer to that. No. The family recognizes the value I add. They would much rather see me maintain my position of authority then have someone like you involved in the running of the city."

"I have no interest in sitting on the Council."

"I'm impressed you can say that with a straight face."

"Are you? I'm so pleased I can impress you."

"You've had nothing but naked ambition your entire life, Daniel."

"Because of you." He needed to continue baiting his father. The longer he could do it, the more likely his father would say something foolish. Even if he didn't, his father had lost. He just didn't know it yet.

"I am surprised you came back here," his father said.

"You wouldn't be if you were paying any attention."

"Indeed? And just what should I be paying attention to?"

"Perhaps had you paid more attention to your family, and those around you, none of this would have been necessary."

"None of what?"

Daniel smiled tightly. "None of this whole conversation, Father."

His father cocked his head, and Daniel smiled to himself. He had often wondered how skilled a Listener his father was, and though he might not find out now, the fact he resorted to using that ability suggested it was not insignificant. He had known his father was a capable Reader, and yet, he had nothing on Cael Elvraeth when it came to that particular ability.

"Do you hear anything?"

His father frowned at him. "And what am I supposed to hear?"

"That would be the sound of your failure. You've lost the Council."

"I've lost nothing."

"You have. The rest of the Council has determined that your role is no longer needed. Considering the impact you had on allowing the C'than to attack the city—and the Elder Trees—others have decided they will no longer work with you."

His father sat quietly. "The rest of the Council was a part of the discussion. Do you think I could take any action independently? Only two families weren't a part of it. The Council had a majority before we acted, as is custom." He leaned back, crossing a leg over the other. "And soon other customs will return. It is long past time."

"Such as exiling those you disagree with?"

"It's more than just that. It's maintaining a certain purity within Elaeavn. Within the Elvraeth." His father flashed a dark smile. "Unfortunately for you, there might be a test case far sooner than we had anticipated."

Daniel glanced over to Rayen. She had been standing there, the shadows around them angled in a specific way, augmenting their voices.

"I'm not terribly concerned about exile, as I once was. In fact, I wonder if perhaps that wouldn't be a better outcome."

"You understand what exile means. We've had that conversation. It means you won't be able to return. You will be stripped of your titles. Stripped of your heritage. You will never see your mother or me again. If you return to the city, you will face a more violent punishment."

"You made it quite clear what's involved in exile. And I have spoken to Galen."

"I'm not surprised you've done that."

"Galen shares a particular insight. Did you realize that there are entire communities of exiles living beyond the city?"

"They matter not to me."

"And yet, if you truly cared about Elaeavn, they would. They are our people. Some of them were like Galen, doing little more than attacking an Elvraeth who deserved every bit of punishment Galen inflicted." Daniel leaned forward. "Yes. I'm well aware of what Galen did to earn his exile. Do you think that Cael Elvraeth did not know?"

"Cael is a foolish girl who dabbles in things she cannot understand."

"I'd be careful about using terms like that around Rayen."

"You would like me to believe that this *friend* of yours"—he said *friend* so derisively that Daniel almost grinned—"is someone that I should fear? What talent does she have? She's pretty enough, and she has lovely full lips, so I—"

His father was suddenly silenced. Darkness swirled around his mouth and throat, and within moments, his eyes began to bulge.

Daniel sighed. "As I was saying, I would be careful around her. You might think that her beauty means she isn't dangerous, but she is one of the deadliest people I've ever met. Look at how quickly you suffer. Think about how she managed to do that in a heartbeat. And look where she's standing."

His father glanced over to where Rayen stood on the far side of the room, leaning casually on the window.

"Have you had enough?"

His father's head bobbed quickly in a nod.

The shadows disappeared. This time, Daniel could practically feel it as they did. The longer he spent around Rayen, the more he began to wonder if he would somehow gain some insight and control over the shadows as well.

His father took a gasping breath.

"So you see, sometimes things aren't quite what they appear." He got to his feet, making his way over to the door.

"You attack me and then you decide to depart? You should've had her kill me. You will find that your fate will be—"

Daniel pulled the door open, and Cael Elvraeth stood on the other side. Deep green eyes blazed with anger, and her blonde hair hung in a braid down to the middle of her back. She was dressed in her formal robes, the heavy embroidery signifying her rank as head of the Council. She was here in that regard as much as anything.

There were a dozen others, all of them watching. Lucy stood among them, her eyes blazing a deep green. Many of the people there looked as if they wished they were anywhere but standing outside the door, but with Cael and with Lucy, they probably had no choice in the matter.

"What is this?" His father said, jumping to his feet.

"Why, it appears that you have admitted to your treason."

"I've admitted to nothing."

Daniel returned and took a seat across from his father. "Rayen has control of shadows. I believe you have felt that most distinctly?" His father pressed his lips together. "Yes. With her control over the shadows, she can modify them so that sound carries."

His father blinked rapidly, his eyes twitching.

"You understand what I'm getting at."

Cael made a motion, and five tchalit came marching into the room. Two of them grabbed his father by the arms, lifting him.

"You're lucky we've forbidden the ancient tradition of exiling. Had we not, you would be a candidate for such suffering."

"Do you think I fear exile?"

"I think you fear losing everything. And with what you have done, you have."

His father stood defiantly. He didn't even make an effort to resist. "The Council supported me in my decision."

"The others have been dealt with. The families have

seen that there is a need for a change in leadership, much like your family has now seen the need for a change." Cael turned to the tchalit. "See that he is secured in the cells."

"You would throw us in the cells?"

"For now. The Council will meet and decide your fate. You'll be lucky if it only involves you serving in Ilphaesn."

The tchalit marched his father out of the room, and the other Elvraeth outside the door quickly dispersed. Lucy entered, closing the door.

Cael sighed. "I wish it hadn't had to come to this."

"It's for the best that we deal with this now."

"Sometimes I wonder," she said.

"You wonder if it's for the best?"

"I wonder if we are weakening Elaeavn through our actions."

"Considering what he did—"

Cael shook her head. "I'm not debating that. There's no question that what he did is unacceptable. His attack on the city and the way he allowed Rsiran to be used are inexcusable, but I don't care for this."

"What will happen with the Council now?"

"What has already happened. The families have chosen, and a replacement will be selected."

"How much influence will you have on who replaces them?" Daniel asked. It was strange thinking about it, especially since there had been a time when he had wanted nothing more than to sit upon the Council, to take over after his father and lead their family. It was one thing that his father had spoken truly about. Daniel had been filled with naked ambition, but that desire had been fostered by his father, built up and strengthened until he had desired only to have power.

"Me personally?" Cael shook her head. "None. Which is how it should be. I served on behalf of my family, as each Council member should. I don't want to choose who sits on the Council. Otherwise, the entire process becomes a farce. We need everyone to serve the way the system is meant to work."

"Obviously, it didn't work this time."

"Didn't it? I think in some ways, it did work exactly as we intended it. The families chose the representative, and the representative has acted. Unfortunately, in this case, there was a desire for power."

She glanced to Rayen. "You really are talented."

Rayen smiled. "I learned from one of the best."

"Galen thinks highly of you."

A slight flush worked across her cheeks and Rayen turned away. It amused Daniel to see her disarmed in such a way. Then again, a compliment from Galen was worth more than gold. It surprised him that he should feel that way, though having spent time around him, he recognized the value the man brought. It was one thing his father had been closed-minded about. He had viewed Galen as a threat—which he was, but not for the reason he had always believed. Galen was a threat because he was so proficient.

"I understand you will be leaving again."

"We need to better understand what the Ai'thol are after," Daniel said. "And if it's another of the Elder Stones…"

Cael sighed. "There are times when I wish I could go.

With my abilities, I can't help but think I would be able to offer some assistance."

Daniel didn't know how much to believe of the rumors about Cael, but if any of them were even remotely true, then she would be an asset when dealing with the Ai'thol. How much else could she offer if they needed to uncover details about the remaining Elder Stone? With her ability to Read, he could come up with dozens of ways she could help.

"Unfortunately, duty keeps me here."

"The people of the city need you," Daniel said.

"There are times when I wonder if I'm doing everything I can. I tried to integrate our people, to bridge the divide, and yet here we are, years later, and it feels as if we are no better off than we had been before. If I had been doing everything I could, we wouldn't have the same division." Cael nodded to Rayen before turning to Daniel. "It was a difficult thing that you did today."

"It wasn't that difficult."

"Anytime you pit yourself against someone you care about, it's difficult. I had to do something similar once, so I understand."

"What happened when you did it?"

Cael motion to her robes. "Unfortunately, I got called to serve."

Daniel laughed. "I have a hard time thinking my family will expect the same from me."

"If they do, it wouldn't be a poor choice. Still, I think you will have another way to serve. In many ways, it is even more important than what you would do here.

Travel well, Daniel, and know that whatever support you need from the city is yours."

As she made her way out of the room, she paused at Lucy, leaning close and whispering something to her. It was said so softly that he couldn't hear any of it, but he realized it didn't matter. That conversation was only for the two of them.

When Cael was gone, Lucy glanced from Daniel to Rayen. "You can transport her wherever you need to go?"

"What about you?"

"Carth needs something from me."

Daniel debated how to answer, but there was nothing for him to say. Instead, he nodded. Lucy turned, and in a flash she disappeared.

"I wonder if she can Slide beyond the palace," Daniel said.

"That was your question?"

He headed over to the window, looking out through the bars of heartstone. "She has become incredibly powerful with her ability to Slide. It makes me wonder."

"You might be able to Slide here."

"I'm afraid to try."

"How will you ever know if you can if you don't attempt it?"

He took a deep breath, preparing for a Slide. Something Rayen had said came back to him. What if he mingled it with his connection to the shadows? They were separate abilities, and yet they seemed to be complementary. If he could somehow find a way to make them work together, would he be able to find a way past the heartstone?

Taking Rayen's hand, he focused on the courtyard on the other side of the window. At first, he felt nothing more than resistance. There was the typical barrier he detected when trying to Slide beyond heartstone, but within it was something else, something he hadn't noticed when he had attempted to do this before.

Could he actually succeed?

He pushed, following a strange contour to the Slide, using that to guide him beyond the barrier.

It felt as if he were twisting and curling, slipping around like shadows slithering through sunlight.

And then he emerged.

He blinked, looking back at the palace, and laughed.

"It worked."

Rayen nodded. "That was interesting."

"What did you detect?"

"You pulled us through the shadows."

"I did what?"

She glanced over at him. "You weren't aware of it?"

"It felt as if I were following a different path than I normally do when Sliding, but it was still a Slide."

"It seems to me that you were following the shadows. I could practically see what you were doing."

That intrigued him, almost as much as it intrigued him that he had managed to Slide beyond heartstone. It would be valuable to have that ability. It was one less way the Ai'thol might be able to trap him.

"Lucy is going off on Carth's mission. Are you ready for ours?" Daniel asked. He had been willing to take on this assignment, though he wasn't entirely sure they would even be able to find anything. Still, having Carth trust him with this made him think he could do it.

"I'm not sure why she decided to punish me by making me go with you, but I suppose if there is no other choice…"

Daniel grabbed her hand, squeezing for a moment, and then they Slid.

9

RYN

THE OUTSIDE OF THE TOWER WAS UNUSUALLY COLD FOR
this time of year, with a bitter chill that swirled around,
forcing Ryn to pull her cloak more tightly around her
shoulders. She resisted the urge to do so, not wanting to
show any signs of weakness, but there wasn't much choice
at this point. If she was to remain comfortable, she was
going to need her cloak.

Standing at the edge of the tower, she stared down
into the city, looking for signs of movement. As far as she
could tell, there were none.

Her eyesight had improved, but then again, much had
improved. She still wasn't quite sure what to make of it,
but she had already begun to accept the changes. What
choice did she have?

Ryn brought her hand up, tracing her finger along the
back of her head, over the implant. It throbbed at times,
serving as a reminder for everything she'd gained. It
wasn't a sacrifice. No—her sacrifice had been made long
ago. For so long, she had thought the sacrifice had been in

coming here, embracing the teachings of the tower, hoping for understanding. But that hadn't been her sacrifice.

Hers had been what her father had given up for her to survive.

"What do you see?"

Ryn turned toward the voice. She wasn't surprised he would come. It seemed he always knew when to arrive, though she still wasn't sure how. He claimed it was his gift, and that he was blessed with knowledge and understanding, and everything she had seen suggested that to be true. How could it be anything else?

"There's nothing down there," she said.

The Great One joined her at the edge of the tower. He kept his hands at his sides, and when he looked up at her, it seemed as if he exuded a sort of power—which she suspected he did. That was what she wanted, and the more she worked at it, the more certain she was that eventually she'd have something similar to his power.

"The others are gone, but that's not what I'm asking. I'm asking you what do you see?"

Ryn stared off into the darkness. An occasional gust of wind whipped around, but she refused to grab for her cloak. She wouldn't do that with him here. It wouldn't do for him to see any weakness in her. He appreciated strength, and she would embrace it. He had earned that much from her. More than anyone else, the Great One had proven himself.

"The city slumbers," Ryn said.

"Slumbers?"

She nodded. "There's silence throughout. I see no

movement. I hear nothing. And the air has none of the typical stench of others out within it."

"Good."

Ryn smiled to herself. Praise from the Great One was always welcomed, and while not necessarily rare, it was certainly something she knew others didn't receive with the same frequency she'd managed. Then again, she wanted nothing more than to serve.

"What else do you detect?"

Since accepting her blessing, Ryn had been asked that question time and again. What did she detect? It seemed to be the answer the Great One wanted from her most of all. Was it a matter of him trying to better understand how the blessing had changed her? He seemed to have expected she would be changed and had known something would happen to her, though he hadn't indicated what exactly that might be. What gifts might her blessing bring compared to others of his followers?

Ryn had been through more than most of them. Few had lived through the loss of their village, at least in the way that Ryn had, having seen Lareth himself attacking, moving through the village, destroying everything. Fewer still had seen lava swallow the remains, leaving nothing but the charred husk of the city.

She pushed away those memories. They did her no good. It only brought up sadness, and this was a happy time. She had been given a great blessing.

"Nothing yet."

"Give it time, my child."

She smiled again. She would take the kind words. Very few were given the opportunity to spend as much time with the Great One as she was, and she was blessed on a regular basis. She knew she needed to be thankful for that, and she was, but more than that, she needed to continue to work. The Great One deserved that from her.

She refused to let him down.

"How much longer should I stay here?"

The Great One touched her arm. Where he did, her skin tingled, leaving her with a thrill of anticipation. She suspected that was tied to some gift he had, but then, the Great One was the most powerful of them all. Eventually, he would come to control all abilities. If everything went well, Ryn would be there with him. She might be young and inexperienced, but she was motivated. The Great One had shown her that motivation counted for much.

"A little while longer, I think. Soon enough I will give you another assignment."

Ryn stood silently, staring into the darkness. Every so often, a pressure seemed to pulse against her senses, and she wasn't quite aware of what that was. Yet. In time, she suspected she would begin to better understand, but for now, it was nothing more than a strange sense.

She had some experience with strange senses suddenly appearing. It had been that way when her enhanced eyesight had first emerged. The suddenness of it had startled her, an ability to make out shapes in the darkness, and then that had quickly faded, receding so that even the darkness was no longer quite as dark as it once had been. Now the daylight and the night weren't all that different. Night consisted of more gradations of gray, but day was merely more shimmerings of brightness.

THE COMING CHAOS | 115

"You are silent," the Great One said. "Do you disapprove?"

"Not at all."

"Good."

He started to turn from her. "When will I see you again?"

"Soon enough," he said.

"Where are you going this time?"

"There is something I must do."

She hoped that he would share more, but that simply wasn't the way of the Great One. If he wanted to share, he would, and it was rare enough for him to say anything, though he was often more forthright with her than he was with many of the others. She figured that came from the fact that he had found her, rescuing her, bringing her to safety. The others had come to him, seeking out his power.

When she looked back, he was gone.

She hadn't needed her eyesight to know he had left. She felt it when he departed.

Perhaps that was the strange pressure she was growing accustomed to feeling. If that was it, there was value in it. The next time he returned, she would have to tell the Great One about that sensation. Perhaps there would be something he could help her learn and understand. She didn't have his skill with traveling, but in time, she hoped she could gain that ability.

Ryn wrapped her cloak back around her shoulders, making her way toward the main part of the tower. It was time to return to her assignment.

Once inside, she paused. The destruction here was

impressive. One man had caused considerable devastation. He had been powerful, but to hear the Great One talk about it, he shouldn't have been. It was a surprising setback, one that was unusual for them to sustain. Ryn wanted to understand what had happened. The disciple who had been responsible for it was gone, but that didn't mean she couldn't find answers.

Heading down a flight of stairs, she reached a small landing and stepped into the room.

A chair lay in shambles, hunks of the sacred metal left as if they were nothing more than scraps on the floor. A body lay broken, twisted, blood splattered all around it. The attacker had done this, had destroyed this Ai'thol in no more time than it would take her to walk down a flight of stairs.

That was not the mark of a weak person.

Given the nature of the attack, she could almost believe it was Lareth himself, but to hear the Great One talk about it, that wouldn't have been possible. Of course, it wouldn't. Ryn suspected the Great One had protections in place that would prevent it, though so far, she didn't have any idea what those protections were.

Eventually he would share them with her. She was certain of it. That was the benefit of being one of his favored.

The blessing gave her gifts, and to hear the Great One talk about it, the gifts came from aspects of abilities she would've otherwise known. It wasn't so much that they were given to her as that they were drawn out from her.

Looking around the room, she tried to understand what had taken place here. The Great One had stopped in here, but he hadn't spent much time. Either he didn't know—and she found that unlikely—or he already knew what had taken place and wanted her to uncover the details. That was far more likely.

She went over to the fallen Ai'thol, rolling him over. He was heavy, and considerably older than her, but he was not blessed in the way she was. He had one of the older blessings, the long scar beneath his chin revealing where the implant had been placed. Ryn was appreciative that she had one of the newer blessings, one that allowed her to slowly gain her abilities, but also one that didn't require such drastic methods in order to be placed. It was painful —there was no doubt about that—but she didn't have the same type of scar. Her hair had already begun to grow around the implant, making it so others wouldn't know.

Searching through the disciple's pockets, she didn't come up with anything. There was likely something she could discover. She sat back on her heels, frowning as she looked around. If not the Ai'thol, was it the chair?

Making her way over to it, she put the pieces of the chair back together, assembling them like some sort of puzzle. That was the answer, though how?

The wood had splintered, leaving fragments of the chair broken and scattered throughout. She found what appeared to be a backrest, and pieced that with other parts, forming it once again. A couple fragments didn't seem quite right. There was something missing.

As she studied it, her enhanced eyesight allowed her to make out the fact that there appeared to be armrests missing.

That was the key. Where were those sections of wood?

She got to her feet and continue to look around the room. There was nothing near the disciple.

That wasn't entirely true. He had the sacred metal near him.

She knew very little about the metal. The Great One kept details of it to himself, and yet the one thing she did know was that it was responsible for granting the blessing. A hunk of it rested on the ground near the disciple. She lifted it, rolling it in her hands, and noticed it felt a little warm. Slipping it into her pocket, Ryn decided she would investigate it further another time. For now, she would continue to look around the room.

There was nothing.

Heading out, she made her way through the staircase and to the altar. It had been a temple, a place of worship and celebration, and the attacker had changed that. He had brought violence and destruction, things she had thought were behind her. They were the kind of things the Great One was supposed to have protected her from.

Ryn pushed those thoughts away. They were dangerous thoughts. Besides, the Great One couldn't be in all places at all times. Regardless of what he claimed, the way he promised he was always watching, she knew it wasn't possible.

Blood was spattered all throughout here much like it had been in the other room. The attacker had come here, but why?

That was the answer she had yet to discover, and as far as she could tell, the Great One hadn't the answer to it, either.

Making her way slowly through the room, she passed

behind the altar, and a scrap of silk caught her eye. It was striped with red and orange, and frayed, but when she picked it up, it remained smooth within her fingers.

It didn't seem the kind of thing an attacker would have on them.

"What are you doing here?"

Ryn looked over. Lorren was old, a man who seemed as if he should have seen and known the world, and yet her experience with him had proven that he was naïve in ways she was not. The long gray robe of one of the acolytes hung along his shoulders, too small for the size of man he had become. Living within the temple had made him fat, and while the Great One never commented on that, she knew that he did not care for such indulgences.

"I'm trying to understand what took place here."

"We were attacked, you fool."

Ryn straightened, crossing her hands in front of herself. She fixed Lorren with as firm a gaze as she could. There was a time when she would've taken an insult like that without argument, but that time had long ago passed. Her experience with the Great One had taught her that she didn't have to fear petty men like him.

Besides, she knew she was favored, much like *he* knew that she was favored. Any comment he might make was bound to place him in danger.

"There was an attack while you were here, and the attacker is nowhere to be seen. It displeases him."

Lorren stared at her. Most looked at her the same way as he did, hating that there was only so much they could do with her. Her connection to the Great One gave her his voice.

"He was here?"

She bowed her head. "He was here."

Lorren licked his lips nervously. "He understands we are doing everything in our power to try to understand what took place."

"I'm certain he does."

"He left you."

She nodded.

"I am at your service, of course. We would do nothing to anger the Great One."

"As is wise."

Ryn made her way to the front of the altar, tracing her hand along the surface. It was smooth and cool, the marble having been polished over the years. There was something formal and stiff about it, but at the same time comforting.

It seemed a strange place to attack, and stranger still to find the scrap of silk that she had.

There was a mystery to be uncovered here, and she would find it for the Great One, reveal that secret, and if she couldn't, then perhaps she was undeserving of the gifts the Great One had provided her.

Ryn was determined not to fail. If she failed, any opportunity to be granted her real desire would be lost. And she *would* be the one to help the Great One find Lareth. He would suffer for all he had done to her people and her family.

"I would like the names of all who were here during the attack," Ryn said.

"Most who were here were not high-level Ai'thol."

Ryn nodded. "I see that. The man lying dead on the other floor was lower ranking than I."

She let the words linger. It was not just a threat, but also a comment on the lack of authority that this temple possessed. They didn't have a connection to the Great One the way they thought they did. They were not like Ryn.

But then, she was something of an outlier. She had been guided by the Great One himself, brought into the fold and welcomed, shepherded in a way. Because of his connection to her, she had been granted a greater understanding of the workings of the Ai'thol.

"What can we do to be of service?"

"I believe I've already told you what you can do."

Lorren nodded, bowing briefly before spinning and leaving her.

As Ryn surveyed the inside of the temple, she couldn't shake the sense that there was something more here than what she understood.

Stranger still was the suspicion that this was somehow tied to Lareth, though she didn't think that it was.

Ryn took a seat in the center of the room, closing her eyes. She was determined to remain here until she had a better sense of what was taking place. Somehow, she felt as if the answer would reach her, but she had to open herself to it.

The question the Great One always asked her rolled through her mind.

What else do you detect?

Nothing, yet. Ryn was determined to change that.

10

RYN

Stale air filled her nostrils, and Ryn breathed it out, frustration flowing through her. During her time in the temple, she had tried to find a place of calm, and yet there were times like this, times when she still struggled with keeping that calm. How could she when there was something she missed?

She leaned forward, resting her elbows on the wide plank table. The surface was rough, unfinished, but it fit her in a way that the heavily lacquered tables she'd been offered did not. And when she ran her hands along the rough surface, it helped her focus her mind.

Not that Ryn needed the additional help with focusing. But after spending days poring over the ledgers, looking through name after name, she was no closer than she had been before. It was almost as if Lorren and the others who worked with him were trying to conceal something from her.

What else did she detect?

There was something unusual taking place here, but

Ryn hadn't discovered it. The more time she spent in the temple, the more certain of that she was. The others always made a great show about offering their help, and they claimed service to the Great One, but there was something about their service she found off-putting. Perhaps she should not. Everyone had their own way of serving the Great One, herself included. Hers was utter devotion, but then that had come from the fact that she'd been saved by the Great One.

Ryn got to her feet, pacing in the small room. She'd been offered larger rooms and even some near the top of the tower where she could look out upon the city. None of them had appealed to her. She preferred to be on the lower levels, closer to the street, and with walls all around her, forcing her to concentrate.

What she needed now was to get out and stretch her legs.

Leaving the ledger behind, she stepped out of the room, closing the door behind her. The hallway swept out from her, and she made her way along it, keeping her senses attuned to the possibility of anything else around her.

As far as she could tell, there was nothing in the hall other than what there was supposed to be. In the last few days, no additional senses had appeared. Part of her was disappointed by that. It hadn't been all that long since she had taken the blessing, and as it pulsed, buried in her skull, she had thought that more might be coming to her. So far it had not.

Ryn should not be disappointed. She could easily imagine the things the Great One would say to her, though more likely than not, he would only admonish her for chasing the gifts she had not been offered rather than embracing those she had. Still, Ryn couldn't help but think there were aspects of her abilities she had not yet touched upon.

Sound came from down a side hallway.

It was a steady, muted tapping, a regular pattern that came and went. Pausing for a moment in the hallway, Ryn listened before realizing it was her augmented hearing that allowed her to detect the tapping. Not only was it farther along the hallway, it also seemed as if it came from somewhere below her.

Where were the stairs?

She tried to remember the layout of the temple, but she had been in so many over the months since she had joined the Great One that they had all started to blend together. This one was like so many others, while at the same time, it had its own curiosities. There was a staircase leading down, but she couldn't recall where it was.

Perhaps that was the challenge she needed to embrace. Focusing on her senses, she not only listened but opened herself up to what she could detect with her enhanced eyesight, and the sense of touch, the way the wind caressed her skin, along with the sense of smell. All of it had been heightened since she had taken her blessing.

A faint stirring of a breeze pulled her to the left when she reached a side hallway.

Ryn headed down there, finding a door at the end of it. She paused, resting her hand on the door, and became aware of the stirring of wind, but also the occasional tap-tapping from the other side of the door.

The door was locked.

That was unusual in the temple. There weren't many places here that the Ai'thol kept locked. While she could go and demand access, the idea that she might surprise them, find her way down on her own, appealed to her. Instead of demanding entry, she withdrew the slender knife given to her by the Great One. It was made of a metal similar to the sacred metal, and when she plunged it into the lock, she felt it changing. It was almost as if it were meant for this purpose, though she had seen it used like that before. The Great One had done so.

The door opened, and she hesitated.

Darkness greeted her, but it was only momentary. Once her eyesight adjusted, she was able to make out the faint shifting of shadows that drifted into the door, leading into a staircase heading down. Lanterns were set into the wall, but none of them were lit. Strange, considering the tapping sound she now heard, louder with the door open.

Ryn approached the stairs carefully, heading down them one at a time, pausing every so often to ensure that the steady tapping she heard didn't veer off in a different direction, though there was only one way for her to go down the stairs.

As she descended, Ryn felt a motion she hadn't experienced in quite some time. Ever since traveling with the Great One, she had felt safe, protected, and even when he left her behind to investigate on his behalf, there had never been fear. She had always acted on his behalf, much the way she did now.

Surprisingly, as she headed down the stairs, there was a sense of fear.

When was the last time she had felt it like this?

Ryn steeled herself. The Great One protected her, even if he wasn't here. She made her way down the stairs, not distracted by the darkness, and when the staircase ended, she looked around. The air smelled different. Stale. Almost hot. There was a pungent aroma she didn't recognize. It moved softly, twisting around her, small eddies that pulled at her cloak. A distant glowing caught her attention, though from where she was, Ryn recognized how the glowing was meant to be masked from anyone who might come down to this level. The one thing they didn't mask was the steady tapping. It sounded like hammering, but why should that be?

Could they be delving deeper beneath the ground?

The temple itself was impressive, like most of the temples the Great One operated. She didn't know for certain, but she suspected the temples had once served a different purpose, especially as each land they visited had temples of different shapes. This one was mostly a circular tower, with smaller arms reaching off and many of the lower buildings interconnected. Other temples were comprised of dozens of spires, or burrowed into the earth itself, or even nothing more than a rocky overlook out upon the sea.

If they were digging deeper into the ground, there had to be some reason. Perhaps it was nothing more than a desire to claim additional power, but she couldn't help but think there was something else she didn't fully grasp.

This was the kind of thing the Great One would like to know about.

Ryn reached the end of the hallway. A door blocked her from going any further, and beneath the door there was a faint red glowing. On the other side of the door came the regular tapping sound, over and over again, and she paused as she had at the last door, giving herself the opportunity to listen. The longer she did, the clearer it was that it came from hammering, almost as if metal on metal.

It reminded her of the blacksmith in Vuahlu.

It had been a long time since she had thought about that. It had been a long time since she had thought about anything from her home village, though even that was not her home village. It had been her living space for a time, a place where they had lived after her father's death, but it had never been *her* home. Her mother had wanted it to be something more than it could be.

If everything went well with the Great One, eventually Ryn hoped to visit the land of her ancestors. She had heard so little about it but knew that it was a place the Great One avoided, at least for now. It was part of his planning, but it was the kind of planning he intended to keep to himself. Every so often, she had heard him speak about what he intended to do with that city, having recognized it when he had mentioned the name, but she had never come to know what exactly he intended.

Ryn tested the door. Like the last one, it was locked.

Unusual for the temple, but even more unusual for the fact that it was so deep beneath the ground. Whatever was taking place here was intended to be kept secret, and that was the kind of thing she knew the Great One would disapprove of.

Slipping her knife out of her pocket, she pressed it into the lock as she had the other. She could feel the metal change, shifting, and she twisted.

The door came open.

Heat flooded outward toward her, mixed with steam that obscured the reddish glowing on the far side of the door.

When it cleared, she peered inside.

What appeared to be a massive hearth glowed at one end of the room. Coals burned brightly, glowing with a violent intensity. She could barely take her eyes off it, but when the hammering returned, she tore her gaze away to see a man standing near the glowing coals, his back hunched, an enormous hammer in his hand as he beat upon metal.

How had she not heard this before?

With the door open, this hammering was loud, a clanging that vibrated through her entire being. It reverberated within her, as if she could feel the changing of the metal each time the hammer struck. Ryn focused on that, trained to search for understanding with every strange experience she might have. The Great One's words stuck with her—*what else did she detect?*

There wasn't anything else there. Ryn approached slowly, carefully, watching the hammering. Every often, there was a pause, and she expected the massive man to turn and realize she was there, but he didn't.

The space was surprising and strange. The walls were all a rough stone, and a massive chimney funneled out the smoke from the coals. She was surprised that it wasn't smokier in here. There was the heat and the steam, but nothing else that pressed in upon her.

"You shouldn't be here."

Ryn turned slowly, keeping her hand locked in front of her. A younger man, someone near her age and smaller than the other blacksmith, met her gaze when she turned. His clothes were dirtied, stains of soot and coal smeared across them. Sweat ringed under his arms and across his chest. His eyes were a deep green.

Ryn took a step back.

In all her time traveling with the Great One, she hadn't come across anyone with eyes like these. She knew there were men like that—her father was one of them—but something about this man reminded her of the story she'd heard from her mother.

"You shouldn't be down here," he said again. "How is it that you got this far?"

Ryn shook the surprise away from her. "I'm here as an emissary of the Great One."

The young man cocked his head to the side. "You're too young for an emissary."

"And you're too inexperienced to challenge me."

She had far too much experience with people like this young man, people who thought her age mattered when it came to the Great One. If they believed that, then they didn't really know the Great One the way they thought they did. To him, it was more a matter of service and willingness than of age.

"Why would the Great One send an emissary here?"

"Why would the Great One need to?" she asked.

"Isn't that what I just asked you?"

She glanced over to where the hulking man continued to hammer at the metal. He was either oblivious to the fact they were there, or he simply didn't care. As he worked, she couldn't tell. Was it her imagination, or did he tip his head slightly to the side as if listening?

"Do you know anything of the attack?"

He frowned. "Attack?"

"Up in the tower. There was an attack, and—"

The young man cut her off with a peal of laughter. "Up in the tower? Do you think we're allowed there?"

Ryn steadied herself. She wasn't about to let someone like this unsettle her, but being down here was unsettling in itself. The coals reminded her of the volcano, and as she looked at them, feeling their heat, she could practically imagine the lava as it flowed down from the mountaintop, swallowing the remains of her village. She tried to push those thoughts out of her head.

"You should still have some knowledge of what's taking place around here. The Great One demands it of all of us."

The boy nodded to the other blacksmith. "And *he* demands my presence. We've been down here working diligently. I doubt I'd even know if there was an attack in the tower."

Ryn hesitated. She had several questions she wanted to ask, and working as the Great One's emissary, she had every right to ask them. As much as she wanted to inquire about the metal they were using and whether he knew anything about the sacred metal, the question that came to her first was not about her assignment.

"Where are you from?"

The young man wrinkled his nose. "Does the Great One demand accountability of such things?"

"The Great One would like to know where his people come from. I would like to know where his people come from."

He shrugged. "I grew up in a small village outside of Thyr. Lived there damn near my whole life, learning how to work at the forge."

"And how did you end up here?"

They had to be leagues from that village, far enough that he might have traveled with someone, but it would be unusual. It was rare for those with that particular ability to take random boys away from their home villages. Unless someone had seen something about him. It was possible that one of the priests had seen potential in him.

"I got kicked out of my village. I needed to find a place that would be a little bit more welcoming."

"Why did you get kicked out of your village?"

The young man glanced over to the other blacksmith. "Are you going to keep asking questions like this, or do you intend to allow me to return to work?"

"I haven't decided yet."

The young man snorted. "Does the Great One send people like you everywhere?"

Ryn shook her head. "I don't know how many others are like me."

"Doubt there can be too many."

She wasn't sure whether that was a compliment or not. It sounded something like an insult, and yet the young man smiled as he said it, taking the edge off the words.

"I got kicked out of my village because I made a play for a girl."

Ryn stiffened. She'd met men like that before, and most of them deserved whatever fate they got. It was one thing the Great One didn't tolerate, though from what she had seen, enough of his followers turned a blind eye to that kind of behavior.

"Not like that."

"Not like what?"

"I see the look on your face. I recognize it. It's the same look the mayor gave me, along with all of the council. They blamed me, convicting me before they even heard my side of it."

"And your side of it would have justified what you did?"

"My side of it wouldn't justify anything. It's just that I didn't do anything to her. We danced. We talked. She let me kiss her. That was it. I thought we might have a chance to be more."

A flush worked up the boy's face, and whatever else she'd thought, he *was* a boy. He might appear her age, perhaps even older, but he acted much younger.

"Don't even know why I'm telling you this."

"Because I'm the Great One's emissary."

"I don't care if you *are* the Great One's emissary. He's not here, so it doesn't matter."

Were it anyone else, she would have corrected him about that. It very much mattered that she was the Great One's emissary, but at the same time, she didn't have the sense the boy had done anything wrong.

"Your village chased you out?"

"They did. Sent me packing, told me not to come back. I had half a mind to go on to Thyr, but they had plenty of blacksmiths there. Wasn't no way I was going to get an apprenticeship in that city. My best bet was heading south, looking for places that had a better need." He shrugged. "Came across a pair of priests when I was starving and exhausted. They thought they could use someone with my skill."

Ryn nodded slowly. It didn't surprise her that the priests would take someone in like that. That was the way they worked. It was how she had been taken in, offered safety and protection, things she valued far more now than she ever had.

"I'm sorry I kept you from your work, Mr...."

"Dillon. Folks call me Dillon around here."

"And what did folks call you around where you grew up?"

Dillon shook his head. "That don't matter anymore. That person is gone."

With that, he turned away, heading over to the forge and joining his master. They fell into a steady pattern, a rhythm, hammering, moving metal, and she got caught up in watching, amazed at the nature of how they worked. There was something of a dance to it, and she could understand why Dillon would have wanted to continue working like this.

It did nothing to explain his bright green eyes. They reminded her of what she had seen when Lareth had attacked her village. Either Dillon was lying about his origins, or there was more to the green-eyed people than she knew.

When she had finished her investigation for the Great One, she would need to get a better sense for where she had come from, and whether there were others like Dillon out there in the world.

Somehow, she had to think that there were.

Ryn watched for a little while longer. There was more taking place here than what she understood, and this seemed to be the answer she was looking for. Dillon might not know it, but that didn't mean that the answer wasn't here.

Her gaze lingered on the blacksmith. She would wait. When he was done working, she would talk with him. She would find out all she could, and perhaps she would finally understand what had taken place here.

11

RYN

RYN WIPED THE SWEAT OFF HER BROW. SHE HAD REMAINED near the back of the stone room, watching as the two men worked. She didn't mind the heat. Having lived so long in Vuahlu, she knew heat and the discomfort that came with it and had learned long ago to ignore it. Then again, when she had lived there, she didn't have the thick cloak or the heavy wool she wore now. Those only trapped heat and moisture, making her feel unpleasantly damp. When this was over, she would have to track down one of the tower's baths, have a soak, and think about what she'd encountered.

"Quench it, and then stack the coals," the larger man said.

As she had watched, the larger man had been generally silent, speaking only in short grunts or single words to tell Dillon how he should be working. They had an obvious familiarity with each other, and Dillon had been able to work without much instruction.

The larger man peeled his leather apron from his neck,

hanging it on a hook near the wall, and made a steady circuit of the room before stopping in front of her. When he did, she realized just how large he was. It wasn't just that he towered over her by a good foot or more; the man was enormous, heavily muscled. And though his shirt was worn and dirty, he still managed to make it seem somewhat formal. He wiped his hands and stuck one hand out, looking at her.

Green eyes.

Why wasn't she surprised?

"I am Ryn Valeron. I am the Great One—"

"I know who you are."

She frowned. "You do?"

The other man nodded. "Heard about you when you came. Supposedly you're close to him."

Ryn bowed her head slightly. "I'm not so sure how close anyone can be to the Great One."

"Is that right?"

"He keeps to himself. He has a plan for all of us, and I am honored that I am included."

"And your plan involves you coming to my forge?"

"I didn't know it was here."

"That's how I like it."

"You don't want others to know you're here?"

"By that, you're asking if the Great One knows if we're here."

She shrugged. "A little bit."

"You don't need to question. He knows."

Ryn considered him for a moment. It wasn't the sort of thing anyone would lie about. Doing so would be dangerous if the Great One caught word, though in a place like this, as isolated as they were, it wouldn't be too much of a stretch for them to take her, perhaps harm her, and then dispose of her. The others within the tower hadn't been terribly welcoming, and she could imagine them helping this man dispose of her.

"How long have you been here?"

"Is that the question you really want to ask?"

"It's the question I'm asking."

The man grunted. "Probably the better half of a decade."

"This temple has been Ai'thol for a decade?"

Most of the temples they occupied had not been Ai'thol originally, so the fact that this one was, or that it had been for longer than most of the others, surprised her. It seemed like the kind of thing the Great One should have warned her about. Then again, maybe he had wanted her to uncover it on her own. It was the sort of thing he would do, challenging her to learn things without his instruction, and she knew enough to recognize that those lessons were often the best ones.

"It wasn't originally."

"You've been here since before."

She flicked her gaze back up to his eyes. Interesting.

"The Great One offered me an opportunity to serve. Seeing as how the alternative was less desirable…"

"What alternative?"

The blacksmith frowned. "What alternative? You've seen what the Great One does to those who don't accept his method of service."

"The Great One teaches."

"Is that what you believe? Perhaps he's shielded you more than you know."

She hid her shock at the way he talked. No one spoke of the Great One in such a way, not if they wanted to live. This man's audacity surprised her, but if he had been here as long as he claimed, perhaps he had a greater freedom than most.

And if the Great One knew about him and continued to allow him to serve, it was something she had to better understand.

"Are you responsible for forging the sacred metal?"

He cocked a brow at her, wiping his hands on his pants and turning away from her. At first, she thought he was going to leave her, but he headed to a table, grabbed something off it, and came back over to her. He held it out, waiting for her to take it from him.

Ryn realized it was a piece of bluish metal.

"Take it."

"What is it?"

The blacksmith smiled. "You don't have to fear it. Take it."

"I don't fear it."

"I see in your eyes that you aren't sure." He twisted it in his hand, smacking it on the palm of the other. "There's nothing dangerous about it. It's metal, nothing more, but when you add a little bit of this"—he pulled a small lump of silvery metal from his pocket, pressing it on the other metal—"it becomes something else. Then you add this." He grabbed another piece of metal. "Or this. And it becomes even more different. Much like we change when it's used on us."

Her eyes widened.

"You see what I'm saying?"

She shook her head. "You're talking about the sacred metal."

"You can call it sacred if you want, but it's an alloy like any other I make, though this one has some tendencies others don't. It's why the Great One works with it. He's found it tends to unlock certain things within people."

Ryn resisted the urge to finger the blessing on the back of her head. That had been given to her by the Great One himself, and it had continued to grant her more and more new abilities, though she wasn't sure whether that would continue forever.

The way the blacksmith looked at her suggested he understood what she had.

"You don't view it as sacred?"

"I've been working with metals my entire life. Some of them have strange qualities, but there's nothing sacred about it. Sacred implies something akin to the Great Watcher, and I haven't seen anything to tell me he gives a damn."

Her gaze lingered on the metal. She knew there was some secret to creating it, though she had never realized it was simply a combination of metals. An alloy, but if it was an alloy and nothing more, that didn't change the fact that they were blessed to be able to use it.

"So you are the one who creates the metal here?"

"I make it."

"Are you aware of the way it was used recently?"

He frowned. "What they do with it up in the tower

doesn't matter to me. I make what I'm asked, and nothing more."

"As the one responsible for the sacred metal, you should be concerned about how it's used."

"Do you think he gives me any choice?" He slipped the hunk of silver back into his pocket and turned back to her. "Besides, do you think I'm the only one who knows how to manipulate these metals? I'm not the first, and I'm not the last. He's not even the first. He's only borrowing knowledge from others."

"The Great One was given a great gift. He was given the understanding of how to—"

The blacksmith started to laugh again, cutting her off. "You don't need to spit out that garbage with me. Down here, under the earth, we work in fact. Not in possibilities. We work with the things we can see and feel."

"You don't think you can see and feel the fact that the Great One has been given gifts?"

"I don't think I care. If he was given gifts, and that's *if*, then they're no different than the gifts many are given. The only difference is how he chooses to use them."

This man intrigued her. Quite a few in the temple seemed willing to be subservient because of the Great One, but this man seemed to be the opposite. It was almost as if he intentionally wanted to make it seem as if he had no interest in serving the Great One.

Then again, it was possible he had no interest in it. If he had been here prior to the Great One taking over the temple, then what sort of things did he believe?

"The attack used your metal," she said.

"I assume that's because it's a weapon."

"Possibly," she said. "Though it is possible there was a reason behind it."

"What sort of reason is that? And is there some reason I need to care?"

"You don't think you should care how your work is utilized?"

"Like I said, I work in fact. I stay beneath the earth, my hammer and my forge as company. I have the coals and the heat as my friends. Those are the things I believe in. I stay focused on how my hammer strikes, or how the heat changes the metal. I know how this metal," he said, holding up the bluish lump, "will change when I add this to it." He pulled out the silver hunk again before slipping it into his pocket. There was something about the fact that he kept the silver metal with him. It was important to him, regardless of what he claimed. "All that is predictable."

"You didn't answer the question."

"If you were listening, you would have heard that I did."

He turned away from her, rejoining Dillon, and then he disappeared. Ryn couldn't see a doorway that led away from here, but there had to be someplace he had snuck off to.

Standing where she was, she watched Dillon for a while. He seemed to be cleaning, moving things around, and then he started shoveling coal into the forge. It didn't take long before the flames burned brighter, the heat pushing outward more intensely.

As much as she wanted to linger and watch, she wasn't sure she could.

There was more for her to uncover, and the longer she stayed here, the less likely it was that she would arrive at those answers. It was enough she had found where the sacred metal was forged, but more than that, she had discovered at least one man who didn't view the Great One the way others did. She would watch him and report back to the Great One. That was her task. She would do it well.

After heading up the stairs, Ryn paused. Here she could hear the steady hammering, and with her enhanced senses, she found it much easier now than she had before. More than that, now that she knew what she was listening to, she would keep track of it so that she could get a sense of what the blacksmith was doing. He was the one she needed to better understand.

Ryn returned to her small workspace. She took a seat, the stack of books calling to her. There was more to learn here, and yet the longer she was here, the more she questioned what exactly she would figure out. The Great One expected answers from her, and if she failed him…

She would not. More than anything else, she was determined to do what was necessary. That involved understanding what had taken place within the temple.

As she turned her attention back to the stack of books, she heard the steady tapping continuing. It became a rhythm she worked to, and when it was done, she pushed her book aside, heading back out of the room and toward the staircase. She hesitated, listening for sounds of movement. There had to be something she could detect. So far, she hadn't determined anything.

As she waited, standing in the darkness and the shadows, concerned that someone might appear and realize she was standing there doing nothing, she focused on the potential for movement all around her. The steady clomping of feet on the steps caught her attention at last.

Ryn waited, standing off to the side, expecting that it would be the blacksmith coming up the stairs, but instead it was Dillon.

He seemed oblivious to her presence, and when he turned down the hallway, she followed him, keeping a reasonable distance. He headed out of the tower, departing through one of the side doors, and Ryn paused for a moment before scurrying after him.

She could follow the blacksmith another time. While Dillon might not know anything—as far as she could tell —he might lead her someplace where she could learn more. That was what she needed. That was what the Great One demanded of her.

Out in the city, night had fallen, leaving darkness hanging like a cloud. The air had a thickness to it, an odor that drifted to her and reminded her of her home. Why should that be? It wasn't like Vuahlu, but the home she had lived in before that.

Ryn hadn't considered that place for quite some time and didn't know whether she should be worried about the fact she had so few memories of it. Then again, her mother had wanted to protect her from the dangers that had befallen her father and had thought that bringing her to the city would do that.

She racked her brain, trying to figure out what it was about the smells that reminded her of home. Perhaps it was the mixture of aromas. Vuahlu didn't have nearly as many smells within it as the city did. There were the scents of Baker Hughes and that of weavers working with the conash fruit, along with the salt coming off the sea. Through it all came the scent of the volcano, the stench of the fog hanging over everything. It had been worse over the last few months, that smell mixing with everything else, practically cloying, and this city had none of that. There wasn't any odor of the sea, and they were far enough from volcanoes that there was nothing here that reminded her of it.

Dillon turned a corner, and Ryn followed. It led into a narrow alleyway, and she hesitated. She wasn't nearly as talented as so many others the Great One had gifted. If someone meant her ill, an alley like this would be dangerous. Not only that, but the protections of the temple didn't extend to her here.

But she wanted to know what Dillon was up to, and it was the kind of thing the Great One would expect her to follow up on.

Ryn took a deep breath, heading down the alleyway.

With her enhanced eyesight, she wasn't nearly as weak as she felt before. She could make out the gradations of light, the faint moonlight providing enough illumination for her to know where she was and what was down here, but little more than that. There was no lantern light glowing in any windows like there was in other places in the city. It would be pure darkness.

It was the kind of place Dillon should not have gone.

Perhaps she'd misjudged him. He shouldn't have come here, shouldn't have gotten involved in anything like this. The fact that he had, disappearing as he did, had her on edge. This was the kind of thing the Great One would like to know about.

Unless he already did.

The Great One had a way of knowing people's intentions, as if he could read their minds. Though she knew that was possible, it had limitations, at least according to the Great One. Then again, having seen the way he worked, maybe he didn't have the same restrictions as others.

She moved carefully now. As she went, she listened for sounds of movement along the street. He had to be here somewhere, but where had he gone? It wouldn't be possible for Dillon to simply disappear.

Ryn paused. There came a sense of movement. She didn't see or hear anything, but she felt it. That surprised her. She shouldn't be able to feel someone moving.

But hadn't she detected someone moving before? When the Great One had been there, she had felt him. Perhaps—and hopefully—it was one more aspect of her abilities that she didn't really understand.

Ryn remained motionless. It was better to observe that way, a lesson the Great One had taught her. For as much as he involved himself, he was an observer first. It was a lesson she wanted to take from him. The more she could observe, the better she would understand what others working with the Great One were after.

As she stood there, the sense of movement came again. This time it was behind her. She noticed it as a stirring from somewhere deep inside her, a fluttering sensation.

Ryn turned only her head, barely enough to look over her shoulder, trying to avoid drawing anyone else's attention. If she wasn't alone in the alley, then she needed to be careful.

There was nothing there.

Ryn frowned to herself.

She was missing something.

If there was one thing she hated, it was the idea that she might overlook something.

Searching against the darkness, she tried to peer through the shadows. With her enhanced eyesight, she knew she should be able to do so, but how?

Waiting there for a moment, she searched for signs of anyone else, but there was nothing.

After a moment passed, and then another, and then another, and still no sign of Dillon, Ryn moved deeper into the alleyway.

There was nothing here.

More surprisingly, there was no way out.

Dillon couldn't just have disappeared, could he?

There was only one way he would have been able to do that—traveling.

Turning around slowly, Ryn looked toward the mouth of the alley. That would be an unusual gift for someone like him to have.

Which meant she had overlooked something about him. Either that, or he was not supposed to have it.

HAERN

DAYS HAD PASSED WITHOUT ANY FURTHER EVENTS, NOTHING that suggested to Haern they were in any danger from other attackers, and yet Haern remained on edge, vigilant, continuing to search for signs of where another attack might come. He was convinced there might be one at any moment, but there had been no sign.

It was late in the day, the sun beginning to set, when he caught sight of a caravan of wagons in the distance.

Haern signaled for them to slow and turned his attention to Elise. "I'm not sure what we might find," he said.

"What is it?"

"Wagons," he said, squinting. His enhanced eyesight allowed him to make out the details of the wagons. There were probably a dozen, which meant there would be nearly a dozen merchants, likely more than that. Enough people that he had to worry about the safety of his.

With each passing day, he felt more and more as if the women were his people.

"Isn't that what we want? Haven't we been looking for signs of others?"

Haern nodded. "We have, but it seems out of place."

"We're out of place," Elise said.

Haern cupped his hand over his eyes as he stared into the distance. "That's not why I feel that way." He looked around, hesitating for a moment before dropping a coin and reaching for Elise. "Join me."

She frowned at him, her brow wrinkling. "Now?"

"Would you rather wait until it's so dark you can't see anything clearly?"

"I don't like the idea of flying with you."

He smiled at the way she said it. She often referred to it as flying, and that seemed as good a way to term it as any. Yet it never felt quite like flying to him. There was much more work involved in it.

"I won't drop you."

She arched a brow. "That's not what I was implying."

He smiled at her. "What were you implying?"

"I don't like heights."

"Then hold on tight."

Haern slipped his arm around her waist and *pushed*, taking to the sky. The strength he had built up working intermittently at the forge allowed him to hold on to her without risking dropping her, and they soared into the air. He was careful not to *push* them too high, not wanting to draw attention to them. At the same time, he needed to get high enough to make out the caravan in the distance.

Wind whipped past them, and clouds filled the sky, obscuring everything with a grayish overcast light. It was the kind of sky that brought the promise of rain, or perhaps more likely the threat of rain. So far, the weather had been decent, and they hadn't had to worry about rain.

"Do you see it?" Haern asked, pointing off into the distance. The wagons continued to move, rolling slowly away from them. It surprised him that the wagons seemed to be moving slower than they were by foot.

"I can see the wagons," she said. "Don't you think they'll see us?"

"They have to be looking in this direction."

"What if they're the ones who attacked you?"

Haern had considered that. That had been his concern from the beginning, and until he knew for certain, he wasn't comfortable approaching the wagons, at least not with any of the others. He needed some sign they were nothing more than simple merchants.

"We never had many merchants come through Elaeavn."

"Why?"

"The leaders of the city, a family called the Elvraeth, preferred to keep us isolated. I think we had some merchants come through, but they were limited to the harbor. Even when they did come, they rarely came into the city. We never had any wagons like this."

"We did," she said softly.

"Why do I get the sense that troubles you?"

"It's not so much that it troubles me. Most of the merchant caravans who came through my home village were smaller than that, though. A couple of wagons. Oftentimes they carried exotic spices, or clothes, or other items the people in the village would trade for. We had skilled weavers, and merchants were always happy to take on our wares."

"Other than the metal, we don't really have much in Elaeavn that merchants would be interested in."

"Seeing the way you can use the metal, I imagine that was prized."

"For a long time, we were forbidden to use it."

"Why?"

Haern shook his head. "I suppose ignorance is the best answer. It was a battle my father fought long before I came around."

"Sometimes merchants would come through and bring musicians with them, sometimes dancers or acrobats, and occasionally we'd get storytellers." She smiled, her eyes looking off into the distance. "It made merchant visits something of a celebration. You never knew what you were going to get when they came, and while they could be nothing more than merchants, it was always the hope for something more that made them appealing."

"That sounds nice."

"Most of the time."

"Most of the time?"

Her brow furrowed, her eyes darkening. "Some merchants weren't as honest as others. Some didn't trade in the same type of goods." She looked down to where the circle of women had gathered and waited for them.

Haern clenched his jaw. He had seen troubling things since leaving Elaeavn, and his experience with the Forgers had been perhaps the most troubling of all, but at least the Forgers were after power. He had lived much of his life wanting more strength and power, so he could understand that.

People who used others like these women had been used were harder for him to understand.

"How often did that happen?"

"Not all that often. We knew to keep an eye out for that sort of trader, and if anyone came that we had any questions about, we observed them, keeping guard."

Haern stared at the wagons as they rolled away from them. "Are you concerned this caravan is something like that?"

She shrugged. "It's possible, but we won't be able to tell until we get closer."

"I don't know that it makes sense for us to get closer if there's a risk to the others."

"We can defend ourselves, Haern. We've been practicing."

"I know we have. You have. It's just they have more numbers than we do."

"What do you intend?"

"I think that I need to figure out what they're doing before we approach."

There was no doubt in his mind they would need to approach. If they had access to wagons, they wouldn't have to travel by foot. With Marcy still injured, dosed with the medication to keep her comfortable, wagons would offer another benefit as well.

"None of us like it when you go off on your own."

"I know, but if something happens to me, the rest will be able to make it to safety."

"You always seem to feel like you need to do things

yourself, but we can help." She looked around before her gaze settled back on Haern. "And if you need to fly, you can at least bring another person with you."

"By that, I assume you mean yourself?"

"If you thought to bring someone else…"

"I don't know that I can bring more than one person." It was times like these that he wished for his father's ability with Sliding. If he could Slide, he could reach the others, and he could easily get to the wagons and then back without having to fear any sort of danger.

"I didn't say you had to bring more than one. I just said that you needed to go with someone else."

He nodded. "We'll go when it's dark."

By the time darkness had fallen, Haern was beginning to question whether he should bring Elise with him. But at the same time, having someone there to watch him and to ensure his safety was beneficial.

Besides, the more he tried to go off and do things on his own, to serve as the protector of these women, the more he wondered if he wasn't falling into the same trap his father had. Too often, his father had felt as if *he* had to be responsible for everyone, and while he believed he was the most skilled in some regards, the others weren't without their own talents.

"Are you ready?" he asked Elise.

She smiled, nodding to him. Jayna and several of the others knew where they were going, and they had set up a watch system, prepared for the possibility that someone might approach. They had decided not to start a campfire tonight, a decision Haern agreed with. Until they knew this other caravan was safe, it was best to exercise caution.

Grabbing for Elise, he dropped a lorcith coin and *pushed*.

They went soaring into the darkness, wind whistling around them. Haern worked quickly, *pushing* and *pulling* on coins. He followed the direction where he had seen the wagons, scanning the darkness for them. They wouldn't have been able to move that much farther ahead at the pace they were going. If they didn't fear other travelers, they would most likely light a campfire, and he should be able to See that from a considerable distance.

As he searched the darkness, he caught sight of it.

They were farther than he would've expected, as if the wagons had picked up pace since he and Elise had seen them. Could the others have been aware of them and of his abilities? They would have been outlined against the sky, too large to be anything but people hovering, much larger than any bird or other airborne creature.

Haern pointed and Elise nodded.

"How do you intend to approach?" she whispered.

"We aren't going to go all the way toward them until we know more."

"How much more do you need to know?"

"It's a matter of listening."

"Is that one of your abilities?"

Haern smiled, though he wondered if she could even see it. "There are times I wish it was. I'm not a Listener—

that's what we call them in Elaeavn. I don't even have any potential for it."

"You say it almost as if you think that makes you weaker."

"I do wish I could have other abilities beyond just Sight."

"Some of us don't have any abilities at all, Haern."

She grinned at him, and he smiled back, knowing he should be appreciative of his gifts. It wasn't the first time he'd been reminded of that, though it was hard for him to feel gratitude after seeing people like Daniel Elvraeth, even Lucy now that she had her significant abilities, or his father.

"It sounds awful of me, doesn't it?"

"I think you've just lived a different experience than others of us. Most of us don't know what it's like to feel so powerful."

"That's the interesting thing about it," Haern said. "I don't know that I would call myself powerful. Some other people in my homeland are even more powerful. The kinds of things they can do are amazing."

She smiled at him, squeezing him a little tighter. "Some of us think you are amazing."

"You're just saying that so I don't drop you."

"I thought that was a good enough reason to say it."

"Are you ready?"

"Are we going down?"

He nodded.

Elise squeezed him more tightly, and Haern descended rapidly, bringing them down on the outskirts of the area where the caravan had camped. They were a good fifty yards away, far enough he doubted that anyone close to the campfire would notice them.

Unless they had enhanced eyesight like he did.

Holding on to Elise, he ducked behind a tree. There were three of them that grew quite high here, as if they had been planted in a pattern, and he hoped the shadows would conceal them.

"What is it?" Elise whispered, leaning toward him and putting her mouth almost up against his ear. The proximity to her sent a shiver through him.

"I didn't consider that some of the people down there might be enhanced."

Elise stiffened, and she leaned close to him. "Do you think they are?"

"It's hard to know, but considering some of the things I've seen over the last few months, it wouldn't surprise me."

And if there was someone with any enhancements, he needed to be careful. He didn't want to put her in any more danger than she already was just by coming with him.

"Maybe you should—"

Elise touched his arm, shaking her head. "I'm not going to stay behind on the chance that I might be in any danger."

He met her gaze and nodded. "Okay. Let's move."

As he went, Haern kept a hold on his connection to lorcith. He needed to use it carefully, wanting to be ready to *push* outward with one of his coins or knives—to attack, if it came down to that.

Thankfully, he had his strength.

As he went, he became aware of something.

Haern froze.

Lorcith.

It was with the wagons.

She leaned in, whispering to him. "What is it?"

He shook his head, motioning backward.

As they headed toward the trees, Haern cursed to himself. He should have been more careful, should have considered the possibility that the caravan would carry lorcith with it, especially after he had been attacked twice and had not seen anything.

When they reached the trees, she leaned in, looking over at him. "What did you see?"

"It's not what I saw. It's what I felt. There's lorcith out there."

She stared into the darkness. Without any enhancement, there probably wasn't much that she would be able to see. "What sort of lorcith?"

That was the problem. He wasn't certain, but from what he could tell, there was a similarity to the sphere that had attacked him. Twice.

He focused, listening to the lorcith. The metal had a certain call to it, though he didn't hear it as a song the way his father and grandfather had described. Perhaps if he could, he wouldn't have been surprised like this.

As he focused on lorcith, he listened.

This time, it wasn't so much of a song as it was a familiarity. It was something that had influenced him once before, and Haern reached for that connection, though he was careful. The last time he had detected it like this, he had triggered an attack.

How had he triggered it, though?

It seemed as if it had been triggered by him *pulling* on the metal, trying to draw it to him, which he couldn't do now. He wasn't even sure he'd be able to. Haern didn't have any idea where the metal was, though he could feel it.

If it was anything like the other attacks, it would be situated all around, possibly on the ground, or perhaps there was someone like him, someone who could *push* on the metal and use it to reach him.

That didn't seem to be the case.

He focused, looking outward, and realized it was in one of the wagons.

Why, though?

Unless they were storing it.

Haern had to be careful. If he approached too quickly or with too much violence, he ran the risk of triggering a response. What would happen if the lorcith was triggered *by* him?

It would put Elise in danger.

He couldn't do that. Which meant that either he had to back away, or he had to break into the wagon to secure it.

Then again, if the lorcith was within the wagon, it wasn't harmful to him. He could trigger it now, force it to explode, to shoot the nails outward, and disarm it.

There was some benefit in that. He wouldn't have to fear the possibility it might explode and harm someone, but at the same time, he didn't like the idea that someone might be in the wagon with it.

He stood in place, debating what to do.

He still needed to get closer but didn't want to approach with Elise.

"Don't think you're going to leave me here," she whispered.

"I was considering it."

"I see that, but I don't think you can."

"I don't either, but what I detect is similar to what attacked me before. I don't know that I can keep you safe."

"You mean to trigger it?"

"I think I need to."

"Then won't I be safer with you than away from you?"

"It might be safer for you to be back by the others."

"You're not sending me back."

"Elise—"

He didn't get a chance to finish. A voice within the campsite caught his attention, and Haern turned, looking out into the darkness. A pair of people, both dressed in cloaks and strange circular hats, started out and away, heading in their direction.

Had they been detected?

Haern swore under his breath. They needed to move.

Dropping the lorcith coin, he *pushed* upward, but at an angle, sending them out and away from the camp. From here, he lowered them back down to the ground, far from where they had been, before turning back toward Elise.

"What are we doing?"

Haern shook his head. "We're going back to the camp."

"Just like that?"

"I don't know that we have much choice. If they have weapons like that, that means they're the ones who set them out. Or they knew I was there." That last seemed a little less likely, for if they had known he was out there, wouldn't they have targeted him again? Which meant they were using weapons like that indiscriminately. That was almost worse.

"When we get back there, what then?"

"Then we avoid the merchants—or whatever they are."

13

HAERN

THE NEXT DAY WENT ALMOST TOO SLOWLY FOR HAERN. HE remained focused on the possibility of lorcith coming toward them, constantly on edge, worried he might miss something as they hurried generally north, but angling gradually to the west. It was in a different direction than the wagons had headed. Every so often, Haern would take to the air, flying overhead to ensure he didn't see any sign of the wagons. If it were just him, Haern probably would have gone to investigate, but he didn't like the idea of leaving the women, and he certainly didn't like the idea of Elise ending up in danger because he left her behind.

It was possible heading in this direction would take them away from where they were going and might veer them through different villages. As it was, they didn't know where they were heading, and Haern hoped they would find someplace to get help—food, clothing, shelter. Anything.

The more they were forced off their intended path, the less certain he was they would reach any of those things.

That night, with a small fire crackling, Haern sat off to the side, his sword resting on his lap. Jayna joined him, sitting across from him, her back to the flames. Elise was sitting at the fire with some of the other women, and every so often she would glance back at him as if to ensure that he remained.

"What did you see?"

"Twelve wagons. They had a weapon like the one that attacked me several days ago."

"Were you attacked?"

Haern shook his head. "No. I think it was in one of their wagons, but I'm pretty sure it's the same thing."

"What happens if they come toward us?"

Jayna was practical, something Haern appreciated about her. With what they were doing and where they were going, they needed someone who had a certain practicality about them. There were times when he needed to be far more practical than he was.

"I keep checking to ensure that they aren't. Eventually, we should be able to move away from them."

"What happens if we don't?"

"I will make sure we stay away from them."

Jayna shook her head. "That's not what I'm getting at. What happens if we approach intentionally?"

"I don't think that's a good idea."

"The weapon is designed to target people like you. What if we approach?"

"We?"

Jayna turned, motioning to the women. "We. Us." She turned back to him. "Not you."

"We don't know anything about them. What if they—"

"You've already told us what they have. If we wait, we run the risk of some kind of attack we can't avoid."

"That's why we're taking a different direction. We're trying to get away from whatever threat they might pose."

"What if that's the wrong approach?"

Haern stared at her. He knew what his father would have done in this situation. It was the shadow he'd lived under his entire life. His father would have believed he was the only one capable of protecting anyone else, and he would have gone after the caravan on his own, leaving the others behind.

Haern didn't want to be like his father. He respected the man and everything he'd done over the years, his way of defending everyone, and yet if he were to behave like his father, the others would be diminished.

Hadn't he seen the effect of that? Hadn't Haern seen what happened when others were pushed off to the side, essentially told that their input and value was not worth as much?

He had.

It was the same issue that had weakened his people. The fact that Rsiran had decided he was the best equipped to deal with the Forgers had made it so that others within Elaeavn did not have the same potential any longer.

"What do you propose?"

Jayna blinked. "You would allow this?"

"I think we need to work together to ensure everyone's safety. If that involves you taking on a responsibility I cannot, then maybe that's the right strategy."

"I would propose that we send five. Enough that we are somewhat imposing, but not so many that we're viewed as a threat. We can assess what's there, and if we find there is some danger, then we escape."

"How do you intend to escape if there is a danger?"

"That will be a different challenge," she said. "It involves you, Haern."

Haern frowned. "How would it involve me?"

"You can fly above us, watching."

"What if the connection to the metal is more dangerous than we realize?"

"Then you have to draw it away."

It involved a risk to the women but also to himself.

They needed to understand whether the caravan was any sort of danger to them, and if it wasn't, then they might be able to get help. If it was...

Then he needed to be prepared.

"When would you like to do this?"

"You don't disagree?"

"I think it's a reasonable plan. Better than what I had come up with."

"And what had you come up with?"

Haern smiled, running his finger along the surface of the sword. "If it came down to it, I thought I would have to rush in and deal with the wagons myself."

"That would be foolish."

"It might be, but it also kept the rest of you out of it."

"There are several of us who don't want to be left out of it."

"I'm aware of that," Haern said. "Who would you recommend go along on this mission?" He knew he would preferably send the women who were the strongest with weapons, but he suspected Jayna needed to plan this herself. Wasn't it similar to how *he* had needed to learn? It wasn't as if he considered himself an expert, but he had more experience than the rest of them, even if his experience was the kind where he had run from danger to danger.

"I would have Elise remain behind."

"Why her?" Haern could easily imagine how Elise would react, and she would blame him for it, but he wasn't about to argue with the idea that she was to stay behind.

"She is skilled at organizing, but she isn't as talented as others with the sword. I would rather have those I know can defend themselves rather than someone who is still working at it." Jayna glanced over her shoulder at Elise. "I'm sure you would prefer to have her with you, though, so I wouldn't argue if you suggest otherwise."

When Jayna looked back at him, Haern shook his head. "I'm not going to object. I think Elise staying behind makes sense. You get to be the one to tell her." He smiled. "And you get to tell her that it was your idea."

"Why do I get the feeling you've manipulated me?" Jayna asked.

"You're the one who came to me with the plan."

"Is it a good plan?"

"We won't know until we try it," Haern said. Jayna stared at him for a moment, and he could see that she was uncertain. "I think it's a reasonable plan. Probably a good plan, but we won't know until we get closer. I think it's a good idea to go and if there is anything there, you may have to modify what you intend."

"That is my concern. None of us want to face the same

challenges again. We have all gone through this enough times and with enough torment that we don't think we can stand by and wait."

"The other choice is to continue what we're doing."

Jayna glanced back at the fire. "We might lose Marcy if we do that."

"What do you mean?"

"Even though she's medicated and much more comfortable, she's still in pain. We can't carry her, no more than we've been carrying her, and if we can't get her to someplace soon, we might lose her."

"Then we should do this now," Haern said.

"Now?"

"It's still early. If we move quickly, we can get to them and back before the end of the night."

Haern got to his feet, sheathing his sword, and headed toward the fire while Jayna went and spoke to the others she intended to invite along on the mission. Haern had a sneaking suspicion she'd already spoken to them.

When he reached Elise, she looked back at him. "What were the two of you talking about?"

"Her plan."

"Her plan?"

"She thinks we should approach the caravan."

"I thought you were avoiding it."

"I was, but she isn't so certain we should."

"And you're letting her decide?"

"I think it's reasonable."

"I get the sense I'm not going to care very much for this."

"She has some who she thinks would be a good fit for this task."

"And I'm not a part of it."

"She feels your organizational skills would be better utilized here."

Haern had worried Elise would get angry, but she surprised him.

"I'm not as quick with the sword as Jayna, and both Stacy and Yolanda are faster with their knives." She looked to where Jayna was talking to others. "Is it a good plan?"

"I don't know. I was going to have us continue veering away, but I'm not sure that's the right strategy, either."

"We need the wagons," she said.

"That's what she says as well."

"You'll be safe?"

Elise slipped her arms around him, pulling him into an embrace. It was more affection than they had shown each other up to this point, and he found himself surprised before sinking in and allowing her to hug him. He hugged her back. "Be safe."

Haern could only nod.

With that, he started off, joining Jayna and the others as they hurried across land. They made their way east, in the general direction where he thought they'd find the wagons. As they walked, he handed a coin to Jayna.

"What's this for?"

"Carry it with you and I'll be able to find you," he said.

"Where will you go?"

"To find the caravan."

As he started to *push* off, she grabbed his wrist,

keeping him from going anywhere. "Don't leave us behind."

"I don't intend to. Let me find out where they are, and I'll return."

Jayna held him with a hard-eyed gaze for a long moment and then released his wrist.

Haern *pushed*, streaking into the air, soaring high above the ground and surveying the landscape. From here, he could make out the campfire they'd started. It was small, controlled, the kind of campfire that would be mostly concealed.

He moved in an easterly direction and scanned for any sign of light. After a while, he began to worry they were aware of his presence. It would be a reason to conceal themselves. But then, in the distance, Haern saw what he was looking for. As he approached, the fire was far larger than he'd believed, the flames dancing. He paused for a moment, watching it before starting to turn.

As he did, he realized that something wasn't right.

Haern turned back.

How many wagons were there?

There had been a dozen wagons before, and now… now there were eight.

Where had the other four gone?

As he focused, searching for the sense of lorcith, he felt it down below, which reassured him. At least one of these wagons still had the lorcith he wanted to find—and possibly trigger so that it couldn't harm anyone else. Then again, what would happen if they had divided up the lorcith they carried? What would happen if there was another danger out there?

He *pushed* himself forward, circling around the campsite.

Where had the other caravan gone?

Haern focused on the coin he'd given Jayna, drawing himself back to it. When he reached them, dropping to the ground, they spun, almost as one.

"I found the caravan," Haern said. "There's a problem."

"What is it?" Jayna asked.

"There were twelve wagons last time. Now there are eight."

"Did you see where the others went?"

Haern shook his head. "I didn't see or detect anything."

"Then we head back to the others," Jayna said.

It certainly was better than him wandering in the darkness, searching for something he might not even be able to find. They had been purposefully trying to avoid the wagons.

They followed him as they marched across the ground. Haern hurried, keeping a rapid pace as the night grew longer. He focused on the sense of lorcith he detected. It was a distinct awareness, and he let it lead him.

"What happens if you need to fight?" he asked Jayna, glancing at the others with him.

"Then we fight," she said.

"I know we don't intend it, but what happens if you need to kill?"

Stacy in particular tensed at the question. They liked the idea of fighting and defending themselves, but were they prepared for the possibility they would have to do something more? Haern wasn't sure.

"If we need to kill, then we do," Jayna whispered.

As the wagons came into view, Haern motioned to the others to slow. "I'm going to watch from above. How will I know if you need my help?"

"You have enhanced eyesight, don't you?"

Haern frowned, nodding.

"Then watch. You'll know."

Haern smiled to himself. Jayna amused him with her practicality.

He *pushed* off with a coin, using it to streak into the air. As he did, he sent another coin out from him but left the first in place. If he needed to move quickly, having the coins arranged around the wagons might provide a quick means of escape.

Haern *pushed* off on two other coins, sending them in either direction around the wagons. With the coins situated in a triangle, he could *push* and *pull*, holding himself in place so that he could hover and watch.

His heart hammered. It was dangerous what the women were doing, but was it any more dangerous than what he had wanted to do?

It wasn't long before the women reached the edge of the campsite. They approached slowly, their cloaks wrapped around them, concealing their weapons. From his vantage, the way they approached was tentative, hopefully meant to appear nervous and scared—which he imagined they were.

He couldn't hear anything but the wind as it whistled around him. He could lower himself closer, but doing so might expose him to the others. It was better to stay high enough where he could still See, even if he was too high to hear anything.

The women were met by three others. It appeared to be two men and one woman, and they were brought toward the center of the clearing, near the campfire. Jayna remained standing, but the other four took a seat, sitting around the campfire. Their backs were stiff with tension.

Someone brought something out to them. It seemed to be water or food, and he could imagine the women eagerly taking offered food. They'd had plenty of water over the last few days, but all they'd had to eat was dried food, so anything offered to them would be appealing.

As he watched, there came a strange sense.

It took Haern a moment to realize what it was. When he did, he swore to himself.

Lorcith.

It was coming at him quickly.

Haern shot upward, streaking into the darkness. He *pushed* against the sense of lorcith but realized that might be a mistake. If another sphere came at him with nails embedded within it, *pushing* on it might cause it to explode and hurt those on the ground.

Twisting in the air, Haern glanced down, but it didn't seem as if there was any unusual activity within the campsite.

Had he missed something?

When he'd come searching before, he hadn't seen anything suspicious, other than the fact that there were eight wagons rather than twelve. There hadn't been any sense of lorcith like this.

Without the triangle of coins he'd placed, Haern wasn't sure he would've been able to manipulate his position so well. With those on the ground, he was able to spin from place to place, with far greater control than he normally had when he used just one coin. He spun around and focused his energy on the sphere, *pushing*, trying to wrap his connection to lorcith around it.

Could he hold it and *pull* it to him?

It would take a level of control he hadn't attempted before.

Haern held his hands outward, focusing on the lorcith within the sphere. His palms tingled where the metal had pierced him.

He tried not to think about what that meant, though he knew it was tied to whatever change had occurred to him following the Forger attack.

The sphere started to slow.

Haern wrapped his connection around it, *pulling* power from himself, sending it swirling around the entirety of the sphere. He was ready for it to explode.

And somehow, he knew it *would* explode.

He *pushed* off the ground, higher and higher. He needed to be high enough so that if it did explode, the nails wouldn't harm anyone on the ground if he lost control.

Haern shot higher than he had before, *pulling* the sphere toward him, holding a barrier around him, a cushion designed to utilize his connection to lorcith so he could force it outward.

Then the sphere exploded.

The suddenness of it almost caught him off guard. Haern had to focus on wrapping his connection around the sphere, and as he did, he started to plummet to the ground.

It took every ounce of energy to keep the nails from shooting through his barrier. It was as if he could feel every single one attempting to penetrate it, and Haern was forced to divert every ounce of focus into *pushing* those nails backward.

And then the explosion stopped.

Haern shifted his focus, *pushing* off the ground once again, realizing he was off center, but also that he had nearly touched the ground. He floated back into the air, *pulling* the sphere to him.

As he did, he noticed something about it.

His effort to prevent it from exploding had kept the nails inside.

Could it launch again?

Haern probed the sphere, worried that something could happen to it, but he didn't detect anything.

As far as he could tell, he was still safe.

Holding himself in the air, he floated back toward the center of the clearing, above the campfire. The women were gone.

14

HAERN

A MOMENT PASSED. THEN ANOTHER.

There was still no sign of the women below, and the longer he went, the more concerned Haern became. Had he taken too long? He wasn't certain, knowing only that he had managed to prevent the sphere from exploding. That had seemed like a victory, and he had been thrilled with it, but now he had lost Jayna and the others he'd come with.

There was a way he could search for Jayna. Her coin should be somewhere. As he focused on it, he detected it off to the side.

Near one of the wagons.

Haern drifted that direction, holding on to the sphere, keeping a surge of his lorcith barrier around it in case it would explode again. If it did, he didn't know if he'd be able to react in time. Hopefully, holding on to it in this way would give him a warning, but even that might not be enough.

The challenge was that he had to *pull* on too much of

his connection to lorcith. In doing so, he wasn't nearly as stable floating in the air. He continued to try to hover, to maintain his position, but it was difficult.

There had been no scream. No shout. And as he drifted toward where he'd detected the coin, he didn't see Jayna.

There was nothing other than the flat side of the wagon.

Haern hesitated. He wanted to give them the benefit of the doubt, the opportunity to defend themselves, but what if the merchants had attacked them? Haern didn't want to wait too long, fearing that if he did, something unpleasant would happen.

He gave it another moment. Then another.

Then he dropped to the ground.

Unsheathing his sword, he held it in one hand and grabbed the sphere in the other. He approached the wagon, waiting for one of the merchants to come running, but there was nothing.

Holding himself up against the edge of the wagon, Haern tapped on the wood softly.

There was no response.

The entrance to the wagon wasn't on this side. He faced outward, away from the center of the clearing, and reaching a door into the wagon would require exposing himself. He would probably have to act quickly.

There was no question in his mind that the coin was within the wagon.

Haern crept along the side of it. It was rough, and though he knew the surface was painted, there was nothing but darkness at this time of night. When he reached the end of the wagon, he craned his neck so he could look between the two wagons and toward the clearing. The flames crackled, disrupting his night vision for a moment, and when he pulled his head back, two darkened figures were in front of him.

Haern blinked, and it took a moment for his Sight to recover.

When it did, he was face-to-face with two men dressed in dark robes. Both of them carried steel swords.

"What did you do to my friends?" Haern asked.

The men didn't answer. They surged forward, swinging their weapons.

Haern danced back, sweeping the lorcith sword around in a quick arc. With his training, he was far more comfortable fighting with the sword than he had been before, but he didn't rely upon it. There were six knives within his pocket, and he focused on two of them, *pushing* outward.

The knives streaked away from him, catching both men in the chest at the same time. Blood blossomed around the wounds, and they fell.

Haern *pulled* on the knives, wanting the weapons if he was attacked again.

He looked around, but there was no sign of anyone else.

Haern poked his head once more between the two wagons. This time, he glanced at the rear wagon, searching for a door.

When he found it, he saw a massive padlock on it.

That wasn't going to be easy to break, which meant he was going to have to unlock it somehow.

Hurrying back toward the two fallen men, Haern checked to see if either of them had keys on them. Other than the swords, they had nothing with them.

Haern took a moment to search them, and when he didn't find any coins, nor any other weapons, he stepped back, frowning to himself.

There was something odd about them, too. It took a moment for him to realize what it was. Lorcith was used here, he was certain of it, and he suspected that these men understood its use, but they didn't have any scars to suggest they were Forgers.

Who else used lorcith like that?

Creeping forward, he pulled one man's eyelids up, looking at his dead and glazed eyes. His stomach lurched for a moment.

Green.

Were they from Elaeavn?

They didn't look like they were, certainly not dressed as they were, but Haern was aware there were others from Elaeavn who didn't live in the city anymore. Galen was evidence of that fact.

And if they didn't live in Elaeavn, were they exiles?

Haern glanced back down. One of the men was older, certainly old enough to have been exiled at some point, but the other man was only a few years older than Haern.

What was going on here?

He needed to get into the wagon. There remained the sense of lorcith coming from the coin he'd given Jayna. Haern decided to try one of his knives.

He *pushed* on it, sending it toward the lock. As it lodged within, he tried to twist it. Lorcith was stronger than most metals and should be able to break almost anything, but it wasn't able to do so with this lock.

Could they have used lorcith in the lock?

Haern didn't think so. He didn't feel any lorcith from it, though it was possible they used an alloy.

But that was giving these people far too much credit, almost as if they were Forgers. Without the scars, they would have no abilities.

If it wasn't lorcith, then it was some equally strong metal. He wasn't going to be able to *push* past it with just a knife.

It was possible that he could *push* beyond it with his sword, but that would involve exposing himself in a dangerous way. But if he didn't, he might not be able to get to Jayna.

A voice on the other side of the circle of wagons caught his attention. He knew he would need to act quickly. It was a mistake that this had taken him as long as it had.

"Find them," a voice said.

Did they know that Haern had dropped two of their people?

If they did, could he act quickly enough that it wouldn't draw any more attention?

And maybe that didn't matter. At this point, all that mattered was ensuring he freed his people. It mattered not at all to him if he had to continue to attack.

Haern didn't wait to see who might be there. He paused for a moment before slipping forward, creeping through the opening between the two wagons. When he did, he came face-to-face with another attacker.

Great Watcher.

He needed to be more careful. He was risking danger time and again—and more than he needed.

The other man reached for something, and Haern *pushed* on the knife.

It streaked forward, catching the man in the chest. Haern didn't wait, *pulling* the knife back and unsheathing his sword, jamming it into the opening and wrenching the blade. Metal screamed. Haern heard others near him.

He ignored the sounds around him, focusing instead on the lock.

As he twisted the blade, the metal crying out against what he was doing, it snapped.

Someone was there.

Another attacker.

Haern spun around, positioning himself so that he could block anyone coming at him, and came face-to-face with no one.

Someone had to be here. He had heard them.

Spinning again, Haern looked between the wagons, but there was no one.

He pulled the lock off the door.

As he did, something struck him.

Haern staggered back, realizing too late that it was lorcith.

He *pushed* on it, but the metal pierced his leg and his shoulder.

Pushing against it involved *pushing* outward and away from himself, but the power to *push* from metal involved drawing from some deep place within himself, and he wasn't sure he would be able to do that with metal stabbing through him.

Haern reached for what had struck him and found only pain. His hand came away sticky and wet. Blood. He reached for his thigh, and it was the same.

Turning, he found no evidence of any attacker.

They had to be there, but where?

Haern spun, looking to see who might have come after him. In the middle of the clearing, near the flame, a silver sphere rested on the ground.

Lorcith.

At least he knew what he'd been struck with. The nails had pierced his shoulder and his thigh. He was lucky it wasn't worse. The fact that he had been hiding between the two wagons had probably protected him. It was unlikely he would get so lucky again.

Haern spun in place, still looking out toward the fire, knowing there was someone out there who had the ability to harm him. He tried to ignore the pain in his shoulder, but it burned, making him wonder if it was poisoned.

There wasn't time to think about that.

There was no sign of anyone here. Nothing other than the empty clearing. Despite that, someone had to be present. There wasn't any way he could have been attacked otherwise.

He tried starting forward, toward the sphere, but the pain in his leg made it impossible.

Haern tried to think of the lessons Galen had taught him about dealing with poisonings. There had been many such lessons, and in all of them, he had remembered how brutal it had felt when he'd suffered. Many of them were painful. This was the kind of pain that came from his flesh torn, metal within it, the same sort of pain he'd felt when the Forgers had pierced his palms with their metal.

If he could focus inwardly, if he could find some way of reaching the lorcith that had penetrated his arms, then he could dislodge it.

Haern reached for the wagon. At least he could open the door. Jayna was inside, and he would do whatever was within his power to ensure her safety. Get them free, and perhaps they could help him. If he could stay awake long enough, he might be able to guide them in finding the right kind of treatment.

The door didn't open.

His mind was starting to get fuzzy. Whatever they had used on him was potent. Would it be slithca? He had some experience with that compound and knew it would cause him to lose his connection to his abilities.

As sedated as he felt, it might not even matter. At this point, he wasn't able to focus on anything other than the pain filling him.

Movement in front of him caught his attention, and Haern tried to stagger toward it but found he could not. He licked his lips. They were dry, another sign of the poisoning. The longer it lingered, the more likely he wouldn't be able to withstand it.

Somehow, Haern had to buy himself some time.

His vision began to blur.

He became acutely aware of the way his heart pounded, the sense of movement around him, and a vague sensation of lorcith somewhere near him. Why should that be?

Could it be *his* lorcith?

Haern didn't think it was lorcith he'd brought with him, but he still didn't know what he was detecting. Whatever it was seemed close.

He spun, and a vague figure appeared. Haern *pushed* out with his connection to lorcith, prepared to cut down more attackers.

He didn't see anything other than shadows.

Crying out, he flung himself forward. This was a mistake. He should have come at this in a different direction. What was he thinking coming by himself? What had he been thinking allowing Jayna to plan like this?

Someone grunted, and he thought that one of his knives hit home.

Haern spun, holding on to his sword, sweeping it in a broad arc.

All he needed to do was cut down whoever was in front of him. Then he would find Jayna. Stacy. Any of the others.

But they weren't here.

Haern swept his sword around in a violent arc.

He staggered. He could barely keep his footing and knew that if he fell, he wouldn't have the strength to get back up.

"Haern?"

Somewhere distantly he heard his name. Why was that?

Could Jayna have come for him?

Haern spun, searching for evidence of Jayna or the others. Everything around him was a haze. Pain throbbed in his leg and his shoulder, pulsing in time with his heartbeat.

It reminded him of how he'd felt when the Forgers had pierced his palms with their bars of metal, the attack that had changed him, turning him into something else.

Haern didn't know what it was.

Why was he thinking about that now?

He should be thinking about getting away from here. He should be thinking about getting the others he had come with away from here.

And maybe there was something he could do.

He still had the sphere in his pocket. He pulled it out and sent it rolling. The awareness of lorcith filled him, near enough that he knew he could *push* on it, trigger the nails to explode away from him. In doing so, he thought he could get to safety.

It wasn't just him needing to get to safety. It was figuring out where the others had gone.

He had no idea, and with his vision hazy, his mind foggy, he wasn't sure he would find them.

Somehow he would have to.

"Haern?"

Someone said his name again, and it seemed almost as if he should recognize the voice, but that couldn't be. It wasn't Jayna, and it wasn't Stacy, or...

Who else was with him?

Haern could no longer remember. All he was aware of was the pain.

His body throbbed.

He took a step toward the sphere.

It might mean sacrificing himself, but wasn't he willing to do that?

"Go, Jayna," Haern said.

At least, he thought he said it. It was possible nothing came out other than a mumbling.

"Haern?"

Who was there? Someone knew his name.

Or they were using him.

He wasn't about to allow anyone to use him. He wasn't about to allow anyone to harm him or the others he was with. He could defend them.

Trigger the sphere.

He could do that.

Haern *pushed*.

It required what he thought was left of his connection to lorcith. It flowed outward from him, striking the sphere. When it did, there came the faint sense of him doing something.

Would the nails fire?

If they did, he could stay low. It was possible he could come out of this.

Power flowed from him.

And then the sphere exploded. Lorcith streaked outward.

Haern smiled to himself, looking up. As he did, his breath caught.

Rayen?

15

LUCY

THE INSIDE OF THE LIBRARY WAS COOL, THE LANTERN flickering with just enough light for Lucy to see, but she didn't even need that.

She sat with her arms resting on the table, staring straight ahead. There was nothing else in the room, and she was left alone, with the library and herself. She didn't have any books in front of her, but she didn't really want any. At this point, all Lucy wanted was to have time with her thoughts.

She needed to Read herself.

And in this place, protected as she was, she knew she wasn't going to be in any danger.

At least she was away from the Architect's influence.

The more she thought about him, the more she realized she'd gained something from the proximity to him.

And more than likely, he hadn't known it.

He would have thought he was too powerful for her to reach into his mind and gather anything, so for her to have grasped anything from him was a great gift.

Now they needed to use it. She would have to continue to focus her mind, trying to find anything of value.

Doing so would be difficult, and yet she was determined to continue to search, straining through her mind, willing to look deep within herself for those answers.

She would start with where she had felt that influence before. She closed her eyes, looking inward, tracing back through where he'd Pushed her. It had been a subtle influence, much different than when he had done it the first time.

This time he had been gentle, as if he hadn't intended for her to know he was there as he tried to Push on her thoughts.

The other difference was that this time, she'd recognized the nature of the influence.

Regardless of what he was trying to convince her, she *had* grown in the time since she'd been with him. Her control and knowledge had increased. She had learned how she could look inwardly and could use that in order to protect herself.

It was going to take her digging within her mind, and given everything she'd experienced, she wasn't sure if she wanted to go that deep into her thoughts.

As she Read herself, she found where he had attempted to Push her.

Why with those thoughts?

The important question was why would he want her to doubt herself. Did he think that would make her look away? He'd been digging, searching, as if he'd wanted to come up with names.

And perhaps that was what he had wanted. He might have been looking for answers, thinking if he could uncover who she was working with, he could target them. The names she'd revealed had to have been Ras and Carth and Galen. All of them highly skilled individuals, people she didn't worry about.

But then there were others. Eve and Marcy and Olivia.

Their names trailed through her mind, a memory of what she'd thought of. Thankfully, she hadn't focused on the village and hadn't revealed anything more than their names, but the fact that she had used those names meant he had access to people she had wanted to protect.

And if she couldn't protect them in this way, how was she going to protect them at all?

Somehow, she would have to find a way to prevent him from doing them any harm.

Lucy focused, looking through her mind for anything that might help her understand what she could uncover from the Architect. His mind had touched hers. A connection would have formed, and she could use that connection to find some way to dig through what he was doing to her and uncover what he wanted.

Names. That was why he had dug at her mind, but why would he care about names?

Unless he was going to target them.

She didn't give him the village. Because of that, there was no reason for her to be concerned about them getting discovered, unless he had managed to rifle through her thoughts and find it, though she didn't think so. She hadn't come up with any image of the village.

What benefit would the names provide?

Other than knowing that they were all working together.

Carth believed this to be some sort of game, believed the Architect was one piece Olandar Fahr was using, which meant they could use him to get to Olandar Fahr.

What she needed was to figure out what he was up to.

Always before, he'd been planning. She knew he'd been a part of Olandar Fahr's strategy and had great influence with the man.

It was the same thing Ras had wanted from her. He'd believed tracing through the Architect's goals would bring them to Olandar Fahr, but perhaps they were working separately.

She paused within her mind, Reading where he had attempted to Push, and searched. There had to be something there, some reason he'd focused on that part of her mind. As she looked, listening, searching, she couldn't come up with anything.

She opened her eyes, looking around the library. He'd been planning something.

She closed her eyes, thinking back through all the times she had worked with him, all the experiences she had with him, from the very beginning.

She'd never given much thought to all those experiences, had never tried to trace through them. Now she thought she needed to. The longer she focused on him, the more certain she was those answers were there.

What had he told her?

At first, she'd been so focused on escape that she hadn't been able to think of anything else. Still, her ability to Read had been there even then, and she had to believe she would have uncovered something.

Then again, the Architect hadn't come to her all that often at that time. She'd been overwhelmed by not only thoughts, but visions. Even now the visions continued to press upon her when she tried to think through them, to the point where Lucy had abandoned any attempt to use them in a meaningful way. There was no purpose in painfully trying to strain through them, to dig them apart, until she better understood whether there was anything useful about them.

But the Architect had stayed near her.

He had Read her then.

It was as if he had wanted to test her.

He had been pleased with her development, her growth, the nature of her abilities.

That was what it was.

He wanted to better understand the augmentation.

She remembered his surprise at how effective it was.

He was working with Olandar Fahr, and with the augmentations the Ai'thol had used. Not the Ai'thol—the C'than.

Had they used any other technique, she would've been left with a terrible scar.

She never would've taken an augmentation voluntarily. They would have had to capture her first, and she never would've left Elaeavn. She would have stayed until Haern came back, if he ever did. Had she not received the augmentation, she might never have left the city, and then Daniel wouldn't have either, and Carth might not have been brought back into the fight.

Why was she thinking about those things?

It seemed almost as if she were guided along that way.

Was somebody else trying to influence her thoughts?

Lucy focused, looking through her mind for any sort of influence, Reading herself.

But she found nothing—those had been her own thoughts.

She wasn't much of a planner. She'd always been a scholar. When it came to Olandar Fahr and everything he wanted, she was going to have to be more than just a scholar. She was going to have to be something more than she had ever been before. She might even have to become something of a soldier.

It was the kind of fighting she didn't want to be involved with, and yet she wondered if she might *need* to have some role in it.

The more she thought about it, the more certain she was she would have to take a greater stand.

The Architect had wanted to know about her augmentation—how it was placed, where it was placed, and what it did for her.

That was why he'd not pushed her at first.

She felt that, which meant she had those memories somewhere within her mind.

She had to find where they came from. If she could, she might even recognize the familiarity of his mind. Then she might be able to trace him, latch on to his thoughts—even Slide to him.

Why would he have been watching?

Unless he didn't know how this augmentation had been placed.

Then again, the Ai'thol wouldn't have known. It was something of the C'than, not the Ai'thol. They had surprised the Ai'thol, suddenly appearing with abilities and augmentations that the Ai'thol didn't understand. Now that Lucy thought about it, she was certain that was the key.

The augmentation was what he wanted to know about.

That was why he'd been there, waiting and listening, searching for any information he might be able to uncover. He'd used that, hoping she might reveal what had happened to her and how it could be replicated.

Lucy had no idea what had been done to her, but he had tested, using her experiences.

Because he'd wanted to recreate it.

That was what the Ai'thol wanted. They wanted the knowledge of the C'than.

Could that be why he was in that town?

They needed to go back.

Lucy got to her feet and started pacing.

She needed to slow down, to think things through, to ensure what she was uncovering was accurate. And if it was, then she had to dig a little deeper, be prepared for the possibility there was something more than what she had already uncovered.

Perhaps she was wrong. Perhaps this was different than just a search for the knowledge of the C'than. Where had the C'than gained that knowledge?

She looked around the library, searching through the books. From what she'd gathered, the knowledge here was different than what was in other places. The books stored within this stronghold were restricted even from those within the C'than. There were places like the university in Asador that were places of study, and yet even there, there wasn't nearly the same type of knowledge stored here.

The fact that they kept some of these books here, restricted from anyone other than very high-ranking Ai'thol, suggested there was danger within them.

Lucy surveyed the books. The only person who really knew what was here would be Ras, and in order to get him to talk about it, she would have to convince him she was right.

She took a deep breath, Sliding within the tower. When she emerged near the main level, she found no one. She Slid again, appearing outside the tower. The sky was dark, and thunder rumbled. Mist drifted down from the sky, mixed with that washing off the ocean. The waves were angry today—chaotic, as Olivia would say. This was the kind of place she would have found relaxing.

And perhaps that was an answer for Olivia.

Lucy had been trying to keep them separate, but perhaps that was a mistake. Bringing someone like Olivia here, someone who needed the time to be alone, to understand the nature of her abilities, might benefit her.

She found a lone figure walking along the shoreline and headed toward them. From here, it was difficult to tell if it was Carth or Ras. Both had dark hair, though Ras's was streaked with more gray. He typically wore a pale white robe that made him almost seem to glow. And he often spent time outside like this.

And yet as she approached, she found that the person

wearing the white robe was Carth. She was glowing in a way that Lucy had rarely seen.

Shadows swirled away from her, as if chased by her sudden appearance.

"Did you uncover anything?"

"I think the Architect's after a way of recreating my augmentation."

"Why would you think that?"

"I was trying to think of why he would have been in that town, and it forced me think back to why he would've been so interested in me."

"He would've been interested in you because you are Elvraeth who had an augmentation placed."

"True, but I had an augmentation he didn't understand." Lucy turned toward the waves crashing along the water. "Mine is different than what the Ai'thol typically place. We all know they generally have scars." She touched the back of her head, running her fingers over the now completely healed surface. There were no remnants of the metal, and yet sometimes she could still feel it. At times, her head still throbbed, the aching leaving her miserable. "I think they've been wanting to know how to do what the C'than have done."

"If they manage to uncover what the C'than have done and recreate it, then the nature of their augmentations will make it difficult for us to identify them."

Lucy nodded.

"You want to return to the town."

"How did you know?"

"It's what I would've done."

"Would have?"

"I think you'll need to go by yourself."

"Why?"

"Because when it comes to this, there is some danger."

She nodded. "You don't want to risk yourself."

"No. I think you are better equipped to find the answers."

"What if it takes me in search of the C'than?"

"Then so be it." Carth turned toward her, and the glowing seemed to ease. "We know there remain others within the C'than who've betrayed us. We need to continue to root them out, and yet, we haven't been able to find anything more about them. I am going to continue to search."

"For the C'than or for Olandar Fahr?"

"For both."

"I know how upset you are—"

"You can't begin to know how upset I am," Carth said.

Lucy watched the other woman. An angry Carth terrified her, but more than that, she worried what Carth might do. She needed the other woman calm and rational so they could prepare for what they needed to do.

"Don't do anything foolish," Lucy said.

"I never do."

"How will I find you?"

Carth smiled tightly. "I think I've revealed how I can reach you if I need to."

Lucy glanced back at the tower. Shadows swirled around it, the way they had since she'd first come here. She still didn't understand why, or what the tower represented, other than that there was some aspect of the Elder Stone mixed within it. It was something she had never really uncovered, and it was possible she never would.

"I will let you know if I find anything."

"I know you will."

With that, Lucy Slid.

She emerged back at the edge of the town, and there was the overwhelming sense of the others around her. She maintained an edge, worried the Architect might've returned. If he had, she needed be careful to avoid his influence, lest he find some way of pushing on her mind.

She started into the town, not wanting to Slide or look out of place. She pulled her cloak off, tucking it under her arm, and looked around as she entered the town.

She knew the way Carth would approach finding information in a place like this. She would go to a tavern. Lucy didn't need to go to a tavern order to find what she needed. She could wander, Listening and Reading.

She hadn't come looking only for the Architect; she wanted to know if there was any evidence of the rogue C'than here. If there was, she needed to figure out why and what they were doing here.

Anything she could uncover would be valuable to her and to the C'than.

And wasn't she one of the C'than now?

She didn't know if Ras would consider her a part of it, but she couldn't help but feel as if she were. It seemed as if she belonged, and the more she worked on their behalf, the more certain she was she was a part of what they were doing.

Reaching the center of the town, she paused, looking around.

She didn't need to linger. She wasn't trapped, since she could always Slide anywhere else she needed to go.

She found a bench near a clearing at the center of the town. Taking a seat on it, Lucy looked around, watching as others made their way through the town. A man pushed carts loaded with food, likely going to a market. As she focused on the man pushing the carts, she could Read how he was hoping for a good day of sales. A young woman scurried along the street, carrying a bolt of cloth, a measuring tape wrapped around her neck. Three men worked along the street in the opposite direction, all of them slightly dirty; she was able to detect that they were loggers.

All of this had a sense of normalcy to it.

What she needed to find was anything that might not be normal. Perhaps she did need to go to a tavern.

She got up and started along the street, reaching a section of town that was a little more run-down. The buildings were less well maintained, some of the signs overhead not as freshly painted as the others she'd passed. Most of the windows were dirty, the road tramped down, with tracks marked through it, not freshly laid cobbles.

Everything about this part of the town left her a little unsettled, and yet she wasn't as uncomfortable as she once would have been. There was a time when she would never have come to a place like this—would never have believed she was capable of protecting herself.

And yet, now that she was here, she recognized she was able to do both of those things. She might not be a fighter, but she could Push, and she could enlist others to fight on her behalf.

She took a deep breath, pushing open the door. Something drifted out to her.

It was a faint thought, barely more than a whisper.

There was something familiar about it, and as she focused on it, she realized where she had recognized it from.

It was like the minds of the women within the village.

It was muted.

Someone here had an augmentation.

16

LUCY

Lucy entered the tavern, her gaze sweeping around. It was dark, dingy, and it seemed as if a haze hung over everything. She watched for a moment, worried there might be shadows twisted, hovering over things the same way Carth used the shadows, but she didn't find anything like that. Unlike some of the taverns she'd visited with Carth, there were no minstrels playing. There was no joyful noise. Even the servants making their way from table to table seemed to have a dreary appearance.

This might've been a mistake.

She focused on the minds inside here, and she Pushed, trying to convince them to ignore her.

She used as subtle a touch as she could, though she wasn't sure she'd been effective. She didn't have as soft a touch as some—not as subtle as the Architect had used when he had been trying to Push on her mind.

She found a table in one corner, took a seat at it, and looked around. Maybe it would've been better to have Carth with her. Then she would have been able to hide in the shadows. But this way, she was forced to work on her own, Pushing, using her talents to protect herself.

Then, if it came down to it, she could Slide.

She wasn't hungry, and yet she worried that if she didn't order something, she would draw unnecessary attention. There were limits to how well she could Push, and she worried whoever was augmented here would realize what she was doing.

She had to use her ability as barely more than a touch. She certainly didn't want to draw the attention of anyone who might be watching for her.

She focused on one of the servants and sent a different kind of Push.

This one was such that it helped to draw them to her.

Lucy waited, sitting on the rickety chair, leaning on the table before realizing how sticky it was and sitting back up.

The old man who approached was missing a few teeth. His hair was long and brushed back. There was something of an angry appearance about him.

"What can I do for you?"

Lucy looked around before meeting his eyes. "I'm looking for some food."

"We got food. You have coin?"

She Pushed slightly, just enough to make him think she had enough coin on her, which she did. She carried money with her, something she never would have done before, and she didn't worry about being able to pay for her food, though he obviously was concerned about her ability to do so.

He turned, heading back to the kitchen.

It gave her an opportunity to sit back, sweeping her gaze around. As she did, she focused on the various minds within the tavern. Most of them were workers—mainly loggers, it seemed—and from what she could Read, it was hard work. They put in long hours, often in terrible conditions.

And there were a few who seemed to be merchants, though they were down on their luck and avoided anyone else's eyes.

That left only a single person in the tavern whom she couldn't easily Read. She wondered if he was one of the C'than.

She tried to avoid drawing his attention. He was near her age and handsome, with dark hair, a square jaw, and high cheekbones. When she tried to Read him, she found his thoughts muted.

That couldn't be a coincidence. Not in a place like this, not with what she had experienced.

She looked away, trying not to draw his notice. If she wasn't able to Push on his mind, it was likely he would already be aware of her.

Would he be able to Read her?

She didn't know what ability someone like that would have, only that the thoughts drifting from his mind were faint, muted, and the more she focused on them, the more certain she was that she'd found what she was looking for.

And now that she had, what would she be able to do with that information?

Lucy nodded politely to the man who brought her a tray of food, glancing down at it briefly. There was nothing that looked appealing. Her stomach might rumble, but the meat looked stringy and dry. The vegetables, if that was what they were, were overcooked, almost mush.

She went through her pocket, double-checking to be sure she had the necessary coins to leave, and then began to pick at the food. The others in the tavern came and went. She listened to their thoughts, focusing on what she could. She waited for the other to disappear, but he didn't.

That told her more than ever that he was one of the rogue C'than. He was here for a purpose.

Sitting alone as he was, with the augmentation he must have, he had to have some reason for being here. Could he have been meeting with the Architect?

Now that the Architect was gone—or at least, she thought he was gone—the C'than might have been disappointed.

What if Lucy pretended to be the Architect?

She pushed the thought out of her mind. It wouldn't work. There must've been rumors of the Architect, and everyone would have known he was male.

It would be better for her to sit and watch, see if she might be able to uncover anything from this man that she could use to learn where more of these C'than were.

His thoughts were too muted for her. The more she tried to focus on them, the more she failed to uncover anything about him.

The waiter came back and glanced at her, but she Pushed on him.

This time, she did it with little more force, and he turned back to the kitchen.

Perhaps that was a mistake.

Movement caught the corner of her eye, and she glanced over to see the C'than getting up. He looked in her direction briefly before heading out of the tavern.

Great Watcher.

She'd made a mistake. She'd been too forceful with Pushing, which meant that now he was aware of what she was doing—and that she was here.

She needed to know where he was going and who he might be with, but if she followed him now, it would be far too obvious.

What choice did she have?

Lucy stacked a few coins on the table and got up, following the man out of the tavern. Once outside, she looked along the street, searching for any sign of him, but he was gone.

Could she trail after his thoughts?

She had caught nothing but a muted image of them, not enough to latch on to, and yet as she focused, she thought she could use what she was able to recall.

It was there. She might not have anything other than the faintest inkling of what he was thinking, but it was enough for her to track him.

He headed north.

She turned, meandering along the street, maintaining that connection, focusing her own mind and pushing away any other thoughts so that she wasn't thinking of anything else around her. In this town, she wondered if that was dangerous. She didn't think there was anyone else here who could pose any danger, and yet there was the possibility she was overlooking something because of her focus on this man.

He headed west now.

Lucy turned, following the path he took, and held on to her connection to him. She waited for the possibility that he might suddenly wink out of existence, disappearing from her. Then she would know for certain that he had some abilities, and more than that, that he could Slide.

He didn't seem to take any specific course. The longer she followed, the more certain she was that he was wandering.

Had he discovered that she was there?

It wouldn't be altogether surprising—if he had some augmentation, he might know what she was doing. He might even be able to Read her. But if so, then why not simply challenge her?

She turned again, realizing she had already passed by this section of town. There was a steady hammering coming from a blacksmith, and she paused.

The rhythm to the hammering was such that she frowned to herself.

A blacksmith couldn't be altogether coincidental, could it?

The rogue C'than would need access to metal. They used it in their augmentations; they would need somebody who had some knowledge over it.

She shifted her focus, attempting to Read whoever was inside, and found she could not.

Odd.

When she shifted back, trying to focus on the man she'd trailed after, she'd lost him.

Great Watcher.

She was making mistake after mistake.

The only other mistake she might make would be if she were to get caught.

And yet, she could still Slide. She could feel that she could still do so, something she had taken to testing every so often, ensuring that no one managed to sneak up on her.

If she was to find out why the Architect was here, she would need to take a few chances. That involved going into this forge, and it involved taking risks.

She pushed open the door and looked inside. It was dark, the walls all made of stone. Lucy had come to know from Haern and his family that blacksmith shops needed to be designed like this. It was safer.

The steady hammering continued, and she looked to see where the blacksmith was but didn't find him.

He must be in a different section of the shop.

Shelves lined the interior of the forge, and she looked around, wanting to know whether the quality was similar to what she was accustomed to in Elaeavn, but she didn't have a chance.

The hammering suddenly stopped.

A door opened, and a man appeared out of the back room. He was a little older than her and had a grizzled beard. He wore heavy leathers and had slung his hammer up over his shoulder, watching her.

"Can I help you?" he asked.

"I just thought I would check out your wares."

"Is that right?"

"It is. I am in the market for a few things…"

She trailed off as he took a step toward her,

approaching with an almost threatening air. She tried to Read him but couldn't detect anything.

Was he augmented?

She glanced down to see if there was anything in his hands but couldn't find anything. He carried the hammer over his shoulder, and she knew from experience that a hammer like that was heavy.

If he swung it at her, could she react in time?

"Why are you here?" he asked.

"I told you that I was—"

He shifted the hammer on his shoulder, and Lucy reacted. She Slid, appearing behind him.

"You don't need to get violent," she said.

He spun, putting his back to the door, effectively barricading her in if she hadn't had the ability to Slide.

Her heart hammered, and she focused on it, trying to calm her nerves. She wasn't in any danger here. She could use anything she could uncover to figure out who these people were and why she couldn't Read them.

If they were with the rogue C'than, then she needed to know.

"Who are you?"

"I would ask you the same thing. What are you working on?"

The man brought the hammer down and rested it on his hand. He looked ready to strike, and Lucy almost missed the sense of movement behind her.

She Slid across the room and spun around, realizing there was another person there.

The man she had seen in the tavern suddenly appeared.

Could he Slide?

She'd been trailing after him and hadn't thought he could, but what if she was wrong?

"What are you doing here?" the newcomer asked.

"I came to the shop to see if there was anything I might be interested in purchasing. I didn't realize I would be assaulted like this."

"Assault?" The man shared a look with the blacksmith before turning her way. "You're the one who came in here looking as if you want to cause trouble."

Lucy frowned, glancing from the blacksmith to the other man. He was handsome, and she stared at him, wondering if he could Slide. If he could, he could follow her, but then again, she could also Read something about him.

The sense of his mind was faint, but it was there. The more she focused, the more certain she was that the answers she was looking for were there within his mind, and yet it was muted to her.

She backed up, keeping the wall behind her. She didn't want somebody else suddenly surprising her.

As she watched, she kept her gaze on the blacksmith. With his hammer, he was the one she feared.

"What are you doing here?" Lucy asked.

"You came to his shop," the other man said.

He took a step toward her, and Lucy watched to see if there would be any telltale sign of someone Sliding. She didn't see any shimmering, nothing that would suggest he'd Slid.

He didn't approach too quickly, and because of that, she thought that she was relatively safe.

Could *she* still Slide?

There was always the possibility they would find some way of trapping her. The Ai'thol had known a way to prevent somebody from Sliding, and even Ras had a way of keeping her from doing so, so she had to be careful.

She held on to the thoughts of Daniel Elvraeth. They were distant, but she used him as she often did, anchoring to him. If it came down to it, she would pull on his mind, drawing herself to him, getting away from here.

The other two simply watched.

Why couldn't she Read the blacksmith?

"Are you with the C'than?" she asked.

She felt it best to get that out in the open, and she watched both of them for any sign of emotion.

The blacksmith didn't move, but the other man did. He took another step toward her. "Who are you with?" he asked.

"It doesn't matter. Not anymore."

"It matters. You're not going anywhere until we find out."

"Do you think you can hold me?"

"I think I would try."

She frowned and attempted a tiny Slide, barely more than a half step over, and found she still could Slide.

"I came here looking for answers. There's a dangerous man here."

"We are dangerous men."

"Are you?" She glanced from the blacksmith to the other. "I see a man holding a hammer, and another man threatening an unarmed woman. Dangerous indeed."

"You might be unarmed, but that doesn't mean you're helpless."

Lucy smiled. "It does not."

And that was perhaps the greatest compliment she could have received. She wasn't helpless, and she was thankful for that.

Whatever else happened, she no longer had to fear.

But she didn't want to fight. That wasn't her purpose in coming here.

"I just came for some answers," she said.

"What sort of answers do you think we have?"

"I don't know. And yet, the two of you look as if you know something."

"Why would we look like that?"

"Because you have augmentations."

She didn't see any spark of recognition.

Perhaps she was wrong.

Most people would know if they had an augmentation, especially the way the C'than placed them. And if they didn't have one, then there might not be any way for her to know.

Perhaps she had been wrong about it entirely.

She didn't think so, though.

There was some resistance to her attempting to Read, and that resistance suggested to her they had some way of opposing what she was doing. The more she focused on it, the more certain she was that there had to be something.

But what if it wasn't an augmentation? What if they had some other way of fighting off what she was able to do?

Carth certainly had a method of preventing her from

Reading, so it wouldn't be beyond the realm of belief that these two had some way as well.

Could it be that she had stumbled across somebody powered by natural Elder Stone power?

If so, she'd made a mistake by trying to chase after them.

She took a step back and bumped into the wall. "Listen. Perhaps we got off on the wrong foot."

"We definitely did," the man said.

"I came looking for people who have been placing augmentations. If that's not you, then I don't need to remain."

The two men shared a look, and with that, the blacksmith suddenly surged.

Lucy reacted and Slid, emerging behind him, near the door. She prepared for the possibility that she might need to Slide away, but she didn't want to do so. She wanted answers.

She hesitated, worried that perhaps this was a mistake. What if she needed Carth?

But the more she thought about it, the more certain she was she had to do this on her own. If she didn't, then how was she ever going to be able to function on her own?

Lucy thought about how she could handle them. She wasn't going to fight them, and she wasn't going to be able to Push on them. There had to be some other way she could use her abilities.

"Now you attack an unarmed woman," she said.

The blacksmith spun and lunged again, bringing the hammer around.

He was fast—faster than she would've expected.

If he wasn't augmented, he still had power. He was considerably larger than her, and if he crashed into her, she likely wouldn't get up.

It was the kind of thing that suggested she needed to keep moving. If she suddenly Slid away, then the answers she needed would be gone.

She breathed out heavily.

The blacksmith neared her, and she Slid, reappearing where she'd been before, with her back to the wall. The other man was there. Lucy attempted to Slide, but he had grabbed on to her.

She pulled, but he was strong.

She felt a faint surge of emotion from him. It was the only thing she was able to uncover. With it, she could feel his triumph, as if he was excited about grabbing her.

She needed to glimpse more of his emotion than that.

She Slid, dragging him with her, and then Slid again. Each time she did, she emerged only a small distance away, but it was enough to unsettle the blacksmith, keeping him from reaching her. With every Slide, she dragged this man with her, preventing him from releasing her. She tried to disorient him. If he had the ability to Slide on his own, then he wouldn't have any trouble with this, but if he didn't—and the longer he held on to her, the more she began to wonder whether or not he did—she expected he would find the jarring sensation of each Slide too much to handle.

She wasn't getting anywhere. Each time she emerged, the blacksmith spun toward her. And so she Slid, emerging outside on the street.

The other man still held on to her, but she kicked, driving her foot into his groin, and he released his grip. She Slid back a few steps, getting away from him, and watched.

He leaned over, and when he did, she searched for evidence of a scar on the back of his head, or anything that would tell her he had some augmentation, but she wasn't able to see anything.

If he did, it had overgrown, much the way hers had overgrown.

"Who are you?" she asked.

"You come to our town and question us?"

"Are you with the C'than?"

He stood up and wiped his hands on his jacket before crossing his arms over his chest. "You aren't going to get any answers from us."

Lucy looked around, worried she might be surrounded by others, but there wasn't anyone else.

It was just this man, and then the door to the shop opened and the blacksmith poked his head out.

Out in the street, he could barrel toward her, but she was able to Slide quickly.

What she wanted was information, not to continue to battle with them, but she wasn't sure she was going to get that information.

She could return. If she brought enough support with her—and if Carth came—she might be able to find out what she wanted, but she worried if she disappeared, they would too.

And here she had come for understanding, but now

that she was close to finding it, she wasn't sure if her efforts were going to be enough.

She focused on the smaller of the two men and tried to Read him.

His mind was muted, shielded, but there had to be some way beyond that. Her mind would've been the same way with the Architect, and yet he had somehow managed to reach inside her thoughts and place a soft Push.

Was there anything she could use from that experience?

She had to believe he had somehow Slid those thoughts into her mind. If so, then could she do the same?

She was able to anchor to thoughts, and in this case, she wasn't trying to Slide to the man but attempting to Slide a Push into him.

It would take something different than she had ever tried before, but if she was ever going to do it, now would be the time.

She focused. It was a strange thing to try to think of, but as she did, she found she was able to do it.

The barrier in his mind fell away, and she forced her pressure inside, Pushing on this man. The request was simple: *Open your mind.*

She didn't want anything more than that, only for him to reveal himself to her and for her to be able to understand what he was doing and what the two of them were planning. She needed to know whether there was anything to fear from either of them, and whether they were working with this man. It was possible he didn't even know. They could've been experimented on the same way she had been.

Thoughts drifted into her mind.

As they did, she felt a moment of victory.

It was short-lived.

The blacksmith barreled toward her, lumbering faster and faster, and without any other choice, Lucy Slid.

17

LUCY

Lucy emerged within the tower and looked around the inside of the library, finding it empty once again. She breathed out heavily, leaning on her thighs, resting her hands there as she panted.

Was there anything she'd be able to uncover from what she'd managed to Read? Anything she could dig up would be faint, difficult, but she needed to try to reach through it, to see if there was anything useful there.

She took a seat at the table, looking around the library. When she'd been here before, she had used this as an opportunity to Read herself, and now she again wondered if she could learn anything.

This time, she had been able to Push on the man in town. She had to be able to find something from him. She closed her eyes, focusing.

The answers were there, deep in her mind.

It had been fast, fleeting, and yet she knew they had to be there.

Images raced through her mind. Lucy struggled to

slow them, trying to get through them so she could better understand what she had encountered, but she could feel only faint stirrings.

There had to be more than that.

The more she focused, the more she could slow down what she'd encountered. She had to dig deeper.

There might be another way.

Could she reach him from here?

Doing so would be difficult, but she had touched his mind, and with the Push, she had a connection to him she didn't before.

She could reach across the distance, the same way she often anchored to Daniel Elvraeth.

And if she could, then she might be able to uncover the answers she wanted without endangering herself.

She focused on him.

From here, he was farther away than she wanted. Could she Slide part of the way?

Doing so was challenging, but she thought about shifting her focus, Sliding only a part of herself, using just her mind to stretch out rather than taking her whole body. Even if she could do that, Lucy wasn't sure it was safe.

And yet, to get the answers she wanted without endangering herself, it might be necessary. She didn't have the skill to do it without getting hurt, and if she approached too closely, she was going to put herself in danger.

She didn't want anything to do with that kind of danger, so she focused.

The faint streamers of his mind were there.

It was muted, but she detected the sense of him, almost as if she could connect to him. She used what she had done before, Sliding her mind.

Doing it again was easier the second time, and now that she had, she was able to bridge the distance between them, and she found his mind opened up to her.

She forced her way in.

It was possible he would know she was there. At this point, she no longer cared. All she wanted was to dig into his mind, to know who had been responsible for placing the augmentations, and to determine whether the C'than were part of this.

As she dug, she found evidence of an augmentation.

It was as she had suspected. The connection was there. The more she thought about it, the more certain she was the augmentation had given him an awareness of others around him. She could tell he sensed everyone, though it was different than her ability to Read. His was more of a connection.

Strange, but perhaps a useful ability.

She pushed deeper. What she wanted was to know whether he was rogue C'than, or at least whether he was with the rogue C'than. Perhaps they had placed the augmentation, or perhaps it was the Ai'thol.

There had been no scar, and without a scar, she had to wonder whether the Ai'thol were responsible.

The Architect *had* been there.

Could he have been running experiments?

It was the kind of thing Olandar Fahr would approve of.

And of course he would be conducting experiments.

He would want to know whether it was safe for others to have an augmentation placed. If Olandar Fahr began to use similar augmentations to the C'than's, it was going to be more dangerous for all of them.

Within his mind, she found the person who had placed it.

It wasn't the Architect.

She didn't recognize the person, though she wasn't sure if she would. The man she was digging into—a man by the name of Ryan—hadn't known the person who'd placed the augmentation either.

He had gone along with it, taking the danger.

He had willingly accepted the augmentation.

Such a thing was not unheard of. The Ai'thol, too, placed augmentations with the permission of the recipient.

Which made it even more likely he was with the Ai'thol rather than the C'than.

She searched for anything else she could uncover, but wasn't able to discover whether he had ties to either group.

He had simply taken the offering of power, and that had been it.

There had been no conditions placed on him, no requirements. It had been the power, and nothing more.

Someone had been watching. She was certain of it, even if she couldn't tell who it was. There had to have been somebody keeping track of what had happened, the same way the C'than had been watching for any change with those they'd influenced.

Which meant that if it wasn't the Architect, somebody

else was still in the town.

And if they were there, would they have known that Lucy had come?

If, like Carth said, they had some way of detecting Sliding, it was possible they were aware of her presence.

She needed to go back.

But she needed to go back with help.

Lucy got to her feet, heading out of the library, and Slid down to the main level before looking around and realizing Ras wasn't there. She Slid again, emerging outside of his rooms. She didn't feel it was appropriate for her to suddenly appear inside of them and wasn't even sure if she would be able to. He'd already proven he had a way of keeping her from Sliding; it wouldn't be surprising if he had a way of keeping her from Sliding into his rooms too.

She knocked and stepped back, waiting. It didn't take long for the door to open, and he stood on the other side, studying her. He seemed to glow as he often did, using his connection to the flames. Lucy had often wondered what purpose there was in glowing like that. Did it somehow allow him a greater control over his powers? Carth did something similar oftentimes, and yet, Lucy didn't know what purpose she had, either.

"You've returned."

"You knew I was gone?"

"Carthenne suggested you might be looking for information."

"I need to reach her. Do you have any way of getting in touch with her?"

Ras frowned, then waved for Lucy to enter. She did so

carefully. The C'than stronghold was mostly empty. There were other C'than who would occasionally come and go, and in the time she'd been here, she hadn't seen too many different people.

"What did you uncover?"

"An experiment."

She took a moment to tell Ras about her experience, sharing everything she had observed. The longer she talked, the more the frown upon his face deepened. When she was done, he took a deep breath, sighing heavily.

"Are you certain of this?"

"When I reach into his mind, I can detect quite a bit. The more I find, the more certain I am of what's there. He was experimented upon, though I don't think it was the Architect. I'm not sure if it was Olandar Fahr or someone else, but whatever is taking place is tied to what we encountered before."

And if she was right, they needed to be equipped for what Olandar Fahr was planning. They needed to know more about these augmentations, so that they could be prepared for Ai'thol who had augmentations they had never encountered. He was up to something more than what they'd seen. While others were looking for the Elder Stones and the way they were planning on using them, she had to do this.

"I can get word to Carthenne, but it might take some time," Ras said.

"Would you come with me?"

He studied her, glowing more brightly for a moment. It was fleeting, barely more than that moment, and yet when it was done, he shook his head.

"I'm not certain it's wise for me to get involved."

"Why not?"

"Anything I might do puts the C'than in danger."

"Doing nothing puts the C'than in danger."

"I suspect it does not. The C'than would suffer far more if I were lost."

From anybody else, it would seem like a strange sort of boasting, but if Ras were lost, it truly would be devastating to the C'than. They needed him, as he was one of the few people who had much influence among the group.

"Is there anyone you think could come with me?"

"You know many people of power, Lucy Elvraeth."

"Everybody else is occupied."

"Everyone?"

She studied him for a moment. She had thought about bringing one of the women she'd been training, but she wasn't sure how they would react. They weren't fully equipped for what was to happen, and none of them had much experience with using their abilities yet.

"They're not ready."

"What do you think it will take for them to become ready?"

Lucy shook her head. "I don't know. I've been trying to get them prepared for what they might need to face, and yet…"

Ras smiled at her. "And yet you fear they will not be."

"Yes."

She didn't really want them to have to be ready for anything in particular. Facing the Ai'thol was something she had wanted to protect them from, and the only way she knew to do it was to keep them from actions that might bring them into greater conflict. None of them were ready for the kind of battles they might be required to fight.

Many of them remained traumatized by what they'd experienced, the attack and torment still so fresh in their minds. It was fresh in Lucy's mind as well, knowing the horrors of what they had gone through.

"What are you doing to prepare them?"

"I'm doing everything I can, but…" Lucy squeezed her eyes shut.

Was she doing everything she could? She'd been trying, but the more she worked with the women, the more she wondered whether she was doing enough. It was more than just training them to know how to use their abilities; it was preparing them for the possibility they might need to fight.

But then, *she* wasn't a fighter, so she found it difficult to demonstrate what they might need in order to successfully resist.

"I can tell you aren't sure whether you're doing everything you can."

"I don't know if I am," she admitted.

"You wish you could do more."

Lucy nodded slowly. "I would love it if I could prepare them for what they might face in the world, but I can't, can I?"

Ras stared at her, smiling. "Do you think the people of Elaeavn once felt that same way?"

"Why are you asking that?"

"Because the power of Elaeavn has been confined to the city for a long time."

"My whole life."

"And one must wonder why."

"I don't know. When I was a caretaker, I looked through some of the ancient records, but I wasn't able to find anything to explain why my people isolated themselves."

It might be only about the sacred crystals, but maybe there was more to it than that. Why isolate themselves when they had so much power?

But then, there was suspicion of power. And with that suspicion, there were some who probably worried the people of Elaeavn would want to rule. The more she knew about people who'd left Elaeavn, the exiles who'd been forced to find a way to survive, the more she wondered whether or not that had been right.

"When we look at people of power over the years, one thing has been true. Some chase power because they want to use it to rule. Olandar Fahr is one such man. The longer we've studied him, the clearer it has been that he seeks power in order to subjugate, and yet, not entirely. We've seen no evidence of him attempting to destroy, only to claim power, nothing more."

"He destroyed in Nyaesh."

"He did, but he did so because they were attacked."

"Are you trying to defend him?"

"Not defend, Lucy Elvraeth, but understand. I find it most beneficial to understand someone in order to know what they might do." He smiled at her. "Knowing what motivates someone is empowering. In the case of Olandar Fahr, I have not been able to fully determine what it is that motivates him. Is it only power? From what we've seen, we certainly could make that claim, and yet I am uncertain. It's possible there is another reason he has been searching for the Elder Stones, one we have yet to uncover."

Lucy thought about the people they'd been dealing with, the nature of the power they'd been facing, and she couldn't help but wonder if perhaps that was what it was tied to.

"And if he's facing another power?"

"That would be reason for him to pursue his own power. If he sees an opponent, he would be searching for an upper hand, a way to ensure success."

"Success in what?"

"In achieving his goal. Whatever that might be. I can't say with any certainty what he might be chasing, but I can say that from what I've seen from Olandar Fahr, there is more to what he's doing than we know."

Lucy watched Ras for a moment. There was always something about him that seemed knowing, and yet there were things he kept to himself, as if he didn't want to share specific information, worried it might reveal some aspect of a greater plan. Ras spoke of Olandar Fahr in a way that described a man plotting and planning, and yet Ras was much the same way. He was a schemer, much as Carth was.

Lucy was not, but then again, that was precisely why Ras was working with her. He wanted her to use her abilities in the way that was most beneficial for her.

He'd already told her she wasn't going to need to play Tsatsun in order to be successful. That wasn't her strength, and Lucy wasn't even able to deny that.

Scheming and attacking and understanding various plans weren't her strongest talents. Not like Carth—or even Daniel.

What Ras wanted from her was to come up with what method was going to be successful for Lucy.

It might be the connections she made.

She'd been helpless once. She had no intention of being helpless again, and having been through that, having known how she'd been used and having been able to look inside, to Read herself, she had come to understand she had managed to protect herself far more than she had known.

What she needed was to empower the others she now worked with.

Maybe it wasn't so much in finding their abilities and trying to help them reach for their power, but more about guiding them through what they had experienced. They all had a shared experience, and that was one thing she thought she could do. She could work with them, help them overcome that, and she could bind them together.

"It all has to do with the Architect," Lucy said. "If we can find the Architect, I think we might find the answers we need."

"And as I've told you, Lucy Elvraeth, you might be the key. I know you don't want to think back upon the time you spent with him, and yet I fear you might need to in order to succeed."

"What about these others?"

"These others must be dealt with, and now that you have a sense of their minds, you can reach them."

"Not all of them."

"Was there one who defied you?"

"His mind was closed to me. I tried, but the more I focused on him, the harder it was to get anything out of him."

"That's interesting. From what I've been able to determine, your ability to Read is unmatched."

"I can't Read you."

"Why do you think that is?"

"I don't know."

He settled his hands on his lap, watching her, everything about him seeming to glow brightly for a moment before fading. "See what answers you can uncover. I will send word to Carthenne, and if she can reach us, we will let her know she is needed."

Lucy nodded. There was nothing else she could do. At this point, they did need Carth, but they also needed to continue to work.

There was no point in returning to that town, not on her own, not without the support she would need in order to survive. She had no idea what it was going to take, only that the people there were powerful enough to pose a danger to her. She had risked herself enough there alone.

Perhaps Carth would return, or perhaps not. Either way, she could still find the man whose mind she had attached to, whether he was there or he had gone somewhere else.

But locating the Architect would be even more valuable. From him, they could reach Olandar Fahr. And that seemed to her to be the most important thing.

18

DANIEL

DANIEL EMERGED FROM HIS SLIDE. THEY WERE FAR ENOUGH from Elaeavn now that his heavy wool cloak along with his long jacket and pants felt too hot for the weather. Humid air seemed to swallow him almost as soon as they emerged from the Slide. He wiped his arm across his forehead, looking around.

It was jungle, but the dense sort of jungle he was uncertain he could Slide through safely. He had reached the edge of it, taking Slide after Slide, traveling so he could get them as far as possible, but now he would be limited in how far he could travel. Without any way of seeing where they were going, they would have to go by foot.

Rayen seemed less troubled by the humidity. She looked around, shadows swirling, and he thought he understood why she wasn't struggling. The shadows must be cooling her in some way.

"I think you're cheating," he said.

"Am I?"

"I can tell what you're doing with the shadows."

"If you can tell what I'm doing, then you should be able to replicate it."

Daniel had tried reaching for the shadows before, and each time, he failed. It was one thing to see them and almost be able to feel them, but it was quite another to use them the way Rayen and Carth did. As far as he knew, they were the only ones with that ability.

"I think you just want to show me I have no ability with them."

"It's not that you don't have any ability, it's just that you refuse to use it."

"What about you? Now that you held one of the crystals—"

"I've already told you that nothing has changed."

Daniel smiled. She might claim nothing had changed, but when he looked at her, he could see it in her eyes. It was almost a glow, a tinge of green that hadn't been there before, as if the Great Watcher *had* gifted her. Knowing Rayen as he did, she would likely not even notice.

"Tell me again how Carth expects to communicate with us if she finds something useful."

Rayen shook her head. "I must admit I don't really know. We have these tokens," she said, pulling a coin from her pocket. It was made of lorcith, supposedly a diminished quantity that would be concealed from most who had the ability to detect the metal, but the simple fact that they were carrying it with them would likely raise suspicion.

"That only works if Haern or someone like him comes looking for us. What if it's Lucy?" She might have many different abilities now that she had been augmented, but as far as he knew, detecting lorcith wasn't one of them. "What if it's one of your Binders?"

"Then I don't know," she said.

Daniel looked through the dense jungle. Carth believed there was a city somewhere in the middle of it, hidden from the rest of the world. It was a place Carth had never visited. She hoped that Daniel might See something she had missed about reaching the city. He found that difficult to believe, knowing Carth missed very little.

"What's the strategy here?"

"Other than simply heading in?" Rayen asked.

"Seeing as how I don't know how to Slide through here, we're going to be forced to go by ground."

"Can you see through the darkness?"

"I can."

"And from what you've said, you need to be able to see where you're going or have been there before in order to safely Slide someone."

"Your point is?"

"Only that you would Slide us through the forest from place to place. If you see an opening, bring us there. If you can continue navigating by the shadows, you might find you can do so even more easily."

Since leaving the palace, Daniel had not tried to Slide using the shadows again. He was nervous to attempt it, unsure whether it would work. What if he needed heartstone in order to navigate?

Instead, he'd tried paying attention to the shadows when he was Sliding, but there wasn't anything within the shadows that revealed secrets to him. If Rayen was right about what he did with the shadows, it was possible he could use that.

If it worked, they might not need to emerge nearly as often. He could imagine snaking around the trees, using his connection to the shadows to slither forward, truly Sliding, searching for an opening where they could appear.

What was the worst that could happen?

Death. Horrible, painful death.

Yet if he didn't try, he'd never know if it was possible.

Taking Rayen's hand, he flashed a smile at her. "I'm going to blame you if we die."

"I don't think that's how it works."

He shrugged. "It doesn't change that I'm going to blame you."

Rayen laughed.

With that, he stepped forward in a Slide. As he did, he focused on what he had done while in the palace, thinking of the shadows. There was a sense of movement, a shifting of darkness, and he latched on to that. He followed the sense, using it in a different way than he had Slid before.

There came the sense of movement that often accompanied the Slide, though it wasn't as rapid as he was accustomed to. Mixed within it was something else—an impression of the trees rising up all around them. He was never aware of trees when Sliding. This time, he could track them, slipping from tree to tree, weaving around them as he went. They were translucent, barely more than wisps of darkness, and when he detected an opening, he emerged.

It wasn't much of an opening. A small clearing spread around them, with the rest of the jungle continuing in all directions.

"Were you aware of it that time?" Rayen asked.

"I felt as if I were following the shadows."

"I saw it. It's similar to when I travel on the shadows, though you were moving far faster than I can."

"You can travel on the shadows?"

"Somewhat. It is a difficult technique, and it requires considerable strength and concentration, but I can use them to conceal myself and travel. I haven't had much success carrying someone else with me, though."

"I don't know if I could have done that for much longer. I felt as if we were in the middle of the Slide for ages."

It was certainly far longer than most Slides. Usually, he stepped in and out of the Slide quickly. These days, Sliding was even more rapid than it had been before, as his strength increased and his capacity to Slide improved.

Having seen Lucy—and having Slid with Lucy—he knew that with strength came even more speed. It wasn't so much a matter of being able to carry more people with him as it was of moving more rapidly. Short distances were easier for him to Slide quickly.

"How far do you think we went?"

Daniel shook his head. "I don't have any idea."

"The jungle is quite vast. When we have sailed past it, it goes on for leagues."

"You can access the jungle by water?"

"The edge of the jungle, but the city Carth believes is here is deep in the heart of the trees."

"And she thinks they have an Elder Stone," he said.

"This place would be as good as any to keep one concealed from Olandar Fahr."

"If Carth is aware of this place, it's likely he is too. What if we don't find anything here?"

"Others are searching other locations," Rayen said.

That didn't reassure him. They didn't really understand everything taking place when it came to Olandar Fahr's plan. It all came back to this Council of Elders, but how did that involve the Elder Stones?

What they needed to do was find Olandar Fahr and stop him.

From the sound of it, Carth had been working on that for the better part of the last twenty years, possibly longer, and hadn't been able to do so.

"Are you ready?"

Rayen nodded and Daniel took her hand, focusing on the shadows. He Slid forward the same way he had the last time. It was slow, but because of that slowness, he was able to weave around to the trees, twisting and turning, winding through the jungle. He continued like that for a while and then found another clearing, stepping out of the Slide. When he did, the trees towered higher overhead than they had been before. No sunlight poked through, casting everything in darkness. The air had a stillness about it, thick and sticky, and the chirping of hundreds of insects kept them company.

"I don't even know if I'm going in the right direction," he said.

"The trees are taller."

"They are, and I'm heading basically south, but I don't know if that's going to help us at all."

"It will have to."

Daniel wasn't so sure about that, but he wasn't going to argue with Rayen.

Holding tightly to her hand, he pulled himself forward in a Slide, following the shadows as he had the last time. Each time he did it, it became easier. He could twist between the trunks of the trees, follow the contour of the forest, all while remaining within the Slide.

There was something else he noticed, something he hadn't paid much attention to at first, but it was almost more significant than anything else. Traveling like this took less energy than he was accustomed to.

Normally when he Slid, there was a sense of fatigue that came with it. The longer he worked at Sliding, the less he noticed that symptom, but it was still there. Now, traveling with the shadows, he had been able to maintain his Slide far longer than he would have otherwise.

Another opening in the forest beckoned him, and he stepped out of the Slide. He immediately noticed that the trees were shorter. Even the air was less humid. More space existed between the trees, as if they were opening up all around them.

"I think we might have overdone it," Daniel said.

"This is different," she said.

"We might be on the far side of the forest now."

"I don't think so," Rayen said. "The far side of the forest is far more arid. This is still hot, but the far side doesn't have the same humidity."

If they hadn't overshot it, that meant that they were

close, but he had a hard time believing they were. "Can you use your connection to the shadows to see if there's anything out here?"

She sent streamers of shadows stretching away from her. They wound in all directions. He thought about suggesting she not expend so much energy but realized he didn't even know if they had been traveling in the right direction. Maybe it was better that she used the shadows like this to determine if they were heading where they were supposed to. At least, having been there once before, he thought he could do so more easily the next time.

Rayen stretched with the shadows. Gradually, the shadows disappeared, the tendrils that had been sneaking away from her fading.

Rayen looked over to him, shaking her head. "I don't detect anything."

"What does that mean?"

"It means I don't detect anything. We could be close, but they might have some way of preventing me from reaching them."

The farther they went into the jungle, the more Daniel began to feel that something was changing. How much further could they go before they uncovered the key to this place? Rayen might not be able to detect the city, but could he?

It was something other than just the shadows.

Daniel searched for where he would target next. He found another opening ahead of him, and he Slid toward it. He held on to Rayen as he did, using the connection to the shadows, winding through the jungle as he went. It was a strange sensation. He could tell that the trees were spaced farther apart, allowing him to travel much more quickly. The shadows guided him, and he pushed outward along them, Sliding on the shadows themselves, and when he finally found another opening, he hesitated a moment before stepping out of the Slide. This time, he focused on how large the clearing happened to be. It seemed considerably bigger than the others. Large enough for a city, perhaps.

Retreating back to the trees, tracing the shadows toward the trunks, he found them and then stepped out of the Slide. He looked toward the clearing, aware of it because of his connection to the shadows.

As he'd suspected, they'd reached the city.

"You found it," Rayen said.

"You didn't think I would?"

"I have to admit, I'm a little surprised."

"It's good I can continue to surprise you."

"It is uncommon."

Daniel smiled. "Not as uncommon these days as it had been."

The city was unlike any other he'd seen. There were no stone buildings, nothing made of wood. Everything seemed to be a part of the jungle, to the point that even the roofs appeared to be made out of branches of the trees. Some of the cottages had thatched roofs. As he stared across the city, he tried to gauge its size but couldn't. It seemed as if the city stretched impossibly far. He marveled at the sheer scope of the place.

"It's enormous," he whispered, keeping his eyes on the city. There were people within it, most of them dressed for the heat, sashes of fabric wrapped around them to conceal their bodies, and many of the men roaming shirtless.

"Carth thought it would be. In all the years she searched, she was never able to uncover the city. She found evidence for it and suspected she'd find something within the jungle, but she wasn't able to discover it herself."

"Now we need to find whether Olandar Fahr hid here. But why would they hide him?"

"Why would anyone follow him to begin with? He represents power."

"These people don't want power," Daniel said, staring into the depths of the city. The city reminded him of Elaeavn. That told him what these people wanted.

"All people want power," Rayen said.

"Look at them. It seems they're more interested in remaining isolated, not the type of power Olandar Fahr chases."

Every so often, he saw some moving off into the trees. Were they hunters? What kind of things would they be after? They'd traveled so quickly through the forest, he really hadn't taken an opportunity to get a sense for what was there.

A part of him wondered whether coming here was the right thing to do. If these people wanted to be separate from the world, why should he be the reason they were forced into it? He didn't want to drag them into the battle that had started with the Ai'thol. They didn't need to have any part in it.

Turning to Rayen, he said, "This is a mistake. They

don't deserve anything we're a part of. We should find Carth and let her know we couldn't find anything."

"I'm not sure we have much of a choice," Rayen said softly.

He frowned and noticed she was flicking her gaze toward the trees.

Turning slowly, he saw they were no longer standing alone. A pair of men pointing long spears at them hid within the trees, standing just off to the side so that he wouldn't notice them quite so easily. They jabbed the spears toward them. With each thrust, Daniel realized that they weren't going to escape—not easily, and not if they wanted information.

"What do you suggest we do?" Rayen asked.

"We can either Slide away, or we can find out what they intend to do with us."

"Well," Rayen said, raising her hand above her head. Shadows swirled around her, though they were tight, confined to her body, as if she placed them there so as to create a barrier around herself. "This should be fun."

19

DANIEL

THE MEN HOLDING THE SPEARS FORCED DANIEL AND RAYEN ahead of them. He kept his hands up, mimicking Rayen, trying to look as nonthreatening as possible. The men made no attempt to remove his sword, and they'd said nothing to him or Rayen since appearing.

Every so often, they would jab their spears toward them. Even then, they didn't say anything, merely forcing them forward. They took a wide-open pathway between many of the cottages, a road that wound through the homes here, and all the people he had observed out on the street retreated at their coming. It was almost as if they realized they were there and made a point of retreating, escaping the newcomers.

The only ones who followed were the children, and they did so at a distance, their voices barely carrying. He could hear their excited chatter and wondered what sort of things they were talking about. He didn't recognize their language.

"Do you recognize it?" he whispered to Rayen.

One of the men jabbed his spear toward Daniel.

He brought his arms up, blocking it from striking him in the groin. The sharp crack slammed into his wrists painfully.

If he were injured, escape would be far more difficult.

When he straightened, the two men pushed them forward along the street.

The cottages started to thin out, and the design began to change. On the edge of the city, the homes were small, compact, but as they continued through the city, they were larger. Many of them seemed to be comprised of multiple cottages built together, a cluster forming a larger home. All of them had the same style of thatched roof, and many had windows cut into the sides, left open. With the heat and humidity of this place, Daniel couldn't help but wonder how anyone managed to sleep.

Rayen whispered to him. "I don't recognize the language," she said.

Her voice carried on a shadow, barely loud enough for him to make out. She seemed to use the shadows to pitch her words so only he would be able to hear them. He wouldn't be able to do the same thing unless he could somehow master a connection to shadows.

Many of the larger clusters of homes had more activity, though that activity began to ease as they neared. Larger structures rose up within the city, and he wondered why he hadn't seen them before. From the edge of the city, he should have been able to make out some of these larger buildings, yet they had been obscured from him. Perhaps it was the thatched roofs, the way they all looked the same, blending together so it looked like an entire field of grass, or perhaps it was some similar mirage to the way the floating palace appeared within Elaeavn, designed so that it would blend into the rock, disappearing to hide the occupants.

"Do you still think we can Slide from here if we need to?" Rayen asked.

"I think so," he whispered.

It wasn't quiet enough, and one of the men swung his spear toward Daniel, catching him on the shin.

He swore under his breath. He needed to be careful that he didn't end up getting hurt before they reached wherever they were taking them. At this point, Daniel was curious as much as anything.

The larger homes began to thin. A tree grew above much of the city from somewhere in the distance. It was this tree the men were guiding them toward. The tree was situated in the middle of the city—at least partly in the middle. More buildings spread out around it, stretching off in all directions. Once again, he marveled at the scale of the place.

The Elder Trees within Elaeavn and the Aisl were impressive, towering high into the air, massive even compared to the surrounding trees. This one seemed to dwarf them. Strangely, he hadn't been aware of it until they had entered the city and were heading toward it. It was as if the city shielded this tree.

As they neared, he saw the base of the tree was as large as several of the larger homes within the city. Gnarled roots twisted, curving out of the ground before diving deep beneath the earth. More people were congregated near the tree than in other places in the city.

What would they find when they got here?

The spear men stopped them near the base of the tree. They tapped on the ground with their spears. Daniel took that as a signal to wait.

He glanced over at Rayen, gauging the distance between them. If it came down to it, he would need to reach and grab for her hand to Slide her away.

Perhaps it would have been better had Carth been the one to come here. This was the kind of thing she would be good at: coordinate a meeting like this, working with strange peoples and attempting to understand them, find a common sort of ground. All fit with his experience with Carth.

Somehow, he and Rayen would have to make it work.

The two men holding the spears backed away, giving him and Rayen a bit of space. He shuffled toward her, moving slowly and still keeping an eye straight ahead of him. "I wish I were a stronger Reader."

"Can you pick up anything?"

"Nothing."

"In my experience, that's strange."

"There are plenty of people who have the ability to block out Readers."

"That's true, but most of them have experience with people who can Read, don't they?"

Were the situation different, he might have made a joke with her, but at this point, he didn't feel as if there were any jokes that could be made. He was scared, if he was honest with himself. Seeing as how he didn't speak the language, he wasn't able to communicate with these people.

A small figure appeared in between two of the gnarled roots, slipping out of them almost as if coming from a doorway. The person approaching had wavy brown hair, deeply tanned skin, and a sash of cloth over her chest and groin dyed a deep green, though there were other colors mixed within, dots of red and orange and yellow, almost making it seem as if it shimmered as she walked. She was short—much shorter than the guards guiding them through the city—and she came unarmed.

She stopped first in front of Rayen, staring at her for a long moment, her lips pressed together in a frown. When she was done, she turned her attention to Daniel, focusing on him.

"Elaeavn."

Daniel blinked. The woman's voice was sharp, lilting, but she had spoken the name of his homeland.

"Child of Ih."

Rayen nodded.

"Why are you here?"

"We're searching for help," Daniel said.

"You will find no help in Ceyaniah."

At least he had a name for where they were, though from the sound of it, it didn't matter. If they weren't willing to help, there might not be anything he'd be able to do.

"You don't even know why we need help," he said.

"I can imagine. You come here together, rather than separately, and there can be only one reason for that."

Rayen studied the woman for a moment. "What reason would that be?"

"You seek the Council."

With that, the woman turned and headed away, leaving Daniel and Rayen staring after her.

They shared a glance. She could mean only one thing by that. And if the woman knew something about the Council of Elders, then they had to find out what it was, in order to understand how the Ai'thol intended to reconstitute the Council of Elders.

That might not be why Carth had sent them here, but it would be equally valuable.

They started forward, but the two men with spears reached them, slamming their spears in front of them, blocking their way. Daniel had half a mind to Slide past them, but he suspected if he did, they would lose the opportunity to ask the questions he wanted to ask, and then they would miss out on gaining insight into this land.

He couldn't shake the sense that Carth was fully aware of what they might find here. It was just the kind of thing she would do.

"We would like to visit with her," Daniel said.

Neither man spoke.

Daniel glanced at Rayen.

"We could Slide," she whispered. Once again, her words were carried on a flutter of wind that was meant only for Daniel's ears.

Perhaps they could Slide past these men. If he did, what might they come upon?

He motioned briefly with his hand, deciding they'd wait. At this point, they could always Slide, but they could just as easily ruin that opportunity if they attempted to run—or break free.

He had to wonder how long they'd be forced to stand there. Neither man spoke, and neither even bothered to look much in his direction, almost as if intentionally avoiding him. It was possible that they were.

The moments passed, stretching longer and longer, and when the woman finally returned, there were several others with her. Each was dressed in the same sash wrapped around their chest and then midsection. Several of them had short, wavy hair, while one had close-cropped hair, shorn nearly bald.

Daniel was surprised to note that it was a woman. She had tattoos along one arm, the markings done with exquisite skill, a series of what appeared to be letters or symbols, something that likely had some meaning for these people. Her other arm had tattoos of animals. He stared at those for a moment, to try to get a sense for what sort of creatures they were. One looked something like a horse, though with a larger head. Another seemed a massive wolf with flames surrounding it. Still another was a serpent with legs.

"Why have you come?" the tattooed woman asked.

Here Daniel had thought the woman who had first come out to greet them was the one in charge, but that didn't seem to be the case.

"We need help. Information."

"And you think that you can find it in Ceyaniah?"

"We didn't know."

"How is it that you came to find us?" This came from the woman near the back. She had deeply tanned skin like all of them and appeared to be a little older. Her dark, wavy hair had streaks of gray running through it, and the lines around the corners of her eyes were deeper, carrying with them the sense of age and wisdom.

"Luck," Daniel said.

"One does not find Ceyaniah by luck," the tattooed woman said.

"Why not?"

"We don't want it to be so simple to find Ceyaniah."

"It wasn't necessarily simple," he admitted. Without the connection between the shadows and Sliding, he doubted he would have found it.

"They seek the Council," the first woman said.

"No one seeks the Council."

"Look at them."

Daniel shared a glance with Rayen before looking at the woman with the tattoos, meeting her intense gaze. She had deep brown eyes, so deep that they were almost black. The way she looked at him carried with it a question—and almost an accusation.

"Is that what you seek?"

"We come for information. There's a dangerous man chasing power, and we want to prevent him from reaching it."

He wasn't sure if that was the right way to describe Olandar Fahr, but it was fitting. He was a dangerous man

—and he was chasing power. Whether or not these people would understand was a different matter.

"You know nothing about the nature of what you seek."

"Help us understand."

"There is no point. As you don't understand, there is nothing to be lost in your ignorance. There is much that could be lost if you begin to learn."

"We want to stop him for good."

"By chasing the Council," the tattooed woman said.

"That wasn't what we were intending."

"The Council of Elders has not met in centuries," the tattooed woman said. "There would be no reason for it to be convened once again."

"None? What if they began to gain the power of the Elder Stones?"

"The Elder Stones were left for the people. The elders recognize the need. If they have acquired those abilities, then all is as it should be."

He couldn't help but feel as if that wasn't quite right. All *wasn't* as it should be, and if the power of the Elder Stones was drawn out by someone with the wrong kind of power, then there was no telling what would take place.

Then again, it was possible that these women knew.

"Help me understand," he said.

"So that you can use it?"

"I have no interest in using that power."

The tattooed woman watched him for a long moment. There was something unsettling about her gaze, and he wanted to turn away but feared that if he did, he'd show weakness. Everything within him told him he couldn't afford to show weakness to these women.

The tattooed woman motioned to someone off to the side, and others carrying spears marched forward. There had to be a dozen, but Daniel didn't dare take his eyes off the women in front of him. The others might have the weapons, but they didn't have the real power here.

She turned away, motioning to the others. "Bring them inside."

20

DANIEL

As he followed the men with spears, Daniel stayed close to Rayen. Every so often, their hands touched, a reminder for both of them that they could Slide from here if it were necessary. Rayen probably wasn't as worried as he was. She had a confidence about her at all times, and he wouldn't be at all surprised to learn that even in a situation like this, she was completely at ease.

The men guided them between the tall roots of the enormous tree before reaching the giant trunk. A doorway that seemed little more than folds of wood blended into the tree itself. The air changed, dropping in temperature and taking on the thick scent of earth and decay. He glanced to Rayen again, but she kept her gaze fixed straight in front of her. The shadows remained tightly wrapped around her.

They stepped inside a massive chamber within the tree with light coming from everywhere. In the middle of the space, an enormous table grew up from the ground. Small stools surrounded it, rising from the ground in the same way as the table.

"What is this?" he asked.

The women shared a glance before turning their attention back to him. "You wanted to see the Council."

Daniel stared. "This is the Council?"

"Not any longer, but this was where the Council once convened."

"You hold it here?"

"We are its protectors. We have long provided oversight to the Council."

Daniel neared the table. A sense of energy surrounded it and pushed against him, as if trying to keep him at a distance. "Why is it here?"

"As we said," the woman with the tattoos said, "there are places like this throughout the world."

"I haven't seen any other places like this," Rayen said. She kept her gaze locked on the table, and it seemed as if she were in awe of it.

"Have you traveled to all places?"

"Not all, but enough I would have known if there were others like it."

The woman smiled at Rayen. "Perhaps they have concealed it from you."

"Or perhaps there are no more," she said.

There certainly couldn't be any place else quite like this room—or this table. How could there be without drawing attention to it? In this place, hidden as it was within the city of Ceyaniah, the tree itself was isolated from the rest of the world.

As Daniel made his way around the table, he was

tempted to have a seat, to see what it might feel like if he was part of the Council of Elders, but the energy pushing against him resisted his efforts.

"There are other places like this, but this one remains pure."

Daniel looked over from the table. "Why are you showing this to us?"

The woman frowned. "Not many have come looking for the Council of Elders over the years."

Not many didn't mean *none*. Could Olandar Fahr have already gotten here?

"What can you tell us about it?"

The woman shared a look with the other, the first dark-haired woman, and motioned for them to follow.

They did, and surprisingly, they departed the massive tree from another angle, heading back out into the clearing. They walked them across the clearing until they reached a building nearby. This one was large, one of the largest he'd seen in the city, and had a steep thatched roof stretching high overhead. The women made their way inside, and Daniel hesitated on the other side of the door, looking around.

After having seen the table for the Council of Elders, he hadn't been sure what to expect. He wasn't sure if this was going to be something similar, but instead he found himself inside a home. Furniture was made of woven branches, covered with furs of some unknown animal, and brightly colored feathers adding to the decoration. The furniture was all flowing lines rather than sharp angles. An enormous animal skin covered the floor, the fur soft and supple beneath his feet. He couldn't imagine what sort of creature it came from.

The woman motioned for him to sit in one of the woven chairs, and Daniel hesitated a moment before doing so. Rayen was slower than he was, more cautious, and shadows swirled around her, probing various aspects of the room before retreating. Finally, Rayen took a seat.

"Are you satisfied?" the woman asked.

"With what?" Rayen asked.

"With your questing."

Rayen tipped her head in a slight nod. Daniel smiled to himself. They had known what she was doing.

Could that be why she hadn't been able to detect anything with the shadows before? Could they have been aware of what she was attempting and have some way of rebuffing it? If so, that suggested even more control and power than he had suspected. Nothing about the city spoke of power. It seemed as if these were simple people, isolated by their location within the forest, but they did appear to have a knowledge of things he and Rayen did not.

The woman pulled a chair up, sitting across from them. The other dark-haired woman stayed near the doorway.

"I am Charlanna, the elder of Ceyaniah. We are not accustomed to having visitors here."

"Obviously," Rayen said.

"Ceyaniah is a difficult place to reach, but then, the elder who founded it wanted it such."

Daniel looked around the room. The other woman was watching, but she had been silent. She kept her gaze fixed on him and Rayen, and there was something about the way she watched that left him wondering if she had some ability of her own.

"You obviously know quite a bit about the Council of Elders," Daniel said, tearing his gaze away from the woman by the door. "We think that someone with knowledge of the Council is intending to convene it in order to gain power."

Charlanna leaned toward him. As she did, he had a distinct sense of power about her, different from the power he detected from others. It seemed to crackle, sizzling against his skin. It was a steady sense that left him with little doubt she was gifted in some way, though he had yet to see anything that would explain how.

"There have been others over the years who have wanted to convene the Council, but they have not remembered the old ways."

Daniel shared a glance with Rayen. "And you do?"

"We don't practice the old ways, but we remember. That was our task."

"Why?"

"Would you ask your Great Watcher why you have the ability to travel as you do?" She glanced to Rayen. "And you, would you ask Ihnish why you were gifted with shadows?" She smiled tightly, shaking her head. "You would not. You recognize you have been handed a gift, and you must utilize that gift in the ways asked of you."

Daniel had suspected she knew more about them than he knew about her, and that answered it. Not only did she seem aware of his abilities, but she knew about Rayen, where she came from, and the nature of her people. Even if they were isolated here in Ceyaniah, that didn't mean they were ignorant of the outside world. He found that intriguing. They were connected to the rest of the world in a way the rest of the world was not connected to them.

"We need to understand what they are after," Daniel said.

"Once you understand, what will you do with that knowledge? How do you think that will help you?"

"We need to stop them." He glanced from Charlanna to the other woman. "There are people suffering because of this."

"There are always people who suffer. That is unfortunately the nature of the world. Those with power use it to maintain their grip, while those without find themselves crushed by the others."

"It doesn't have to be that way," Daniel said.

"Perhaps not, but that is the way of the world."

"Is that why you keep yourself here?"

"We are here because we are people of Ceyaniah."

"What does it mean to be a person of Ceyaniah?"

"You are a descendant of the Great Watcher, and yet you have failed to see?"

Daniel frowned. "What does that mean?"

"It means that you should be quite aware of what it signifies. The children of the Great Watcher have long observed."

"You really don't know anything about the world?" Rayen said, glancing toward Daniel. "The children of the Great Watcher have isolated themselves, keeping themselves apart from the rest of the world."

Charlanna frowned. "Why?"

"I suppose my people have felt it was dangerous to be too deeply involved with the rest of the world." He didn't know the history of Elaeavn as well as some, but it was the answer that made the most sense. For as long as he could remember, they had been isolated. Elaeavn had been not quite as difficult to reach as Ceyaniah, but it had been closed to visitors, allowing only those from within Elaeavn to spend any time there.

He'd never really considered why. When he was growing up, he'd believed it was on behalf of the safety of their people, done so that those without abilities didn't find themselves surrounded by people who had them. Considering everyone—or nearly everyone—within Elaeavn had some ability, it would be a reasonable thing to want to protect others from.

"You should not have been isolated. The people of the Great Watcher have been meant to observe and report, to ensure that if the Council was needed, they would be there to call it."

"What is the Council?"

Charlanna looked at them, frowning deeply. "You really don't know?"

"We really don't," Rayen said.

"And yet you came here seeking answers about the Council."

After watching him for a moment, Charlanna got to her feet. She disappeared, and Daniel glanced to Rayen. "I'm not sure what we hope to find here," he whispered.

"I'm not either. I think Carth wanted us to find information about the missing stone, but I have a sense that either they don't know anything about the stone or, if they do, they won't share it with us."

Daniel had that sense, too.

"Are you still prepared for the possibility we'll need to travel from here?"

He nodded. "I don't think there is anything restricting me from Sliding."

He glanced back at the woman standing at the door. She had been silent ever since their arrival here, and he couldn't tell what she did, or what powers she might have. The fact that she alone stood guard over them suggested she had some sort of power. The people of this place obviously knew about the nature of their abilities, which meant they wouldn't be surprised by what he and Rayen could do.

After a few moments, Charlanna returned, carrying a slender wooden box.

She rested her hands on top of it and looked up, holding his gaze. "You know nothing about the Council, but do you know anything about the stones?"

Daniel stared at the box. Could she have all of the stones?

"We know about the stones," he said.

"As you should." Charlanna pressed on the top of the box, and somewhere within it, a lock clicked. She flipped the lid open. The inside was lined with a red velvety fabric. A ring of five smooth-looking rocks rested inside the box, another one in the middle of them.

"This represents the stones," she said, tapping on each of them. "And this represents the Watcher. An oversight above the stones. Separate."

"Which stones do they represent?" Rayen asked.

"Which stones do you think they represent?"

Rayen said nothing, and Daniel understood what she'd been trying to do. She was testing Charlanna, trying to understand just how much she knew. It was possible Charlanna didn't have the same knowledge of the stones that they did.

Charlanna smiled at her. "This box represents the stones present in this world, the ones I suspect you know about. Unfortunately, the knowledge of stones has been lost to Ceyaniah over time. We know only that there are five. As I said, sitting above the stones is the Watcher."

There was something about what she said that troubled him. "You said the stones in this world."

Charlanna nodded. "That is true. There are five stones in this world, five that comprise the Council."

"Are there other stones?" More than that, was there another world?

Charlanna studied Daniel for a long moment. "As a child of the Watcher, you can travel, and yet you wonder if there are other worlds?"

"What other worlds?"

"There are some that are difficult to reach, and some that are easier." She nodded to Rayen. "She has traveled. She has the look of knowledge to her."

Rayen met Charlanna's eyes for a moment. "I don't deny that I have traveled."

"And in your travels, what have you seen?"

"I've seen lands influenced by these stones."

"Of course you have. Your own is included, is it not?"

Rayen frowned and then slowly nodded.

"Are there limits to where you can travel?"

Rayen shrugged. "There were limits to how far we were willing to go. The sea is vast and endless."

Charlanna shook her head. "Not endless. Vast, true, but not endless, not at all. And if you were to push far enough, travel beyond, you would find that there is more."

Charlanna reached beneath her and pulled out another box, similar to the last. She pressed on it, triggering a lock somewhere within it, and pulled open the lid. Like the other one, it held a ring of stones with another in the middle.

"This represents the Council in another land."

"And the center stone?" Daniel asked.

"That is the Watcher."

"Why does the Watcher oversee both councils?"

"The Watcher oversees all councils," she said. "The Watcher is outside of all, unable to take part, and yet able to influence."

"How many are like that?"

Charlanna reached beneath the table again, pulling out another box. She pressed on the top, prying it open. "How many do you think?"

He stared. They had been so focused on the Ai'thol gaining access to each of the Elder Stones, thinking there were only five. But if there were more, the danger was far greater than they had known. What would happen if Olandar Fahr obtained access to each of the stones? He was already dangerous enough with the power of the known stones in this world.

"What happens if the Council convenes?" he asked. There had to be some reason for the Council to gather, and considering what he'd seen of the table in the middle of the tree, whatever reason there was would be powerful.

"When the Council comes together, power comes with it. And with that power comes an understanding." She tapped each of the stones from the box in front of her, and when she was done, she tapped on the center one.

He started to work through what she was telling him. For a long time, they had believed that the Great Watcher had gifted his people, the people of Elaeavn and the Elvraeth in particular, with the abilities they possessed. If so, did that mean they were somehow meant to have powers similar to this?

Or was there another reason?

If he tracked through what he'd learned, the crystals within Elaeavn didn't represent an Elder Stone at all.

His gaze drifted to the box, but not the surrounding stones. This time, he looked to the stone at the center of it.

"How many boxes do you have like that?"

She frowned, watching him. "Why?"

"How many?"

"There are five."

Five Councils. Twenty-five Elder Stones.

Five crystals in Elaeavn.

And if Olandar Fahr gained the kind of power that would come from all those councils, how powerful would he be?

It would be incredible. He would be unstoppable. It was the kind of thing they couldn't allow. While they'd already slowed his reach, delaying him from using his power to draw the energy from the sacred crystals, he wondered if that would even be enough. Would Olandar Fahr have some way of compensating for what they had done?

Olandar Fahr was already a step or more ahead of Carth, and if he knew how many stones existed, how much power there was, then he could be unstoppable.

Only, the more he thought about it, the less sense it made. Why would the crystals of the Great Watcher be in Elaeavn?

"Do you know where to find the stones in this land?" he asked.

"I know where most can be found, but not all. There's a reason they are difficult to find, and a reason they are difficult to bring back together."

"Can you show us?"

"I thought you said you weren't after power." She closed the box, pushing it off to the side, and then reached for another, closing it. When she was done, she moved on to the third box, closing it much like the others. Finally, she looked up at him, fixing him with a stare that bored into him.

Daniel watched her a moment. "I'm not after power, but I'm beginning to think we need to convene the Council before he has the opportunity to do so."

21

DANIEL

THE CITY NO LONGER SEEMED QUITE AS IMPRESSIVE AS IT had been when they had first arrived. Daniel Slid, moving between the trees, using his connection to the shadows to practice how he could navigate among them, uncertain whether he was doing so as effectively as he wanted. It was easier each time he did it, the sense that he could continue to use the shadows, to navigate within them, and to Slide using that connection in a way he had never considered before.

When he emerged back at the edge of the forest, Rayen was there. Shadows swirled around her, and he suspected she did it so she could mask herself.

She glanced over at him. "You are just as unsettled as I."

Daniel flicked his gaze to the center of the city where the massive tree rose. He couldn't shake the sense of the table there, the Council of Elders, and everything he'd learned.

"We've been thinking we were chasing after five Elder

Stones. If there are that many different councils, how much power is out there?"

"I think Carth has always suspected there's more than one council," Rayen said.

Daniel frowned. "Why would you say that?"

"She's traveled far more extensively than I have. In the time that she was gone," she said, her eyes taking on a faraway look and the shadows within them deepening, "she wasn't anywhere the Binders could find."

"She wanted you to think she was dead."

"Sure, but even then, she shouldn't have been able to conceal herself so easily from the Binders. The network is extensive. In order to hide from us that effectively…"

"You think she was somewhere else."

"I think she had to have been."

"Why wouldn't she have shared this?"

"Because we are pieces to her."

Daniel didn't have that impression. He agreed that Carth played a grander game than they did, but he didn't feel that she didn't care for them.

"What if the other councils aren't necessarily different pieces?"

"Why?"

He frowned, and on a whim, he grabbed her hand and Slid.

They emerged in Asador, in a small room he knew Rayen had long occupied, and darkness shrouded everything. The sudden change startled her, and she blinked, looking at him. "You already gave up on Ceyaniah?"

Daniel shook his head. "I've been there, so I can return."

It would be a simple matter to do so, nothing more than stepping forward in a Slide, and though he had just traveled an incredible distance in little more than a blink of an eye, he didn't feel fatigue the way he once would have. More than ever, he was certain that his connection to the shadows had changed him, strengthening him.

Lighting a lantern, pushing back some of the darkness, he went to the table taking up most of the center of the room. He hadn't been here all that often, but enough that he knew Rayen would have this here. It was a Tsatsun board, and the pieces were arranged on either side of the game board, waiting for a player.

"Look at the board," he said.

Rayen frowned as she stared. "You mean the Stone?"

"The Stone is the goal, but that piece isn't played until the endgame."

"Maybe I've been giving you too much credit," she said.

"Why?"

"The entire purpose of Tsatsun is to move the Stone. When you control it, you win."

"You win, but look at the pieces. What do you notice?"

Rayen studied the game board for a moment, frowning. "What are you getting at?"

"Many of the pieces are the same."

"And?"

"And some are sacrificed. Have you ever played a game of Tsatsun where you didn't have to sacrifice any pieces?"

"I have not. Carth has."

Daniel couldn't imagine what would be involved in a game where one wouldn't have to sacrifice anything in order to win. In every game he'd played, and particularly in those he'd won, he'd been forced to give up certain pieces. He'd never attempted a game where pieces weren't forfeited in order to reach the Stone. At the same time, he'd never really noticed there was a symmetry to the pieces.

Daniel slid one of his pieces forward. It was a solid first move, but it was one that wouldn't place him in danger of losing it on the next. He focused on playing out the game, thinking through the various possibilities as Carth had taught him. How would he play if he didn't want to sacrifice any of his pieces?

When he had first learned how to play, Carth had shown him that in order to win, certain pieces needed to be forfeited. Could that have all been part of her game?

He could see Carth using that strategy to try to convince them of one thing while playing a very different game. He frowned for a moment, looking at the board. Rayen hadn't made a move, and he turned the board around, choosing a piece and sliding it forward.

Carth had described playing it out like that before, explaining to him that was how she had learned to grow her skill, and she had used games with herself in order to continue to improve. Doing so meant he would have to keep the possibilities of both sides in mind while playing.

Could he do that and still try not to sacrifice any pieces?

As he went, playing one side and then the other, focused on the nature of the game, he found there really wasn't any move that wouldn't involve a sacrifice.

Sitting back, he stared at the game board for a moment. "I don't know if I can do it," he said.

Rayen joined him on the sofa, glancing from the board to him. "I've seen Carth play like that, but it's been a while."

"Like what?"

"Lost in the moves. I think I *have* underestimated you, Daniel."

He waited for the expected insult, but it never came.

"Are you sure you've only been playing for a short while?"

Daniel nodded. "Only since I first came across Carth, but my father had always wanted me to understand how to play similar games. To him, everything in Elaeavn was a game of strategy and positioning."

"Which is why he just lost."

"He did, but think about how long he maintained his position. With everything he's done over the years, it didn't matter. He has managed to stay ahead of the rest of the Council."

And in doing so, he'd made sure that he had stayed in a position of power.

Daniel started resetting the pieces. In that game, there hadn't been any way for him to win without making a sacrifice, but what if he tried another approach?

Eventually, he was sure he would find some way to play out the game without sacrificing pieces. He still didn't know whether that mattered. It was just a game, and yet, the more he played Tsatsun, the more value he saw in it. He understood why Carth appreciated the game as much as she did, and he thought he understood why she treated it as something more than just a game.

"We should go back," he said.

"If you need to try again, you can."

"I don't know that it's going to help me find out anything more."

"I suppose I could play out with you," she said.

"Then I definitely don't know that it will help."

She laughed softly and went to sit across from him. She quickly placed the game board back into the starting position. Rayen took the first move, and Daniel stared at the board, analyzing the various possibilities. He wasn't as quick as Carth, but in her case, it was a matter of memorizing the various movements she might make. In this case, he wanted to try something other than mere memorization. He wanted instead to find out whether he could succeed if he applied a specific strategy.

It involved taking a less aggressive approach. That had never suited his style of play, but then, his father had taught him to play aggressively Rather than applying his father's method, Daniel needed to come up with his own.

What if he made moves based on grouping similar pieces together—as if he were moving one Council?

Surprisingly, doing so allowed him to frame the Stone in a different way than he had expected. He surrounded it and thought that perhaps he would be able to hold it.

Then Rayen moved forward.

She was playing aggressively, the way he normally did, and she wasn't playing with any intention of holding back, not trying to keep from sacrificing pieces.

Rayen smiled at him. "You are applying an interesting technique."

"Am I?"

"I've seen Carth play like this before, but never so tentatively."

Daniel slipped one of his pieces forward, needing to barricade it behind another. If he didn't, he would have lost the piece—Rayen would have been able to remove that one along with quite a few others. Holding out here allowed him to defend and maintain a certain safety.

"Not so much tentative as it is playing cautiously."

"Cautious and tentative are the same thing."

"Not exactly. Tentative would mean I'm afraid of making a move. In this case, I'm taking my time to consider the various options and positioning my pieces so that I have the greatest likelihood of success."

"Do you really believe you can replicate what Carth has done?"

"Play without sacrifice?"

Rayen nodded.

Daniel shrugged. "I don't know."

"Sometimes, seeing it from a unique perspective is all that matters. I think even Carth would say that. She might win most games she plays, but even she has weaknesses."

The times he had played with her—especially as his skill had improved—he'd never known Carth to have weaknesses to her game.

"What do we know about Olandar Fahr?" Daniel asked. "When it comes to Tsatsun, what sort of style of play does he favor?"

"I don't know. Carth claims she's played him, though I don't know if she's played him in an actual game or if it was more a real-world type of setting."

For Carth, either would be gameplay.

Daniel thought about what he knew of Olandar Fahr, the way he'd used the Ai'thol. He'd sent them to attack, maneuvering them in a way meant to overpower the defenses on this side of the world.

"Something about this doesn't quite make sense," he said, staring at the board. Something was off—though what was it? It had to be more than a matter of the strategy.

How would the game play out if he focused on bundling the various pieces together?

He shifted them around. Rather than lining them up in a traditional setup, he held them in place so he could position the pieces to get a better sense of how things would play out were he to go about this from a different direction.

"What are you doing?" Rayen asked.

Daniel started maneuvering the pieces. There were five clusters of pieces on either side of the board.

Somehow, that didn't make complete sense. If he were to use the pieces in order to play the same way the councils would, the clusters and the number of pieces represented by them would be significant. It had to be, didn't it?

He tried maneuvering them, no longer trying to ensure he didn't sacrifice all the pieces, but even playing in that manner didn't make a difference. After a while, he sat back in frustration, staring at the board. No answers came to him.

"I'm missing something."

"Why did you try it like that?" Rayen asked.

Daniel waved his hand at the board. "I'm trying to set

up a play that would be similar to the various councils."

Rayen leaned forward, staring at the board for a moment. "You have ten different councils. I thought we heard there were five."

"There are five." He motioned, indicating the five on one side.

"But in the way you have this set up, there are five on either side."

Daniel leaned back, smiling to himself. "I didn't say it was a perfect system. In fact, I'm probably way off when it comes to this."

"It seems to me you've latched on to something."

"I think I need to talk to Carth."

"Even if you're right, we still don't know what to make of the fifth stone." She grabbed five of the pieces, holding them. "But say you *are* right and this is what he's after. We know there are five seats on the Council of Elders, and those five seats will allow us to do… what?"

"According to Carth, they thought it was a matter of power, that by maneuvering the pieces, that they would gain the power of the Great Watcher."

"You don't think so?"

"Honestly? I'm not really sure what to think. I'm probably reading too much into all of this at this point. Tsatsun is designed to play out in a way that gains control of the Stone. If it is tied to the Elder Stones"—and he wasn't even sure if it was or if he was simply reading far too much into things—"the game isn't won by having the Great Watcher—the Stone—taking control the other pieces. The game is won by having the other pieces maneuvering in such a way that they're in control of the board." Which meant either he was way off, or what they believed the Ai'thol were after was wrong.

Daniel shifted the pieces back into place once again, resetting the game board. This time, he placed the pieces around it back into their traditional locations. He stared at the board, his mind racing, trying to work through various scenarios, but the longer he stared, the less it felt as if he could come up with anything that would explain what was taking place.

Perhaps he wouldn't be able to understand.

Rayen was right. They did need to take things one step at a time. If he could figure out what stone Olandar Fahr was after, there was a real chance they could stop him. Seeing as how Carth knew the locations of the other Elder Stones…

"We need to go to the other stones," he whispered.

"What?"

Daniel stared at the board. "I think… I think we need to go to the other stones."

"You've been in Nyaesh and know that one of the stones is there. You have now been to the chamber of shadows."

Daniel nodded. And he had been to the wisdom stone. "You mentioned that there was another Elder Stone you're aware of."

Rayen watched him for a moment. "Why?"

"I think we need to visit it."

"Daniel, what you're asking is for—"

"You to show me where one of the Elder Stones can be found."

"What happens if you get to it and decide you want its

power?"

"I don't know that its power will make a difference to me."

"Are you so sure?"

"When I was influenced by the chamber of shadows, I wasn't given much. It's added to my ability to Slide, but even that isn't all that dramatic."

"Not all that dramatic? The way you now use your ability is far different than how even Lareth does, and from everything I hear from your people, he is the most talented among you with that ability."

Daniel nodded. Lareth was incredibly gifted with Sliding, but part of it came from his control over the metals, not just lorcith but heartstone and others. It had changed his connection to Sliding, much like how his connection to the shadows now gave Daniel the opportunity to trail along them in a new way.

"That's just it—I don't know having access to one of the stones even made a significant difference to me."

Rayen glanced down at the game board. "I've seen how those who acquire one of the Elder Stones change, Daniel Elvraeth. There is much different about them. Power changes everyone."

"And yet, it's strange, but when we went to the chamber of shadows, there wasn't much changed for me."

"You doubt going to one of the other Elder Stones will change you."

"What if there's something about me—or my people—that prevents us from gaining the benefit of the Elder Stone?" The more he thought about it, the more likely it seemed than anything else. If it was something about the people from Elaeavn, the fact they were touched by the Great Watcher anyway, could that be why they didn't seem to take on dramatic changes when they were around the other Elder Stones?

Rayen looked up from the board. "I will show you this."

Daniel blinked. "You will?"

Rayen shrugged. "I might be wrong, and if I am, Carthenne may decide to cut you down so that you don't have the influence of another Elder Stone, but that will be her choice. This is mine." She got to her feet, waiting for Daniel.

He hesitated, watching her. "Cut me down?"

She smiled at him. "You know how Carthenne can be."

"She wouldn't do that."

Rayen smiled at him. "Of course not, Daniel Elvraeth. Carth is nothing but a gentle soul."

He didn't know what to say. Maybe Carth would be willing to cut him down if it came down to it. She would do whatever it took to ensure the protection of the stones. He had seen that from her. Yet he didn't want to find the Elder Stone for power. Rather, he thought he needed to. As he stared at the board, noticing the way the pieces were clustered, he couldn't help but wonder if perhaps there was a different key to the game than the one he'd been considering.

The purpose of the game was to control the Stone. At least, that was how he had always viewed it. What if control wasn't the key?

It all came back to understanding what Olandar Fahr wanted.

RYN

THE INSIDE OF THE TOWER WAS DRAFTY. THAT SURPRISED Ryn given the value of the artifacts kept within it. In one section, a massive library stretched from wall to wall, stuffed with books that would be incredibly valuable, and yet elsewhere within the tower, someone left windows open, the humid breeze drifting in, the danger to the books more than what she thought the Great One would tolerate.

It wasn't any of her business, not really. While she had been sent here to ensure the Great One had answers, she wasn't expected to solve the issues others created.

In the two days since Dillon had disappeared on her, she hadn't found him again. She had gone looking, thinking she would figure out what he was doing out in the city, even if she had to ask him directly. She wasn't above a pointed question that might provide information. As the Great One's emissary, she protected from dangers such direct questioning might otherwise draw to her, especially within the tower.

Only, she hadn't seen Dillon since that night. She had no idea where he'd gone, and she hesitated to approach the blacksmith with that question. While he might answer —she was the emissary, after all—there was something about him that made her reluctant. And here she'd thought that the blacksmith was the one she needed to figure out.

She hadn't abandoned that search, either, though the blacksmith was predictable. He started early in the morning, usually at sunup or shortly after, and he worked until late in the day, the steady hammering audible throughout the entirety of the tower now that she knew how to listen for it. It was continuous, a regular rhythm, and considering the nature of his work, Ryn didn't think it made sense to interrupt what he was doing, if he would even allow her to do so.

About noon, Ryn headed down the stairs, once more toward the blacksmith. She had made her way there often enough over the last few days that she was comfortable on the stairs, and when she came across someone else, she froze for a moment.

"Emissary. Are you lost?"

Ryn nodded to Lorren. "Do I look as if I'm lost?"

"It's not a question of appearance, it's more that I was not expecting you to be heading this way."

"Because you thought I would have no interest in your blacksmith?"

Lorren frowned for a moment. "The Great One knows all about the blacksmith."

"So he tells me."

Lorren's eyes widened. Ryn smiled to herself. Her

response was ambiguous enough that she suspected the priest believed she had spoken to the Great One about the blacksmith.

"Do you mind if I ask what interest you have in him?"

"I don't mind, but I'm not certain I will share with you."

"We are only here to help."

"If that were the case, then you would have offered me assistance from the very beginning. Instead I had to force my way along." She smiled. Having the protection of the Great One meant she could speak freely like this, though she really should be careful. It was just as likely that she would lose it.

"It was a mistake, emissary. Surely you can understand that."

"Because I have made so many mistakes?"

"That is not what I was implying."

"What were you doing heading down to the blacksmith?"

"I was checking on the nature of his work."

"And?"

"And I have found it satisfactory."

She smiled to herself. "Satisfactory? That's all?"

"He works diligently on behalf of the Great One, manufacturing more of the sacred metal."

"He doesn't seem to view his work as quite as monumental as others within the Ai'thol would."

Lorren's face clouded for a moment. "Unfortunately, that one cannot be reformed. We have tried, but…"

At least Ryn wasn't wrong in her impression of the blacksmith. "Do you trust him?"

"Trust?"

Ryn nodded. "Do you trust him?"

"There is no reason not to trust. He has served us well."

"And he served the previous masters of the temple, too."

"He told you that?"

"I get the sense he doesn't keep much to himself."

The priest shook his head, chuckling. "Unfortunately, there are times when he would be better served if he did, and yet he does not."

"Does that trouble you?"

"Why should it? He has served us without question."

Ryn's gaze darted past Lorren, looking down the stairs. "And what of his apprentice?"

"He is a young man in need of some stability. He was found—"

"I know what story he tells us about how he was found."

"You question whether he was found the way he tells us? I have spoken to the priest, and I can assure you he was encountered nearly dying, starving because his own people had abandoned him."

"That's what he told me."

"It's a shame, really."

"What is?"

"What happened to him."

"He's safe, now."

"Now, and he still struggles to find himself."

"Don't you think assigning him to work with the

blacksmith might have been problematic, considering the man's lack of faith?"

"I suppose one could see it that way, and yet, the blacksmith offered a certain level of stability that Dillon was missing. In the blacksmith, he found an ally who was willing to offer him friendship, and mentoring, and much he didn't have before."

Ryn smiled. She wasn't going to continue to argue with Lorren about it, but she imagined that the Great One would see things differently. He wouldn't have wanted to have his people so influenced by men like the blacksmith.

"If you don't mind," Ryn said.

"Of course." Lorren stepped aside, and Ryn started down the stairs.

It surprised her when Lorren followed. She glanced back at him, but he stared straight ahead, as if determined to avoid her gaze. What was he playing at?

Then again, what was *she* playing at? She might have the approval and authority of the Great One, but she needed to be careful not to offend those who served him. That was one thing he would not tolerate, and with her, she thought he would tolerate quite a bit.

At the bottom of the stairs, the heat struck quickly. She hurried toward the door leading to the forge, pausing at the locked door. Slipping the knife out of her pocket, she stuffed it into the lock, feeling the way it changed, and twisted.

Ryn didn't bother to glance back at Lorren as she made her way into the room on the other side. She didn't need to—she could practically feel the question he wanted to ask burning into her back. It did no good for her to worry about Lorren. He might be a high-ranking priest within the Ai'thol in this city, but he was not one of the disciples, and therefore there were limits to his reach.

As she continued forward, the steady sound of the hammering drew her. The rhythm to it was different today than it had been before, the pounding almost a slightly different frequency.

"You do not need to accompany me," she said to Lorren.

"I am curious."

As it was his temple, she didn't think she could refuse him access, but at the same time, she didn't like the idea of him tagging along behind her.

"What do you think you can learn?"

Lorren smiled at her. "The better question is, what do *you* think you can learn?"

Once inside the forge, she paused for a moment, orienting herself. As they had before, the bright red coals glowed intensely. Heat radiated from the forge, and she didn't see any sign of Dillon working at it, building the coals up higher than they had been before. There was nothing there. All that she noticed was the blacksmith, his enormous body hunched over as he hammered repeatedly.

She could feel Lorren watching her. A part of her was tempted to do nothing, to stay where she was and simply observe, but at the same time, she had questions. While she didn't know if the blacksmith would be able to answer them, she felt that he was the one who most likely could.

When he paused, she stepped forward. She started to clear her throat, but he shook his head.

"I know you're there," he said.

"I suspected you did."

The blacksmith grunted. "I thought we had our conversation the other day. I didn't realize we had more to go through."

"It's not so much that there's more we need to go through as there is a need for me to better understand you."

"What's there to understand? I've told you all about me."

"I'm not so sure you have. You told me what you want me to know about you, but that's not the same as telling me what I need to know."

He grunted. "Is that right? What more do you think I should be sharing with you?"

"There will be time for that later." She had already begun to think about what she wanted to say to him, and the question she wanted answered. The problem remained how much he would be willing to answer. It was possible he wouldn't answer anything for her.

"If you're not here about that, then why?"

"Where's your apprentice?"

"Dillon? He wasn't feeling well."

"Is it common for him to miss working with you?"

"I'm not so sure that he'd say he's missing it."

She eyed him strangely for a moment. "Is it common?"

"No. Why?"

"Just a curiosity I have."

"Do you get them often?"

"Often enough."

"I saw him out in the city the other night."

"Is that forbidden by the Great One?"

"I lost sight of him."

"Is that unusual for you?"

"It is these days."

She waited, letting that sink in. He watched her, frowning for a moment, and she noticed how his hand went to his pocket—likely the same pocket that held the small hunk of silver metal. There was something about that metal that she needed to better understand, and if it were possible, she needed to find it.

That might not be why she was here, but Ryn couldn't help wanting to better understand the sacred metal.

"You might as well just come out and say it," he said.

"Say what?"

"Say whatever you plan on accusing him of."

"I'm not accusing him of anything. I just have questions."

The blacksmith met her gaze for a moment before shrugging. "You can find him near the tower. He has a place where he stays."

Maybe that was all it was. She had followed him out into the city, and from there, when he had disappeared, she had questioned whether there was something more to it. If there was nothing more, then she had made a mistake. It was uncommon, but with everything else going on these days, she needed to be cautious.

"Interesting," she said.

"Do you intend to keep harassing me, or will you be heading on your way?"

"I didn't realize I was harassing you."

"You come in here with concerns about my apprentice,

disrupt my work, and you watch me with a look that tells me you doubt me. I'd say that you have been doing plenty of harassment."

She held his gaze for a moment. She could practically feel the smug satisfaction coming from Lorren, though he was wise enough to keep it to himself. He was a man she would have to be careful with and watch.

"When you're done, I would expect you will come find me. Anyone in the tower can tell you where. I have questions for you."

She spun and left him before he had a chance to object. When she was done, she breathed out, happy to be back out of the hot air. She made her way back up the stairs, not bothering to determine if Lorren followed. She didn't need to. She could feel that he was still down near the blacksmith, and when his hammering returned, the steady pounding that she had become all too familiar with, she suspected Lorren had departed.

Back in the room, she sat there, flipping through her pages. Every so often she took notes, documenting something she had uncovered, scratching a reminder about something else. She couldn't help but wonder if the blacksmith would come talk with her. After a while, the hammering stopped, and she listened, waiting for an indication that it would resume, but it did not.

She got lost in her notes, making marks in her records, and when a tapping on her door startled her, she looked up.

"Enter," she said.

The blacksmith stood on the other side of the door. He

leaned in slightly, his gaze sweeping around before frowning at her. "Is this the right place?"

"You doubt it is?"

"It doesn't look quite like I was expecting."

"What sort of thing were you expecting?"

"For an emissary to the Great One"—he said *Great One* with a hint of scorn, and she couldn't help but wonder what sort of interaction they had, and whether this man really did serve the way he was supposed to—"I thought you might take a bit of a nicer place."

"This has everything I need. A table. A chair. A bright lantern." Even that wasn't necessary anymore. She had found that she could work when the lantern had burned down to nearly nothing, though she liked having the extra light. "And access to people like yourself." She motioned to a chair, and when the blacksmith sat, he practically swallowed the chair with his body.

"Why did you want to talk with me here?"

"I thought it was best to get you out of your workshop."

It was a little more than that—not so much that she wanted him uncomfortable as that she needed him to be less settled than he was within his forge.

"What do you want to know?"

"To start with, your name."

"It doesn't matter."

"Names matter."

"Is that right? And what is yours?"

"Ryn." She paused. Perhaps it would help this man if she shared a little bit about herself. "The Great One found me. My home had been destroyed. Everything I knew was lost. I was broken. He helped me find something better."

The blacksmith stared at her. "I suppose you think I should share with you some great story about how I was found, but there isn't one."

"I'd be interested in hearing how you ended up here."

"I needed a place to stay. I needed work. They offered both."

"You weren't a believer?"

"I'm not much for religion. It's never served me all that well."

"What has served you well?"

"Myself."

"You don't care very much for the Great One."

"It's not that I don't care for him. It's that I recognize he preaches a brand of religion that can be dangerous. I've seen it before."

"And where was that?"

"It doesn't matter."

"Why not?"

The blacksmith grunted. "What's your question?"

"I would like to know whether you serve the Great One faithfully or not."

"I serve as I'm asked."

"If you don't believe, then why do you serve?"

"I have a place to stay. That's all that matters."

That idea seemed strange to her. How could a place to stay be all that mattered?

"What about Dillon?"

"What about him?"

"What else do you know about him?"

"If you have anything to accuse him of, you might as well do it."

"No accusation, I'm just curious."

The blacksmith leaned forward. "Why did the Great One make you his emissary?"

"I wonder that all the time."

"Do you?"

She nodded. There were days when she sat and contemplated why the Great One would have chosen her. What set her apart?

The only answer she could come up with was that he had seen something special about her, or maybe it was the fact that she remained devoted to him when others did not. Either way, she wasn't going to challenge it. She was thankful she had been given the opportunity.

"I've learned with the Great One that it doesn't make sense to question."

"It's been my experience that it is best to question everything. When you act without questioning, you are acting on blind faith."

"It's not blind faith if you have seen."

The blacksmith smiled at her. "And yet, from some of your comments, I can tell you haven't. If you had, you wouldn't be asking some of the questions you have been. There is much you haven't seen. How could you at your age?"

"How old do you think I am?"

"Not old enough. Not nearly old enough."

"I'm old enough that the Great One chose me."

"You hang on to that. If that's what matters to you, then you should hold on to it and use that. Me, I prefer to take a different approach. I prefer to trust the things I have experienced and know." He flashed a smile. "Are we done here?"

"I will have the answers I seek."

"Have I been preventing you from reaching them?"

"You haven't been helpful to my finding those answers."

"That's not my responsibility. Everybody has to ask their own questions, and everybody has to find their own answers. I can't be the reason you find them." The black-smith got to his feet, standing in front of her. "Maybe when you're older, you'll better understand."

With that, he turned and left, and Ryn didn't even bother to chase him. There didn't seem to be any point.

There was something about him that left her troubled, though she wasn't quite sure why. Perhaps it was the confidence about him, or perhaps it was that his confidence seemed to be tied to his questioning of the Great One. Either way, she thought she had enough information.

At least about him.

She still had questions about Dillon. She was determined to find those answers, and now she knew where to look.

RYN

RAIN PELTED HER. RYN PULLED UP THE HOOD OF HER cloak, keeping her from getting drenched, but she was already soaked by the onslaught, so it didn't. What she wouldn't give to keep from getting wet. Her enhanced senses didn't do her any good here.

Somewhere distantly, thunder rumbled, the steady sound drifting to her and reminding her of the thunder that had preceded the volcano's eruption.

There was no lightning—the storm hadn't been severe enough for that—but the rain had been dumping on them so much that she wondered if it would ever end.

Still there had been no sign of Dillon.

She remained motionless, vigilant, willing to suffer a little if it meant she would find the answers she needed. That was the kind of service the Great One demanded. Ryn was determined to do everything the Great One would require, find the answers he needed, and if it involved her standing outside in the rain, getting soaked, then she would do it.

What else did she detect?

His question lingered in the back of her mind. So far, she hadn't sensed anything else, but she thought that there should be something.

What had she noticed when she was around Lorren?

There was a sense of the man. Even now, she thought she could track him. She could practically feel him up in the tower, though she suspected it was little more than her imagination.

If only she had a similar sense of Dillon.

There was no sign of him. There was nothing. There had been no sign of him for the hours she'd been watching, and as she remained there, she couldn't help but think she would eventually find some evidence of him.

Another peal of thunder rumbled toward her.

Ryn shifted the hood of her cloak, just enough that she could shield herself from additional rain, but not enough to stay dry. She sat there for a moment, debating whether she would leave, thinking she had been here long enough.

How much longer was she willing to wait?

She should wait as long as it was necessary.

The Great One had taught her patience. It hadn't been her strength before meeting him. She had been impulsive, and she could only imagine what her mother would think of her were she still alive, to learn about the person she was now, the way she served.

Her mother had wanted her to have comfort, her own life, and to be happy. Was that what Ryn could claim now?

As she stood there, the blacksmith's words intruded. Question and find her own answers.

Didn't she have her own answers? She had questioned

as much as she thought she could and had seen much while working with the Great One, but she wasn't always with him. There were things he was accused of that she tried to ignore, and many of those things she believed him innocent of, though others claimed differently.

Ryn thought she knew better, but then again, she thought she knew what kind of person the Great One truly was, the part of him others did not get to see.

Other questions began to roll through her mind. Maybe the blacksmith was trying to distract her, to guide her so that she would make a mistake. This was a dangerous kind of man. She wouldn't be at all surprised if he was trying to set her up for failure.

He didn't think much of her as the emissary. That much was clear.

The rain began to intensify.

Great. It was just what she needed to be stuck out here, dumped on by the rain, and though she wasn't necessarily trapped, she didn't feel as if she would be doing a thorough job for the Great One if she didn't search for as much information as possible. In this case, that meant finding out what Dillon knew.

The rain in front of her started to fold.

At first she wasn't sure what she was seeing, or whether it was real, but the longer she stared, the more certain she was that it had *folded*. It was a strange sensation, as if the raindrops that had been pounding down had stopped, and suddenly, Dillon appeared in front of her.

When he did, she could feel something change. It came as a deep sensation from within her stomach, a quivering, almost nausea, but not quite. She thought she might be imagining it, but the longer she was aware of it, the more certain she was that it was real.

What was it she detected?

There was a lesson that the Great One had taught her. He had wanted her to work on what she detected, trying to train her to observe the same way he did. It was the reason he had made her his emissary in the first place. Not because she had some great insight—she knew she didn't, and regardless of what the blacksmith said, she was fully aware of her limitations—but because of her ability to observe and report back what she had seen. It was that ability that had made her valuable to the Great One. Without it, she never would have helped him. She never would have helped herself.

She didn't have any way of retreating, and as much as she wanted to slide back into the shadows, she couldn't.

There was a faint shimmering, little more than a swirling of color around him, and the folding of the rain. The shimmering was something she recognized. She'd had enough experience with those who could travel and had seen it around the Great One himself.

"What are you doing here?" Dillon asked when he appeared.

"You can travel."

"What?"

"Appear and disappear. You don't need to walk."

"Transporting. Yes. I can."

She would never have called it transporting, but maybe the fact that he did meant he really was from the village he claimed. A part of her had questioned it, mostly because she wasn't sure whether she could trust him. She still wasn't.

"Does the Great One know?"

"My ability isn't from him."

"It's not?"

"Some people are born with it. It's... it's the reason that I got in trouble. They found me with the mayor's daughter."

Ryn shook her head. "You just appeared with her?"

"I would have disappeared with her too, but I don't have much strength with it. Or didn't."

"Didn't?"

Dillon looked behind him, as if he were expecting someone to appear, but they never did. "Didn't. You know, no strength beforehand. It seems the more you use it, the stronger it gets. I don't know if I can travel with another person or not, but the more I practice, the more likely it is I can."

"I'm told it's like any other talent. Practice makes you stronger with it."

"How is it that you know?"

"I'm the Great One's emissary."

Dillon glanced over his shoulder again.

"Are you expecting someone?"

He shook his head. "No, it's just..."

"I have some questions for you." She said it more assertively than she intended, and as she wiped the rain from her eyes, she felt as if she looked small—and young. It was bad enough looking young next to the blacksmith. He had something about him that spoke of age and experience and a hint of anger, as if something had happened to him long ago that he refused to let go of. Dillon was different. If she were too aggressive, she worried that he would refuse to answer her questions, and in order to find out what she needed for the Great One, she couldn't offend him too soon.

"Out in the rain?"

"Do you have someplace we can go?"

"You're the emissary."

Ryn glanced to the tower. Lanterns glowed within windows. "We certainly could return. My office isn't all that impressive, and it's lacking a hearth, so we won't be able to warm up."

"Fine. You can come with me."

She had half expected him to travel the same way that the Great One did, but instead he pushed past her, heading down the street. She hurried along, worried she'd lose track of him. If she did, she didn't know whether she would find him again. He had disappeared from her once; now that he knew she was tracking him, would he try to evade her again?

Instead, he reached a door partway along the street and paused. He fished a key out of his pocket and slipped it into the lock. Ryn followed him inside.

It was dark, but her eyesight quickly adjusted, taking in the various items within the room. It was sparsely decorated. A table and two chairs pushed along one side. A bench and another chair rested near a hearth. The floor was all stone. A single lantern rested on one table, and Dillon headed to it, lighting it.

"Are you going to let the rain in?"

Ryn closed the door and turned back to him. "This is your place?"

"Being a blacksmith's apprentice doesn't pay all that well. It's lucky I have a place of my own. Torry offered for me to stay in the forge, but I wasn't interested in staying there. Too hot, you know, even when I quench the coals. I need a little bit of a breeze."

Ryn stuffed away the name. Torry had to be the blacksmith. She could use it to find more about him. "You could stay there?"

"When I was apprenticed in my village, I stayed there. It wasn't much. A cot in the back. At least it was separated from the rest of the forge. I don't really care for the heat."

"You said that."

"Did I?"

Ryn looked around before taking a seat on the bench near the hearth. "I could use some warmth now."

It didn't take long for Dillon to get a fire going. Ryn breathed out, thankful for the warmth, and curled her arms around her. Water pooled from her cloak onto the floor.

"I'm sorry for making a mess in here."

Dillon shrugged. "Water dries. Besides, there's nothing here that can be damaged. And it's not mine. I pay a man two coppers a week to stay here. If anything's ruined, I'll just send him over to the Great One."

She could only imagine the way the Great One would reply but realized that Dillon was joking. He smiled as he stood from near the hearth and held his hand out to her.

"What?"

"Your cloak. Are you going to give it to me or not?"

"What are you going to do with it?"

"Are you always this suspicious?"

"I serve the Great One."

"That doesn't mean you need to be suspicious. I'm going to take your cloak and hang it near the fire. Hopefully it will dry out a little bit. Don't you want to dry out?"

She pulled the cloak off her shoulders, handing it over to him.

Everything within her told her she needed to be cautious with him. He hadn't told her the truth. If he had, she would have known he had the ability to travel, but then, perhaps he was keeping it from others.

That didn't seem likely. If he was hiding it from others, he wouldn't have done it so openly. More likely was that he was suspicious of her as the Great One's emissary. She couldn't blame him for that, either.

"How long were you waiting?"

"A few hours," she said.

"Hours?"

She shrugged. "I have patience."

"You would have to, to wait that long. Why were you standing out there, anyway?"

"I saw you along the alley. I wanted to know whether or not you could travel."

"You decided to wait for me?"

"Is there another way I should have gone about it?"

"You know, asking me?"

"You haven't been at the forge. Your master didn't know when you would return."

He turned away. "I haven't been feeling well."

There was something in the way he said it that troubled her. Not feeling well could mean many different things, and from what the blacksmith had said, it seemed as if it was unusual for Dillon to disappear like that. Why would he have suddenly done so at the same time as she had begun to look for him?

"I hope you're feeling better."

Dillon turned, nodding slowly. "A little."

Ryn studied him for a moment. His fingers twitched, almost as if he were flexing them. There seemed to be a hint of tension in his posture even though he stooped.

What was Dillon keeping from her?

The Great One had taught her to be observant, and she used that now. He wanted her to understand when others were deceiving her, and that was part of the reason she doubted that the Great One himself was deceiving her. Why would he have trained her to pick up on those things if he was going to try to use them against her?

Ryn sat up, ignoring the water pouring off her. Even though she sat in front of the fire, she still felt a chill from the dampness and the rainwater.

"Where have you been?" she asked.

"I told you I wasn't feeling well."

"That's what you say, but your body language tells a different story. You move your hand as if to prepare to escape. You're tense, as if you were trying to hide something from me. And there's the fact that I just don't believe you."

"Why not?"

"With your ability to travel, you could go anywhere. I have a hard time believing you chose to come here, when you had so many other options. Why this place, why so far from where you knew?"

"I told you about my village—"

"Your village. It's the same story you told others, and yet something about the story changes with each telling, doesn't it?" She leaned forward, fixing him with an intense gaze. "You aren't really from Thyr, are you?"

Dillon stood up, clasping his hands in front of him as he watched her. She had thought him young, partly from the way he interacted with her, but partly from the way he looked. As she studied him, she realized that wasn't quite right. Was he as young as he seemed?

It was hard for her to tell. As she watched him, she couldn't shake the sense that he didn't look to be quite like she expected. His deep green eyes blazed as they stared at her, and as she watched, it seemed as if they flashed slightly brighter.

Ryn sat rigidly, hands resting on her lap.

"I told you I was from near Thyr."

Ryn thought about what the Great One had taught her of geography, and it was considerable. He had wanted her to know the land, if only so that she would be ready when she departed him, prepared to serve as his emissary. Thyr was far from here, near the north, and in a place that had once held significance for the Ai'thol but had not for many years. It was a dangerous place, at least according to the Great One, who had warned her that she was not quite ready to visit it. At the time, she hadn't known what he'd meant by that, but the more she began to understand her abilities and what he wanted from her, the more she thought that she did understand. He was trying to protect her, keeping her from the dangers of places like that. Even here, within the temple, it was dangerous for her to serve as his emissary.

Why should that be?

It was something she hadn't considered much before now. There should be no reason for her to fear places that the Great One influenced. They should want to serve, and the fact that there was danger anywhere was a suggestion that perhaps his control wasn't as great as it needed to be.

Was that the lesson he was trying to teach her?

With the Great One, it could be difficult to know what he wanted her to learn. Part of that was because he wanted her to experience it herself, to understand aspects of the world in ways he didn't feel he could teach. There was value in it, and she had seen that herself. It meant she could study and learn, gain insight into the inner workings of various places, and in time, she would be better equipped to observe.

"You would like me to believe you traveled all the way to the south from near Thyr, while at the same time nearly dying and needing to be escorted away by priests."

Dillon watched her, saying nothing. The darkness swirling around his eyes made it difficult for her to fully understand what he was thinking.

"While all that time, you had the ability to travel. If you have that ability, and having seen it myself, I know that you do, why would you have needed the priests to rescue you?"

"It was early. I didn't have much control over my ability—"

"Other than the fact you were able to use it around your home."

Dillon grabbed a chair, pulling it toward the hearth, where he took a seat. "What do you know about transporting?"

"Traveling. That's what the Great One calls it."

"I don't care what the Great One calls it. What do you know about it?"

The dismissive way he referred to the Great One troubled her. "I've traveled with the Great One many times. I understand he is able to transport," she said, leaning toward him, holding his gaze, "but I don't have the same ability. That doesn't mean I don't recognize what it can do. The Great One has taught me to pay attention and observe, which I've done in studying the way he transports. I saw the same from you."

"If you were paying attention, you would know I need to have traveled someplace in order to visit it. Otherwise, it's dangerous."

She frowned. That was something she wasn't aware of when it came to the Great One. Was it a piece of information he didn't want her to have? More likely, he simply hadn't shared it with her because he had wanted her to uncover it on her own.

"How is it dangerous?"

"Imagine if I tried to transport myself where there was nothing but rock. Or imagine if I transported myself to the middle of an ocean. Or—"

"A volcano," she said.

His face wrinkled and he shrugged. "Sure. A volcano. Not that I've seen many of those."

He offered at least a believable reason for why he would have needed the priests, but once he had found them, why had he stayed with them?

She couldn't shake the sense that there was something he wasn't telling her, and that it was important to her understanding what had taken place here and what the Great One needed to know.

Whatever he was hiding was significant, she was certain of that, though she wasn't quite sure what he would need to keep from her.

What she needed was to look at it from a different angle. Why would he keep something from her?

She was the Great One's emissary, which meant she was his voice in this place. She had seen there was less regard for the Great One here than she had anticipated. While the blacksmith was the most open about it, she had noticed a certain disregard for her stature even with the priests.

"Who are the priests who found you?"

"Back to that? I've already told you I can't transport myself to places I haven't been. Too dangerous."

"That wasn't the question. Who were the priests who found you?"

He glanced around, almost as if he were looking to find help. She smiled to herself. She was sure she had it right.

"One of them was the man who runs the tower."

Why wasn't she surprised?

"And who is the other?"

"It doesn't matter."

"I think it does."

"No. It doesn't. He's gone."

"Gone? Where did he go?"

"Not like that. Not as if he ran off and disappeared someplace. He's gone as in he died."

Her mind raced, trying to come up with what to say. Why would one of the priests have died? They had lost quite a few priests over the years, at least according to the Great One. Could it have anything to do with Lareth?

"How long have you been here?"

"The city, or here in front of you? If it's the last, then you know that as well as I do. If you're asking about the city—"

"The city, Dillon."

The other man shrugged. "A year. Not much more."

Not long enough for him to have fully become a part of what the Great One was doing, but long enough for him to understand his role within the temple.

"Thank you for your conversation."

"That's it?"

"I might have more questions for you later, but for now, that's it."

She stood, and Dillon scrambled to his feet and positioned himself in front of her.

"Do you intend to block the emissary of the Great One from leaving?"

Dillon shook his head quickly. "That's not what I was trying to do."

"I will take my cloak."

"You don't have to go. We can continue to talk."

"About what? Do you have more you think I need to know?"

When he didn't say anything, she reached for her cloak.

A part of her worried he might try to restrain her. She wasn't a fighter, so she didn't know what she would be required to do in order to get free. She didn't want to have to fight Dillon off, but at the same time, she wasn't about to let him restrict her from leaving. The Great One would be disappointed in her if that happened.

And she still had questions.

Everything circled back around to Lorren, though he had made it seem as if he were innocent in what was taking place—as if he were nothing more than a faithful servant of the Great One.

What if he was not?

That was the answer she needed to obtain.

Ryn didn't know how much longer she had before the Great One returned, bringing her to some other place to observe and report. It was possible he would come in the morning, or the next day. It was equally possible he would leave her here for weeks. He was unpredictable, and most of the time it didn't matter. Eventually, he would come for her. He always did.

When she grabbed her cloak, pulling it off, she shook it, feeling a bit of moisture still present on it. It was drier than it had been, and she was thankful that Dillon had been willing to start the fire, giving her an opportunity to warm herself in front of the hearth. It was an unexpected kindness from him, though he was still keeping something from her. Maybe it was nothing more than the fact that he could travel. There was danger in others being able to travel whom the Great One didn't know about.

"That's it?"

"For now," she said. She backed toward the door, continuing to watch him. "If I need you again, I'll send word."

Reaching the door, she pulled it open, stepping back out into the rain and letting out a sigh of relief. For whatever reason, Dillon had made her nervous. It was the same way the blacksmith had made her feel.

That couldn't be a coincidence, could it?

And yet, the one person who hadn't made her nervous was the one she now questioned.

It was time for her to visit with Lorren.

RYN

WIND WHISTLED AROUND HER AT THE TOP OF THE TOWER, and Ryn stood staring outward, looking at the city spread around it. The view really was quite nice, and as she took it in, she couldn't help but feel as if there was a sense of connection to the city itself. This wasn't her city—at this point, Ryn no longer knew what her city was—but it was a place where she felt the connections.

It stirred within her, a mixture of her ability to see along with what she could hear and smell. Her enhanced senses triggered a very different perception of this city than she'd had when she first had come.

Her fingers found the back of her head, running along the blessing. It was circular, but there were irregularities along the edge, grooves that she often traced. The metal itself was slightly warm, though not unpleasantly so. It was as if her own body had warmed it, and yet it seemed even warmer than the rest of her. The longer it was there, the smaller it seemed to be. That didn't make much sense to her, but she was trained to observe, and in this case, her training had shown her that it seemed to be different than it had been before.

As she felt along the surface of the blessing, she couldn't help but wonder why it would be changing. It was one of the things she thought she could ask the Great One when he returned, and yet he had been gone now for quite some time. It had already been longer than his usual departure. Then again, it was possible that he knew she was struggling to find answers and was giving her the opportunity to succeed. If so, she should be grateful for it.

From the top of the tower, Ryn watched children racing along the street, chasing a small animal—possibly a dog or a cat, the size and her distance making it difficult to tell—and laughing. The sound of their joyful voices drifted to her ears, and she pushed away the swell of emotion that flooded into her.

"You asked to see me."

Ryn turned and nodded to Lorren. The priest stood at the entrance of the stairs, his hands clasped in front of him, his dark robes draped over his body. She studied his face for a moment, searching his eyes for any sign of green.

There was none.

Then again, when she looked in a mirror, she didn't have any green in her eyes. Hers were pale, almost blank, and yet she knew where she had come from. She should have green eyes much like Dillon.

"I did want to see you."

Lorren approached, joining her at the railing looking down over the city. She couldn't help but think of when the Great One had been here, standing alongside her as she looked out at the city. Lorren was nothing like the Great One, and though she suspected he wished for that sort of power, he would never rival the other man.

"Why out here?"

"I enjoy the view."

"And the cold?"

Ryn wrapped her cloak around her shoulders, cinching it tight. The cold didn't bother her much, though for as long as she had spent in Vuahlu, she had grown accustomed to the heat, and there was something comforting about it.

"Do you mind the cold?"

"This isn't all that cold," Lorren said.

She smiled to herself. It was another piece of information about the man she needed. "I understand you are one of the priests who found Dillon."

Lorren nodded. "There was a time when the Great One sent me to explore. I followed his direction, as you, as emissary, do."

"I don't wander as much as it sounds like you do."

"Did." When she glanced over at him, he shook his head. "I don't wander like that any longer. My task is to remain in the city and work with as many as we can here."

"Do you know why the Great One asked me to remain here?"

"You are his emissary. I wouldn't think to question."

"And yet, I suspect you have."

"It is only natural for one to have questions about the nature of service."

"I suppose that is true."

"Have you discovered something?"

"Are you concerned I might have?"

"I understand that the Great One has wanted information about the attack. If you have uncovered something, I would be pleased if you would share it with me."

Ryn turned her attention back to the city. Standing next to Lorren, she could feel his presence. She wasn't quite sure what that meant, only that she had been much more aware of those she had spent any time around. It was almost as if she were connected to him. In the case of Lorren, she wasn't sure that she wanted such a bond. In the case of others, like Dillon and the blacksmith, it was more intriguing than anything. Standing here as she was, she could still pick up on the distant sense of the blacksmith, although he was deep beneath the ground. More than that, now that she understood what it was, she could hear the hammering. It was a constant sound, and she could ignore it for long stretches of time, but when she began to think about the blacksmith, she became far more aware of the hammering.

"I have wondered why the Great One didn't share with me that your temple manufactures the sacred metal."

"Does the Great One share all things with you?"

"No. Often, he wants me to discover them on my own."

"Why?"

"It's in his nature to question, but also to observe. He wants that for others as well. He is an observer of many things, and through that, he has an understanding of the way the world works."

"And what has he asked you to observe?"

"Everything." She turned toward him. "The attack on

the temple occurred because of experiments with the sacred metal."

"There were no experiments—"

Ryn raised her hand, cutting him off. "I saw the metal in the room where the attack took place. Such a thing would be unusual. Either the Great One knew that you were using the metal in such a way, or he did not, and you were hoping to conceal it. Given that the Great One would've mentioned to me if such use of the metal was allowed, I suspect the rest was something you were hoping to keep from him."

She watched Lorren and saw no expression on his face, nothing to reveal what she suspected. The more she had learned in the city, and the more she had begun to understand about both the blacksmith and Dillon, along with Lorren, the better understanding she had of what they were attempting here.

It was secretive, and it was their intent to defy the Great One by maintaining those secrets. It was the kind of thing the Great One would be disturbed by. Then again, she suspected that they wanted to keep it from the Great One.

"As his emissary, I will be reporting what I have observed."

Lorren stared at her for a moment. "No."

She cocked her head to the side. "No?"

Lorren glanced behind him, and Ryn turned. The door opened, and there were two priests standing there. She didn't recognize either of them, not having met them in her time here. One was tall and slender, his dark hair cropped close, thick eyebrows on a sloping forehead, and a wide nose. Bluish metal pierced either side of his temple.

The sacred metal.

The other person was shorter, her long hair swept over one shoulder, and yet she appeared muscular in a surprising way. Ryn searched for any evidence that the woman had the sacred metal on her but didn't come up with anything.

It was possible she had an implant much like Ryn did.

"What is this?" Ryn asked.

"This is me intending to have words with you."

"Were we not having them already?" Ryn tried to steady the hammering in her chest. Her heart seemed to be fluttering, pounding loudly. Lorren had to know how anxious she was, and yet she was forced to try to keep her face as serene as possible. She didn't want him to know what she was feeling.

"You were accusing me of behavior that would force the Great One to take action."

"I think you are forcing the Great One to take action through what you are doing now."

"Only if he finds out."

"You don't think he will?"

"I think that by the time we are done working with you, it won't matter."

Lorren nodded, and the man and woman hurried forward, grabbing for her. Ryn tried to fight but couldn't.

"You're making a mistake."

"The mistake was not acting sooner."

They dragged her away, and she craned her neck, trying to watch for Lorren as she disappeared back into the temple, but he stayed out on the tower. Ryn didn't bother shouting or crying out. Neither of the two holding her made any attempt to speak to her. She wasn't surprised, as it seemed as if they were deeply involved with whatever Lorren had planned.

She should have known better than to linger there. Then again, she had thought herself safe, thought that her role as the Great One's emissary had granted her protection, instead of recognizing the danger that her position placed her in.

"What do you intend to do with me?" she asked.

Neither of them answered.

Ryn found herself carried into a side room. In her time in the temple, she had investigated all of the rooms, stopping in them, sweeping her gaze around, looking for anything that might help her understand what had taken place here, but there had been nothing.

This room reminded her of the one she occupied. The walls were paneled, but it was small and windowless.

The woman forced her into a chair, and when she was done, she pulled one of Ryn's arms out, binding it to the armrest. It took Ryn a moment to realize she was using the sacred metal in order to do so. They shouldn't have this much here. When she was done, she did the same thing with her other arm, wrapping a band of the sacred metal around it, strapping it to the armrest.

Pain coursed through her, starting at her arms, rolling along her and reaching her shoulders. When they strapped her legs in, the pain increased, and she cried out.

Tears streamed down her face, and when they cleared, she realized she was alone. They had her bound, strapped into the chair, and there was nothing she could do to escape it.

She forced herself to think, to try to clear her mind and come up with an understanding of what was taking place here. *Observe and detect.* The Great One's words came to her even now. What else could she detect?

The room was small. She was alone, as far as she could tell. Her arms and legs throbbed, the sacred metal causing pain to work its way along the surface of her skin, a reminder of the experience she'd had when they had placed the implant the first time. That had been powerfully painful, overwhelmingly so, and yet this was similar.

She couldn't think about anything else. The pain made it difficult to focus.

Lorren had been the one involved all along. And here she had questioned his role with Dillon, when instead she should have been questioning the role of the sacred metal and why they had it here. She had wondered about it but had never thought they were manufacturing it. Having a blacksmith—two, actually—should have raised her suspicions long ago, and yet she hadn't questioned the way that she should have.

The Great One would be disappointed that it took her so long to learn this lesson.

Ever since coming to serve the Great One, Ryn had known no danger. He had protected her, welcoming her, and when he had made her his emissary, she had been granted a place that she otherwise would not have. Now she was suddenly thrust into danger again.

Everything throbbed within her. It seemed to be

beating in time with her heart, pulsing, and she focused on the bands around her wrist.

Observe and detect.

With her heightened senses, she suspected everything the sacred metal did to her was more intense than it would otherwise be. If only she could reach with one hand, she might be able to move the metal. She wouldn't be strong enough to unwind the bands and was surprised they had managed to wrap them around her arms and legs as if they were no more than leather strips.

The strips of metal prevented her from moving her hands much, starting around her wrists and working their way up her forearms. Each place the metal pressed into her skin seemed to burn, though she knew that had to be her imagination. Even if it wasn't, it was likely nothing more than her heightened senses from the implant placed in the back of her head.

Why use the sacred metal for this?

Did they think she could travel? If they did, metal like this might have the potential to restrain someone from traveling the way the Great One did. And yet, she had shown no sign of being able to travel, so unless Lorren was being overly cautious, there had to be another reason.

Ryn lost track of how long she was here, losing herself to the pain, trying to force her mind to focus, but failing.

"You hurt."

Ryn blinked her eyes, looking up and trying to see who was standing across from her. Could it be Lorren?

Rather than Lorren, it was the blacksmith.

"What are you doing here?"

"I came to check on you."

"Release me and I will ensure the Great One knows you helped free me."

"Release you? I don't think so."

"You would oppose the Great One?"

"Why would I oppose him? He has given me access to what I could not get on my own."

Ryn tried to look up, but the pain picked up in intensity, making it difficult for her to focus. "You're responsible for this?"

"I've been here for many years."

"I knew you did not view the Great One the same as others, but I thought…"

Ryn wasn't entirely sure what she had thought. Only that he was different than what she had expected. She certainly didn't expect the blacksmith to be responsible for what was happening to her, not having seen any sign of that from him. It surprised her that he would be so blatant about opposing the Great One.

"When he suppressed the temple, I acquiesced. What choice did I have? I fell into line, allowing myself to serve."

"The Great One will find out what you've done."

"Perhaps, but I think that he will not. In time, it won't matter. We will use his knowledge and his control against him."

"Why?"

"Because I serve another." Ryn started to shake her head, and a blacksmith approached, resting his hands on her forearms. "I find it interesting that you suffer so much from the effect of this. You shouldn't feel it like this, but then again, everyone has a different reaction when they are touched by it."

"Let me go, and I will not share with the Great One what you've done."

"I think it's too late for that. There was a mistake here, and now he's aware of us. Leaving you here was another sign. Unfortunately, I don't think I can continue to make that mistake."

Ryn thrashed, trying to break free of the metal. It didn't budge. She wasn't strong enough. She might have augmentations, she might have gifts that the Great One had given her, but she was now at the mercy of the blacksmith.

"You're responsible for what happened here?"

"Not me. That was a mistake, and it's one that should not have happened. The man responsible for it paid the price."

"Then what?"

Her head felt like it was growing heavy, thoughts beginning to swim within her mind. She couldn't concentrate on anything, and although she knew she needed to gain that focus, it didn't come to her the way she needed it to.

"You will find that service here is easier if you relent."

"What?"

"Relent."

There was pressure, and as she felt it, Ryn became aware of where it was coming from.

The blacksmith.

Not only was there pressure there, but it seemed as if it were trying to force her thoughts. She had seen others within the Ai'thol do that. The Great One had trained her to fortify her mind to avoid the influence of others. She couldn't be an effective emissary and his steward if she had no strength to withstand an internal attack like that.

As she struggled, she realized the sacred metal was pushing against her, making it more and more difficult for her to maintain her resistance.

That was the reason behind it. He was using it against her.

"When you begin to relent, you will find you can serve."

She blinked away the tears, trying to fortify her mind. The blacksmith would use her?

No. She wasn't about to be used. She had seen far too many others get used. It was the reason she served the Great One as willingly as she did. He wanted to free others from a similar fate. She wanted to ensure none suffered the way she had suffered. And the Great One would be the end of Lareth.

Somehow, she had to fight.

The blacksmith smiled at her. "Perhaps you need more time. I have no problem allowing you that time to consider. Eventually, you will find that the metal changes you. And whatever your Great One has given you to resist will fail."

She didn't see him leave. The only thing she was aware of was the door closing.

Pain pulsed through her, and somehow—some way— Ryn knew she was going to have to escape.

The only problem was she didn't know if she could.

RYN

RYN LOST TRACK OF TIME. SHE SUSPECTED THAT WAS intentional. Every time she started to drift off, someone would come in and jostle her, keeping her awake. Most of the time, it was little more than harassment, nothing more, and certainly she could handle a little pestering, but it prevented her from resting. Sleeplessness was its own sort of torture.

She welcomed the pain. She had no choice but to do so. It was a constant companion, the steady and persistent burning working through her arms and legs, a sense of torment that she couldn't shake. Instead, she focused on what she could control. Her breathing. Her mind. Her response to the pain.

Through it all came the Great One's reminder for her to observe.

There was nothing here for her to observe other than her own reaction to the events. As much as she wanted to ignore those pains, she decided to embrace them. How else would she be able to report to the Great One what she had experienced?

The question rolled through her mind: what did she detect?

It was a burning sensation, starting deep within her wrists, and it worked up her arms, ending in her shoulders.

It wasn't just her arms that throbbed. Her legs did as well, a steady pulsating sense that she couldn't shake. Agony rolled through her, and she tried to ignore it, but there was no ignoring. It was all she knew.

That was part of the intention. It was the way the blacksmith meant to disrupt her thinking, and yet if she could hold on to herself, she could continue to maintain her focus, to prevent him from getting inside her mind and using her.

That was what he wanted.

The lesson the Great One had taught her about preventing that stayed with her. It was difficult, but she knew that she could withstand it. She had no choice but to do so.

Ever since her blessing, it had been easier for her to fortify her mind as the Great One instructed. What she needed now was to ensure that it was stout, that it remained a firm barrier, blocking anyone else from reaching into her mind. She would not allow that.

When the door opened again, Ryn looked over. She wasn't surprised to see Lorren enter. He had been one of her frequent tormentors, and the joy he took in doing so surprised her.

"You still fight," he said.

"And you still allow him to use you."

"Do you think he uses me?"

Ryn grunted. "I know I can prevent access to my mind. The Great One himself taught me."

"Did he? Or is the Great One himself the one who is controlling your mind?"

Ryn didn't think that was the case. Why would he teach her how to protect herself if he intended to control her? No. This was another way they wanted to force her to ignore the teachings of the Great One. She wasn't about to get caught up in that. She knew the Great One had taught her, that he had helped her, and she was not about to think otherwise.

"You fear him," she said.

"The Great One? He's powerful."

"Not him. Him." She nodded toward the door. She didn't need the blacksmith to be inside for her to recognize that he was standing on the other side of the door. She could feel him. Regardless of what they did to her, the way they used these metal bars wrapped around her forearms, that awareness of him remained.

The only one she hadn't sensed since her capture was Dillon. She supposed that should be a relief.

"You don't understand."

"What's there not to understand? He controls you, and others within the temple."

"Are you so sure? He has freed us. Because of him, we do not have to fear the influence of others like the Great One. We recognize that he has given us a gift."

Ryn smiled to herself. The Great One had been curious about this place, and she had wondered what it had been before the temple had been taken over by the Ai'thol, but she never would have expected that a black-smith would be the one who controlled the people within it.

"I will fight him."

"How long do you think you can fight? Eventually you will get hungry. You will get thirsty. Eventually you will need what he can provide."

"I'd rather die."

Lorren held her gaze. "If that's the case, then so be it."

He backed away, and Ryn tried to spit at him, but she had no saliva in her mouth. "You can tell him I know he's on the other side of the door."

Lorren hesitated for a moment, frowning, and then he shook his head. "He wouldn't remain behind for you. He is an important man and busy, and there are many things he needs to do and prepare for."

"He won't be able to overpower the Great One."

"Overpower? That has never been his intention."

When the door closed, Ryn was left in darkness once again, and yet her eyesight allowed her to make out the various gradations of shadow. She had begun to give up hope of escape. There was no way for her to do so. They had her bound too tightly.

If only she could break free from the chair.

A memory drifted to her. Hadn't that been what she had come to investigate?

She tried to stand but couldn't. She was weak, her time confined here having stolen strength from her, and the longer she was here, the weaker she was going to get. She needed to act soon. Otherwise, any opportunity to escape would be lost.

Ryn put pressure on her legs. She had to ignore the pain surging through them, the increased intensity that burned within her as she put weight down on them, the throbbing that rolled through her from the metal wrapped around her ankles.

For a moment she hovered, holding herself upward.

And she dropped.

Ryn threw all of her weight onto the chair. It was stout, and she was not heavy, but the sudden drop was enough to cause the chair to creak.

She took that as a positive sign. Standing again, she held on, trying to ignore the pain that rolled through her, knowing she had to hold out, though uncertain how she would be able to do so. The pressure was enormous, the pain intense, and everything within her hurt. As she stood, it rolled up her legs through her thighs and into her midsection. It was almost enough to make her…

Ryn crashed back down to the floor, slamming into the chair again.

She sat there for a moment, her head spinning, tears streaming from her eyes, surprising her that she still had the moisture to cry. She swallowed and tasted a coppery flavor in her mouth. Had she bit her tongue? It was difficult to determine what hurt since everything did.

When there was no other sound, and when her head began to finally settle, Ryn stood once again. She was determined to keep doing this until she passed out, or until someone else came in.

This time, the pain shot all the way through her,

heading from her toes all the way up into her head before rolling back through her chest and down her arms. It was almost as if the pain from the two places she was bound worked together, intensifying it, and she could no longer stand. As much as she tried, she found that she couldn't hold out.

Ryn collapsed into the chair, sagging backward, and she looked around.

Not the chair.

She sat on the floor.

Splintered wood lay all around her, reminding her of the scene she had gone to investigate.

Unlike that moment, the sacred metal was wrapped around her. Now that her arms and legs were free, she tried to slip the sacred metal off her wrist, but it wouldn't move. They had it wrapped too tightly. Ryn tried to unwind it, but it wouldn't budge. She rolled over, looking down at her legs, and found the same thing there.

Worse, where the metal had been wrapped, the ends now pierced her ankles. Blood oozed around the piercings. She didn't think that had been the case before.

When she looked at her wrists, she noticed something similar.

Her head felt heavy.

What would happen to her?

She had been so focused on escaping, getting free of the metal wrapped around her, that she hadn't considered what she would do when she finally managed to get free. There wasn't anything on either side of the door that she could escape to, and though she didn't detect Lorren or the blacksmith nearby, she knew they had to be some-where here.

The advantage she had was that she had studied the temple. In the time since she'd come here, she'd pored over records, over the books, and had focused, searching for answers about the place.

What she needed to do was get out of the room, find someone who could help pry the sacred metal off her wrists and ankles before it did anything more to harm her.

Ryn got to her feet. With each step, pain coursed through her, and she tried to ignore it, but it was intense. Spots shone in front of her eyes, and every so often, it felt as if the room was spinning around her, forcing her to focus.

She paused at the door, leaning on it a moment to gather herself.

As she rested there, she tried to ignore the pain, but it was more than just the pain she had to overlook. There was something else—another sensation—and she wasn't entirely sure what it meant.

What was it? She needed to understand that. If she could understand what she detected, perhaps she could use it.

There came a stirring sense within her stomach.

Nausea. That was what she detected.

She'd known nausea quite well in the time since her capture. Had it only been a day? Could it have been longer? She'd lost track, and with the number of disrup-tions they had made with her, it was their intent to ensure she couldn't recover and focus on maintaining her mental barriers.

Ryn took a deep breath. She pushed away the sense of nausea, the throbbing in her legs and arms, and pulled open the door.

There was no one there.

She would've expected a guard or someone to be keeping an eye on her, but they must have believed her trapped.

Perhaps she should have been.

Ryn staggered out into the hallway. She leaned on the wall for support, running her hand along the stone, feeling the smooth surface beneath her fingertips. As she went, her heart racing, the nausea threatened to return, and she pushed it away again.

She found stairs. Up meant to the top of the tower. She wouldn't go there.

Down ran the risk of encountering others within the temple, but she also had a chance of escaping. Then she could get word to the Great One.

She started down the stairs. She had to pause to rest on the walls, putting her head down, as everything continued to spin around her.

As it did, she felt a throbbing, a pulsating sense, that came from everywhere within her. It took a moment for her to realize that pulsating focused on the back of her head.

She reached back, fingering the blessing, but it was gone.

Had they removed it?

Such a thing was not possible. If the Great One said it

couldn't be done, she had a hard time believing the black-smith would have managed to do so. It meant it had fully integrated into her skin. She knew that it was happening anyway but didn't know what that meant for her. Now that it was there, there was no removing it. Not that she would want to do so. It was a gift from the Great One himself. It was a return of her powers, a return of what she would have been had she remained in the land of her parents when she was younger.

When the pain abated, she continued on the stairs, hurrying cautiously along. She took the stairs one at a time, and when she began to wobble, staggering a little bit, she paused to gather herself. Every so often, there came a sense of nausea, but she pushed it away. She managed to ignore that sense and focused instead on the pain. She welcomed it, embracing it. As she did that, it seemed to become less.

Where were Lorren and the blacksmith? Those were the two she was most aware of, but she didn't detect them.

That was odd. They should be here, shouldn't they?

She tried to think when she had last been aware of them but couldn't come up with an answer. As far as she could tell, the last time had been when Lorren had tormented her, moments before she had started to drop into the chair, attempting to break herself free.

He wouldn't have been able to disappear so quickly… unless he could travel.

Had she seen anything from him that would suggest he could travel?

Dillon could. She didn't know if the blacksmith could, but the idea that it was possible lingered. If they both could, then there wouldn't be any place they couldn't go.

She reached the base of the temple.

She needed to get out of here and find a way to get word to the Great One. If she did that, though, she would leave behind her records.

Her room was only one floor above.

When she reached the door leading outside, she decided to turn back. Hurrying up the stairs, Ryn felt waves of nausea threatening to spill over her, and she pushed it away, forcing that queasiness from her.

This hallway was empty as well. When she started down it, she expected to find someone, anyone, but she didn't. Throwing open the door, she found the room much as she had left it. Her cloak was there, and it surprised her they would have brought her cloak, but then, they might have wanted to search it the same way they probably had searched everything in this room.

Ryn took it, slipping it on, covering the metal. It did nothing to ease the pain, but she continued to embrace that sensation, welcoming it, thinking that if she could accept it, perhaps she could overpower it.

There were only a few books that were important to her. They were the observations she'd made in the time she had served the Great One, and she found them stacked near one corner. Ryn grabbed them, stuffing them into her cloak pocket, and started to turn when nausea rolled over her.

It was almost too much. She sank to the floor, the sickness slamming into her over and over again.

"No!"

She forced it away from her, and it slowly eased off.

Getting to her feet, she hesitated, afraid the nausea would return, but it didn't. Instead, she found that she was steadier than she had been in a while. She headed toward the door, staggering, the pain making her gait strange. She took step after step, and with each one, she felt stronger. At the stairs, she looked down. There seemed to be some shimmering movement, and with it came the sense of nausea, which she forced away.

The shimmering disappeared.

Maybe it was only her imagination, or related to the sickness that she was feeling. She had seen the way people often shut down when suffering from severe pain.

At the door leading out of the temple, she paused, looking outside. The sky was gray. She couldn't tell what time of day it was, the sun hidden by the clouds, and people moved along the street in the distance. She could hear and see them, smelling their presence along with that of their animals.

Ryn started toward the sense of the people. She wanted to get out into the crowd, wanted to disappear, to fade into that, and do anything that would help her escape.

She stumbled with each step, dragging herself.

Nausea washed over her, and as she tried to push away, she failed.

Something shimmered in front of her. Ryn staggered forward, trying to run, fearing there might be someone here who would attack. She couldn't help but feel as if someone were traveling toward her, and that the shimmering was the preceding effect from someone traveling, but as she moved forward, that sense faded.

Maybe it was nothing more than her imagination.

Nausea rolled through her again, and she tried to force it away, hurrying toward the distant sense of people, and failed.

Ryn collapsed on the ground. She couldn't keep her head up, and as the pain and nausea continued to roll through her, she felt herself failing.

If the blacksmith found her, he would overpower her mental barriers.

She couldn't have that. She didn't want him to get into her mind, to force her to act against the Great One, but she was in no shape to fight.

Scrambling to her knees, Ryn tried to move forward, to make her way from where she had fallen in the street, when another surge of nausea rolled over her.

This time, she couldn't fight.

She sagged down to the ground, the sense overwhelming, and blacked out.

26

HAERN

WITH THE REALIZATION THAT RAYEN WAS THERE, HAERN tried to *pull* on his connection to the metal, attempting to withdraw the lorcith, to prevent it from hitting her or anyone who might be with her, but he wasn't strong enough.

He fell back, everything within him hurting.

As he stared upward, mouthing an apology to Rayen that he knew wouldn't matter, darkness swirled around him.

It lingered for a moment. Then another. And then another.

When it cleared, he realized he was still alive.

Hands reached underneath him, grabbing him, pulling him along. Someone tried to lift him, but they set him back on the ground.

What was taking place here?

His mind remained a haze. He tried to think through what was going on, and whether there was any way for him to understand it.

There wasn't anything.

Rayen was here, and she should not be. There was no reason for her to be.

He couldn't make sense of what was happening. Everything throbbed, and when someone pressed something to his lips, he spat against it, determined not to be poisoned.

"Drink," someone said.

He thought he recognized the voice, but he wasn't entirely certain. If it was Rayen, why was she here?

None of this made any sense.

Somebody brought something else to his lips, and Haern spat again.

Pressure on the back of his neck forced his mouth open, and something was poured into it. It was thick, unpleasant, and he tried to spit, but he couldn't.

"Drink."

Again, he thought he recognized the voice.

Who would it have been?

"If you want to live, you need to drink."

Galen?

That couldn't be, either. They weren't anywhere near Elaeavn. But then again, Galen had been with him, hadn't he? He remembered the attack, much like he remembered how Galen had taken on several Forgers at once. There was no way he should have been able to get away from the Forgers, no way for him to have survived.

Haern drank, swallowing the liquid.

It burned as it went down his throat. There was something unpleasant about it, but then there was often something unpleasant about the things Galen offered him.

He lay there, a part of him expecting that poison would work through him, that he would pass out from it, another part thinking that perhaps Galen had given him a restorative. He didn't know which it was going to be. All he knew was that everything hurt.

After a while, there was pressure in his shoulder, as if someone were digging around within it. If they were, he needed to ignore the pain.

The pain in his shoulder began to ease, and he felt something on his thigh as well, where he had sustained his other wound. Hands pressed down on either side of his thigh, clamping down with a firm grip, holding his leg in place. Haern tried to move, feeling a surge of fear at being trapped like this. Panic set in, sending his heart fluttering.

"Just relax," somebody whispered to him.

Haern lost track of who it was, but at the same time, he didn't think he could relax under the circumstances.

Sharp agony worked through his leg again, the same sort of pain he'd experienced in his shoulder, and as he tried to pull away, the hands holding down on his leg prevented him from doing so.

"There's something else, but I can't get to it," a different voice said, one Haern didn't recognize.

"What else is there?"

"It appears something injured his hands."

"Lorcith," Haern muttered. "Or something like it."

Someone grabbed his hand, squeezing. Warmth washed through him, the kind of Healing warmth he had felt when Darren had worked on him. Could Darren be here?

Why would he have come outside of the city?

Unless someone had come for him, Sliding him back to Elaeavn.

If that was the case, then what would happen to Jayna and the others?

He tried opening his eyes, needing to look around, but couldn't.

All he saw was darkness.

It was a wonder his mind still worked, and that there wasn't more confusion. He felt off, though he wasn't able to explain why. It was a strange sensation where everything seemed wrong. The longer he experienced it, the more worried he became.

Would the attack have taken his ability to use lorcith?

As strange as it was, that was his greatest fear. After having finally begun to see the value in lorcith, he didn't want to lose it.

Another wave of Healing washed over him.

"It's like the other."

"Lucy?" someone said.

"Somewhat like that, though different. This has burrowed beneath the skin. I can't take it out without harming him."

"Leave it," Haern said. At least, he tried to. He wasn't sure how much he was saying clearly at this point.

"What happened?" someone said. Galen?

Haern wasn't sure. His vision was blurry, darkness all around him, and he suspected that came from Rayen. With her control over the shadows, he wouldn't be surprised if she was the reason he couldn't detect anything.

"Forgers," Haern said. "Trapped me. Metal broke off."
It was more than that, though he wasn't sure how to explain it. Much like he wasn't sure how to explain why the metal had seemed to be absorbed within him. He doubted that was the Forgers' intent. From what he could tell, that had surprised them as much as it had surprised Haern. More than that, it seemed as if the side effect, that of his increased connection to lorcith, was not intended.

Had it been intended for Lucy?

It was possible it wasn't.

But then, from what they knew of it, what happened to Lucy was different. The attack had never been the Forgers in the first place. It was someone else.

"How long will it take him to come around?"

"I don't know. I've given him everything I can to restore him, but it might take some time."

Haern let out a shaky breath. He could already feel the effect of whatever had struck him beginning to fade. His mind had been a fog before, and that seemed lessened. Now whatever it was that afflicted him only impacted his connection to his abilities.

He tested, searching for whether he could reach for lorcith. If he could, he might be able to relax, to lie back and wait for the rest of the poisoning to clear—if it would.

For a moment, he wasn't sure if it would. But the longer he focused, the more certain he was that he could detect lorcith.

It was there in his sword, though it wasn't near him. It was there in the knives still within his pocket. It was there in something else, a strange sense near him, though it was something he didn't entirely understand.

What was that?

The longer he focused on it, the more uncertain he was.

The pressure on his leg eased off, and he had the sense that he was no longer being held down. He couldn't hear anything, but there seemed to be a faint murmuring nearby. Haern focused on his breathing, on the sense of pain, but even that was beginning to fade.

It might be that it would leave him altogether.

Slowly, his eyesight began to clear. As it did, he looked around, thinking that if nothing else, maybe he would be able to make out movement, something that would confirm that Galen was here, but there wasn't anything.

If it was Galen—and Haern hoped that it was—where was he?

Had it been Rayen?

There was a possibility that it wasn't.

There were others who had the ability to control shadows. Carth came to mind, but Haern had a hard time thinking Carth would be here, either. Then again, it didn't make any sense that Rayen would have been here.

He rolled his head from side to side, trying to focus on where he was. It seemed to be a narrow room, with wooden walls on either side and a planked wooden ceiling. There was no decoration, nothing that seemed to adorn the walls.

A wagon.

That had to be where he was, but how?

"Easy," a voice said.

Haern blinked, and some of the haziness cleared. He looked over, his eyesight starting to return. "Galen?"

"I didn't expect to see you here."

"What happened?"

"I'd like to ask you that, but I'm not sure how much you will remember."

"I remember everything."

27

HAERN

HAERN CLOSED HIS EYES AGAIN, TRYING TO THINK ABOUT just how much he did remember. Everything about the attack had been something of a blur, and the moment he'd been struck by the nails, he'd started to lose track of everything else.

The spheres.

"Were the lorcith spheres yours?" he asked.

Haern looked over to Galen, and the other man leaned in. He smelled of spice, heat, and something else that Haern couldn't quite place.

"They weren't ours. That's why we're here." Galen watched him until he seemed satisfied that Haern was still awake. "We've been tracking those spheres. There have been a dozen or so explosions, all throughout various empty fields. We've been trying to understand what the Forgers have been after, but we haven't been able to determine anything."

"I don't think it is the Forgers."

"Why?"

"These spheres are pure lorcith, not an alloy like I'd expect from the Forgers." Haern's hand went to his shoulder, fingering where the nail had penetrated. The skin was smooth, Healed over. There wasn't anyone else here other than Galen, so if Darren had been here, he had disappeared. "They have these spikes, nails, and those nails explode. I managed to stop one, but…"

"About that," Galen said.

"What?"

The older man leaned in. His bright deep green eyes met Haern's. "How is it that you were able to contain one of those spheres?"

"My control over lorcith."

"The force of the explosions is considerable."

"It is."

"We have someone from your smith guild who has tried to contain it but failed."

"Who?"

"Your grandfather."

Haern's breath caught. His grandfather was here?

It was strange thinking that he would want to see his grandfather, but at the same time, after everything he'd been through, a familiar face, especially one as caring as his grandfather's, would be welcome.

"What about my grandfather?"

"Neran made it clear he wasn't able to contain one of those explosions. He thought it was quite unlikely anyone other than your father would be able to do so."

"Was Darren here?"

Galen shook his head.

"Someone Healed me."

"Not Darren. It was Della."

Haern blinked. As far as he had known, Della was gone, maybe dead, but certainly not available to help heal someone like himself. But apparently...

"You heard what she said about the metal in my hands."

Galen nodded.

"I was in some southern city, helping others—"

With the thought, Haern started to sit up. What had happened to Jayna and the others? He needed to find them, to see if there was anything he could do to help them, to ensure they weren't harmed. But Galen was there, pressing his hand on his shoulder, trying to get him to lean back.

"There were others with me," Haern said. "I don't know what happened to them, but I need to—"

"They're fine, Haern. We found them. We have them sequestered."

"Sequestered?"

"They were a bit feisty."

"How long have I been out?"

"Quite a while."

What would've happened to Elise? They were only supposed to have been gone for a night, no more. Would Elise be worried about him?

He knew she would. Would she have stayed in place, waiting for Haern and the rest of them to return, or would she have gone onward, trying to move away? If she had done that, would she have come into contact with the other four wagons he'd detected?

"I was captured when I was trying to help them,"

Haern said, trying to relax. He clenched his hand, feeling the strange metal beneath it as he often did. "The metal became a part of me. When it did, it changed my connection to lorcith."

"That's how you were able to contain the explosion?"

"It seems that way."

"That's useful."

"That's not all," Haern said.

"What else?"

"I've been able to use the metal in a far more effective way ever since the explosion. It's sort of like what happened to Lucy, though I don't think mine was intentional the way hers was."

"Yours was the Ai'thol?"

Haern nodded. "I think it was. Listen, Galen. I appreciate that you're here. I need to check on the others, and I need to get back to the rest."

"The rest? Haern, we have quite a lot to talk about."

"And I will be happy to talk with you about it, but I can't leave them."

Galen frowned, studying him. "What happened to you?"

"More than I could imagine, and since my father is gone—"

"What?"

"I captured a Forger. I forced him to Slide me to where they were holding my father. He's gone. Whatever they did to him killed him."

Galen stared at him for a moment. "I'm sorry."

"I know. I am too, and yet, I haven't allowed myself a chance to grieve. There hasn't been an opportunity. Even if there was, my father has been absent for so much of my life that it's hard for me to know how I'm supposed to feel."

"You're supposed to feel sadness, Haern."

"I do feel sadness. And I worry about telling my mother, especially as I don't know how she's going to react to knowing he's finally gone."

"Did you see his body?"

Haern blinked, meeting Galen's eyes for a moment before shaking his head. "That is a little bit morbid, even for you, Galen."

"Morbid or not, if you didn't see the body, then it's unlikely your father is gone."

"What?"

"If he's anything like Carth—and from what I've seen of Rsiran, he is—it means either he wants others to think he's gone, or the Ai'thol still have him, trying to convince you he's dead. Either way, this is all part of some larger play."

Haern swallowed. If it was possible that his father still lived, what was he supposed to do? He couldn't go after him, not without having any idea where his father might be, and not now that he had another responsibility.

"I promised the others I would ensure they got to Asador safely."

"Why Asador?"

"Because they can find safety with the Binders."

Galen flicked his gaze toward the far end of the wagon, and Haern turned to see a door there.

"They were captured, Galen. I'm sure Carth won't like to hear this, but there are women who claim to be the

Binders in other places, and they are using the threat of the Binders to make others believe they're something they're not."

Galen whistled softly, leaning back. "Maybe it's best you be the one to tell Carth that."

"You don't want to?"

"Knowing how seriously she takes the Binders, I don't know that Carth will appreciate it all that much. She will probably go to investigate."

"She would need help."

"They have it. They're working with others who can Slide."

"Daniel?"

"Him, but it's more than him."

That meant Lucy.

"Maybe I should just let them take care of it."

"That might be for the best," Galen said.

Haern sat up, ignoring Galen as he tried to hold him down. He shook the other man off, and he looked around, feeling how cramped he was inside this small wagon.

"What happened to the people who had the wagons?"

"You took out some. The women with you took out some. And we finished it."

"Why?"

"Well, considering that we don't know who they're with, we did our best to try to eliminate the threat of them, but I'm not sure we got them all."

"We're missing four wagons," Haern said.

"Four?"

"There were twelve when I came to investigate, and there were only eight when we returned."

"How did you investigate?"

Haern pointed up. "With my connection to lorcith being what it is, I can travel a whole lot more easily than I used to be able to."

"It seems as if you *have* been through quite a bit in the last month."

"More than you can know."

"Would you care to tell me about what you experienced?"

Haern looked around. What was there to tell? So much had happened to him, and he had changed. All this time he had wanted more power, and it wasn't until he had gone to the Forgers, nearly losing himself, that he had been able to get it.

"Another time, Galen."

Galen studied him for a moment. "I think I understand."

"Do you?"

"You're concerned about others. I understand that."

"I'm worried about what will happen if I don't get to them."

"Then don't let me hold you back."

Haern pulled the door open, stepping outside. It was early morning. Light had crept over the top of the wagons. He took a deep breath, feeling surprisingly well despite everything he'd been through. As he looked around, he saw the remains of the fire, now burned down to coals. Stepping out toward it, he felt the sense of lorcith surge, power that came from the sphere he'd exploded, the small nails scattered all around.

And yet, they hadn't scattered nearly as far as he had

expected. That had been Rayen's doing. He was certain of that. Rayen had somehow held the nails in place, keeping them from striking anyone.

Why would they have needed his grandfather if Rayen was so capable?

Unless they weren't sure.

Galen joined him, looking around.

"Where are they?"

He pointed to one of the wagons, and as he did, Haern focused on the sense of lorcith, recognizing the coin. He didn't even need Galen to point, the ability to detect the lorcith guiding him as much as anything else.

"They're unharmed?"

Galen glanced over at him, arching a brow. "Do you know nothing about me?"

"I wouldn't have expected you to have harmed them, but if they attacked…"

"They're skilled. I should have known where they obtained their training earlier."

"I wasn't going to leave them helpless," Haern said.

"I think Carth would appreciate that."

"Do you think she would take them in?"

"You could talk to Rayen after you speak with them."

"I don't know how long I have here. There are others waiting for us."

"Perhaps you should go to them."

"Not without speaking to Jayna and the others first."

Galen considered him for a moment before nodding.

Haern followed the sense of lorcith, reaching the wagon. Once he was there, he pulled the door open. Inside, the five women sat on the benches along the wall.

Jayna saw him, and everything within her seemed to tense.

"Haern?"

"You can come out," he said.

"What is this?"

"Some of these are my people."

"They attacked us."

"The merchants—or whatever they were—weren't my people, but they helped."

Jayna followed him out of the wagon, stepping into the daylight. She blinked, looking up at the sky.

"I know," Haern said.

"They will be worried."

"Most likely."

Jayna frowned at him, studying his shirt. It took him a moment to realize why.

Haern fingered the injury, tapping his chest. "I was caught by one of the nails."

"You don't look injured."

"I was Healed."

"Healed?"

"You asked about the abilities people from my home-land have?" She nodded. "One of them is Healing. It's an ability that allows us to restore people to a certain point."

"And this ability was used on you?"

"It seems that way."

Haern glanced to Galen. "I'm going to see if I can't find the others."

"We have someone who can Slide," Galen said. "If you can wait—"

"I'm not willing to wait until someone returns."

Galen studied him for a moment. Haern wasn't sure if he was going to tell him not to go, but instead, Galen only nodded. "Go quickly."

Haern glanced over to Jayna. "I won't be long."

He dropped a coin and *pushed*. With that, he went soaring into the air. He focused on the sense of lorcith, drawing the coin he'd dropped to him, and found he was *pulling* on some of the nails as well. They would work just as well as coins, and he sent them streaking in front of him, tied to him in a way that would allow him to move faster and faster. Healed as he was, he found that he could move quickly, and he raced back in the direction of the camp from the night before. As he went, he focused on lorcith, searching for the knife Elise carried.

He found it, but it wasn't where he expected.

It was quite a bit farther away.

Thankfully he was able to move quickly enough that he could chase the sense of lorcith. He streaked toward it, toward Elise, and as he did, he realized something was amiss.

There were the four wagons.

The sense of lorcith came from within them.

Great Watcher!

He hadn't expected the others would've been attacked by the remaining wagons.

Haern hung suspended in the air for a moment, using his connection to lorcith to try to detect where Elise was within the wagons.

She was in the middle one.

If these people were anything like the others—and he

suspected they were, considering they had traveled together—they would be just as likely to attack.

Maybe he should have brought Galen with him.

There was no point in hesitating, no point in slowing himself. He dropped near the front wagon. Two men sat atop horses, guiding the wagons, and Haern *pushed* on a bundle of nails he'd been dragging with them. The nails streaked forward, crashing into the riders, who fell off the wagon.

Someone cried out, and Haern *pushed*, dragging a coin toward him before spinning higher into the sky, sending himself streaking away from the wagons. He hovered, looking at the people down below, and as he did, he continued to *push* on the nails. He used his connection to lorcith to *push* and *pull*, dragging it, knocking down the people on the wagons.

They fell quickly.

Haern had a hard time finding any remorse. These people had attacked his friends. He had no idea why, or what they had in mind, but he wasn't about to sit back and wait, hoping nothing happened. They had proven their intentions already.

Haern went wagon by wagon, using his connection to lorcith to destroy everyone he came in contact with.

And then there were no more.

Even though no others remained, he still didn't know if he'd removed the entire threat. He waited, worried there might still be others who could reach him, but when no more appeared, Haern dropped near the wagons, heading toward the one where he felt the lorcith. He would get to Elise first, and then he would see about the others, looking to see why these attackers had come after his people. His friends.

Like the other wagon's had been, the door was locked.

Haern jabbed his sword into the padlock and pried it open. It came slowly, snapping open, and he jerked the remains of the lock free.

When he pulled the door open, there was a part of him that worried he'd been mistaken and there wouldn't be anything inside.

Elise was there.

When she saw him, she jumped toward him, wrapping her arms around him.

"When you didn't come—"

"I know. I'm sorry."

"What happened?"

"We were attacked."

"I thought…" She shook her head, turning away.

"You thought what?"

Elise smiled at him, and Haern knew he would do whatever he could to ensure that nothing happened to her.

"We were attacked around dawn. We'd been safe, thinking you and the others would return any moment, but when you didn't, we started to get worried. And then we saw the wagons approaching."

"And you thought it was us."

"We did. We didn't know who else it might have been."

The timing would have been right. "I'm sorry it wasn't us."

"It's not your fault."

"It is, though. We knew there were four wagons

missing when we approached the other caravan, but we didn't think as much of it as we should have. We thought perhaps we could figure out where the wagons had gone, and once we did, we could deal with them later. We didn't know they'd come for you."

"What happened to them?"

Haern shook his head. "I took care of them."

He worried that Elise would be offended, but she just nodded. "Good. They hurt Marcy."

"How?"

"They tossed her into one of the other wagons. They were unmindful of the fact that her leg was broken."

He should have left one of them alive, if only to question him.

They needed to understand where these attackers had gotten hold of the lorcith spheres. They seemed like the kind of weapon the Forgers would use, but he didn't think this was their work.

"We need to move these wagons and bring them over to the others," Haern said.

"The others?"

"We're now in control of all twelve of the wagons. I'm not really sure what's in them—"

"Haern," she said.

"What?"

"Let me show you."

They made their way over to one of the other wagons. When he reached it, he had to pull it open the same way he had the other ones, forcing his sword into it and prying off the padlock.

Inside, he found the wagon filled with women. They

were of all ages, reminding him of the others, the women he'd discovered when he had found Elise.

"Again?" Anger rolled through him.

"It seems so," she said.

"Why?"

"I don't really know. They grabbed us, but I don't know if they knew we were here."

Looking at Elise, he knew what he had to ask next would be difficult for her. "Do you think you can help me gather up the people I took care of?"

"Why?"

"Because we need some answers."

"I think so," she said.

Elise jumped back into the wagon and whispered something to a couple of the other women. Together, they joined Haern and went wagon to wagon, pulling the fallen wagon drivers off and dragging them toward the front. Once they were all laid out, Haern realized one of them still lived.

It was an older man, gray-haired, with pale eyes that were almost silver. He coughed, blood burbling to his lips. Haern had a hard time summoning any sympathy for the man.

"Is this it?" he asked.

Elise nodded. "This is all that we found."

"What about the other two wagons?"

"We only knew about the one. They were let out as we were forced in, almost as if to show us what our fate was."

"We need to check the others," Haern said. "Will you watch them?"

"We will."

When he left Elise, he made his way toward the front two wagons. Stopping at the nearest, he pried the lock open. When he pulled it off, he hesitated, worried about what he would find. But if there were other women inside, he was determined to get to them, rescue them, free them from whatever fate might otherwise have befallen them.

Much like the last two wagons, he found women inside. They were in various states of poor health, and he realized they needed the help of a healer. If he could find Della, maybe he could get them that help.

If the remaining wagon was the same, he needed to free them.

When he pulled the door open, a familiar sense drifted out, but it was too late.

Lorcith.

And it exploded.

HAERN

HAERN *PUSHED* AGAINST THE EXPLOSION AS FIRMLY AS HE could, worried he wasn't fast enough. Shards of lorcith streaked toward him. Had he not been healed and well rested, he wasn't sure he would have survived. Instead, when the explosion slammed into his barrier, he was able to repel it by *pushing* against it using his connection to lorcith.

He was helped by the confines of the wagon. He didn't have to encircle the spheres the same way as he had when it was outside. But if he could somehow trap the explosion, it was possible he could use one of these spheres.

Haern *pushed* even harder, trying to force the explosion back around the spheres he detected, and there were several of them.

He wasn't sure if he was fast enough.

The metal strained against him, exploding outward, and despite his every intention to hold it within the sphere, he didn't think he'd be able to do so.

Instead, Haern let the nails drop to the ground.

When the pressure from the explosion eased, he took a step back, breathing heavily, and stared at the inside of the wagon.

It had somehow been triggered.

There was no one inside the wagon, at least no one that he could see, which meant that either someone nearby had triggered it, or it had been set off by the only remaining living wagon driver.

Haern closed the door, slipping a knife into it to keep it shut until he had a chance to better examine it, and stormed over to where the old man lay coughing. Crouching down, he glared at the man.

"What did you do?"

The man rolled his head over to the side, looking up at Haern. When he saw him watching, he grinned. "You won't be able to stop this."

"We already have stopped it."

"Have you? You are children playing at war."

Haern grabbed the man by the shirt, forcing him to look at him, and shook him briefly. "What did you do?"

"Only what had to be done."

"You think your lorcith spheres will stop me?"

The man coughed, blinking. For a moment, clarity returned to his eyes.

"That's right. I know exactly what you're trying to do with those lorcith spheres. And let me tell you: I can stop it. I will stop you."

"Will you?"

The man coughed again, bloody phlegm burbling from his lips, and then he took no more breaths.

Haern let him go, and the man sagged to the ground, dead.

Haern got to his feet, looking around at the others. So many were dead, killed because of him, but there was something he was missing.

Had he not acted in such anger, maybe he would've figured it out. Instead, he'd slaughtered all of them, rage filling him, driving him to act in a way that would ultimately prevent them from acquiring the answers they needed.

It was a mistake, and he knew it was a mistake, and yet he had done it.

"It's okay," Elise said.

Haern got to his feet, staring at the others. "It's not."

This was the kind of thing his father wouldn't have done. His father might have discovered what they were doing, and he would've figured out some way of stopping them, using his control over lorcith and Sliding in order to better understand what they were after. Haern had lost control.

Maybe the old man was right. Maybe he was nothing more than a child playing at war.

"We should rejoin the others," Haern said.

Elise turned away. Haern didn't have to worry. She would organize the rest, getting everybody together, prepared to depart. It didn't take long for her to establish order. She was good at it, and in very short order, the wagons were reloaded, though none of them had their doors locked. Slats over windows were open, letting air flow into the backs of the wagons. Haern, Elise and the others who had traveled with him from the beginning took up seats on top of the wagons, leading them.

Haern said nothing as they traveled. Every so often, Elise would glance over, and she patted him on the arm before taking his hand and squeezing it. It did little to comfort him and instead left him feeling as if he had let her—and the others—down. It was ridiculous, he knew it, but he couldn't shake the sense that there was a greater plot afoot than he understood. By slaughtering the wagon riders, he'd lost the opportunity to uncover what that plot might be.

When the other wagons came into view, tension rose up within him.

They slowed as they neared, and for a moment, Haern had a sneaking fear the attackers had somehow escaped from Galen and Rayen. But when they approached, Jayna, Stacy, and the rest of the women who had left the camp with Haern all came slowly forward.

Jayna looked up at him, and he shook his head.

Haern *pushed* off, heading toward the center of the camp. When he dropped down, Galen joined him.

"You look as if you have just made a bad kill," Galen said.

"Is any kill a good kill?"

"You and I have talked about how there are some people who really shouldn't live."

"I think I found them."

"What happened?"

"There was another attack. I found them locked in the back of the wagon."

"And you rescued them."

"I did, but I'm not sure it was the right thing to do. In rescuing them, I killed the attackers. When I did that, we lost the opportunity to understand what they were after."

"What do you think they were after?"

"They had a wagon filled with the lorcith spheres."

"And you want to know why?"

"I think we need to. I've encountered enough of them during this journey, I think we have to understand why."

Galen looked around. "It looks like you have someone there waiting for you."

Haern glanced over to see Elise watching. He waved her over. "Galen, this is Elise. She is—"

"Important to you. I see that." Galen reached out his hand, taking Elise's. "Sometimes you have to leave home to find something to care about."

Galen was looking at Elise, but it felt as if the words were meant for Haern.

Haern smiled to himself, thinking that Galen had left Elaeavn and met Cael Elvraeth.

"You're the one who taught him."

Galen shrugged. "I've done what I can, but Haern has a mind of his own."

"He says you're a Healer."

"There was a time I could claim that, but lately my talents have been used in a different way. Unfortunately, it's not always for healing."

"I have you to thank for the fact that Haern knew enough to save us."

"I think you can thank Haern."

As he looked around the clearing, Haern couldn't help but wonder about what the other man had said. There was something Haern was missing. Why would the man have seemed so smug?

Elise glanced over at him, seemingly noticing his discomfort. "I'm going to check in with Jayna," she said. Turning to Galen, she nodded politely. "It was wonderful to meet you."

When she was gone, Galen frowned at Haern. "What is it?"

"It's something a man said."

"I presume this is one of the men you killed."

"It is. What's going on with these spheres?"

"That, unfortunately, is a long story."

"Do you think we don't have the necessary time to tell it?"

"It's not so much about having time." Galen sighed, looking around. "You've been gone a while. There have been a few developments."

"In Elaeavn?"

Galen nodded. "Daniel Elvraeth discovered why the C'than attacked the Elder Trees."

When Haern had been there last, the strange metal burrowed into the trunks of the trees had solidified, sinking even deeper into them. In that regard, it was similar to what had happened to the metal that had absorbed into his hands, changing not only him but the nature of his abilities. With the way it had worked on Lucy, he couldn't help but worry that the metal would somehow change the nature of the Elder Trees, and yet, other than his father, there wasn't anyone who could do anything about it. Even Rsiran hadn't known whether anything could be done. Now that Haern had a greater connection to lorcith, he had to wonder if perhaps he could influence that lorcith.

"What reason is that?"

"They were drawing off the power of the sacred crystals, funneling it away. And they would have succeeded, but he uncovered what they were doing."

"Why would they do that?"

"I don't really know why the Ai'thol do anything."

Only, it wasn't the Ai'thol who'd attacked the trees. It wasn't the Ai'thol who'd attacked Elaeavn. It had been scholars, presumably, the C'than, and they existed in order to protect power—at least, that was what they claimed.

"If you uncovered it, were you able to stop it?"

"We stopped part of it, but the power is still being funneled away." Galen scanned the clearing for a moment before turning his attention back to Haern. "It really should be someone else speaking to you about this. Maybe your mother. But there's something more taking place, something much greater."

"We have suspected the Forgers had a plan."

"This is more than just a plan."

Haern spun to see Rayen approaching. There was a hint of darkness swirling around her, the shadows she controlled. It had been a while since he'd seen anything like that, and now when he looked at her, he couldn't help but think that the nature of the shadows seemed to be more tightly controlled than it had been. Was that because his connection to his Sight had changed, or was it because she was stronger with the shadows than she had been the last time he'd seen her?

"I'm glad you found me," Haern said.

"You tried to kill yourself."

Haern focused on where the sphere had fallen in the center of the clearing. There were still nails staggered around here, regardless of how many he had pulled on and used in his attack on the remaining wagons. "I wasn't trying to kill myself. I was trying to stop an attack. I've been escorting several dozen women, hopefully to Asador, where they could get shelter."

He held Rayen's gaze, worried that perhaps she would decline his request. If she did, it was unlikely that Carth would agree. This was what he'd wanted. He'd hoped they would allow him to bring these women to Asador, to reach the Binders, but if they didn't, then everything he attempted would be for nothing.

Haern wasn't going to leave them. He would find some other way to ensure their safety, but it would be more difficult. Then again, Haern had some experience with difficulty these days.

"So I have come to understand." Rayen glanced toward the wagons. "And now you have brought more."

"If that's a problem, Rayen, I—"

Rayen shook her head. "You really don't understand the nature of the Binders, do you?"

"Probably not as well as I should."

"When Carth started them, she did so in a similar way to what you're doing. Perhaps not quite so messy or violent, though even I'm not sure I know the thruth about that. I haven't heard all of the stories. It's a way for us to offer an element of protection."

"That your way of telling me you'll help?"

Rayen smiled sadly. "Unfortunately, my task is not yet complete. I need to go with Galen and the others in order to end this, but you may continue your journey."

"I didn't realize I was asking your permission."

"Is that not what you were doing?"

Haern shook his head. "If the Binders weren't able to offer any protection, then I was going to have to find some on my own."

Rayen stared at him for a moment before glancing to Galen. "He's more like you than Rsiran."

"Is that such a bad thing?" Galen asked.

"Your influence is clear."

"I have been working with him."

Rayen chuckled. "Obviously." She spun, turning to Haern. "When you reach Asador, go to the Red Thistle. You will recognize it when you see it, and inside, there will be an older woman—heavyset, short, good with the spoon—who will offer you all the help you need."

It would've been easier had Rayen been willing to come with him, but then, he understood that she had another role.

"What is it you and Carth are up to?" he asked them.

"There is another Elder Stone."

"I thought there were quite a few Elder Stones."

"This one is different," Rayen said. "This is one that we haven't identified."

"Is that why you're here?"

Galen glanced to the wagons. "We caught word of items transported, and we thought to investigate."

Haern was thankful they had. If they hadn't, it was likely he wouldn't have survived. The fact that they had someone with them who could Slide them here made it so much easier. Given Lucy's new powers, she could Slide all of them to Asador, couldn't she?

Even if she could, Haern wasn't sure that was the right strategy. There might be a better way.

The other women wouldn't enjoy being transported by a Slide, and he couldn't force them. Besides, with as many as there were, even with Lucy's enhancements, it was possible she wouldn't be able to Slide all of them at one time.

Then again, he didn't know the limits Lucy had. If her abilities were augmented the same way his had been, with her power becoming so much greater, it was entirely possible that she could Slide everyone at the same time.

"Were you expecting this?"

Rayen's face clouded. "Not this. We thought this sort of thing had been curtailed."

Galen grunted. "You can't curtail men's baser desires. I learned that lesson quite well on the streets of Eban."

In all the time that Haern had been working with Galen, he hadn't uncovered much about what Galen had experienced in Eban. The other man was quiet about it, as if he didn't want to share too much, but Haern had a sense Galen had been through quite a bit when he had been exiled. He doubted his mentor would ever share everything he experienced, though the other man had referenced the events often enough he had a suspicion about what he had gone through.

"We had controlled it."

"You thought that you controlled it. Unfortunately, we also thought we had the Ai'thol controlled."

Rayen frowned for a moment before turning her attention to the collection of women. "Perhaps. It is even more reason for Haern to reach Asador. Unfortunately, I don't know that I can be there with you."

She'd given him enough information to find the help he needed in Asador, but he couldn't deny that having Rayen there, someone who knew the people of Asador, the same people he would be going to for aid, would be helpful. Without Rayen, would he find the assistance he needed?

As he looked at the wagons, Haern couldn't help but worry that they would have too many people to bring with them. It had been almost overwhelming to begin with, but now the sheer numbers traveling would be far more than he felt he could safely accommodate.

The trek would involve Jayna and the others who were able to fight doing just that.

"Where will you be going?" he asked.

"Our journey is not yet over. Our search for the Elder Stone will take us quite a ways from here."

"What if the Forgers already know about the Elder Stone you're searching for?"

Galen frowned. "It's possible they do. Carth is certain we need to find it before they come across it. Otherwise, Olandar Fahr will gain incredible power."

"What sort of power does he want?"

"The power of the Great Watcher."

Haern started to laugh until he realized they weren't joking. "How is he supposed to get the power of the Great Watcher?"

"There are some who suspect your father is the key."

"Of course he is," Haern said.

"Not like that," Galen said. "It's more that he's held each of the crystals, and because of that, he has a unique perspective."

"What kind of unique perspective?" Haern asked, smiling.

"The kind that gives him an understanding of what was once called the Council of Elders."

Haern regarded Galen for a moment. "What is it?"

"We don't really know. Carth has been looking for information about it, but what she has uncovered tells her that the Council of Elders was comprised of those who were gifted by Elder Stones."

"It's more than that." Rayen met his eyes. "Whether or not we believe matters little when it comes down to what we're dealing with. All that matters is that he believes, and in this case, everything we've uncovered tells us that he very much does believe."

The desire for power, the nature of what the Forgers had done over the years, made sense. If it was all about gaining access to the Elder Stones so he could recreate this Council of Elders, then he could see what they might be attempting.

What did he know?

Not only had Elaeavn been attacked, but Asador as they searched for the wisdom stone. There was the stone nearly lost in Nyaesh, but as far as he knew, Carth had protected it. There seemed to be one for the shadow power, and how many others?

"He has to have nearly acquired all of the stones," Haern said.

"Nearly," Rayen agreed.

"What happens when he does?"

"When he does, then he will begin to create his Council of Elders."

"And what does that mean?"

No one answered for a moment. After a while, Galen glanced from Rayen to Haern. "We don't know. If he's after the Elder Stones so he can recreate the Council of Elders, the next step for him would be to oversee it, and yet we haven't been able to determine what that means. We're trying to prevent him from acquiring the final stone, and if that fails, then we need to understand the purpose behind his actions."

For some reason, Haern suspected there was more to it, but at the same time, it was unlikely there would be anything they could do until they understood just what this man intended.

"It sounds as if what you need to do is important." He looked behind him, seeing the women gathered there. There had been a time when he had wanted to fight, to do the same things his father had done, to face the Forgers and to defeat them, the same way he thought that his father had managed to defeat them.

At some point, much had changed for him. He no longer felt compelled the same way as he had before. While there was value in defeating the Forgers, and he thought he had a role to play in it, he also felt a calling to work with and help these women.

That as much as anything motivated him.

"I see you have something you must do," Galen said.

"You aren't going to have me go back to Elaeavn?"

Galen cocked his head at him. "And why would I do that?"

"I don't know. I suspected my parents would have said something to you."

"Your mother would be thrilled if you returned. At the same time, if she hasn't come to terms with the fact that you continue to mature, she will. There comes a time in every man's life when he needs to decide what's important to him and what he's willing to fight for."

"It's not that I don't want to fight for my people."

"I know," Galen said with a hint of a smile. "You would fight for them. It's just that you also recognize others can't fight for *them*," he said, nodding toward the wagons.

That was a part of it, and maybe that was all of it. For as long as he had known, the fight that mattered to him was one where he matched up with his father, learning how he had managed to withstand the Forgers. Now that his father was gone and Haern had come into a power of his own, he wasn't sure that was the same fight he wanted to engage in. Galen was right. His fight was a different one.

"When I get them to Asador…"

Galen smiled. "When you get them to Asador, you decide what you need to do."

Haern wasn't entirely sure what that would be, and perhaps that was the point. Perhaps it didn't really matter what choice he made so long as he decided for himself.

RYN

WHEN SHE CAME AROUND, RYN BLINKED OPEN HER EYES. The pain was still there in her arms and legs, but it was less than it had been before. Everything throbbed, the pain moving along her arms and legs, working toward her midsection. This time, even her head throbbed, a pulsating sensation that sent more waves of pain rolling through her. It seemed timed to her heart, as if every beating of her life blood caused more agony to work through her.

At least the nausea was gone.

She looked up, expecting to see the gray sky, but saw a paneled wood ceiling.

Panic struck her, and she jerked up, sitting up as she looked around, afraid that they had recaptured her. Where were Lorren and the blacksmith?

She could feel them. Through the pain and the nausea that she still suffered, she could feel where they were, but thankfully they weren't anywhere near her.

That didn't mean she wasn't their captive again. They

had already proven they were able to capture her and torment her. When she'd escaped, she had barely done so, and she wasn't sure she would succeed if they caught her once more. With the pain she experienced in her arms and legs, it was possible she wouldn't be able to tolerate it.

"You need to relax," a voice said.

Ryn turned, surprised to see Dillon.

"Where am I?"

"I found you on the street. I brought you here."

"You're with them."

"With them how?"

"With the ones who are tormenting me."

Dillon watched her, and she couldn't read the emotion behind his eyes. There was something there, and as she waited for him to refute what she said, he only shook his head. "I'm not with them for that."

"You know what they did?"

He motioned toward her arms. "I saw what happened."

Ryn brought her arms up. Dillon had removed her cloak, and her arms were exposed. The bands of metal wrapped around her forearms still, though there wasn't the same burning as before. One end pierced her wrist, closest to her hand, and there was no blood coming from it. "Can you remove it?"

"I don't think I can."

"Then you're with them."

Dillon shook his head. "It's not that. It's already starting to set."

"What?"

"I've been watching and learning from Torry. When the metal begins to set, there's nothing that can be done. It stays fixed within the person. There's been no one able to remove it."

"Why?"

"I don't know. It's something about the nature of the metal."

Ryn looked down at it and realized she was wrong. She had thought that only one end had pierced her skin, but the other end had as well. It pressed into her forearm up near the elbow. Was it the same way on her legs?

Leaning forward, she saw that it was.

"Did they do this on purpose?"

"I suspect they would use it as a way to hold you," Dillon said.

"Hold me?"

"The metal prevents those who can transport from doing so. Seeing how you serve him, I imagine they feared you could travel the same way he can."

Ryn shook her head. "I can't." She stared at the metal on her arms and legs. This was nothing like the blessing the Great One had given. When the Great One offered it to her, she had viewed it as a great reward. It had been anything but a reward. It had been torture, painful, and yet it had done everything he'd claimed it would.

And now all she could think about was what this would do.

If the metal was setting inside her, she could imagine it changing her much the way that the blessing had.

"What is this?"

"This would be Torry's creation. He's been studying it for years. Ever since he first encountered the Ai'thol, he's tried to understand it."

Ryn blinked. She had thought they were using the sacred metal, but it wasn't. "It's not the same?"

"It's not even the same metals, at least from what I can tell."

She looked at Dillon for a moment. "Who are you?"

Dillon smiled. "I'm no one."

"That's not true. You're not really from Thyr, are you?"

Dillon scooted toward her. "I was once, but all that changed."

"Why are you here?"

"For information."

"What kind of information?"

"The kind that will help others stop them."

"Stop Lorren and the blacksmith?"

Dillon held her gaze. "No. To stop your Great One."

Her heart skipped. "You don't serve him."

"They don't serve him, either. It's how I was able to fit in. I think if they knew, they would have expelled me long ago. There's something about my abilities that allows me to avoid their influence, though they continue to try to force me."

Ryn didn't know what to say. He was with them, but he wasn't. At the same time, he wasn't with the Great One.

"Why?"

"Because I've seen what happens if he's not resisted."

"What does that mean?"

"How long have you served as an emissary?"

"A year or more."

"You're young to be serving in such a capacity."

"He found me broken and lost. He gave me purpose."

"Yeah? My people were broken and lost, too."

"How?"

"Because of your Great One."

"He would do nothing to harm your people."

"I disagree. I've seen the kind of things he's done."

"The Great One saves. He offers protection. He offers his comfort."

"Your Great One wants to control. He wants power. He wants to rule."

Ryn held Dillon's eyes for a moment. She'd seen the kind of things the Great One had done. Very few understood the Great One. The Great One didn't need that sort of recognition. All he wanted was to ensure that others were given the freedom her family had been denied.

"You don't understand what you're talking about. I know the Great One. I've traveled with him. I've seen the things he's willing to do."

"My homeland was destroyed by your Great One. At least, by his people. They marched in, pretending to be someone else, and I spent a long time believing this other person was responsible for what happened. But I learned the truth. I've seen it myself."

"What have you seen?"

"I have seen the way that the Ai'thol destroy in order to gain more power."

He sat in silence, and she became aware of the fire crackling in the hearth, giving off a warmth. Why hadn't she noticed it before?

The pain.

It was a constant presence, a persistent sensation that rolled through her, and it seemed to push away her awareness of everything else around her. As much as she wanted to ignore the pain and the throbbing in her body, it intruded.

It disrupted even her ability to seal off her mind the way the Great One had taught her.

Perhaps it was a good thing she was here with Dillon rather than still captive within the tower. If the blacksmith were around her now, he would find it all too easy to overwhelm her mind, to burrow beneath the protections she had placed and force her to do whatever he wanted her to do.

"How long?" she asked Dillon.

"How long for what?"

"How long until you turn me back over to them?"

"What makes you think I will?"

She tore her gaze away from the flames, looking at Dillon. "You want to ingratiate yourself, don't you?"

"I already have ingratiated myself to them. I don't need to do any more."

"And yet you'd still turn me over to them."

"I have no intention of doing that."

"I have a hard time believing you."

He shrugged. "Believe what you want. I'm telling you what I will do, and I have no intention of handing you over. As far as I'm concerned, you can depart, return to your Great One, and do whatever it is he wants of you."

Ryn glanced down at her wrists. She didn't think she could get very far. It would be hard for her to get anywhere without being overwhelmed by the pain.

Dillon watched her, and she couldn't tell how old he was. He seemed so young when she first met him, and the longer she looked at him, the more she questioned whether he was far older than she believed.

Worse, she didn't know anything about him.

Despite that, he was the only one who had been decent to her. He hadn't harmed her, and he had actually helped her.

"Why?" she asked.

"I don't get to choose for you. Just because you serve him doesn't mean you're bad."

"I'm not bad," she said.

He smiled. "See?"

"If you would serve the Great One, you would understand that he is—"

Dillon leaned forward, smiling. "I've already told you what I've seen about your Great One. I understand him in a way you don't, much like you understand him in a way I don't. Two sides, same story. Either way, it doesn't matter."

"If you dislike him so much, why help me?"

"Because you haven't done anything."

She looked down at her wrist, feeling the throbbing, the pain that lingered, wanting nothing more than to shake that pain away. The pain in her head was still there as well, and that blessing had been placed months ago, long enough that it should have resolved.

"Why can't the metal be removed?"

"That's something he's tried to determine," Dillon said. "It's part of his experiments. He wants to know if he can pull power off once it's been given."

"And what happens?"

"People suffered."

"Suffer?"

Dillon arched a brow. "Suffer. Die. Basically the same."

"It's not the same."

"It's not, and yet it is. They suffer before they die."

"You've seen this?"

"Not that he knows."

"You've kept it from him?"

Dillon smiled slightly. "There are many things I've kept from him. This is but one of them."

"Why?"

"These are the kind of questions that you want to ask?"

Ryn blinked. "I don't know what type of questions I want to ask. All I know is that I don't understand why you're helping me."

"Consider it my penance."

"Why would you need to pay a penance?"

"Because I've done nothing. I have seen the kind of things he's done, and yet, even though I had the opportunity, I haven't done anything to stop him."

"If he's as powerful as you say, then it might be there's nothing for you to do." And there was something else about the blacksmith—a memory of what he'd said to her. He served someone else.

The Great One would need to know.

Dillon leaned back, breathing in deeply. "Perhaps that's the case. It's what I tell myself, at least. I've seen too many people suffering. Seen too many deaths. All to experiment."

"Why is he experimenting?"

"He wants to understand."

"Why here?"

"This isn't the only place he experiments."

"He can travel."

"He can. And he's incredibly powerful. I didn't realize that at first, but the longer I've worked with him, the more I've come to understand the nature of his power. There's nothing I can do against it."

"You can fight."

"I don't think I can. I don't think you could. It's possible the Great One would be able to oppose him, but that's only if the Great One managed to catch up to him."

Ryn sat back, resting on her elbows. She thought about what the Great One wanted of her. He'd sent her here to observe, to understand what had taken place, and instead she'd uncovered something more.

A part of her couldn't help but think the Great One had known she would.

If he had, what purpose would there be in sending her here? This wasn't the kind of fight she could handle. This wasn't the kind of thing she could even survive. This was far beyond her capacity.

The Great One would've known that, too.

Unless he had hoped to challenge her. It was possible he was using this as a test, perhaps to gauge whether she was ready for a greater task, or perhaps it was his way of forcing her to develop increased abilities.

If that was the case, then it had worked, but not in the way he had intended.

That was if the metal in her arms and legs would grant her additional abilities. She still didn't know if that was the case. Why would she be able to be augmented further?

"I need to get word to him," she whispered.

"To your master?"

Ryn looked over to Dillon. "He's not my master. He's been working with me. Teaching me."

"He's your master. You serve him. You serve at his leisure. And you have taken on an augmentation because of him."

She didn't have a good response. She didn't feel as if the Great One were her master, and yet, she had come here on his behalf. She was his emissary. It was a position she was proud of, a position that gave her an opportunity to understand him, and yet… it *was* a position that meant she served.

"Regardless of what you want to call him, I still need to get word to him. He needs to understand what's taking place."

"The moment you do it, the temple will be destroyed."

"What makes you say that?"

"As I told you, I've seen it. Your master will come here, destroy the temple and everyone in it if he can. It's the same thing he's done elsewhere."

Ryn shook her head. "That's not what he would do."

"Unfortunately, it is. But you get word to him if you have some way of doing it. And if you don't believe me, stay behind and watch. Wait and see what happens. When you do, you'll realize your master is far more violent than you believe."

That didn't fit with what she knew of him. It wasn't the kind of thing he would do.

And yet, it was possible she didn't know what he would do. The Great One wanted her to observe, detect, and report back to him.

That was what she needed to do.

Ryn sat up, looking around. The pain was beginning to retreat, and as it did, her mind started to clear, enough that she thought she would be able to stand. She got to her feet. The throbbing was much less than it had been before, and she glanced over to Dillon. "Thank you for your help."

He watched her. "Eventually you're going to find out your master isn't what you think he is."

"I doubt that."

Dillon shook his head. "Unfortunately, you will. Unless he prevents you from seeing it, you'll come to know exactly what sort of person he is. And when you do, you're going to have questions. Know the things you think you know, the facts you believe, aren't at all what's real."

Ryn held his gaze for a moment. She had seen enough over the years to know the truth. She'd seen the way Lareth had destroyed her village. She'd observed the way he continued his attacks, and she understood his power destroyed, and because of that, others suffered.

All of those were things she knew. Regardless of what Dillon wanted to tell her, she understood the Great One was responsible for protecting others. Because of him, many had been saved.

"One day you might recognize that you've been wrong," Ryn said.

"Perhaps. And if I do, at least I'll have an open mind about it. Can you say the same?"

She stared at him for a moment. "Thank you again."

"Where will you go?" Dillon asked.

"I've told you. I intend to get word to the Great One."

"So you said. But how? Where do you intend to go in order to get word to him?"

The temple wasn't safe for her, and that was the way she would have gone normally. Now what would she do? Where would she go?

"There's a temple in another city I can go to."

"Are you sure?"

Ryn thought about the places she'd visited with the Great One, all of the temples, and every place he'd brought her in the time she'd been working with him. She had seen that some places were less safe than others. For the most part, the temples were places of safety. They were all places where the Great One had been welcomed, where she knew and recognized the nature of the power there.

"I've been many different places. All of them are safe."

Dillon watched her for a little while, and then he shook his head. "I'm going to regret this, but…"

"But what?" She tensed, fearing that Dillon might do something that would harm her. She had to be prepared for whatever he might do, and yet, if he attacked, there wouldn't be anything for her to do. She wasn't a fighter. She was trained to observe, to witness, to report.

"I'm going to show you."

"Show me what?"

"Show you the kind of things your Great One has done."

RYN

DILLON HELD HIS HAND OUT, WAITING, AND RYN LOOKED AT it, not certain what he wanted her to do. The fire crackled softly, and it pushed back the chill within the air, but with the pain throbbing through her, there was a different kind of chill. She couldn't shake the steady throbbing in her wrists and ankles. The sense of it was overwhelming.

"What do you expect me to do?"

"I expect you to let me guide you."

"You don't want to help me get word to the Great One."

"If you manage to do so, I'm not going to stop you, but at the same time, I think there's something I can show you."

"Why should I trust you?"

"Because I could have turned you in before now. If I wanted to harm you, I would have."

"Why don't you want to harm me?"

"Because I see in you the same thing that is in me."

"Your homeland was destroyed."

"It was."

"And you blame the Great One for this."

"I do."

"I don't blame him for what happened to mine."

"Who do you blame for that?"

Ryn stood, twisting the fabric of her jacket between her fingers. It felt strange, and it took her a moment to realize it was because the burning in her hands changed the way the fabric felt. Somehow, she could feel the way the fabric rubbed against her fingers, almost as if it were attempting to wear off the tips of them. It seemed rougher than she remembered.

"I know what happened. I was there when my village was destroyed. There was one man who was responsible. He made his way through the village, ravaging everything there."

Dillon watched her. "One man?"

Ryn nodded.

"One man wouldn't be able to destroy a village."

"This one would. Everything I've learned about him since then tells me he's incredibly powerful. He's powerful enough that even the Great One is cautious with him."

Dillon lowered his hand. "Rsiran," he breathed out.

"Who?"

"His name. It's Rsiran Lareth. I've been looking for him, wanting to find him, but…"

Lareth. The name burned in her mind, the memory of when she'd first heard of him coming back to her. She hated that name. He was responsible for what had happened to her father. He was responsible for them moving, going to the village for safety. And he was responsible for the destruction of the village.

She had been taught by the Great One to observe. And yet, despite her observing, there remained within her the strong desire to get vengeance. She was determined to do so, and yet in all the time she had been working with the Great One, she hadn't been able to figure out how. She didn't think the Great One wanted her to get revenge, but he also didn't want her to suffer.

"Why are you looking for him?"

"Because my people need his help."

"Help? If you know anything about Lareth, you'll know he doesn't help. He destroys. He kills indiscriminately."

"You know him?"

"I don't know him. I know of him. I've seen him."

"You saw him destroy your village?"

She closed her eyes. As she did, she swayed in place for a moment. The pain in her wrists and ankles was there, a companion to her, but she ignored it as she thought back, her mind drifting to Lareth. "I saw the way he tore through the village. My mother was crushed. People I knew destroyed. All because of him. He slung metal throughout the village, using it to destroy everything."

There was silence for a few moments.

"Let me tell you my experience," Dillon said. "When my homeland was attacked, it was caught in the middle of a battle. There were a dozen men. All of them with eyes like mine, and all of them with dark hair. They wore black cloaks. Black jackets and pants. All of them controlled metal."

Ryn opened her eyes. "What?"

Dillon sighed. "All of them. There were a dozen men. They looked similar, and they all claimed to be fighting on behalf of Lareth as they destroyed the village. And yet, when they were gone, I followed them. I saw where they went. I saw who they were with. I know what they did."

"Who were they with?"

"Your Great One."

She shook her head. "I don't believe you."

"You don't have to believe me. I believe what I saw, much like you believe what you saw." He held his hand up again. "If you want, I'll take you from here and you can reach out to your Great One. And like I said, watch and see how he responds. See what he does. And see the kind of violence he brings."

Ryn hesitated. Did she dare go with him? She wasn't sure if it was safe to do so, but at the same time, she thought that she needed to in order to understand. More than that, she needed to get out of the city and away from the tower in order to get word to the Great One. As soon as she did, she could return here and wait for him.

Regardless of what Dillon said, the Great One wasn't responsible for destroying his home. And yet, the way he had described the attackers—it was the same as what she had seen.

She shook away that thought.

Reaching her hand out, she took Dillon's hand.

Nausea struck her, and she pushed it away.

There came a strange swirling sense, and Dillon cried out.

And then they were falling.

Ryn opened her eyes and saw that they were dropping toward the ground. How was that possible? They were outside, the sun was shining overhead, bright and warm, and then they struck.

The air burst from her lungs. Pain hit her, but no worse than it had been before. She let go of Dillon's hand and lay there, trying to collect her thoughts and figure out what had just happened.

Rolling over, she looked at Dillon. His eyes had a glaze to them. She'd seen something like that before and was reminded of when her village had been destroyed.

She looked around. They were well outside of the city, though she couldn't see any evidence of it in the background. There was a road somewhere nearby, and clumps of trees grew up all around her. Flowers scattered the plains, lending their fragrance to the air.

"Dillon?"

He took a gasping breath and blinked, rolling over. "What... what happened?"

Ryn shook her head. "You traveled us, but where?"

Dillon shook his head. "I started to, but something happened. I felt as if I lost control of it."

"You lost control?" What was she thinking, traveling with him like that? He'd already told her that he didn't have as much control as some, and here she had been willing to risk herself by going with him. In doing so, she'd nearly died. She very well *could* have died.

"I've never experienced anything quite like it. I was starting my transport, and then all of a sudden, it felt as if I were thrown out of it. Almost as if I were pushed."

Ryn swallowed. Everything within her hurt, though it

was no different than the pain she had been experiencing over the last few days. "Pushed?"

He nodded. "I don't understand it." Dillon got to his feet, leaning forward and resting his hand on his thighs. "I'm going to try a small step."

With that, he started to move. Colors swirled around him.

Nausea rolled through her again, and Ryn pushed it away.

Dillon cried out.

He lay on the ground a dozen paces from her, his body bent, and he slowly got to his feet, shaking his head. "It happened again."

"What do you mean?"

"I lost control again. I don't really understand it. This has never happened before. I've been working on trying to increase my ability with it, trying to improve my control. It's almost as if someone is forcing me along."

What had been the common features?

Nausea.

Not only nausea, but she'd been pushing it away.

Ryn glanced down at her wrists. Could that be the key?

It would be an unusual ability if true, but she had experience with unusual abilities.

"Try it again."

Dillon shook his head. "I don't want to. If it happens again, I don't know that I can stand the landing."

"I think… I think *I'm* the reason you've been ending up somewhere else."

"How?"

"Just try it again."

Dillon took a deep breath, and colors once again swirled around him. When they did, the nausea returned, rolling through Ryn's stomach. This time she ignored it, letting it wash over her, and when he disappeared, the nausea vanished.

He appeared a few feet in front of her.

"It's fine. It didn't happen that time."

"I didn't push the nausea away, either."

"I don't understand."

"To be honest, I don't understand either. I was feeling nausea when you started your traveling, and I'd learned it to push it away."

"You pushed away the nausea?"

"I don't know how to describe it other than that, and it seemed to work."

"You think you can pull on the nausea?"

Ryn frowned. "Why?"

"Just try it."

Dillon jogged away from her before turning and facing her. He nodded.

As he did, color swirled around him again, and the nausea came, rolling through her. This time Ryn pulled on it rather than pushing it away. A wave of pain throbbed through her, striking her wrists before ending.

When it cleared, Dillon stood in front of her.

He was panting. He leaned forward, resting his arms on his thighs. "There it was again. This time was different. It felt as if I were drawn rather than pushed."

Could that have been her?

If it was, how was she able to do that?

"I don't know why that should have been possible," she said.

When she had been traveling with the Great One, there had been no sense of anyone getting pushed or pulled along. It had always been safe. But then again, the Great One had always been the one doing the traveling. No one would dare interrupt his movement.

"I didn't even know such a thing was possible," Dillon said, looking around. "We need to practice this."

"Practice? I don't want to do it. What happens if I force you like you said? What happens if I push you in the middle of some tree or into the earth?"

"That's why you need to practice. You need to gain control so you don't accidentally influence anything—wait. What if you can control where we travel?"

"I don't know what you mean."

"Well, one of the limitations to transporting the way I do is that I have to have been there before. If I haven't, I'm not able to reach it, at least not easily. It takes longer. I have to have a line of sight, and I can make my way where I want, but it's slower than simply stepping into a transport."

"Why would I be able to control it?"

"I don't know. It would be helpful, though, especially for one of the Great One's emissaries."

She frowned at him. "I feel like you're mocking me."

"I'm trying to help you understand your abilities, Ryn."

"This isn't an ability I knew I had." And it certainly wasn't an ability she wanted to have.

Yet, the more she thought about it, the more she thought an power like this would be useful for her to possess. While she might not have the ability to travel, she could draw on others.

If it were possible for her to control where someone traveled, all she needed was to have access to that person, and she could use that ability, couldn't she?

Observe and detect.

This was the kind of thing that the Great One wanted her to do.

They would have to work on it later. For now, she wanted to get word to the Great One.

"Can you take us to Blaspher?"

"I'm not familiar with it."

"What about Yzern?"

Dillon shook his head.

"Horch? Vren? Cernal?"

With each name, Dillon continue to shake his head.

He didn't know any of the places she had been.

Unless he did, and he wasn't telling her the truth, but she didn't get that sense from him. She trusted her instincts when it came to this.

Ryn sighed. What choice did she have but to work with him, to practice this, and to see if she could perhaps gain some control over whatever ability it was that she had developed?

She glanced down at her wrists, looking at the metal as it pierced her skin. She traced her fingers over the other wrist, feeling the warmth. It was strangely soothing to touch it, and it was far smoother than her cloth had been.

Why should she develop this ability?

It was the kind of question she should be asking. It was the kind of question the Great One wanted her to ask.

Observe, determine the reason behind something, and use that knowledge.

And yet, there might not be a reason. It didn't seem as if they had intentionally placed the bars around her wrists and her ankles in order for her to acquire this ability. They had used it to trap her, to hold her from being able to transport.

Strangely, it had done the opposite.

Perhaps that was the key.

"Why don't you see if we can try this?"

Dillon smiled. "I think it's safest. That way when we do transport, I don't have to worry about you sending us someplace dangerous."

"You don't have to do this. You don't have to stay with me."

"I told you I would get you somewhere safe."

"Why help me?" As she watched him, she thought it wasn't so much that he was helping; it was that he was willing to work with her to help her understand this ability, too. He had no reason to do so. If anything, he had every reason to abandon her, to leave her behind and let her stumble through this and figure it out on her own. And it wasn't that she thought she couldn't figure it out. She suspected that with enough time—and with access to those who could travel like this—she would be able to do so. But it also involved practice, and without knowing who else could travel, she wouldn't be able to practice as well as she wanted.

"When I was first learning about my ability, someone helped me."

"Who?"

He shook his head. "It doesn't really matter. Like I said, let me help you figure this out."

She took a deep breath. "What do you think we should do first?"

Dillon looked around. "It's wide open here. We can practice in small steps, and it should be relatively safe. It's the kind of place where I learned."

"What do you propose we try?"

"First I would suggest we see if you can control how you push and pull me."

That was something she thought she understood, however slightly. When the nausea had come, she had been aware of it, and when she had pushed it down, that was when they had ended up in the wrong place. When she had pulled the nausea toward her—something that was far stranger for her to have done—it had controlled where Dillon had traveled.

"Let's try it."

"Focus on pushing me across the clearing," he said.

She nodded, staring off into the distance. With her enhanced eyesight, it was easy enough for her to make out what was out there, and she waited for the nausea to start, the colors starting to swirl around Dillon, and then she pushed that nausea. She tried to push it in a specific direction, though she wasn't sure she was effective. When she had done it before, she had pushed it *down*.

As the nausea disappeared, Dillon emerged a hundred yards from her.

It had worked.

It wasn't the first time she'd pushed nausea away. She had done it in the tower, and she'd wondered why there wasn't anyone else there. Could she have been doing it then? Could she have been pushing the blacksmith and Lorren away from her? If so, she had somehow saved herself without even knowing what she was doing.

And then out on the street, when she had finally managed to escape from the tower, she had done the same thing. It was possible that was Lorren and the blacksmith, but it was also possible it was Dillon, coming to try to help her.

Nausea started to work through her, and this time, she pulled on it, drawing it toward her. She cut off about midway, wondering if she could direct how far she was pulled, and Dillon appeared about fifty yards from her.

It had worked.

When the nausea came again, this time she pushed to her right and gave a stronger force to it, trying to send him farther than she had before. She slammed it away from her, and as the colors swirled around him, she could feel as he drifted away from her.

That was different than before.

Why should she be able to feel him drift away from her?

Dillon cried out. He was several hundred yards away, far enough that he looked small, and he leaned down, his hands gripping his thighs, panting.

Nausea rolled through her again. This time she pulled, drawing it all the way to her.

When it cleared, Dillon was once more in front of her, panting heavily.

He shook his head. "I don't know how much longer I can keep at this. It's hard enough for me to transport when it's just me, and I've already brought you wherever it is that we are. Now it's almost like I've been fighting."

"Do you resist when I've pushed and pulled?"

Dillon straightened, leaning back and locking his hands behind his back. "I don't know that I'm fighting intentionally, but it's such a strange sensation I don't know what else I could be doing." He looked over at her, arching a brow. "Do you have a better sense of what you're doing?"

She sighed. "I think I was able to control it somewhat, but I'm not sure I have enough control not to be a risk to you."

"Does it weaken you?"

She didn't think it did. It didn't seem any harder each time she tried it, not the way she had heard others describe their abilities. Then again, when it came to her vision and her hearing and listening, there hadn't been anything like that, either.

"I don't think so."

"I guess that's good."

It was strange that it wouldn't weaken her. She didn't have as much experience with blessings as others, but what she'd seen working with the Great One had shown her that those who had various blessings did have some limitations. They weren't able to use them extensively before growing tired. It had been described to her in the past as if the person were running. The more they ran, the easier it became for them to run longer distances at a greater speed.

"Can we try again?"

"We can, but I need to rest."

Ryn looked around the landscape. There was nothing here, and if Dillon decided to rest, there would be nothing for her to do.

Dillon made his way over to a nearby cluster of trees and took a seat, with his back against a tree trunk. He leaned back, closing his eyes, clasping his hands over his stomach. When he sat like that, she thought him younger, at least young enough he could be only a few years older than her. There were other times when she found it much more difficult to know how old he was.

Ryn paced, looking around, weaving between the trees as she did. Her mind raced, struggling to figure out what she should be doing. All of this was challenging to her. She was now outside of the city that the Great One had wanted her to observe, well beyond the borders of the tower, and now that she was here, she didn't know whether she could even get word to the Great One. If she couldn't, how would the Great One respond?

She'd seen the look on his face when others had disappointed him, the mixture of sadness and irritation, and she didn't want that for herself.

"You can take a seat next to me."

She glanced down at Dillon. "I'm just thinking."

"You're making me tired."

"By walking?"

"It's not so much that you're walking. You look agitated."

Ryn shrugged. "Perhaps I am."

"Which is why you need to take a seat."

She shook her head. "I won't be able to get anything accomplished by doing that."

"You can rest. After everything you've been through, don't you want to rest?"

After everything she'd been through, she wanted nothing more than to finish her assignment.

Slowly she made her way back to Dillon and took a seat next to him. He rested his head back against the trunk of the tree, closing his eyes, and soon his breathing began to slow. Ryn took one of the books out of her pocket, looking through the pages as she read through observations made in the time she'd been working with the Great One. It hadn't been all that long, and yet she had seen quite a bit in the time since she had started working with him.

As she read through her notes, she couldn't help but think about what Dillon had said. She didn't think the Great One was responsible for what had happened to Dillon's home, but at the same time, she didn't know who was.

It was strange that he viewed Lareth as something other than the monster she knew him to be.

What had Dillon said? Two sides to a story.

As much as she hated to agree with him, she couldn't help but recognize the value in what he said. It was all part of what the Great One wanted her to know. Observing something meant trying to look at it from all angles. In order to fully document what she experienced, she needed to have insight she couldn't gain by seeing it from one side and not the other.

Even if she disagreed with him, that didn't mean that she couldn't listen, perceive things from her own vantage, and add those observations into what she witnessed.

Ryn continued to flip through the pages. Everything stopped when she reached the tower. Some of her notes were here, comments she had made about what she had observed when she'd first reached the tower, the things she had seen and the people she'd spoken to. At the time, she'd not recognized the danger the blacksmith and Lorren had posed. If she had, would she have been able to avoid this?

She might've played things are little differently. She'd been too blunt.

Sitting back, making a few notes on the page, she documented what had occurred in the time since she had left the tower. She left nothing out, including her conversation with Dillon. There was no point in excluding anything. All observations were beneficial, and when she came back to them later to review them, she might see them in a different light, especially when taken as part of a greater experience.

Dillon began to snore.

She watched him, smiling to herself. If she were to be dependent upon his abilities, she would be limited by his strength and weakness. It seemed he did have some limitations, regardless of how much he claimed to have worked with his traveling. If that was the case, she would need to be careful with how much she practiced. Her first goal was to get word to the Great One, and then they could practice. Until then, she needed to be less concerned about how this new ability would work for her.

While thinking of it, Ryn began to document her observations of her new ability, too. She added that to everything else, and when she was done, she set down her pen, closing the notebook.

Strangely, there was a surprising comfort in simply sitting here. There was no danger out here, at least not acutely, and she couldn't deny how peaceful it felt to simply sit out in the shade, a warm breeze blowing through, twisting her hair, and someone who had been friendly to her sitting next to her.

For a moment, she was able to think back to what it had been like before Vuahlu had been destroyed.

But only for a moment.

Nausea rolled through her, the sense of someone traveling, and she stuffed her notebook back into her pocket and turned to Dillon to wake him. Regardless of how tired he was, they might not have time for him to get much rest.

RYN

THE CITY OF LEXA SPREAD OUT BEFORE THEM. IT HAD taken a long time to reach it, and Ryn had a growing sense of agitation with each passing moment. In order to get word to the Great One, they needed to act quickly, which had prompted her to force Dillon to travel much faster—and farther—than he wanted.

They had paused from time to time during their travel to Lexa, and each time they did, Dillon would quickly fall into a deep slumber. She allowed him to rest as long as it was safe. Ryn had taken to keeping guard over him while he slept, all the while looking around and focusing on the sense of nausea that might warn her of someone traveling toward them.

Each time she felt it—and was certain it wasn't coming from Dillon—she pushed it away. She didn't even consider where she was pushing it, knowing it didn't matter. All that counted was that they bought time.

It continued to work. For some reason, her pushing

away that nausea seemed to keep others from traveling to them, and while she knew there would be limits to how long she could do it, she was determined to maintain their safety. When the sense of nausea came with increasing waves, suggesting there was more than one person attempting to travel to them, she would wake Dillon, and they would travel.

He needed far more sleep than he'd managed so far, and she worried that she was pushing him too hard. Part of it was selfish. If he grew too tired to offer her any assistance, then she'd have to worry about what her attackers might do. She had no idea who they were, or whether they were even with the blacksmith and Lorren. There remained the possibility that it was the Great One and others with him.

"Where are we?" Dillon asked. His voice was weak and his words slurred. He sounded as if he had been drinking too much ale.

He didn't have much left in him. Ryn was thankful they'd reached Lexa. It was a place she'd been before, and generally safe, though it had been the better part of a year since she'd visited. It was close enough to Dreshen and where the tower and the blacksmith were, but far enough away it should still be under the Great One's control.

What would she do if it wasn't?

She tried not to think about that, or about the fact that she no longer knew who to trust. She trusted the Great One, and as they continued to travel, she found herself beginning to trust Dillon more and more, especially given how hard he was pushing himself on her behalf.

"It's called Lexa."

"Lexa?" He lifted his head, straining to open his eyes, as if the light was too bright for him. "I've never heard of it."

"It's quite a bit south of where we were."

"How do you know of it?"

"I've visited before."

Dillon could only grunt, and even with that, he barely got the sound out. He wasn't going to be able to travel the rest of the way to Lexa.

Ryn slipped her arm around his waist, keeping him upright, and they started walking. She was tired too, and yet she refused to allow herself to drift off. Every time they had stopped, she had forced her eyes open, straining to keep awake, and the effort of that had begun to wear on her.

As the city grew closer, the palace at the heart of it drew her in. It was different than the temple in Dreshen. The palace was all pale white stone, intricately carved cornices, sculptures that were staggered along with peaks. It was hundreds of years old, and she remembered the awe that had filled her when she had first come here. She and the Great One had spent the better part of a month here, long enough that she had come to know the palace and the people within it. It was as safe as any place they might go.

They reached the wide road leading into the city. There were other people out, and as the day grew longer, the sun dipping down, she was thankful they had a place to end their travels. Hopefully this would be an end for now. If not, where would she go?

Lexa was a wealthy city. It was a place of heavy trade, situated in between a nexus of roads that led to various parts of the world, and it brought peoples from all over through the borders of the city. Through her tired eyes, she noted the dress of a dozen different places, her mind naming them briefly, still observing the way the Great One had taught her. Regist. Inlar. Neeland. Grovl. Kresh.

Ryn pushed those thoughts out of her mind. It did her no good to continue to think about the various peoples. She had to focus on the palace. And as she neared it, there was a heavy presence of guards. Most of them wore dark jackets and pants, and at least in that they were familiar. They were the markers of the Ai'thol. Many of them bore the scars of the older style of implant. What she needed was someone she recognized.

Unfortunately, she hadn't been a part of the Ai'thol long enough to recognize anyone. More than that, she had served as the Great One's emissary and hadn't remained in any one place for any extended period of time. She hadn't gained the knowledge and experience to know these people all that well.

"We're going there?" Dillon asked.

Ryn slowed, putting her back up against a building. The smooth stone was cool and slightly damp. From here, she could peer along the street, look at the palace rising up on a hillside across from her, and consider how she was going to approach. She had her markers of the Ai'thol, but she realized that she didn't look the same as others, and because of that, her age gave her a disadvantage.

"That is the Palace of Nevelar. Rumor has it that the

Nevelar family used to rule in Lexa long ago. Eventually they lost favor, and the palace turned over multiple times before we took control."

"We?"

Dillon looked up at her, blinking. As the moments passed, he seemed to be regaining his strength. That was good, as they might need it to get into the palace. She could use it to find the help she needed. If he could travel across the borders, from there she could reach one of the higher-ranking Ai'thol, find one of the disciples, and get word to the Great One.

"The Ai'thol. The city was poorly run prior to the Ai'thol presence. We provided stability where there had been lawlessness. We provided organization where there had been none. Now there is prosperity here."

Dillon shook his head. "What if your people didn't do any of that?"

"You would accuse me of lying?"

"Not you, but did you see this yourself?"

"Well, no—"

"I thought you were trained to observe."

"I am. And I have observed the stability and coordination within the city. It's a place of peace."

"Or a place of fear." Dillon straightened and looked around. "There isn't any energy here."

"Energy?"

"There's a vibrancy to a city. When it's alive, you can feel it. It's as if the city itself has its own sort of life to it. This place is cold, almost sterile. The people here go about their day, but can you say they do so with any real zeal?"

"I'm not sure it matters."

"Really? When you see a place that is alive, you'll know the difference. It's… it's like nothing else."

"Like Thyr?"

Dillon swept his gaze along the street. "Thyr was different a long time ago. Everything I've heard about it tells me it was a place much like this. The people were scared, ruled over by men quite a bit like your Ai'thol. When they were destroyed, when their presence was removed from the city, the city rebounded. It took some time, but now it's stronger."

"Let me guess, Lareth was responsible for destroying these people."

"I don't know."

Ryn continued to look across the street. Ai'thol patrolled along the wall leading into the palace. It was a low wall, no more than six feet tall, and with the palace situated on a hillside behind it, the wall didn't block any view of the palace grounds or the palace itself. It did little more than create a minor barricade, a separation between the people within the city and those who lived on the palace grounds.

"You believe you'll find safety there?"

"I hope so. When I was here the last time, the people here treated us well."

"They had to."

"They didn't have to."

Dillon smiled. "I doubt they were willing to risk the wrath of the Great One."

"You don't understand. He has—"

"I know what you think he's done. I'm just offering an alternative explanation."

"It's a wrong explanation."

"Perhaps. You can prove to me it's wrong."

Darkness had begun to fall. A sliver of moon overhead cast a little bit of light, but barely enough for them to easily see. The city itself was quiet, even quieter than what she had experienced in Dreshen. There she had noted the sound of children and, when night fell, that of music and the occasional shout that rang out. Every so often, voices drifted along the streets, whispered conversation that she wouldn't have heard were it not for her enhanced hearing.

It was different here.

There seemed to be nothing. It was almost as if everything was in perfect silence; there were only muted sounds like that of the occasional boot on stone. Even that was diminished, as if the people who were marching did so carefully so as not to draw attention to their passing.

"Do you think you can manage another traveling?"

Dillon looked over at her. His lids were heavy, and he seemed to be struggling to hold them up, but he nodded. "I think so. I don't know how far we can go, but I think that I can get us one more. After that…"

Ryn pointed across the street. "It doesn't have to be far, and afterward, you should be able to rest."

"You intend to take us there."

"Actually, I intend for *you* to take us there. I just hope the disciples will recognize me."

"And if they don't?"

She had her sigil, and she had the fact that she served

the Great One, so she thought that was all that was necessary. If she needed more, she was going to be in trouble.

"They will."

"But if they don't?"

Ryn didn't answer. Instead, she held out her hand, waiting for Dillon to take it. When he did, he entwined his fingers into hers. For a moment, he squeezed her hand, and then she nodded across the street. "Take us near the door."

Dillon squeezed his eyes shut. She didn't think it was necessary for him to do so, but perhaps with as weak as he'd become, he needed to. A wave of nausea started through her, building slowly. She resisted the urge to push or pull it away. She didn't want to influence him in any way, worried she would send him somewhere else, far beyond where they intended to go. If she did, they might not be able to get back without giving him a chance to rest.

The nausea built differently than it had before. It was slow, a roiling that rose steadily from deep within her, and then it washed over, spilling out.

When they stepped free from the traveling, the palace suddenly looming overhead, she leaned forward, vomiting violently.

Dillon collapsed.

It took a moment for the effects of their travel to pass. When they did, Ryn looked around, half expecting several of the Ai'thol to come strolling toward her, but no one did. The palace grounds were mostly silent. The patrols were on the other side of the wall, not on this side, as if they didn't expect anyone to attempt to cross. Perhaps they didn't.

"Get up, Dillon."

He groaned, rolling off to the side, but he didn't open his eyes.

"You need to get up. We need to get into the palace so that we can get you some rest."

"I'm going to rest here," he said.

"You don't want to do that," she said.

"I do. This is fine."

"I just threw up right near you."

Dillon cocked open one eye. "You did?"

She nodded and pointed to where she had vomited. "That felt different than the others."

"It was harder. I… I think I've pushed myself farther than I ever have before."

"Maybe that means you'll be stronger the next time."

"Or maybe it means that I won't be able to transport myself ever again."

"I doubt that's the case."

Dillon got to his knees and looked around the courtyard. Ryn followed the direction of his gaze. Even in the darkness, she was able to make out the garden and the various paths leading around it. It had fallen into somewhat of a state of disrepair, though there were patches of the garden that still bloomed vibrantly with flowers of many different colors, as if a reminder of what had once been here. It seemed as if the Ai'thol didn't care so much for the beauty that could be created in the garden.

Grabbing on to Dillon's hand, she pulled him to his feet.

"Do you think you can walk?"

"A little while longer, but I don't know how much more I can do. I doubt I'd be able to transport us again."

"Let's hope it's not necessary."

"Even if it were necessary, I don't know that it would work. I… I worry it would kill me."

Ryn nodded. The palace would be safe. It had to be.

She guided Dillon toward the main entrance of the palace. Once there, she expected to find Ai'thol guards, but there were none. Pulling open the doors, stepping inside, she paused. The floors were all a slick marble, and massive pillars rose up, framing a wide staircase that swept around, leading to the second level. A catwalk led along the upper level, looking down at the main hallway. Sculptures and paintings and exquisitely designed carpets adorned the palace.

"Look at all this," Dillon breathed out.

"This was all here before."

"I'm not surprised, I'm just… look at it!"

Ryn nodded, heading toward the staircase. When she reached it, she hesitated. She had been here for a month with the Great One, long enough for her to know how to navigate, and finding where one of the disciples would be located shouldn't be difficult, and yet, she wasn't sure where to start her search.

It was still early evening, and she remembered the exquisite meals they had had, though she didn't know if that was for the benefit of the Great One.

Ryn turned away from the staircase.

"Where are you going?"

"The dining hall."

"There's a whole hall for dining?"

"This is the palace, Dillon. It was designed for entertaining."

"It was designed as a pompous display of wealth."

She frowned at him. "Sometimes there's value in such displays of wealth. It demonstrates power."

"Where do you think they got the money from?"

Ryn looked around before shrugging. "I don't know."

"I imagine from the people living beyond the wall."

She thought he might elaborate, but he didn't. Instead he followed her wordlessly as she wound through the main level, turning down a side hallway and heading toward the dining hall. Memories of staying here came flooding back to her, and she barely had to think about where she was going, so that when she turned off onto the wide hallway that led to the dining hall she started to feel relaxed.

Reaching the door, she hesitated, listening.

Several voices drifted out, and she didn't recognize any of them.

"What is it?" Dillon whispered.

She raised a hand, quieting him.

"How much longer will we have to keep up this charade?" a voice from the other side of the door said.

"It's not a charade. We do what's necessary."

"There's an alternative."

"You know the alternative is useless, the same as I do."

"It's not useless. You've seen what he's demonstrated."

"We've seen how he claims his additions are effective, but we have no proof of it."

"According to him, we will soon."

Ryn stepped back, glancing over to Dillon. The conversation was a strange one, and it didn't make sense to her. Why would they be having a debate about this? It sounded... almost treasonous.

Could the Great One have lost control over the Ai'thol?

She thought that was unlikely. He'd led the Ai'thol for a long time, certainly long enough that others had seen the nature of his thinking and planning. It was because of him that the Ai'thol had taken such a prestigious role within the world.

The sound of movement on the other side of the door caught her attention, and she turned away. Hurrying down the hall, she grabbed Dillon's hand, pulling him along with her.

When they turned a corner, he looked over at her. "What is this?"

"I'm not sure. I heard—"

Ryn didn't have the chance to finish. The sound of the door opening behind her caught her attention, and she slipped away, winding through the palace. She reached a staircase that headed down and took it.

With each step, her fear grew. Could she have left one dangerous place and ended up in another?

"What do you intend to do?"

"I intend to get you some rest."

"Why?"

Ryn glanced up the stairs. From here, she couldn't hear anything that suggested they were being followed, which reassured her a little bit. If they'd been followed, then she would need to move more quickly, and it was possible she'd need for Dillon to travel one more time, which wasn't what she wanted.

What she wanted to do was to find answers, and having Dillon with her meant she had some measure of safety. She could escape if it came down to it.

If there was something more taking place, some plot against the Great One, she needed to know about it in order to report to him.

As she raced forward, hurrying along the hallway, she glanced back every so often, looking to see if there was anyone following her. So far, she didn't detect anything, and she paused every so often to listen.

There was no sound.

She didn't really expect there to be any noises down here. They were deep beneath the ground, far below where anyone would normally come. The walls were narrower here, and there was a dampness she recognized. It would be a good place for them to hide, though how long would she be able to do it?

She couldn't sleep, not while there were others approaching, and not while there was danger coming her way.

When she reached the door, she paused, throwing it open. Standing there in the doorway, she hesitated for a moment, thankful she didn't detect anything or anyone.

It was a closet, a storeroom. A row of shelves held buckets, and a mop leaned against one wall. It was enough to hide them. It would have to be good enough for her.

Motioning for Dillon to join her, she headed into the storeroom, pulling the door closed.

"Here?"

Ryn nodded. "For now. Get some rest."

"And what are you going to do?"

"I'm going to keep an eye on you."

"Ryn—"

She shook her head, though she didn't know if he would even be able to see it. "I don't know what we might encounter when we go to them, but I'm determined to find out what they're doing. I need you to be fully awake and ready to help."

"I don't know how long it will take me to recover."

"Take what time you need. I'll keep an eye on you."

He watched her, but his lids were heavy, and every time he blinked, she could tell he struggled to stay awake. It wouldn't be long before he drifted off completely.

Dillon laid his head back, sliding along the far wall until he was situated beneath the shelves. From here, the shadows concealed him for the most part.

Ryn sat, her arms wrapped around her legs, watching him.

As he drifted off, his breathing becoming steadier and more regular. She tried to focus her mind, but she was tired. After everything they'd gone through, after the hope and promise of reaching here—reaching safety—had been crushed, she wasn't sure how she was going to stay awake.

Somehow, she would have to try.

With each passing moment, she listened for sounds outside the door that would suggest to her that they had been discovered, but there was no sign of that. There was no sign of anything.

Gradually, she found herself beginning to relax, to find a moment of peace, and despite her best effort to resist the urge to drift, she couldn't help it. She started to slip away, fighting as sleep attempted to claim her. After everything she had experienced, it was a fight she couldn't win.

32

DANIEL

REACHING KEYALL WAS DIFFICULT.

Part of it came from the fact that Daniel had never traveled this far to the south, though Rayen had. Part of it came from the fact that he had finally begun to reach the limits of his powers. Rayen had guided him continually south. At a certain point, they had to go by sight, since he had never traveled this far.

"How long do you think you need to rest?" Rayen asked.

It had been a little while since Rayen had gone off on Carth's behalf, helping Haern with his issue—something he still wasn't entirely sure what had happened. Lucy had coordinated it and now she was back with him.

Daniel sat with his legs crossed in front of him, staring out at the water. He took a few deep breaths, trying to gather himself, wanting to be prepared for the next step.

"I don't know. It's been a while since I've pushed myself like this."

"If the shadows for you are anything like what they are for me, they should offer some restoration."

"It would be nice if they did." He breathed in deeply, thinking about the shadows and what he detected when he was Sliding, but he felt no sense of renewal.

Perhaps it only worked for her.

His ability was different than hers. He couldn't control the shadows the way she could, manipulating them to mask himself in darkness. He couldn't even imagine using them as a barrier the way she did. The one thing the shadows offered him was a connection to his Sliding.

He lay back, resting his head on his arms. Wind whistled around him, gusting up out of the south. Every so often, he caught a hint of something mixed with the sea breeze, a strange and pleasant aroma. It was a warm wind, reminding him of their journey into the jungle and toward Ceyaniah. He felt a little guilty that they hadn't returned to Ceyaniah, though now that he'd been there, it shouldn't be difficult to return.

"Why do you think the shadows are different for me and you?" he asked.

Rayen took a seat next to him, crossing her legs and sitting upright as she stared out into the distance. "There are probably many reasons, but the most likely would be that I grew up influenced by them."

"You didn't live near the chamber of shadows."

Rayen shook her head. "No. I didn't, but my family had."

"They did?"

Rayen nodded. "It was a long time ago, but they didn't live all that far from where we'd been. I think that's part of the key when it comes to the gifts the Elder Stones grant. Some of it is proximity to the stone itself. With enough time, the stone changes someone."

"By that, you're saying that I needed more time with the stone."

"Possibly. I don't know if you would gain control over shadows if you were to remain in the chamber for longer."

He thought about what he knew of his abilities. There were some who suggested that people born outside of Elaeavn didn't have the same strength with their abilities as those born within the city. In that case, proximity to the sacred crystals made a difference.

Why, though? If what they believed was true—that the crystals were not an Elder Stone but something else—then why would it make any difference?

"You still have control over the shadows," he said.

"Mine is because my people lived in that land for as long as they did. Carth speculates that if I had been raised within our borders, my powers might have been even more potent."

Daniel glanced at her. "Even more?"

"I know it's hard for you to imagine me even more impressive than I already am," Rayen said, smiling at him.

"What about Carth?"

"Carth isn't all that different from me. She didn't grow up in our homeland. By the time she was born, our peoples had begun to depart. War forced us away."

"And yet, Carth is powerful with her connection to the shadows."

"I imagine you wonder what it must be like for others, and how powerful they might be."

That had been what he was thinking about. If there was such benefit to growing up in the land where the Elder Stone gave strength, what would have happened if Carth had done so?

"There simply aren't that many who are shadow born," Rayen said.

"That's what you call yourself?"

"It's how our people refer to us. Many were given the gift of the shadow blessing, and even that is considered incredibly valuable. Those who were touched more deeply, those who were truly shadow born, are rarer still."

It was different than what he knew in Elaeavn. The Elvraeth had always been powerful, though wasn't that capability tied to the fact that his people had had access to the sacred crystals all these years? Those crystals granted their people the abilities of the Great Watcher, strengthening the bonds.

"I wonder what I would have been able to do if I had been there. I've often considered what it would've been like had I been raised in my homeland. Just how much would I have been able to accomplish? Just how much power would I have been able to summon?" As she said it, she used the shadows, wrapping them tightly around her. Daniel marveled at her control, as he often did, amazed at how much she could do already.

"Have you ever considered returning?"

Rayen nodded. "I've contemplated remaining in those lands, but every time I consider it, I realize it's not my destiny anymore. I have another purpose."

"The Binders."

"That has been part of it," she said.

Daniel rested his head, looking outward as he did. There was something quite comfortable about sitting with Rayen. They weren't isolated, though it felt that way. Regardless of where they went, he always had the knowledge that he could return. Surprisingly, as he lay there, he realized his strength was replenishing more rapidly than he'd expected. Perhaps Rayen was right, and his connection to the shadows did grant him additional strength.

He glanced over at Rayen. "How did you and Carth meet?"

"It was chance, nothing more. She has long served the role that she does, protecting the Binders, and there was a time when she came across me. I didn't have much purpose at the time. I was using my shadows in ways I probably should not have been. Carth recognized something in me. That's not surprising now, but at the time, there weren't many who had ever seen anything useful about me."

"Why do you think that?"

"I didn't have an easy childhood," she said.

Daniel waited for her to elaborate. In all the time he'd traveled with Rayen, he had struggled to get her to open up, and she had always been reluctant to do so. He had known not to push. There was no reason for him to do so. Pushing would only drive her away, and he enjoyed her company.

"I think that isn't all that unique," Rayen went on. "When I hear Carth talk about her childhood, I recognize a shared trauma, though she came out of it strong. I came out of it broken."

"You don't seem broken."

"Not now, but I was." She let out a heavy sigh. The shadows swirled around her, colors flickering. "My parents died when I was young. We were travelers, sailing on massive ships that spent most of their time out at sea." She nodded to the distant ocean, and a hint of a smile curled her lips. "Those were happy memories. I can easily recall my father working the wheel, guiding us through storms and swells, my laughter as we rolled through seas that could claim us. My father shared in my laughter, never minding the storms or the wind or the waves, not the way Mother did." Rayen swallowed, and she wiped the corner of her eye. "Life was good. But then, life on the sea is unpredictable. That's something I've seen even in the time I've been traveling with Carth."

When she didn't go on, Daniel looked over at her. "What happened?"

"Not everyone who sails is kind. It's the same as what you find throughout all lands. It's the reason for the Binders. We offer protection to those who need it, and we offer safety, especially as so many don't have it."

"Were you hurt?"

"Many times," she said. "I didn't have an understanding of the shadows at that time. I think I was aware of them, sort of like someone can be aware of the night, but even if I knew what I was able to do, I had no control over it. They were deep within me, buried. My parents didn't have the shadow gift. They may have been blessed, but if they were, they didn't know how to use it either."

It was interesting how she spoke of her parents. She, who had been given joy and happiness but had not been guided on the use of her powers, still spoke fondly about them. Then there was Daniel, who had been trained by his father, taught to plan, to prepare, to use the powers the Great Watcher had given him in order to lead in Elaeavn when it came time. Even though he'd been taught, he had no happy memories from that time. There had always been a sense of disappointment, a sense that he had to perform in order to please his father and convince him he was worthy.

Where had that gotten him?

He had never considered it a tormented childhood, but perhaps it was. Perhaps his childhood was just as difficult as Rayen's, though for different reasons.

"When did Carth find you?"

"I lost my parents when I was seven or eight. It's hard to remember, but there were several years where I can fondly remember the ocean and the waves and the ports we visited. I recall the games my father taught me, a way of passing time as we traveled, and even Mother would get in on it. She didn't love the games the same way Father did."

"My father liked to play games, but they were ones where he wanted me to try to figure out what he was thinking and how to manipulate others."

"A form of Tsatsun," she said.

"Maybe, though he never called it that, and I don't know that I would have considered it Tsatsun at the time."

"When my parents were killed, I was taken on board another vessel. We traveled for several years, and each day was a new sort of torment. I went from knowing the freedom of being with people who cared about me, the freedom of wandering the ship, climbing the mast, exploring below decks and enjoying every port we visited, to being confined to a single room and trotted out at each port for a very specific purpose."

Rayen shuddered, and the shadows swirled back inwardly for a moment before she breathed out, releasing her hold on the shadows.

"It was in one of those ports where Carth found me. I was young. Twelve, maybe thirteen, I don't even know anymore. She rescued all of us. Offered us her protection. A promise of safety. Perhaps something more. When she slaughtered the captain, I wondered if that promise was an empty one or if it really was a chance to hope for something more." Rayen trailed off near the end, and she turned away from him. "I don't talk about it. Carth knows, and I suppose the women who were rescued with me know, though very few of them stayed on to serve the Binders. Most were content to be freed, and they were resettled, given an opportunity to have a new life. For the most part, they wanted that and were more than happy to take advantage of that new existence. I wanted something different."

"What did you want?"

"At first, revenge."

"Only at first?"

"Eventually, Carth got through to me. Revenge is hollow. When it's over, what are you left with? What I needed instead was purpose, and she gave that to me. And then I very nearly betrayed her."

"You were trying to protect your people," Daniel said.

"I should have known that Carth deserved my trust.

She had earned it dozens of times by that point, and yet, I still abandoned her, and in doing so, I…"

Rayen sat with her back to him, and Daniel got up, scooting around and slipping an arm around her shoulders. "Thank you for sharing with me."

"I didn't share with you so you would pity me."

"Why would I pity you?"

"Because of what I told you."

"You told me you experienced trauma. I can't say I have any idea what you went through, nor can I say I understand. All I can say is that I'm sorry. And I guess I can say you're strong."

"I won't allow it to happen to me again."

He thought he understood now why she acted the way she did, and how she had grown. It certainly made sense that she shared Carth's sentiments about the Binders.

"It's too bad that in all the time you were with Carth, she didn't make you a better Tsatsun player," he said.

She turned toward him. Her eyes were reddened, and the corners were moist. She rubbed a knuckle in her eyes and started to laugh. "That's your takeaway from all of this?"

"I guess I would have expected you to learn something from her during all the time you spent together."

"I did learn something."

"Really?"

She sent the shadows swirling around him and pulled him toward her.

The suddenness of it was disarming, and he chose not to resist. There had always been something appealing about

Rayen, though it had been hard for Daniel to move past Lucy. Then again, Lucy had made it clear she was not open to such advances. His entire young adult life had been spent pining over Lucy Elvraeth, wanting that connection. He had let himself believe that it was his choice, and that he was attracted to her because of who she was. Having known Lucy as well and as long as he had, he couldn't deny there was an appeal. Yet, the more he thought about it, the more he wondered how deep his feelings truly were. He found Lucy both more and less appealing now that she had been given her augmentation and had changed as much as she had.

It was different with Rayen. When he looked at Rayen, he saw strength despite what she had gone through. He saw a powerful woman. He saw a woman who still found humor in the world despite everything she had experienced and seen. He saw someone who understood strategy, regardless of her skill at Tsatsun.

This was someone he found appealing now.

How much had he changed since leaving Elaeavn?

He might have ventured into the chamber of shadows, but there had been other changes within him. It might not have been as stark as what had happened to Lucy, but he had changed.

"Why have you told me all of this?" he asked.

"You didn't want to know?" Her voice was soft, husky, and she was close to him. He could smell her breath. Feel the heat of it. The warmth of her body radiated off her along with the strange sense of the shadows.

"I'm glad you finally shared," he said.

"We have been traveling long enough I thought you should know."

"Is that the only reason?"

"What other reason should there be?"

Daniel leaned toward Rayen and kissed her.

She was the one who had pulled him close to her, and he suspected she was open to affection, but he wasn't certain how she would respond. That was part of Rayen's appeal. Not knowing what she might do, or how she might react.

She kissed him back.

As she did, he could feel the shadows swirl around them. They pulled him closer to her, drawing them together. They stayed close, wrapped in shadows, lying on the seashore, the sound of waves crashing around them, winds swirling everywhere around them.

33

DANIEL

THE CITY OF KEYALL RESTED ALONG AN IMPOSSIBLY HIGH peak. Daniel stared up at it from the shore, ignoring the ships behind him, many of them lining the docks, the sounds of sailors and merchants and seagulls all mingling together. Instead, he looked up at the rock towering high overhead, amazed.

"This is Keyall?"

Rayen remain transfixed, looking up the same way as he did, her jaw clenched as she stared. She had grown somewhat quieter the farther they had come, as if she had disliked the idea of coming to Keyall. She hadn't said, but he had to wonder if perhaps this was the place where she'd been abducted.

"It's an interesting city," Rayen said. "Carth spent quite a bit of time here when she was younger, and I think she even found herself imprisoned here."

"What would it take to imprison Carth?" Knowing Carth, he couldn't imagine her being easily subdued.

"The magic of the Elder Stone here." With that, Rayen

strode forward, heading along the shore until they reached the road going up. It wound past merchants, dozens of them, many of them simply sitting outside of their shops, occasionally hollering at passersby, otherwise staring blankly as if they had nothing to say.

It would've been easier for him to Slide up to the rest of the city, but Rayen wanted them to walk, and so they did. There had been a closeness between them since that afternoon spent on the shores, and yet it had not been repeated. Neither of them spoke about it, though they would need to address it eventually. For now, he enjoyed the closeness with her.

When they reached the top of the cliff, he looked back the way they had come. It was incredibly steep, a surprising place to build a city, but what was more surprising was the way the city spread out from the top of the cliff. Most of it was here, and he marveled at the sheer size of Keyall.

"I don't know anything about this city," he said.

"Keyall is isolated here. It's the way they like it."

"Like Elaeavn?"

Rayen shook her head. "The people of Keyall don't keep themselves closed off to outsiders. You saw how many ships were out there."

"I did."

"They have dozens of merchants moving through each week, and all of them have items to trade. Because of that, Keyall gets word from outside of the city. They might be separated geographically, but they aren't isolated from the world."

Daniel stared down at the shoreline. From here, he

could make out the ships more easily. There were dozens and dozens of ships. Some were making their way toward Keyall, while others were sailing away, the wind catching their massive sails and guiding them out and away from the city. Most of the ships were in different styles, and he marveled at the fact that many of them were quite a bit different than even those found in Elaeavn. Most of those were narrow, with sleek hulls designed to travel along the shoreline rather than in the deep water. When he had been in Asador, he had seen other sorts of ships that had other purposes, and these were even different than those.

"Where do we need to go here?" he asked, turning back toward Keyall.

"I'm still not completely convinced this is the right plan."

"I thought you agreed with me."

"I agreed to accompany you, but that doesn't mean that I agree with you. The caretakers in Keyall can be very protective about the Elder Stone they possess."

"Is there a way for us to get to it without their knowing?"

Rayen's mouth twisted in a frown. "It won't be easy."

"Which means there is."

She nodded. "There is, but I think it's better if we approach the caretakers and see if they would be willing to allow us access."

Daniel wasn't about to argue with Rayen when it came to this. She would know better than he, though he wanted to know if he was right. The first step would be getting to the stone and spending some time around it. Once he did, he could determine if there was anything about him that changed after handling it.

It was possible nothing would change. When he had been around the chamber of shadows, he hadn't known that anything had changed for quite a while. Even now, his connection to the shadows continued to evolve.

What would happen when he managed to reach the stone here?

So far, Rayen hadn't even told him what the stone in Keyall was like.

"What's the best strategy for approaching?"

"When I came here before, I came with Carth, and even that visit was brief."

Daniel glanced over at her for a moment. "You do know how to find the Elder Stone here."

She met his gaze for a moment before shaking her head. "Unfortunately…"

Daniel laughed. "All of this and you don't even know how to find it?"

"I know that the stone is in Keyall. Carth has been protective of its location."

"Which means *we* have to find it now."

"It seems that way," she said.

"You know, it would be easier if we simply found Carth and asked her."

"Do you think you can?"

Daniel shook his head. "I have no idea where she'd be. Even if I did, I don't know that she's going to offer us much help."

"That would be typical for Carth."

He looked around the city. It wasn't all that dissimilar

to places like Asador and Elaeavn, though the buildings were spaced a little farther apart. They all seemed to be made of a dark stone, and there was something strange about it. It seemed to give off shadows, but at the same time, it swallowed them.

Looking over to Rayen, he watched as she used her shadows, letting them swirl around her. She often did it without any awareness of her actions, letting the shadows stream away from her. It was a unique feature to her, and he suspected it was a way to ensure that they were safe, to maintain her connection to them, but the more he had come to know about her, the more he wondered if perhaps there wasn't another reason for her to use the shadows like that.

"Do you notice anything about this place?" Daniel asked.

"What should I be noticing?"

When her shadows reached one of the nearest buildings, they disappeared. "Look at what your shadows are doing."

Rayen turned her attention from him and focused on her shadows. They swirled out from her with increased power, drifting until they reached one of the buildings. When they did, they faded again.

"I suspect you're not doing that?"

Rayen clenched her jaw before shaking her head. "No."

"That's why Carth didn't tell you anything about Keyall." He looked around again, curious if he could even Slide, and tried, slipping forward, but as he attempted to do so by using the shadows, that connection failed. He could Slide, but he couldn't use his new connection to them in order to do so. "Why was Carth imprisoned here?"

"I'm not entirely sure. I do know that whatever she experienced here was tied to Olandar Fahr."

"We need to find someone who might be familiar with Carth and her time here."

"How do you propose we do that?"

"What is one place Carth always goes regardless of where she is?" Daniel asked.

Rayen grinned. "Taverns."

It was something he always found amusing about Carth. She did visit taverns in pretty much every place they went. There had to be some reason for it, though with Carth, he was unlikely to be able to discover that key. She kept things like that to herself, though according to Rayen, it had something to do with what she had experienced as a child.

They headed off, moving along the street. Daniel glanced from side to side as they went. Usually, finding a tavern wasn't difficult. Within Elaeavn, there were many different types. The ones in the old Lower Town were more raucous, the kind of place he enjoyed visiting. There was music and dancing, and loud conversation that mingled with ale. It was so different than what he found in the Upper Town, where the taverns were full of muted, whispered conversation. The drinks were different, too. Few people drank ale, most preferring the more refined exotic spiced wine.

What would they find here?

In Asador, the taverns he'd visited had reminded him more of those in Lower Town. There had been a certain chaos, an energy, and there had been loud voices and music, but not as much dancing. The women running the taverns in Asador—and even in Eban—had done so with a tight sort of control to ensure the safety of the people within. That was another difference between Asador and Elaeavn: there were no Binders offering themselves to men in exchange for secrets.

He glanced over to Rayen, frowning. "Do the Binders operate in Elaeavn?"

"We have operatives in all places."

"In the taverns?"

"In the taverns. Other places throughout the city. Any place we can find information."

Why wasn't he surprised that Carth had managed to secure her network in Elaeavn? The city wasn't as fortified as those within the floating palace thought.

Rayen pointed, and they headed toward the sound of music. It was loud and vibrant and drifted out of an open door. Several people headed in as they were making their way there, and he realized this was reassuring. A place with some activity was better than one without any. When they reached the door, Daniel paused for a moment, looking inside. There were several dozen people inside, most seated at tables staggered around the room. Women meandered from table to table, servants similar to what he had found at other taverns. Daniel tapped on Rayen's arm, nodding.

"We don't have a presence here," Rayen whispered.

"You don't?"

She shook her head. "Apparently, it was some agreement Carth made."

"You don't hear anything out of Keyall?"

"We do, but it's not through our network. That was another part of some agreement she arranged."

"Why would Carth make an agreement like that?"

"I never learned."

"Why didn't anyone try to establish their network here?"

"We were told that anyone who tried would find the constables angered. It's simply safer not to risk it. No one needs the danger of a city where we aren't welcome."

"I don't know that you're necessarily welcome in other places, and yet…"

"We did what Carth asked," Rayen said.

Her tone suggested she wasn't willing to discuss it any further, and Daniel decided not to push.

They made their way into the tavern and found an open table near the back. Taking a seat, he tried to twist his chair around so he could pay attention to the people here but found it was a bit difficult. Rayen didn't have the same challenge. She made certain that her chair was along the wall, and pushed shadows out from her, sending them swirling. The wooden walls of the tavern did nothing to obstruct them.

With his newfound connection to shadows, Daniel found it difficult to know what purpose Rayen had when she used them like this. Before, he would know when she was trying to mask herself within the shadows, but now he was less aware of that.

"What are you doing?" he whispered.

"I am making us less visible."

"Don't you want to be visible so we can see what we can learn?"

"Eventually, and I'm not completely making us invisible, just… muting… us."

"How does it work?"

Rayen glanced over. "Do you now have a connection to your shadows that you can use like that?"

"Not really, but I'm curious. Besides, what happens if I gain that ability?"

"If you gain it, I will teach you. I wonder if you'll be as inexperienced in that as you are in other things."

Daniel coughed, leaning back as heat worked up his neck. "You didn't seem to complain."

"Inexperience can be sweet." She rested her head back on the wall, smiling, and he shook his head. She was trying to get to him. What was worse, it was working.

Daniel looked around the tavern, searching for anything that might help him figure out where the Elder Stone would be hidden within the city. Carth would come to taverns like this for a variety of reasons, but one thing he'd often seen her do was playing games. Then again, with her abilities, she rarely lost. Most of the time, Daniel was impressed to find she did so out of skill rather than trying to sneak her way through, using shadows or her connection to the flame in order to win. Then again, there were times when he suspected she did use those abilities. How could she not? Someone simply didn't win that often at dicing without some extra help.

At a table near them, four men sat with a couple of dice resting on the table. Every so often, one of them would roll the dice, and they would begin to laugh.

Money was moved around the table as they played, and Daniel wished he better understood how to dice.

Another table had a circular board with small figurines placed upon it. It reminded him somewhat of Tsatsun, though there didn't appear to be the same level of strategy with it. Money changed hands at that table, too.

"Do they gamble on all of these games?" he whispered.

"What's the point of playing if there's nothing at stake?" Rayen asked.

"Isn't the point just to win?"

"For some, but others need to risk something. Think about how much more it will matter when they win."

Daniel leaned forward, watching the men nearest him as they diced. It seemed to him a great disservice that in all the time he had grown up around the palace, he'd not learned anything about a game like dice. Then again, regardless of his father wanting to teach him strategy, he hadn't learned anything about Tsatsun, and that seemed to be a game that would have intrigued him. As Daniel watched, he tried to get a sense for the strategy involved. As far as he could tell, they were trying to get the highest roll on three dice, and it seemed they had three rolls with which to do so. There didn't seem to be any skill to this game at all. It was a matter of luck. Then again, perhaps there was some skill with how the matchings were chosen.

Daniel turned his attention to the game board, looking at the pieces. The men there moved more deliberately, taking their time in between each move, lifting their pieces as they slid them across the board. From what he could tell, most of the pieces looked the same, though not

424 | D.K. HOLMBERG

all. There was no central piece as there was in Tsatsun—
the Stone—and as they moved, nearing their opponent's
pieces, they removed piece after piece from the board.

Daniel frowned. A game like that would have some
strategy, though as he watched, he couldn't detect what it
might be.

"Are you sensing anything?" he asked Rayen. With her
shadows, she could tilt them, manipulate them in such a
way she could listen to conversations around her that he
had no access to.

"Not so far. There is mostly conversation about
gambling, and about the inventory on ships. It seems
many of these men are merchants."

Daniel looked around the tavern. This wasn't the right
kind of place for them to uncover what they wanted. He
motioned for Rayen to follow him, and got to his feet,
heading out the door. Once outside, he glanced back at
the tavern.

"That's not where we need to be."

"It's the kind of place Carth would have gone."

"Perhaps, but what we're looking for is someone
familiar with the city. We need to find someone who
knows things here. If we can uncover that, then we can
figure out what they know about the Elder Stone." As he
looked around, he tried to think about what they would
need. It would be a more refined tavern—one more like
those in Upper Town in Elaeavn.

It would be a place where locals gathered, not
merchants. Even in Asador, Daniel had noticed many of
the locals preferred to go to taverns where they wouldn't
have to be surrounded by outsiders. There weren't as

many places like that, and those they found weren't as well marked.

Normally, he would ask Rayen to help, using her connection to the shadows to listen, but perhaps that was a mistake here. And maybe he wouldn't even need to have Rayen use her ability in order for them to figure out where to go.

There was another way for him to find someplace more typical for Keyall. He'd seen it when he'd first reached this upper section of the city.

It was the stone.

People from the city would prefer a building made from their stone. If it was impervious to shadows, it was likely special to them in other ways, and perhaps it was connected to their Elder Stone.

He looked around, searching for something that would tell him where they needed to go.

"What are you looking for?" Rayen asked.

"A tavern with the dark stone."

"Why do you think you'll find one?"

"Just consider it a hunch."

She laughed, glancing over at him. "I didn't take you for the kind who played by hunch. I always figured you preferred skill and strategy."

"In this case, I think they'll be the same." He nodded to the building they'd just come out of. "Look at that one. It's made of wood. It's filled with merchants. Outsiders. It didn't have anything about it that struck me as unique to Keyall. What we need to find is a place less well marked, but more likely to be considered local."

He started along the street, looking and listening as he

went, glancing from building to building. Some of them were built partly out of the same dark stone. Those that weren't were typically made of wood and were shorter than those made from the stone.

It took a while, but Daniel finally found a row of buildings that all seemed to be constructed from the same dark stone that he found immune to the shadows. He started toward it, but Rayen grabbed his hand.

"We should be careful," she said.

"What are you worried about?"

"Only that we don't know enough about Keyall."

Daniel squeezed her hand. "I know you're worried that your abilities aren't working like you think they should, but I can Slide us out of here if I need to."

"Are you able to do so even without a connection to the shadows?"

"It's not that I don't have a connection to the shadows, it's just that when I tried to use it around the buildings— at least, around these buildings—I didn't have the same capability."

"I haven't seen anything I suspect is a tavern," she said.

"Then we should watch."

"How would you propose we watch?"

Daniel pointed to a nearby rooftop. Rayen looked over to him and nodded.

34

DANIEL

DANIEL WAS GETTING TIRED FROM SITTING ON THE rooftop. It felt as if they had been here for most of the night, though he knew that wasn't the case. He tried to mimic Rayen as she remained crouched next to him, scanning the darkness. She had said nothing about experiencing discomfort positioned as she was.

"We haven't come across anything," he whispered.

"That's not true," she said, nodding to the street. They had followed dozens of people throughout the night, staying along the rooftop, using Daniel's ability to Slide. Each time they followed someone, they found they didn't go quite where he had expected. No one seemed to be a local, or if they were, they were heading away from this section and deeper into the city.

They had found quite a few merchants who traveled from place to place, often going into taverns, but just as often traveling deeper into the city, likely to trade their wares, before disappearing altogether.

All in all, it was an entirely frustrating turn of events.

Finding a local—and someone who was able to guide them to a tavern—had proven more challenging than he had expected.

"I can't believe Carth has managed to uncover so much by following people throughout the city."

"Most of the time, it's relatively easy to find a tavern," Rayen said. "Even if you start at the wrong one, it doesn't take long to hear about others."

"We could have used that strategy."

"I don't know that it would've worked."

Neither did Daniel. It wasn't a matter of just finding any local. They wanted to find the right kind. Someone who had information—real information.

It was nearing midnight, late enough that anyone who might go out for the night would already have done so, and the longer they waited, the less likely it was that they would come across anyone. It might be better for them to get some sleep and then come back out the following night. He considered finding a place in Keyall, but it would be just as easy for them to Slide back to Elaeavn or Asador or any other place where they had rooms. More than that, they would be safe rooms. In Keyall, he had no idea what sort of safety he'd find.

"You see that?" Rayen whispered.

"No."

She shot him a look. "You're the Elvraeth. Don't you have enhanced eyesight?"

"Yes, but I'm not seeing what you think I should."

She pointed along the road. "Look. Movement."

They'd had several false alarms already. Each time, they thought they had come across movement, but it had been little more than merchants or visitors, and once even a trio of constables. He had been careful not to follow too closely, not wanting to draw the constables' attention.

Daniel stared at the street, peering through the darkness. His eyesight was good, but not as enhanced as others from Elaeavn. It was one of those gifts he'd never cared all that much to develop, but now he couldn't help but think it would've been nice to have more capability there.

As he stared, he took a moment to see what Rayen referred to. A man skittered along the street, slipping from one pool of darkness to the next. He seemed to have an awareness of how to conceal himself within the shadows as he moved. Daniel couldn't help but think that wasn't chance.

Grabbing Rayen, he Slid, reaching the end of the street, emerging on the rooftop and looking down.

The man was gone.

No—he was still there, but he had moved to the far side of the street, still hiding within the shadows. As he went, Daniel found himself smiling at the man. It was impressive that he was able to conceal himself. The fact he traveled the way he did couldn't be chance. No one moved that discreetly.

He strained to look through the darkness, searching for any sign of how the man was dressed or others who might be with him, but it was difficult to tell.

Could he have some way of negating Daniel's ability?

He'd never seen anything like that, but perhaps that was the key.

Rayen leaned in. "He's sneaky, that one is."

"Why do you say that?"

"I can barely make him out. I think he knows what he's doing, but it's a different tactic than I've seen before."

Daniel continued studying the man as he went along the street and realized he seemed unaware of the fact that he was observed. The man seemed to be oblivious to the fact that Daniel and Rayen were there.

He stayed with Rayen, moving them along the street, and when they reached another intersection, he watched as the man made his way along the street before veering off.

Now that he knew what to look for, Daniel was better able to keep track of where the man went. They continued to follow him, and Daniel noted how he made his way deeper into the city, heading along various side streets. Every so often he would pause, glancing back as if he wanted to ensure no one was following him, but he would continue on. It was almost as if he did so at a very cursory level, not really expecting anyone to follow.

He paused at another intersection, glancing in either direction—but never looking up. When he was done, he hurried forward. Darkness swallowed him, and as Daniel stared, he realized that part of that darkness seemed to be from the long cloak he wore. Almost as if the cloak itself helped to shield him. He'd never seen anything quite like that.

The man reached a building. It was standalone, not combined with other buildings like they had seen in other sections of the city, and made entirely of the dark stone. As Daniel stared at it, he realized that Rayen was pushing shadows toward the building. Every time the shadows got near the building, they disappeared, fading away as if the stone made them dissipate completely.

The man pulled open the door, heading into the building. As he did, he cast one more glance over his shoulder, looking back along the street. This time, his gaze did dart up.

Daniel remained fixed in place, fearful that the man had caught sight of him, but he turned and headed back into the building.

"That was strange," he whispered.

"That he looked back at us, or that he didn't see us?"

"Both?"

"Hopefully I've concealed us in shadows, though given what happened with him, I'm not entirely sure it worked."

"He only looked up the one time," Daniel said.

"That we noticed."

"I don't think he did it any other time."

Rayen sighed. "It is unfortunate that we aren't able to tell any better than that."

"Where do you think he went?"

"It's the kind of building you were looking for, isn't it?"

Daniel nodded. They had been searching for a building made entirely of the black stone; at the same time, they wanted a building that seemed preferred by the locals. Given the late hour, it was hard to know what kind of place this was. It could be nothing more than this man's home. If that was the case, then following him would have revealed nothing.

"I hope this was worth it," he whispered.

Rayen shrugged. "If it wasn't, then it's only been a waste of time, nothing more."

With that, she jumped, landing on the side of the road, and backed up along the wall, waiting for him.

Daniel chuckled to himself. He Slid, not quite as comfortable jumping from a height as Rayen. Out on the street, they started toward the building. He glanced around, and when they finally reached the building, he hesitated.

There was no sound of music, nothing that gave off the sense of a tavern. He didn't even notice any voices. No murmuring or shouts or calls, or anything that would suggest there was activity within.

Daniel glanced over to Rayen before taking her hand. Then he Slid.

Emerging on the other side of the door brought him into a dimly lit room. A couple of lanterns hung on hooks from posts around the room. A haze of smoke filled the space, and there was a hint of an aroma with it, one that left him thinking of spice and cinnamon rather than burning firewood. Some of the smoke drifted out of the hearth itself, but most of it seemed to be coming from vents cut into the floor. It was almost as if the occupants of the room wanted the smoke.

It certainly provided a masking effect. He tried to See through the smoke, but other than making out the faint shapes of various forms, he wasn't able to tell all that much. He had a sense of how few people were here, but even that was difficult.

"Can you make out much of anything?"

"Not really," she said.

"Have you seen anything like this before?"

"Like smoke?"

"Smoke used to conceal people inside the tavern."

"There are many ways people conceal themselves in places like this," Rayen said. "Sometimes they prefer smoke, sometimes they use abilities like I have, and other times they simply dress themselves differently. If nothing else, this is exactly the kind of place we wanted to find." She held on to his hand, weaving through the smoke, managing to avoid bumping into anyone.

Daniel tried to see through the smoke, but it seemed to have a weight to it, almost as if it were designed to be difficult to see through. Not just to see through, but to navigate through as well.

They reached a table and chairs, and Rayen helped him find his way so he could sit. Taking a seat, he put his back to the wall, mimicking what Rayen had done in the last tavern. She shot him a look of annoyance, and he grinned.

Leaning toward her, he lowered his voice. "If we can't see or hear anything, what sort of benefit will we gain by coming here?"

"Probably none, other than we should be able to determine whether there is anyone here that we want to see."

They had already seen the man entering, and now Daniel wondered if they'd be able to follow him if it came down to it. More than that, could they figure out if there were any others here they should be tracking?

"I might have to use the shadows to see if I can't disperse some of the smoke," she said.

"Do you think you can?"

shadows aren't responding as well as they

strange, but Daniel could detect the same thing.

The stone outside had disrupted the shadows, but while there was the stone in the walls surrounding them, the shadows should be able to work inside, not limited by whatever was taking place within the walls.

How much of it was from the smoke? Even though he wasn't able to penetrate the shadows, he had to wonder if there was something within the smoke that made it difficult to see through them.

Regardless, it suggested whoever was here had familiarity with the shadows—and they knew how to overpower them.

As he leaned over to say something to Rayen, a figure appeared before them. Daniel could make him out as little more than a darkness that formed within the smoke, but this figure sat at the table with them.

"You'll find your ability is limited here," the man said. He had an accented voice, and his words were slightly clipped, giving a strange contour to them.

"And what ability is that?" Daniel asked.

"Not yours. Hers."

Daniel looked over to Rayen. Shadows coalesced around her, sweeping outward, but they faded rapidly as they met whatever strange resistance was formed by the smoke.

"As I said," the man said.

"Who are you?"

"The better question is who are you and why are you here?"

"We're just passing through," Rayen said.

"Indeed? An odd location for one like yourself. Then again, as you aren't the first person to have visited Keyall with your particular abilities, I'm not altogether surprised."

Daniel sat up, leaning toward the man. Even as he did, he couldn't make him out any better than he had before. "Who do you know who visited here with these abilities?"

The man said nothing. "As I said, you'll find your abilities are not quite as effective here." He started to get up when Daniel surged toward him, Sliding. When he grabbed the man by the wrist, he Slid him from the tavern, emerging on the street. He waited a moment for Rayen to follow, concerned she might hold off, but she stepped out into the night only a few moments after he did.

Out in the street, he was able to make out the man more clearly. He was thin, dressed in a long cloak, and the jewelry on his fingers spoke of wealth, though it was gaudier than anything Daniel would have preferred.

It was the man they'd followed. Daniel had not gotten a good look at him, but he was certain this was the same person.

"Interesting," the man said, looking around. "You were able to take me out here that quickly?"

"Who are you?" Daniel asked.

"You might find that Keyall is less than welcoming to strangers who attempt to assault individuals within the city."

"And you might find we aren't forced to stay here for whatever justice you might exact. Who are you?" Daniel said again.

The man's gaze drifted past him and over to Rayen. He

studied her for a long time, and after a while, he smiled. "You look like her."

Daniel frowned. "Who does she look like?"

The man sniffed. "Don't play games. If you're with her, I suppose you can't help it. Regardless," he said, waving his hand.

Rayen started to smile. "You know Carth."

The man nodded. "I know her. It's been some time since I've seen her, but I know her." He looked around the street, frowning. "Come now, before the constables decide to make their presence known." He started off, unmindful of the fact that he put his back to two people he didn't know, and seemingly unconcerned about how Daniel had simply dragged him from the tavern.

He glanced to Rayen. "Do you think we should follow?"

"If he knows Carth, he can provide us information about what we're looking for."

"Or he has a grudge against her, and he's using this as an opportunity to pay it back."

Rayen smiled. "You really do think like her."

"I'll take that as a compliment."

"She sees danger in every shadow, sort of like you appear to."

"Only she can see deeper into the shadows than I can."

"With practice, I suspect you'll be able to see deeper into the shadows, too." They followed the man as he turned a corner, and Daniel reached for the hilt of his sword. He didn't know if this man would attempt anything or whether he would guide them someplace dangerous, but the street opened up, and a massive estate spread in front of them.

Daniel blinked. "This is your place?"

"It is now," the man said. "Keyall is uniquely situated. We have merchants come from all over, which means that trade comes from all over. When you learn to maneuver it, you gain skill." He flashed a smile. "With skill comes wealth."

The man reached the gate leading into the estate grounds and nodded to the guards standing on either side of it. The wall surrounding the estate seemed to be made of the same dark stone, which made Daniel question whether they would be able to Slide beyond here if they went inside.

So far, he hadn't seen any reason to believe that the stone would prevent him from Sliding, but if it did, he wanted to be prepared. He still could fight if necessary, and he doubted they would have any way to keep him from Sliding if it came down to it, but it was much better for them not to need such defenses.

Rayen grabbed for his hand. As they walked through the gate, shadows continued to swirl around her, but as soon as they were through, they spread out, stretching across the ground. She relaxed, letting out a pent-up breath.

The man guided them up to the main entrance to the estate, and once there, he paused, glancing over his shoulder at them. "There's no need to fear."

"We're not afraid," Daniel said, though he suspected that wasn't completely true. Rayen losing her abilities in this place would make her nervous. The Great Watcher knew it made him nervous.

"Why don't we have a drink, and then we can talk?"

"Maybe we can talk first," Daniel said.

The man grunted. "So direct. There is advantage to taking one's time and enjoying the experience."

He pulled open the door. A grand hallway opened up in front of them. Portraits hung on the wall, one of the man they were with, and another of an older gentleman. They faced each other, and there were similarities in their features. Both wore the same style of dark cloak that this man wore, and the older man had a cane, whereas the man they were with carried a walking stick that was pointed at the end, almost like a sword. Would he have that on him now?

He guided them up a wide staircase, turning down a carpeted hall, and reached another door at the end of the hall. Once there, he stepped inside, waving his hand with a flourish. "Take a seat. I will see that you are brought wine, and then we can talk."

The man closed the door, leaving them for a moment. Daniel looked around and noticed they were in a massive library. Shelves lined the walls, books stuffed within them. There were globes and spyglasses and other items of intrigue resting on many of the shelves. He wandered over to one shelf, scanning the titles, curious what sort of books a man like this would have. Many of them seemed to be in a different language, though the titles he could understand suggested they were historical documents.

"How do we even know this man knows Carth?" Daniel asked, looking at the shelves. "What if he's only encountered someone with the shadow blessing and not someone like her—or you—who's shadow born?"

"I suspect he's actually met her."

"Why is that?" Daniel asked, pulling a book off the shelf. He glanced at the cover, realizing that it was a story about Asador. It would be interesting to learn more about the history of Asador, though it would be intruiging to learn about many different histories. With everything he had been experiencing, having a greater knowledge of the past would be beneficial.

"Look," Rayen said.

Daniel pushed the book back into its spot on the shelf, staring at the others around it for a moment before turning back to Rayen. She was leaning over a table.

An ornate Tsatsun board rested upon it.

35

DANIEL

THE DOOR OPENED AS DANIEL WAS HOLDING ON TO ONE OF the Tsatsun pieces, rolling it between his fingers, marveling at the quality of the piece. They were made of the same stone as the walls, polished, and the detail was incredible. Rayen had tested the pieces to see whether she could use her shadows on them, but she found she could not. Even the game board seemed to be made out of the same stone—at least partly. The darker squares were the stone, whereas the lighter squares were a polished marble. The entire thing suggested incredible wealth.

"Ah, I see that you have found the board."

Daniel glanced at Rayen before setting the piece back down where he'd found it. It was a game in progress, and he didn't want to disrupt it, though from the way he could see the game playing out, it would not take long to end it. One side was far stronger than the other.

"How do you know Carth?" Daniel asked.

The man pulled a bottle of wine from his pocket and

grabbed three stacked glasses from the other. He set them on another table and began filling them. When he was done, he turned back to them, offering both Rayen and Daniel a glass.

He took it but was hesitant to do so. The other man watched them for a moment before tipping his own glass back and swallowing. "Not poisoned, if that was your concern."

"A little bit," Daniel said.

"If you are anything like her, then poison won't work on you anyway."

Daniel stared at him. "How do you know her?"

"I was here when she was. My role was a little different, and my hair not so gray," he said, touching his hair and smoothing it back. "And I don't think she cared very much for me at first, but the more we got to know each other, the better we got along."

"That still hasn't answered my question." Daniel held the glass of wine in one hand, staring down at it, swirling it. It was a deep red, and while he wasn't a wine connoisseur, living in the Elvraeth palace had taught him about such things. He brought it to his nose, sniffing it, noting various hints of flowers within it. There was an edge of cinnamon, a spice that reminded him of what they'd noticed in the smoky tavern.

"I told you I was here when she was here."

"Why was she here?" Daniel asked.

"Are you the only one who speaks, or does her daughter speak as well?"

Daniel glanced at Rayen. Carth and she had similar features, but as far as he knew, they were not related.

"You have her eyes and her nose. Even her hair. When I saw her last, she styled hers much like you do."

Rayen smiled tightly. "She is not my mother."

The man brought his hand up to his mouth. "No? My apologies."

"There's no need for apology. It would be my honor if she were, it's just that she is not."

"Regardless, you are as lovely as she. The two of you…" He waved his hand from Daniel to Rayen.

They shared a glance. This was not the kind of man he had expected.

"Who are you?"

"Why, I am Alistan Rhain. I would have imagined Carth had told you about me."

"Carth doesn't speak of her time in Keyall," Rayen said.

"Perhaps that's for the best. It was part of the agreement."

"About that," Daniel said, glancing from Rayen to Alistan. "Why?"

"Carth did not make many friends when she was here. It's surprising, considering how she saved us, but not all see it that way. I suspect even she doesn't see it that way. She had a unique experience within the city, having spent considerable time in our prison."

"Your prison?"

"Indeed. As you can see, we have a particular gift with suppressing those with her ability."

"How?"

Alistan eyed him for a moment. "Carth really didn't say anything?"

Daniel shook his head. "I'm sorry, but she did not."

"A shame. I thought perhaps I meant more to her than this."

"The fact that she hasn't said anything doesn't mean that you didn't mean anything to her," Daniel said. "When it comes to Carth, my experience has been she shares only what is necessary and protects those she cares about."

"Ah, in that I suspect you are right. My experience with her has been the same. Why, I know how much it troubled her when she lost that friend of hers while she was here."

"Who did she lose?" Rayen asked.

"Perhaps it was before your time. It was a man, an albino, who went by the name of Boiyn. She was quite fond of him, and I know that she was most distraught when the Collector caused his death."

"The Collector?" Daniel asked.

Alistan smiled. "Another story Carth has kept to herself? I suppose that's just as well. The Collector caused enough trouble over the years. It was most fortuitous Carth arrived willing to take on the challenge."

"Why was Carth here?" Daniel felt as if he were talking in circles, and he glanced at the wall of books before looking down at the Tsatsun board. So far, he hadn't taken a drink, and it seemed almost as if the man wanted to talk him into doing so.

That couldn't be coincidental.

It was a delaying tactic, but why? What did he hope to accomplish by delaying Daniel from asking the questions he wanted to ask?

Was there someone else here?

He took a step toward Rayen, prepared for the possibility that they might need to escape. He tested his ability to Slide, starting to do so before withdrawing. Thankfully, that capacity remained intact. Whatever this stone did to eliminate Rayen's ability with shadows, it did not do the same with his control of Sliding.

"As I said, she came to deal with the threat of the Collector. It disrupted her trade, and it placed those she cared about in danger. She is most particular about those she cares for."

"That has not changed," Rayen said.

"You haven't asked why we are here," Daniel said.

"Must I ask?" He glanced from Rayen to Daniel. "You're here for the same reason many others have come to Keyall, and fortunately, none have succeeded."

"What reason is that?"

The man tapped his chin and then took a slow drink of his wine. "To find our secret." He glanced over at the Tsatsun board. "Would you care to play a game?"

Daniel glanced over at Rayen. "Stay near me," he whispered.

She nodded, and when he took a seat—purposely choosing the weaker side of the board that had already been played—Rayen rested her hand on his shoulder.

"Why don't we finish this game?" Daniel said.

"This game? It's already ended."

"Has it?" Daniel said.

"Perhaps you won't be much of a challenge," the man said, smiling. "And here I thought that you knowing Carth meant you might know her most favored game." He looked up and met Rayen's eyes. "You, in particular. I would have expected she would have taught you the intricacies of the game."

"It isn't a game for everyone," Rayen said.

"IImm. Perhaps you're right. As Carth was happy to tell me, not all are capable of playing. Those who can aren't always that skilled."

"How about if we finish this, and if I can win, you answer my questions?" Daniel said.

The man glanced to the game board, and there came a moment of clarity, one that lingered for no more than three heartbeats, long enough for Daniel to realize that the man's flighty demeanor was little more than a ruse. He was calculating, and regardless of how he might seem, he still had his wits about him.

"It would be a shame to beat you so quickly, but perhaps you aren't much of a challenge anyway," Alistan said.

"Probably not," Daniel replied. He smiled at Alistan, looking at the board. "Do you get to go first?"

"I think I do," the man said.

It would be good to see how he played. There was one thing Carth taught him about observing while playing Tsatsun. It was helpful to know how each person would respond, and the more you watched, the better you would be able to understand their tendencies. Carth was often able to determine someone's tendencies in a few moves, taking in as much information as she needed in order to decide if she would be able to easily defeat them, or if she needed to work a little bit. It was part of the game that had always impressed him. Not so much the ability she had with strategy. Daniel believed she overemphasized seeing the board and the hundreds of possibilities that existed. In his mind, you could know the various possibilities, react to them, and make plans as needed, but there was also a need to understand your opponent. While he still had quite a bit to learn about the various moves, evaluating his opponent was something he had already begun to master.

Daniel credited a lifetime of learning from his father. It was all a part of his father's strategy with understanding the different people who might pose a challenge to his authority in the future. His father had used every bit of guile he had to ensure he knew who he might be facing. Daniel had learned that strategy from him.

Even though Alistan had a strong position on the board, he made an aggressive move, sliding one of his Bowmen along the edge of the board. It was designed to weaken Daniel's position, though it was already weak. Most of the pieces had been sacrificed already, and there was very little chance of him securing the Stone through traditional means.

Rayen squeezed his shoulder, and he wondered how much of the game she had already worked out. Probably as much as him. For all the teasing he gave her, she was a skilled player.

He made another move, this time designed to simply fortify his position. Daniel slid back one of his Archers, keeping it off to the side, away from Alistan's pieces. It would keep him from getting attacked as quickly, but it didn't do anything to move onto the offensive.

Considering the way this game looked, Daniel wasn't sure if he would even be able to go on the offensive. It was possible he would have to play completely defensively, looking to isolate Alistan before he was able to remove a piece. Depending on how skilled a player Alistan was, isolating him might not be possible. If he was skilled—and considering how long ago he would have met with Carth and learned about the game, Daniel suspected he was—he would be prepared for various maneuvers Daniel might make, all of which were designed to separate him and his players from the rest of the board.

That meant that Daniel had to get creative. Draw him out.

Would there be any way to do it while testing the questions he had about the game? He didn't think he'd be able to do so while trying to test his ideas about not sacrificing another person's players, but perhaps he could do it while testing his theory about not sacrificing his own. It was possible he would need to play in such a way.

Alistan made another move, this time equally aggressive. It brought another Bowman along the other side of the board, as if he intended to squeeze Daniel, forcing his pieces together.

There were several different maneuvers Alistan might be making, and they were interesting, many of them similar to moves he'd seen Carth make over the years.

"Perhaps we should have started fresh," Alistan said as Daniel made another play. This one was designed to protect his pieces, and in doing so, he collected them toward the center of his side of the board. All he was doing at this point was running from Alistan's attack, but so far, he thought he could avoid the other man getting another of his pieces.

"Perhaps, but you agreed."

"What did I agree to?" Alistan asked.

"You agreed that if I won, you would answer my questions."

Alistan arched a brow, looking up from the board. "Did I agree to that?"

"Look at my side of the board," Daniel said. "It's unlikely I would be able to win this game."

"Perhaps that's true. What do I get if I win?"

"Seeing as how you started with the much stronger side?"

Alistan smiled. "You recognized that?"

"I recognized I was taking a chance."

"And still you decided to sit on that side?"

"Where's the value in winning otherwise?"

Rayen squeezed his shoulder, and he wanted to smile.

"Indeed. I suppose my victory would be too easy. Then again, I would have been content to beat you from a neutral board. Perhaps I would have negotiated more information about what Carth has been up to over the years."

"You can still negotiate for that," Daniel said.

"I get the sense from your friend she is not too eager to share anything about Carth."

"There's only so much she knows. She doesn't travel with Carth anymore."

"No? And what does Carth do these days? The last time I saw her, she was attempting to secure safe transportation for her people. While I believe she was successful in it, I had hoped to see her more frequently than I have."

"We can talk more about that if you win," Daniel said.

Alistan chuckled. "We might as well talk about it while I win. And you might as well enjoy your wine."

"After," Daniel said.

"After you lose?"

Daniel shrugged. As he did, he pushed one of his pieces forward, one space away from the Stone. It was a safe move in that Alistan wouldn't be able to attack that piece, but it also was a strong move in that it gave him proximity to the Stone. Having that proximity allowed his pieces to be protected. They couldn't be easily removed from the board when they were so close to the Stone. There were still ways in which to do so—Carth had destroyed him one time when he had thought to move a couple of his pieces up along the Stone—but the likelihood of it was much lower.

Alistan studied the board for a moment. "An interesting maneuver."

"Is it? I still have quite a bit to learn about the game."

"It is one of lifelong learning. The only master I know of is Carth."

"She has played a long time," Daniel said.

"Not just played it, but she teaches it. There is benefit in teaching. You must understand the intricacies of something in order to teach it."

"And yet, some teachers are terrible players."

"You think so?"

"It's been my experience that some of the best instructors are those who understand technique, even if they don't understand the best way of putting it together."

"What sort of instructors have you had over the years? You are a young man."

"Mostly with the sword."

Alistan rested his hands on the table, looking up at him. "I would think an excellent swordsman would serve as an excellent teacher."

"There are things you can learn from an excellent swordsman, but there are many more things you can learn from someone who understands the technique, even if they aren't as skilled at utilizing it."

He made another move, sliding his piece up and near Alistan's. It was positioned in such a way that Alistan wouldn't be able to attack, but it would force him to continue to move in order to ensure that Daniel didn't claim one of his pieces. More than that, it gave him additional proximity to the Stone.

Alistan studied the board. "How often have you played Tsatsun with Carth?"

"Not as often as I would like. She's busy most of the time."

"How long have you played?"

"The better part of a year." With that, Daniel claimed one of Alistan's pieces, setting it off to the side.

"Ah, that explains it, then."

Daniel glanced up, holding on to his pieces. "What does it explain?"

"Explains why you chose that side of the board. It takes a long time to gain skill at Tsatsun. Some never progress beyond the basics, whereas others quickly become skilled players, though rarely masters. True masters take—"

"A few months," Rayen said softly.

"What was that?" Alistan asked, moving one piece to the other side of the board.

"True masters take only a few months. Carth learned to play in only a few months."

"I believe that is merely legend. It's difficult for me to believe Carth became as skilled as she was by playing that short a time."

"It doesn't matter what you believe," Rayen said. "All that matters is what happened."

"Were you there?"

Rayen shook her head and squeezed Daniel's shoulder a little harder. She was getting frustrated, and he didn't know why that would be. Did she dislike this Alistan that much? He thought he understood. Alistan came off as arrogant, but Daniel didn't know how much of that was real. It was possible most of it was only for show.

"If you weren't there, then you wouldn't know how much of Carth's playing was from when she initially learned and how much of it came from later on in life. As I believe she's told you, she has played the game for a long time."

Daniel made a move, taking another of Alistan's pieces. He had claimed five now, and Alistan had yet to take one of his. He continued to position his pieces in such a way that he was defended not only by his place-ment on the board but also by the Stone, preventing the other man from maneuvering around him.

Alistan glanced at the board. When he was done, he looked up at Daniel. "Interesting. You've only been playing for a year?"

Daniel nodded. "We don't have Tsatsun in my homeland."

"Elaeavn, I believe?"

Daniel nodded. "You know it?"

"I'm afraid not many people are allowed into Elaeavn. It's closed, though I suspect you know that better than most. It was the eyes, you see. The deep green eyes of Elaeavn are widely renowned."

"Sometimes for the wrong reasons," Daniel said.

"You be surprised. There are plenty of people who have green eyes who weren't born or raised in your city, but they still are impressive individuals."

Daniel hesitated, faltering with his move. How many people from the city were there outside of Elaeavn? It was something he hadn't given much thought to, but that seemed significant. All those years, they had been exiling people, and many of them—most—had remained outside of the city. As far as he knew, Galen was the only one who had returned.

He should have given thought to what had happened to all those exiles over the years, where they had gone and what they were up to.

Could all of this be tied together?

Was even Olandar Fahr an exile?

That seemed to be too much. He knew the Hjan attack had been about that, but the Ai'thol were something else.

He slipped his piece over, completing his move. In doing so, he eliminated another piece from Alistan and strengthened his position on the board even more. Within a few more moves, Daniel would be well positioned to ensure his survival, but it would take quite a few more in order for him to defeat Alistan. The longer he played, the more likely it was that he was going to conquer the man.

He had started on this side on a whim, doubting his skill was such that he would be able to outplay him from such a weakened position, but the more he played, the more it seemed as if he were increasingly likely to succeed.

Alistan made another move. This was a shift in tactics, and he switched from trying to play aggressively—a strategy that had backfired—to backing up and becoming more defensive. The challenge with such a change in strategy was that it was difficult to rearrange the pieces to move from steady attacking to a defensive posture. Daniel made another series of moves, and with each one, he claimed another of Alistan's pieces.

"You were playing me," Alistan said.

"How was I playing you?"

"How long have you really been playing Tsatsun?"

"Ever since I met Carth," Daniel said.

Alistan leaned back, crossing his arms over his chest. "She put you up to this, did she? I suspect you've been playing with her since you were a child."

"Unfortunately not. I grew up in Elaeavn, as I told you, and it wasn't until about a year ago that I began playing Tsatsun with Carth."

Daniel made another move. At this point, he had pieces nearly encircling the Stone. He thought he might be able to finish far more rapidly than he had believed. He'd never tried the strategy of circling the Stone, and he doubted he would have had he not been hoping to better understand the Council of Elders.

"That is a technique I've not seen before," Alistan said, leaning forward over the table. He studied the placement of Daniel's pieces. Daniel had thought the other man might be angry with the way he played, but Alistan seemed more intrigued. His demeanor changed. "Why play like this?" Alistan asked.

"There is a benefit to positioning the pieces in such a way," he said.

"I see that," Alistan said. "With you surrounding them like this, it strengthens each position. That is most interesting."

And it was something Daniel hadn't even considered. He had recognized he could maneuver the pieces like this, sliding them around so that he could surround the Stone, but even as he had played it out, he hadn't realized doing so would create a level of strength to his position. The pieces were additive.

But only in this way. It wouldn't work if he had used similar pieces. They had to be dissimilar, and there was a specific arrangement that mattered.

Studying the board, he focused on what placement would be necessary, looking to see if more than one approach would work. It was possible that it would.

Then again, as he studied it, it seemed almost as if the pieces demanded that they be arranged in a specific fashion.

Daniel frowned. That was not a coincidence. While there might be hundreds upon hundreds of possible moves when it came to Tsatsun, and the nature of the game would allow those various moves to play out in an equal number of patterns, the fact that this pattern around the Stone was important was surprising.

Maybe Alistan was right. It could take a long time to truly master Tsatsun. Certainly his experience had been that the game took years to really learn.

But this was something different. This was not only seeing that the game board played out in a way he hadn't expected; it also was a matter of how the pieces worked together.

Alistan sat back, watching Daniel. He shook his head, smiling. "I can't believe it."

"What?" Daniel asked.

"It appears as if I don't have any additional moves I can make. You have managed to isolate me. I am most impressed with how you played."

"Does that mean you'll tell us the answer to any question we have?"

Alistan smiled at him. "I suspect there's only one question that you have, and only one reason you've come."

"That's not true."

"Isn't it?"

"What do you think we came for?"

"I think that you came for the same reason Carth stayed."

"Which is?"

Alistan smiled widely. "Come, friend of Carthenne Rel. Let me show you."

36

LUCY

WAVES CRASHED ON THE SHORE, AND LUCY STARED OUT AT them. It felt to her the chaos continued to build, rising all around her, swirls of not just the waves, but the thunder rolling in the distance, mixing with the wind whipping at her hair and her cloak.

And still there was something comforting about it.

It was a strange thing for her to enjoy the chaos and the cold as it whipped around her, but she did. She had always appreciated structure and organization, and that was part of the reason she had wanted to be a caretaker, but it was unlikely she would enjoy the same thing were she to return to Elaeavn. It was hard for her to even think about going back. If she were to go back, what would she be able to do? She doubted she'd welcome the same quiet and solitude as she once had. Now she savored the questions, the chaos, and the change.

Lucy breathed in the salty air, listening to the waves crash along the shore, the rumbling of the thunder as it rolled toward her. The swells slamming against the rocky coastline suggested this would be a particularly violent storm. As she looked into the distance, searching for any sign of other ships as she often did—and finding none—she couldn't help but wonder if perhaps she should go inside.

At least there was no rain—yet.

The chaos of this place seemed a fitting time and location for her to look deeper inside her thoughts, to search for anything that might help her find answers about the Architect.

Ras was right—if she could uncover that, if she could find anything that might help her understand where he was going and what he was doing, they would be able to reach Olandar Fahr.

The more she focused on him, the more certain she was those answers would be there. Now it was a matter of finding them.

It was a question of locating a familiarity within her mind, of reaching for that knowledge. She knew it was there. It was difficult for her to parse through the various thoughts she'd encountered, but the Architect was one she had enough familiarity with that she thought she could.

Her experience with him was significant, and his mind was unique enough that she thought she could uncover it. The more she focused, the more she believed she could find him. Once she did, would she be able to reach him from a distance?

That was going to be the real challenge. Her time with him had taught her many things, but mostly that he had a way of protecting himself—and his thoughts.

She focused on the most recent connection to him.

There were aspects to it that she thought she could reach, and by delving deeper into her mind, she thought she could reach deeper into his as well.

The touch was there.

She recognized it. How could she not when she'd felt it so many times before?

The Architect had a subtle touch, barely brushing along the surface of her mind, but it was enough that she was able to feel him and his influence.

Lucy used that, gaining familiarity with it, recognizing it.

A particularly loud peal of thunder shook her. She jerked, looking up at the sky.

Rain streaked down, slamming into the ocean, and the waves picked up, crashing violently.

She wasn't going to be able to stay out here much longer. Soon she would have to go inside or risk getting drenched, and though she didn't mind the water, she had no interest in getting soaked.

Using what she had detected of the Architect, she focused, stretching out her awareness, probing to see if she could find where he'd gone.

Would she be able to recognize those thoughts from a distance the same way she could with Daniel Elvraeth? His thoughts were familiar to her, and she was able to latch on to him, anchor for each of her Slides, but part of that came from knowing him for the entirety of her life. She hadn't known the Architect that long.

But she *had* known him well.

More than that, his mind had mingled with hers, and with the way he had Pushed on her, forcing her thoughts, she had interacted with his mind far more than she had with some others.

And she knew what that felt like.

The sense of him was out there.

And she focused on it.

Lucy breathed out, holding focus, and reached for that awareness.

When she found it, she Slid.

She traveled a great distance, farther than she had expected, and emerged inside a small room.

Stone walls surrounded her. The portrait on one of the walls drew her attention, a painting of a pale-skinned woman with dark hair hanging to her shoulders. Eyes of a deep green caught Lucy's notice, but there was something else about it. Had she seen her before?

She hesitated, looking around. This was where the Architect had brought her, but why? His mind was tied here, but he wasn't here.

Had he known she was using his mind to anchor?

If he had, it suggested an even greater awareness of Lucy.

Something felt off.

It was a pressure upon her, an unfamiliarity. The more she thought about it, the more unpleasant it was.

She wanted to be somewhere else.

She thought about the tower and Ras and Slid.

Or attempted to.

She didn't go anywhere.

Was it some sort of trap?

It was possible she'd made a mistake, though how would the Architect have known she was coming? He might've been aware of her presence within his mind, but he shouldn't have been able to prepare a trap for her so quickly.

That suggested to her he was still here.

Only where was here?

Lucy found the door and tested it.

Finding it unlocked, she pushed it open, glancing along the hallway. It was narrow. Had she been with someone else, they would have a difficult time going side by side. She attempted to Slide, testing whether she could travel short distances, and found she could, which let her know this trap was either confined to that room, or it was confined to this building—wherever she was.

It intrigued her.

It was the kind of thing she once would have feared. Getting imprisoned like this should terrify her, and a part of her was nervous about getting stuck here. But the longer she was here, without finding anyone, the harder it was for her to believe she would be truly trapped. There had to be some way to escape if it came down to it.

She found no one. There were doors along the hall, and she tested each of them, finding them unlocked. She thought about Sliding beyond them but decided against it.

A staircase at the end of the hall circled around, and she took the stairs two at a time, moving carefully but wanting to travel quickly as well.

At the next landing, she paused. She focused on the Architect, searching for his mind, but didn't find him anywhere near her. There had to be some way of picking him up.

Perhaps her pounding heartbeat meant she couldn't

focus on him as well as she wanted to. It could be that the threat of capture was so much that her ability to Read, to reach out beyond her own mind, was limited. There was also a rising curiosity in her about where she was.

She attempted to Slide again, and though she felt some resistance, there wasn't as much.

What was strange was that she felt pressure upon her, the same sort of pressure she'd experienced ever since coming here.

It left her with nausea rolling through her and a slight headache.

It was almost as if the implant throbbed. In the time since she'd received the augmentation, it had throbbed often enough for her to recognize that sensation. It was unpleasant, but this was worse.

The stairs continued down, and Lucy hurried down them, no longer worried about the noise she made. As she focused all around her, she didn't detect anyone else.

The Architect could Slide, but with a trap that restricted her from Sliding, he should be affected as well. Unless he was the one holding the trap, but if he were, he should be here.

Hurrying down to the bottom of the stairs, she focused, Reading.

There was nothing.

It was a strange absence of everything. While she felt that, there came the continuing pressure on her, the sense of her augmentation twisting.

Was there something happening to change it?

Maybe that was the nature of the prison that the Architect intended. He would know her augmentation from the time they had spent together, and if anyone would understand just how to harm her through it, it would be the Architect.

The throbbing began to intensify.

As it built throughout her, it left her head aching.

She attempted to Slide.

There was resistance, but now there was also pain.

If she didn't get away from here soon, she doubted she'd be able to escape.

Lucy took a deep breath, looking around her, and focused. There had to be some way she could Slide away. As she locked on to the tower, she found it was slipping away from her.

It was almost as if her ability to Slide were being torn away.

What about Daniel Elvraeth?

When she anchored to him, she should be able to find him, but as she searched for his mind, it wasn't there.

Panic set in.

Her heart hammered, and the nausea rolling through her intensified, a painful sensation, but more than that, it was terrifying.

What would happen if she were stuck here?

There didn't appear to be anyone around, but whatever was happening seemed to be taking place without anyone else influencing her. Whoever was tormenting her managed to do so from a distance, and without her having any way of Reading them.

It was possible they were there and somehow masked their thoughts from her, the same way Ras did. The same way the strange man in that town had done.

And if they were able to conceal their thoughts from her, it was possible the entirety of the building she came through was filled with people—and all of them could be augmented in the same way.

More than anything, that sent her panicking.

If they were powered in some way, and if they did have those augmentations, and some way of preventing her from Reading them, she wanted to be anywhere else.

Sliding was going to be difficult, but the more she focused, the more certain she was she was going to have to fight her way through this. She was going to have to force herself beyond what she could do. It would take all of her strength to escape.

And if she didn't have the tower to lock on to, and if she couldn't find Daniel Elvraeth, then she had to find some other anchor.

It wasn't going to be Carth. It wasn't going to be Ras.

The only other anchor she could consider using would be someplace in Elaeavn, but what would she use?

There were options within it, but she feared she wouldn't be able to reach anyone effectively. The people she knew in Elaeavn were her parents, the caretakers within the library, and people within the forest.

If Haern were there, then she might be able to use him.

She had enough experience with Haern and his mind, she thought that she could reach him.

She pushed away everything else, the sense of anything beyond her, and found stirrings of thoughts. There was fear, but there was also something else. Something had changed.

Haern was muted.

Muted didn't mean she couldn't reach him at all.

He was there, and yet he was still far away from her.

As she focused on Haern, she grasped for his thoughts and held on to them. She anchored as tightly as she could and started to Slide.

There was pain.

It was unlike anything she'd ever experienced before, a ripping and tearing sense. It felt as if everything exploded within her.

The implant within her throbbed, pulsating, leaving her crying out.

Where was the Architect?

How had he managed to trap her like this?

She held on to Haern's mind. She needed him, and she could feel herself moving, Sliding only a little. The pressure on her continued to build, squeezing her. It felt like she was going through a tight tunnel. The tearing threw her outward. The longer she went, the more she felt as if she were being stretched apart.

But she was Sliding. It was slow, painful, but she was moving.

She held on to her sense of Haern and could feel him there in the back of her mind.

She couldn't Read anything about his thoughts, but they were there.

And it wasn't anything that she needed to Read. All she required was to focus on him.

Gradually, she was torn free of this place.

The squeezing sensation eased, the throbbing receded, and she was left with an emptiness. Sliding remained a struggle but gradually became easier. The longer she held on to the Slide, the farther she felt herself going.

But fatigue set in.

Lucy burst through, tearing through whatever resistance was holding her here.

She lost control of the Slide.

A different sort of panic struck then.

She'd never lost control of the Slide, though she'd heard of others who had and knew it could be devastating. She switched the focus of her Slide, focusing on the tower, trying to find someplace she recognized.

Even that didn't seem like it was going be enough. She changed her focus again, and rather than heading toward the tower, Lucy focused on moving toward the village. She had enough experience with the village that she thought she could find it more easily than she could the tower. The tower had some natural protections tied to the shadows that defended against her capacity to reach it.

And now, she had to think there would be some way for her to find the village, but what was it going to take?

Lucy didn't know. The more she focused, the harder it was for her to reach where she intended to go.

She strained, scrambling for the different minds she knew were within the village.

Doing so involved pulling with every ounce of strength she had, focusing on the various minds, anchoring in a way she hadn't before.

The sense of them was there.

The more Lucy focused, the more certain she was that she could reach them.

She managed to regain control of the Slide, emerging

at the edge of the village, overlooking the water. Waves slammed into it, chaotic and violent, and she breathed out heavily.

Somehow, she'd have to figure out what had happened. If she couldn't, then she'd have to fear the same thing happening again and again.

And she had to be careful. Searching for the Architect meant she was going after someone dangerous, someone who had a greater control over Sliding than what she possessed. She had to believe he would be able to over-power her, but she would be ready for it.

Not only did she need to train the women here in the village, she had to train herself, prepare for the next time something that dangerous took place.

LUCY

The wind whistled around her, and Lucy ignored it, focusing instead on what she could Read. She was determined to find the Architect. The more she focused on him, the harder it seemed for her to ensure nothing unfortunate happened again. When she had been trapped by him the last time, he'd somehow forced her into a place where he could confine her, but this time, she was determined to ensure he wouldn't.

She reached deep into her mind, connecting to what she could uncover of the Architect. His mind was there, his touch on her mind giving her enough of a sense of him. The more she concentrated on him, the more certain she was that she could find him and piece together what he was up to.

She'd spent the last week working with the women in the village. That time had been well spent. She had been trying to help them reach their abilities, and the longer she spent with them, the more certain she was that she needed to return more frequently. There was value in it, not only for them, but for her.

She benefited just as much as the women did by her presence. In going to them, trying to understand the way they could use their abilities, she was able to try to better understand her own.

Though she might not have the capacity to Slide, she had aspects of each of the other abilities. Working with them made her better able to explain. The one she really wanted to understand was how to See, to have visions.

As far as she could tell, none of the women in the village had that ability, though it was possible none had yet developed it. It was rare enough within Elaeavn.

Lucy had no control over it, gaining only snippets of visions, certainly not enough to be useful.

To work through what was going to come, to plan what she would need to do, she thought she would need a better understanding of those abilities. If she could use them, then she had to hope that there might be something she could uncover, an aspect of what the Architect planned, a way to unravel his goals. As it stood, she had no idea what he intended.

Reaching for the sense of his mind, she focused on it. She was able to home in on it, using the sound of the waves crashing around her. It was something that Olivia had helped her find, the silence of the chaos.

Using that, she was able to put everything else away, to ignore all the other voices that threatened to intrude, all the other aspects of her abilities, and focus only on what she could Read within herself.

The more she did it, the easier it became.

She thought he was aware of what she was doing, which ran the risk of greater danger to her and the others. She would hide that from them, if she could. It was almost as if he knew she was looking.

His mind was there. The other advantage of the waves was that they crowded out everything else. Within that chaos, she could be anywhere. Because of the chaos, he couldn't uncover anything about her—which meant he couldn't influence anyone she cared about and had vowed to protect.

Lucy held on to it.

That sense filled her, and she reached for it, embracing it, drawing an awareness of the Architect to her.

In doing so, she could feel his mind.

It was time to uncover what he was doing. After learning everything else that was taking place, she needed to understand him.

She Slid, emerging near a darkened shoreline. There was an energy upon her, similar to what she had felt before. Within that energy, she could practically feel the nature of the power, enough she thought there was something she needed to be cautious with.

She attempted to Slide, worried he might have tried to trap her again. There were times when she wondered if she should wait for Carth, but this was something she needed to do. She believed she could find the Architect. More than that, she believed she knew of some way of incapacitating him. She might be the only one capable of it. With her ability to Push, she could control him.

She looked all around and listened. There were strange sounds. That of hammering, of rumbling, and the chaotic waves that crashed along the shores. The air stank of a bitter ash, but there was something else mixed with that, an odor she didn't fully recognize. Lucy focused on it, trying to better understand, but the more she did, the harder it was for her to know if what she was detecting was real.

It was dangerous for her to be here.

The longer she was here, the more the pressure continued to build, pressing upon her. Lucy tried to ignore it altogether but wasn't sure if she was able to do so effectively. She strained against what she was able to uncover, but there was something mixed within it that made it difficult for her.

When she had Slid, she had been certain that she had detected the Architect, but there was no sign of him. It was the same way as the last time.

Would he be testing her?

She wouldn't put it past him. So far, she had Slid toward him twice, and both times he'd managed to evade her.

Lucy Slid, emerging back near Asador, and then Slid again, emerging near Nyaesh, and then Slid again, emerging near Elaeavn, before taking one more Slide and returning to the village.

Each step came more quickly than the last. The first one had been the most difficult, almost as if she were nearly stepping into a trap, but she hadn't lingered long enough to end up stuck as she had before.

Not only had he anticipated that she would come, but he had prepared some way of trying to hold her.

She needed to be more careful. If he had the ability to

do that, and if he was that aware of her reaching for him, then she had to be more cautious with him than she already was. She didn't want to end up manipulated by him, tormented by his ability to reach her. He had already used her enough times.

"You weren't gone long."

Lucy turned, and she noticed Eve watching her.

The other woman stood at the edge of the shore, lorcith spinning around her, twisting overhead.

"No. I was just investigating something."

"I watched you. You were here, and then you blinked out. I've seen you disappear like that before."

"It's called Sliding, or some would call it traveling."

"Whatever it is, it means that you can travel without walking, doesn't it?"

"It does."

"And you can just appear and disappear like that?"

"You know I can."

"Why did you go for such a short time?"

Lucy took a deep breath, turning her attention out toward the ocean yet again. In the last two days, she had taken to spending considerable time there, looking for answers that never came to her. It was almost as if staring out over the waves, watching the water crash into the shore, might give her some solutions, but the longer she stared, the less it seemed she had the answers.

"I've been looking for the man responsible for tormenting me."

"Only you?"

Lucy shrugged. "I don't know how much he's been responsible for hurting anyone else here. It's possible he didn't have anything to do with the rest of you." As far as she knew, the Architect had only targeted her, and yet, there likely were others. There were the two men she'd detected in the town far from here. There had to be more like them, though she had yet to return. "He's close to Olandar Fahr, and we need to find him, and so—"

"You thought by digging through his mind, you might be able to learn something."

Lucy nodded. It might be her imagination, but there was a ship out on the sea, bobbing with the waves. The sea had been angry over the last few days, the skies perpetually dark, though they'd only had rain once. Every so often, thunder rumbled, a promise of something more.

"I need to know where he and Olandar Fahr plan to go next."

"What if you can't uncover it?"

"Then others will suffer."

"Others like us?"

Lucy took a deep breath. "I've been looking for others like you. Searching for the ones who were responsible for it."

"The C'than."

Lucy shook her head, turning toward her. "Not the C'than, at least not all of them. They were a subset of the C'than, influenced by someone else."

She still had yet to know who was responsible for influencing the C'than and understood that piece was perhaps the most important of all. If they could determine it, they might learn who was to blame for the rest. The more she thought about it, the more certain she was that they needed to understand whether there were others who were responsible. Somehow, there was someone else who was working against Olandar Fahr. Seeing how they were willing to use these women, and the violence they were willing to commit in order to do so, she didn't know if they could be allies or not.

If she understood their motivation, then perhaps they could. She was looking for the C'than who had broken off, but what she needed was to learn who was responsible for the rest.

"Why are you defending them?" Olivia asked, heading toward them along the road.

Lucy tensed. She hadn't realized that Olivia had been there. Of all of them, Olivia was probably the one most likely to recognize something going on with Lucy. Not only could she feel the emotion within her, but she would sense Lucy's uncertainty. When it came to how she felt about the C'than, Lucy didn't know how to express that emotion.

"I'm defending them because not all of the C'than are responsible for what happened." It was time that the truth came out. "The C'than who used you violated their beliefs. There are others who work to maintain a balance."

"That's what they told us," Olivia said.

"They told you that they worked to maintain a balance?"

"They said that they were responsible for the balance. They wanted to use us to help them achieve it."

"They were using you—and me—as an experiment."

"You were used differently," Eve said.

"I was, but I was still used." She didn't want the others to think that she had welcomed her augmentation. Hers had come about differently, and she hadn't been held, tormented by the C'than, as the others had, but she had been used nonetheless.

"How do you know?" Eve asked.

"I know many of the C'than," she said. Olivia gasped, and she could feel Eve tensing, but of all the women within the village, these were the two she thought she needed to convince first. If she got them to understand, they would be able to sway the others. "One of the strongest people I know is with the C'than. She's part of the reason that you all are here."

"Carth," Olivia whispered.

"Carth. She has been with the C'than a long time, and I have come to know her mentor, another powerful individual, and another person who wanted nothing to do with what happened, who is angered by the way the other C'than used you and the rest of these women."

"How can we trust any of them?" Eve asked.

"We can trust them because we know them."

"We don't know any of the C'than."

"You know me."

Eve held her gaze. "Are you telling me you are with the C'than?"

Lucy inhaled deeply, and she glanced from Eve to Olivia. "I'm telling you that you can trust me."

"We can't trust anyone, and apparently we can't even trust you."

Lucy shook her head. "I haven't done anything to harm you. I've been working with you, trying to train you, helping you understand the nature of your abilities."

"If you're with the C'than, then you've been hiding it from us."

"I haven't been hiding it from you. I've been trying to help you understand."

She wished there were a way to show Eve, to show Olivia. As she thought about it, she decided there was.

She grabbed them and Slid.

It happened quickly. When she emerged in the tower, she released the two of them, and Eve looked around suspiciously. Olivia sucked in a short breath, her gaze taking in everything around her.

"This is one of the strongholds of the C'than," Lucy said.

"Why would you bring us here?" Eve asked.

"Because you wanted to know."

"We might have wanted to know, but we don't want to be trapped by the C'than again. You know what we've gone through," Eve said.

"Nothing like this."

Lucy could practically feel it as Ras made his way down toward them. As he did, she realized he must be allowing her to know he was coming. It was the only way she would be aware of it. He flowed down the stairs, gliding on bright light, his entire body glowing.

Once again, Olivia gasped.

"Olivia, Eve, this is Ras. He is one of the C'than. He leads here in the stronghold."

He took a step back, and Lucy realized he'd cut the other woman off from her lorcith. It might be for the best. If Eve had access to it, there was no telling what she would've done with the metal. It was possible she would've spun around to attack Ras.

Then again, it was also possible Ras would have been impervious to any attack. With his ability with the flames, he might be connected in such a way that anything they did to him would be deflected.

"It's a pleasure to make your acquaintance," Ras said, nodding to each of them.

It seemed as if the heat radiating from him retreated, though he continued to glow. The control he had over his power left her marveling. Even when she was around Carth, it was nothing like what she saw with Ras. Then again, Ras had only this ability, so he would have mastered it the same way those within Elaeavn who had only one ability would have mastered theirs.

"I take it that Lucy has been talking with you of the C'than. You had the misfortune of being held by those who violated their oath."

"How do we know they violated it and that it's not what you wanted of them?" Eve asked.

It didn't surprise Lucy that she was the one to speak up, but she did marvel at the way the woman adapted. She was a strong woman, and with her growing control over lorcith, she could eventually become powerful. She would be an asset, and yet the darkness within her would have to be honed.

In order to help her, Lucy would need to better understand the other woman, to gain an understanding of where that darkness came from. It would be better to master it now rather than to lose control in some situation where they might need her to have it.

"Lucy, if you don't mind guiding them to the library."

"Why the library?"

"I believe you brought them here with the intention of demonstrating the nature of the C'than."

Lucy nodded.

"I think that can be best done in the library."

She frowned but grabbed the two women and Slid. When she emerged in the library, she found it empty. Eve scanned the inside of the room, saying nothing, while Olivia studied the books.

"This is a library?" Olivia whispered.

"It is."

"I've never seen anything like it."

"The C'than have several like it. The largest would probably be the library at the University in Asador, but this rivals it in some ways."

"How does it rival it?" Eve asked.

"Because the knowledge stored here is restricted even from those within Asador," Ras said, strolling through the door. His hands were clasped in front of him, and he no longer seemed to glow quite as brightly. "We have done our best over the years to ensure that only those who have the necessary abilities and mental fortitude are given access to this knowledge. Unfortunately, in the case of the ones who tormented you, they managed to uncover knowledge they should not have."

"The knowledge of the C'than?" Eve asked.

Ras gazed at the shelves. "Even that isn't the knowledge of the C'than. I have spent many long days looking through these volumes, searching for anything that might have contributed to what was done to you, and I can't find anything."

"So it wasn't the C'than, then?" Eve said. "Are you trying to deflect it upon somebody else?"

Ras smiled sadly. "If only it were so simple. The C'than were involved, at least a subset of them. And because of that, all of us are responsible for what happened to you. But at the same time, not all of us are responsible, if that makes sense to you."

"How would they have known how to do this"—Olivia rubbed the back of her head as she asked—"if they didn't have the knowledge from here?"

"How indeed?" Ras took a step forward and swept his gaze along the shelves, and Lucy could practically imagine him trying to catalog the various volumes, as if trying to find the answer written in those books from here where he stood. "It makes me wonder where they uncovered it. We cannot blame the Ai'thol. The Ai'thol did not have the knowledge before they acquired it from us, and I don't know where the C'than acquired it."

"That's what you have Lucy looking for," Eve said.

"Lucy is looking for information about Olandar Fahr, primarily so that we can understand what move he might make, and how that will influence our next decision."

"What decision do you have to make?" Eve asked.

"We must determine where we focus our attention. It's possible it needs to be upon Olandar Fahr, but it's possible it needs to be focused somewhere else."

It was the first time Lucy had heard Ras say that. Where else would they focus if not on Olandar Fahr? Wasn't that why they were doing all this? It seemed to her that everything she was doing, and all the times she risked herself searching for the Architect, had been because she was trying to uncover what the Architect might know about Olandar Fahr. If that wasn't the case, then what were they doing?

It had to do with what she had uncovered in that town.

"I am deeply sorry for what happened to you and the others with you," Ras said. He turned back toward them and started glowing a little more brightly. "If there were any way to undo it, I would. From what Lucy Elvraeth tells me, what was done to you cannot be undone. That is unfortunate. Even more unfortunate is that it was done by those who should know better. And yet, when I see the two of you with Lucy Elvraeth, I see the strength you possess, and the way you carry yourselves, and I understand why Lucy has been dedicating so much of her time to trying to help you."

"She hasn't helped us that much," Eve said.

Olivia ignored Eve, glancing at Lucy. "She helped me calm the chaos. And she helped you learn how to use the metal. Isn't that helping?"

"I suppose," Eve said.

"Each of us has our own way," Ras said. "And when it comes to what you've gone through, you must find your own methods, and your own strength. But I fear you may be pivotal in what is to come."

"How so?" Eve asked.

"You have been changed. You have been touched by a great gift, and it has made you something more than what you were before. Who knows where that will take you, and where you want it to take you? Only you can decide that. When you do, I suspect each of you, along with the others in the village where Lucy hides you, will become far more powerful than you are even now. Know that the C'than will not attempt to harm you. Know that the C'than are trying to find answers as to what is taking place. And know that the C'than were not directly responsible for what happened to you."

Ras nodded to Lucy and then departed.

When he was gone, Olivia stared at the shelves. "I would love an opportunity to read here," she said.

"You enjoy books?"

"I enjoy the quiet found within them," she said.

That was something Lucy understood. When she had been working to become a caretaker, she had never minded the silence the way so many others did. It gave her an opportunity to think, to work through what she needed to do, and an chance to better understand herself.

"If it wasn't the C'than, then who was it?" Eve asked.

"The C'than weren't the ones who harmed you," Lucy said.

"Right, I understand that, but they weren't responsible, not directly. Somebody gave them that information. If it wasn't the C'than, then who?"

Lucy shook her head. "I'm trying to find that out now."

"And it's not the Ai'thol?" Eve asked.

"The Ai'thol had abilities, but they placed augmentations differently, leaving quite drastic scars. I don't know if they do the same any longer now that the knowledge of the C'than has been revealed, but for as long as I've known, the Ai'thol have used a different way of placing that augmentation."

"And that's what you are trying to find?"

"I'm trying to find one person who could lead me to another. Unfortunately, every time I try to Slide to him, I find myself trapped."

"How does he trap you?" Olivia asked.

Lucy smiled to herself. It was the most they had engaged in any sort of conversation.

"The first time I found him, I almost didn't make it out. I have no idea where he was, only that I found his mind, and he guided me to a place that made it difficult for me to Slide away. The last time I went, there was nothing there. Both times, there was some strange pressure upon me. I think that pressure is what made it so I couldn't Slide."

"Why do you have to go to him?" Eve asked.

"Because she's chasing him," Olivia said.

"I realize that, but why can't she make him come to her?"

"It doesn't work like that," Olivia said.

Lucy frowned, thinking. *Could* it work like that?

She had been chasing the Architect, thinking she needed to use her connection to his mind to track him down, but what if there was another way? She'd been Sliding to him, and each time she did so, she ran the risk that she might not be able to escape. The first time, she had been lucky she had; the second time, she had recognized that something was off in time to get away.

If she kept chasing down the Architect, it was possible he would find some way to fully trap her.

What if she tried a different approach?

She had been focusing on Reading herself, and in so

doing, she was able to find the Architect's mind and reach him.

If she could reach him, couldn't she Push him?

"You might be on to something," she said to Eve.

"See?" She turned to Lucy. "What might I be on to?"

"I've been trying to chase him down, and it's time for him to chase me."

"And if he catches you?"

"If I'm prepared, then I'm going to *want* him to catch me."

The challenge was finding the right preparation. For that, she was going to need Carth. Hopefully Ras's word had gotten to her.

HAERN

THE WAGON CARAVAN MOVED SLOWLY, WINDING ACROSS THE hilly road. It had been two days since Haern had left Galen and Rayen, and in that time, he had contemplated whether his mission was what he wanted. So far, this seemed to be exactly what he wanted to do, and yet he couldn't deny there were times when he questioned. Was he making a mistake?

All that mattered was continuing forward. They would reach Asador eventually, though he had started to wonder how long it would take them. It was something he should have asked Galen before leaving, but the other man had disappeared with a rapid Slide the moment Lucy had returned.

Sitting on top of the wagon, Haern smiled to himself as he thought about Lucy. She had changed so much from the girl she'd been. His friend and companion all those years in the forest, and now she was something else. He still wasn't entirely sure what she had become. More than she had been before, and yet, Lucy might have been the only one who didn't understand how impressive she had always been. It was one of the things about her that always made him a little sad. For some reason, Lucy never saw herself the way others did. Haern didn't know if that had changed. It was possible she still viewed herself the same way.

Then again, he'd seen the confident way she'd appeared. Not just confidence in her presence, but in the way she carried herself. He couldn't help but feel a sense of pride. She was amazing, and it was good that she saw that about herself.

"Why are you smiling to yourself?" Elise asked.

"Was I smiling to myself?"

She chuckled. "Very much."

"I don't know. I was thinking about my friend and how different she is than who she had been before."

"That makes you smile?"

Haern could only shrug. "When we were younger"—he realized how strange that sounded, considering that he didn't view himself as all that old at this point—"we used to dream about getting out of the city."

"Why?"

"I've told you about my homeland."

She nodded. "You told me some."

Haern smiled. "Someday if you're interested, I'll take you there."

"I'd like that."

"One of the things about my homeland is how isolated we are. Growing up, I didn't think much about it, but I mentioned to you we never had merchants, not the same way you did. We didn't have outsiders come to the city. It was just us. My father was about the only one who would leave the city for any extended period of time, and most didn't care for the fact that he did that."

"Why?"

"Many in the city have a complicated perception of my father. Partly it stems from how he went against the traditions of others within the city, but partly it's because he continues to be… well, I guess he continues to be himself."

She chuckled, glancing at him. "And what do you mean by that?"

"What I mean is that my father continues to oppose the Forgers. At least, he did. That made him some enemies."

"Why?"

"There are quite a few people who feel he's gone beyond his responsibilities." Haern shrugged. "I can't even say I disagree. Like I said, my father has a complicated relationship with those around him." Haern's gaze drifted off for a moment, and he shook his head.

"Anyway, Lucy and I had always dreamed about leaving the city. We spent lots of time talking about what it would be like, what the rest of the world might look like, and when we did, things were never quite like we imagined them to be. And yet, I can't help but think that Lucy has found a sort of happiness."

"What about you?"

"I've found my sort of happiness," he said, smiling at her. How could there be anything but happiness when it came to his connection to Elise? She was nothing like anyone he had ever known. In so many ways, that was a good thing.

"You don't always look as if you've found your happiness," Elise said.

Haern glanced over to her. "I don't?"

She shrugged. "I don't say that to upset you. It's more that you still seem to be searching, if that makes any sense."

"When your father is like mine, I don't know if it's possible to ever stop searching."

"At what point do you step out of his shadow?"

Haern smiled. It was a question he asked himself frequently, but he still didn't have an answer. When would he step out of his father's shadow? For years, he'd had a desire for more power, to be able to do the same things as his father, but he'd also known that he never would be the same as him. In all that time, Haern had come to terms with it, recognizing that while he wasn't powerless, he certainly wasn't as powerful as his father, either.

Was that the case anymore?

He couldn't Slide like his father, but with the things he could now do, the way he could now use the lorcith, it was possible he shared his father's skill.

Even if he didn't, Haern wasn't sure it mattered.

"I think I need to stop worrying about it."

"If it's not something that you can change, there is no sense in worrying."

Haern grunted, taking her hand. "You know, you make a lot of sense."

"Most of the time, it's my mother's sense."

"Do you miss her?"

"Every day," Elise whispered. "My experience was much like the others'. I returned to my home to find it gone. Destroyed. I didn't have anything, so when I wandered off, thinking I had managed to find safety, I…"

She looked away, and Haern wished there was a way for him to take away her pain, and yet, he suspected she needed that pain, the same way he needed to strive to be something more than what he was.

"This is a good thing," Elise said, looking around her. "When we went with you, I wasn't sure." She glanced at Haern, smiling sheepishly. "We didn't know you, and we didn't know what kind of person you would be or what you would do to us, but now that we know you… this is a good thing."

Haern looked back at the wagons trailing after them. Much like theirs—the lead wagon—several people sat on top of the wagons, most of them women they'd rescued from the so-called merchants. Each shared an expression of determination. Strength. And it was one that gave him a sense of hope.

"I only wish we could make better time," he said.

"From the sound of it, we don't have that much farther to go."

He hoped that was the case. Supposedly, they only had a few more days before they reached the outskirts of Asador. As a city-state, the Asador holdings extended quite a ways from the city itself. When he had traveled there before, he had Slid, and he didn't have any experience with any of the surrounding areas. He still found it surprising there were no villages along the way, nothing that would indicate anyone else lived here, and that troubled him. Why *wouldn't* there be others out here?

"I still worry that we might come across more of these spheres."

Haern took the lorcith sphere from his pocket along with a handful of the nails. As far as he could tell, they seemed to be pure lorcith, and there shouldn't be anything dangerous about them.

If only he had his father's connection to lorcith. If he did, then he would know with certainty whether or not they were pure. If not, then he had to be careful. And as far as he could tell, the nails were laced with poison, though what sort of poison had been used on them?

Galen hadn't known. He'd treated him with the general restorative, not anything targeted to a specific agent. And then Della had Healed him, purging the remaining effects of the poison so that anything that would harm him would be burned out of his body.

"What are you thinking about?" Elise asked.

Haern glanced over. "Just this sphere."

"It looks like you're trying to reassemble it."

Looking down, he saw that he had been shoving some of the nails back into the sphere. It was something like a puzzle. Not all of the nails fit. He hadn't realized it before, but the nails all seemed to be a different diameter, and when he tried pushing them back into the sphere, he found he wasn't able to do it very easily. There was a pattern, and until he knew that pattern, he wasn't sure he would be able to finish this.

"I don't know if I can completely reassemble it."

"Why? I've seen you working at it."

Haern held out the sphere, pointing to the four nails he'd managed to replace. "This is the same sphere I somehow triggered." Not only had he triggered it, but he'd suppressed it from triggering against him. In that regard, he should be better connected to it than he was to any of the others. "And these nails were gathered from it." Haern had done his best to collect as many of the nails as possible. There were nearly one hundred, and all of them were slightly different. Not only did whoever made this sphere have some talent, but they also must have had a certain level of patience. "I'm trying to figure out in what pattern these nails go back into it."

"Are you sure you should?"

He focused on the sphere. The steady sense of pure lorcith pulsed against him. That had to matter, didn't it?

If he were more skilled, better connected like his father, he had to think he would be able to determine where the lorcith came from. He remembered his father telling him how he could distinguish the lorcith mine from the song of the metal. At the time, that had seemed strange to him, but the longer he worked with lorcith, and the greater his connection was, the less odd that seemed. Now it was almost understandable.

"I'm trying to understand it. Until I do, I'm not sure we'll know who's responsible for this."

"Are you sure we will ever be able to determine who is responsible?"

"Someone created this," he said, looking at the sphere. "And there is incredible skill in its making. Whoever did this knows lorcith as well as I do, and I wonder if they know it as well as my father." He looked up at her. "If you met him, you'd understand. My father is better connected to the metal than anyone I've ever known."

She was silent for a few moments. "You seem to be quite well connected to it, too."

What if there was another way for him to try to reassemble the sphere?

It was something he should've contemplated before. He could probe for the various openings within the lorcith, use that to help him determine where each nail needed to go. It might be cumbersome and slow, but could it be any more so than trying it by hand? He lost track as he went, so he suspected he had used the same nail on the same hole more than once. It was a wonder he'd matched up four of them.

"I should've tried that before," he whispered.

"Tried what?"

He focused on one of the nails. As he did, he held it up, hovering in front of him. Using his connection to the metal in that way allowed him to recognize the size, and then he shifted his attention over to the sphere, wrapping his awareness around that. Combining the two, he could feel for the slight dimpling within the sphere, the openings that were meant for the nails, and in doing so, he…

There.

Haern moved the nail and slipped it into the corresponding hole.

It would be time-consuming going like this, but certainly less time-consuming than what he had done before.

Even if he did this, it still didn't provide him with answers. It didn't help him know how the sphere had been made, and almost as much as anything, he thought he needed that knowledge. If he could uncover the how, then maybe he could uncover the who.

Perhaps recreating the sphere, using the nails and slipping them back inside, would help him. Then again, it might not.

Elise said nothing as he worked. Haern went nail by nail, focusing first on the nail, then on the sphere, matching one to the other using his connection to lorcith. While it was slow, he made much better progress than he had. He continued slipping one nail into another hole and lost track of time as he worked, focused as he was on the process.

When the horses slowed and the wagons came to a stop, Haern looked up and realized much of the day had passed. The sun was beginning to set, and they had reached a stream.

"I thought this would be a good place for us," Elise said. "I didn't want to bother you while you were working."

Haern smiled and nodded. There were only a few nails remaining, and yet, there were still several dozen holes. With the nature of the explosion, the way the nails had been blasted in all directions, some of them might have ended up buried in the earth. But then, Haern had used his connection to lorcith to try to gather them all together.

"I'm going to see if I can't finish this."

"We'll get the wagons situated," Elise said.

He finished the few nails he had remaining, and when he was done, he held the sphere. Joined together like this, there was a strange sense from it. The weight had changed. It was an unusual shift, almost as if it were doubled, not what he would have expected from just slipping the nails back into it.

Climbing down from the wagon, he joined the others at the campfire. They still didn't have enough food, but one of the wagons had been stocked with more items than they had before, so they weren't starving as they had been. Eventually they would need to resupply, unless they reached Asador quickly. A village might not even be enough with the number of people who traveled with them now.

"What have you been doing?"

Haern turned to see Jayna watching him.

He held out the sphere. "I'm trying to reassemble this."

She reached for it, and he reluctantly handed it over, concerned that something might happen to her. It had been his project, and he'd spent considerable time trying to piece it together, but she could help.

"You're missing some," Jayna said.

"I thought I'd gathered all of the nails, but…"

"Even the ones that stuck into the sides of the wagons?"

Haern frowned. "What was that?"

Jayna glanced back at the half circle of wagons. They used them for a bit of shelter, but they didn't circle themselves entirely. Doing so would block off access to escape if it were necessary.

"When we were captured"—Haern had heard about what had happened to them, the way they had been poisoned, something slipped in the water that had incapacitated them quickly—"we were trapped in the wagon when you came back. I heard the knocking, and then the sound of the nails slamming into the side of the wagon."

Haern had thought Rayen had suppressed most of them, but what if she hadn't?

He focused on lorcith. Within the camp, there were other items of lorcith, enough that he could detect it from many places near the campfire itself. Then there was the lorcith within the wagons. The one that had carried the spheres that had exploded remain untouched. Haern wanted to investigate it, but there were far too many nails collected in there to sort through them.

There was some metal near him that wasn't within one of the wagons.

That was what he needed to focus on.

Haern *pulled*.

It came away, but it did so slowly. The longer he *pulled*, the more he realized this was exactly what he wanted. There had to be a dozen or more similar items, all of them staggered and spread out around the wagons.

With one more hard *pull*, the nails came free.

As soon as they did, Haern shifted the direction of them, sending them up into the air, ensuring no one was targeted. He squeezed, bringing all of the nails into a tight cluster, and then slowly let them descend until he could *pull* them from the air.

"You did all of that from here?" Jayna asked.

Haern nodded. "As much as I could. There might still be some remaining."

"Impressive." She handed the sphere back to him and then turned away, heading back to the fire, taking a seat next to Stacy and Beatrice.

With another cluster of nails, Haern had more to work with, and he began to focus on them, testing one after another until they were all placed within the sphere. Even with these, there were still a couple missing.

Haern couldn't help but feel as if there was something he was close to understanding. Stuffing the sphere back into his pocket, he went and rejoined the others.

Elise glanced over at him. "You look as if you need something."

"Just a sense of understanding."

"You weren't able to figure it out?"

He shook his head. "There are some nails missing."

"That's not the only sphere you have to work with."

Haern glanced over to the wagon containing the lorcith that had exploded. It wasn't the only sphere, but the problem was that drawing from the spheres within that wagon would be even harder. There had to be seven spheres, and all of them had exploded, which meant figuring out the puzzle there would be even more difficult than what he had tried with this one.

Yet he felt as if he needed to attempt it.

"Great," Elise said, watching him.

Haern looked up. "What?"

"I have a sense I'm not going to see you for a while."

39

HAERN

THE WAGON JOSTLED ALONG AS THEY TRAVELED, AND Haern tried to sit carefully, not wanting to get slammed around, but the wagon didn't make for a comfortable place to sit as they traveled over what was apparently rough terrain. Seven spheres circled him, each of them set within a box, giving him the opportunity to test each of them, though even as he worked, Haern wasn't sure he was uncovering quite what he wanted.

Somehow, he would still have to figure out which of these nails went to which sphere. It had taken him the better part of the morning to remove the nails from the walls, and he still didn't know if he'd missed any. It was possible some had broken free, shot through the wood, and were long gone.

He had to hope the nails could be sorted, but the complexity was far more than what he thought he was capable of doing.

It took incredible concentration. That was never one

of his greatest strengths, but while working, he continued to go nail by nail, holding it and then moving on to the sphere. It took considerably longer to match each nail to the sphere, but he had been successful. Each of the spheres inside the wagon had several dozen nails already placed within it. The longer he went, the more certain he was he would be able to replace all of them.

More likely than not, this was a great waste of his time. If it was, then he would have simply expended unnecessary energy, but he couldn't shake the thought—and the hope—that by doing this, he could figure out something about the construction.

Besides, it gave him a way to pass time. It would've been better to do so sitting next to Elise and talking, but she was busy working with some of the rescued women. With their numbers having swollen to well over fifty, her work was important. More than ever, Elise's organizational skills had been crucial. Because of her, they had organized the amount of food that remained. They had set aside casks they filled with water at each stop, and they had started to help those who were injured and sick.

He needed a break. Sitting up, he looked around the inside of the wagon. A pile of nails rested in front of him, and he had resisted the urge to count through them, knowing that the task would feel overwhelming. The spheres were set into boxes, hay resting beneath them to prop them up and keep them from rolling around.

There were other items within the wagon, several of them made of lorcith. He found a section of chains and cuffs that looked as if they were meant to confine someone, but no key. He was hesitant to try them, not certain whether he would end up trapped.

Other things within the wagon were less likely weapons. He came across stacks of flattened steel, something that would've been useful when he had still worked in the forge, but it wasn't clear what purpose there was for those. He didn't find anything else that was similar to it. No other flattened sections of metal, and nothing else quite as strange. There were pots, dozens of them, each of them made with reasonable skill, and it seemed to him they were gathered for someone to sell or trade them. With something like that, the wagons could give off the real appearance of a merchant.

He came across a drawer full of jewelry. He had been hesitant to reveal that to others before finally showing it to Elise. She had agreed with him that they needed to keep it to themselves, mostly because others might be tempted to sneak in here and claim them. Much of it was gold or silver chains with jewels attached to them. Haern didn't know much about the value of such items, but Elise suspected they were worth quite a bit. If they didn't get the help they hoped they would in Asador, the jewels might buy them safety. And if for some reason they weren't able to make it to Asador, Elise thought that they could sell them and ensure their survival.

Haern had never had much skill with creating jewelry. He'd seen some of the things his father had made, mostly for his mother, but he had stopped doing that over the years. His father's exquisite creations would have been unrivaled by any jeweler within the city.

He leaned back, staring at the nails. There was something about this he still didn't get. Someone would have to have exquisite control over lorcith in order to effectively create these explosive spheres. The Forgers couldn't have that type of control, could they?

He had been around the Forgers a little and had seen the kind of things they were able to do, but none of it seemed quite *that* well controlled.

What if he was going about this the wrong way?

He was trying to shove the nails back into place, forcing them into the holes they'd come out of, but what if the person who'd created this hadn't done so in that manner?

Haern frowned. If not, then they would have used some way of creating circles within a sphere of lorcith.

He didn't have any idea how that might be possible.

There came a tapping on the top of the wagon, and Haern pulled the door open and climbed on top. Elise guided the horse, staying near the forefront of the procession. She had taken it upon herself to lead the journey, and no one had argued. For the most part, everyone seemed to agree Elise was the right person to do so. She was so organized that others just fell into line behind her.

"What is it?" he asked.

"Look up there," she said.

Haern scanned the horizon. They still hadn't managed to find any road, and because of that they traveled across rough, uneven ground. The long grasses slowed them and seemed to irritate the horses, but they were still making reasonable time. When they found a roadway, they were all in agreement that they would take it.

"I don't see anything."

"Nothing?"

Haern shrugged. "It slopes too much. There's a pretty considerable hillside, and then beyond that is…" Haern frowned. From there, it looked almost rocky, quite different than the landscape they'd been traveling along.

Was that her concern? It made sense if it was. Then again, he hadn't expected her to be able to see that.

"Can you make it out?" he asked.

She shook her head. "Not very well. I can tell there's something there, but…"

"I can go and investigate, if you want."

Elise looked behind her. "It might be helpful. If we're heading in the wrong direction and need to change course, it would be nice to know it now."

Haern hadn't traveled off on his own since they had gotten the caravan together. Every so often he would fly overhead to try to orient them, but he hadn't ventured off, partly because he didn't want to leave the others, and partly because there wasn't any benefit. There had been no signs of movement to suggest they were in any danger.

"I won't be long."

Grabbing for a pocket full of coins, he tossed them out and *pushed*.

He went quickly, soaring into the sky as rapidly as he could. He didn't want to be gone from the wagons for long, but now that he had a connection to the lorcith within them, even if he was separated, he'd be able to find them quickly. Then again, if something happened to Haern, the others wouldn't have the same advantage.

He needed to stay airborne, use that to—

Lorcith streaked toward him.

Having spent the last few days around lorcith, trying to puzzle over the nature of the nails and the spheres, when this one came shooting toward him, he recognized it, even if he didn't recognize where it came from. It shot up from the ground, almost as if drawn to him.

And maybe it was. Haern had been *pulling* on lorcith when it came to him.

He dropped, wrapping the sphere in a barrier of his connection, squeezing it tightly. As he did, he forced the nails back inside. If he could prevent it from exploding, he might be able to study it.

It took considerable effort, but he hadn't been taxing himself all that much by working on the nails. Because of that, he had enough strength to push them back inside, overriding whatever had triggered them in the first place.

When he dropped to the ground, Haern looked around. He didn't see any sign of an attacker like he would've expected.

Why would this sphere be here?

The better question would be *how* had this sphere gotten here?

He debated whether to take it with him, worried that if he did, it might explode while he was carrying it. Taking it might involve holding on to a connection to the lorcith, forcing it around it in a barrier. One wrong move and it could explode.

He could maintain a barrier around it until he had something he could place it inside. The pots within the wagon would serve for that.

Haern took to the air again. He turned in place,

looking around, distantly aware of the wagons. He focused, worried there might be another sphere heading toward him, but he didn't detect anything there.

Haern made his way northward, moving away from the wagons. As he went, he remained cautious, on edge for the possibility of another attack. He stayed high in the air, much higher than he would otherwise have gone, but by remaining as high as he was, there was the added advantage that he would be equipped to respond quickly.

Nothing else came.

That should have relieved him, and yet it didn't. He worried he'd overlooked something. Not just that he'd overlooked something, but that there was someone else out there he needed to find.

Haern headed toward the rocky prominence he'd noted when sitting atop the wagon. When he reached it, he discovered that it led toward the shore.

They were heading in the right direction. They could follow the shoreline, make their way north, and from there they could reach Asador.

If they were near the shoreline, how far were they from Elaeavn?

He hadn't considered returning to his home, other than the few moments he'd contemplated it when he'd seen Galen. Other than that, he'd been focused on making it to Asador, though perhaps that was a mistake. There were other places that would be equally likely to be safe, where they could find branches of the Binders. Rayen had done nothing to disabuse him of the notion of heading to Asador. Either she supported it, or she'd been too distracted with what had been taking place to suggest an alternative.

When he reached the water, he hesitated for a moment. He wouldn't be able to travel over the water the way he could over land. It wouldn't be possible for him to trigger lorcith into the water and then *pull* it back out. That was one disadvantage to his method of traveling compared to the Forgers and those who could Slide.

Haern followed the shoreline for a little longer, searching for more lorcith and signs of another possible attack, but came up with nothing.

Turning back toward the wagons, he went quickly. As he did, he focused on the sense of the sphere in his pocket, worried it might explode, but he was able to maintain a connection around it, holding it wrapped in a barrier. As he did, there was another sense, a twitching, as if the lorcith were trying to break free.

He needed to get back to the wagons quickly so that he could place it into one of the pots that would keep it from exploding.

The wagons came into view.

As they did, Haern realized that something was off.

They had stopped.

His heart began to skip. Could they have been under attack? Typically, the wagons continued throughout the day, rarely stopping. It was too much of an ordeal to get them up to speed, and with the casks of water they now had, there wasn't generally a need to stop.

He didn't see anything.

That didn't change his worry, and Haern moved carefully.

As he went, he held on to his connection to the lorcith, squeezing that around the sphere, worried he would release it before he got back to the wagons.

He couldn't help but feel as if, in his brief absence, something had happened to the others. Could that have been the plan?

No one else would've known that he was going to go off.

Whatever happened would be incidental, nothing more than that.

As he neared, he realized what it was.

One of the wagons had a broken axle.

Haern breathed out a sigh of relief. It was a wonder they hadn't experienced anything similar before. With as rough as the going had been, they'd gotten lucky not having encountered trouble before now.

Haern dropped to the ground, looking for Elise, but didn't see her anywhere.

He came across Stacy and got her attention. "What happened?"

Stacy waved her hand at the wagon. "We were going along at a rapid clip when that one crashed. We didn't see anything, and it just stopped going."

"Is everyone okay?"

"We are, but the wagon is going to be of no use to us." She had a thick accent that had taken him time to understand.

Haern headed toward the wagon, still looking for Elise. When he reached the broken wagon, he circled around it. The axle appeared shattered, the wheels bent off on either side, but there was something about it that struck him as odd.

It wasn't just that the axle had been shattered; it was that it had been done with such force.

That was more than just hitting something.

Haern's breath caught. He dropped to the ground, focusing on lorcith, but came across nothing.

Could there have been another type of explosion?

He got to his feet and looked around.

The wagon would be useless to them. They would have to scrap it, move everyone to another wagon, and continue on. Considering how much the wagons were carrying, that wouldn't be all that difficult, other than the delay.

"Did you see anything?"

Haern turned to see Elise, suddenly relieved. "There wasn't anything other than this," he said, holding out the sphere.

Elise's eyes widened as she looked at it. "Where did you find that?"

"As I was heading out to see what was ahead of us. It's nothing but seashore, so I think we're heading in the right direction," he said, "but I'm not sure what's responsible for this."

"Did you see anyone?"

Haern shook his head. "There wasn't anyone. It was triggered and drawn toward me, and I think it was only because I was *pulling* on lorcith that it attacked."

Elise looked back, turning her attention to the wagon. "What if they were just setting them down, preparing for the possibility someone like you would come along?"

"Why?"

"I don't know. If there wasn't anyone there, it doesn't make a lot of sense. They wouldn't have known you were there, and even if they did, would they have been able to hide before you could see them?"

"I should have been able to See someone," he said.

She nodded. "That's what I thought."

"I understand the wagon basically exploded?"

Elise frowned, her face wrinkling in as she did. "We hit a massive hole we hadn't noticed before."

Haern looked back down to where the wagon was. That was a better explanation than what he had begun to fear. At least it wasn't anything magical in origin.

"I imagine you've already started to make preparations to move people."

Elise nodded. "It shouldn't be much longer before we have it taken care of."

"Then I'm going to take care of this." He held on to the sphere, still maintaining his barrier around it, and headed toward the lead wagon, pulling open the door.

One of the pots was larger than the others. He placed the sphere inside, carefully replacing the lid, and looked for some rope or twine. He found that at one end of the wagon and looped it around the pot until the lid was fully secured.

Haern breathed out, releasing his connection to lorcith. Holding it like that had been more tiring than he had expected. Gradually, he eased off completely and focused, worried there still might be an explosion, but none came.

When he was done, he debated what to do with the

pot. If he left it here, the jostling of the wagon could trigger it, and he didn't want it to explode in the back of the wagon. If he were working back here, he absolutely didn't want it triggered. He might be able to suppress it, but he didn't know if the pot would be able to confine the lorcith.

Without much choice, Haern decided to carry it with him.

Eventually, he would find a place for it, even if it meant carrying it with him on top of the wagon, holding on to his lorcith connection the entire time.

It didn't take long before Elise had everyone organized, and the caravan began to move onward once more. Haern kept the pot with the sphere tucked alongside him, nervous to let it out of his sight.

Elise took her place next to him on top of the wagon, glancing over in his direction. She frowned as she looked at him. "You look troubled."

"I'm trying to better understand these lorcith spheres. I can't really figure out anything about them."

Whoever had made them had incredible skill with lorcith. And they targeted him. He couldn't help but feel as if that was what was happening. Somehow, the spheres seemed as if they were finding a way to reach him.

Haern turned away, looking at the pot, tracing his hand around the surface of it. He ignored the metal of the pot itself, focusing on what he could detect within it. The answer was there, though he didn't know what he'd be able to determine from it. All he could think of was that his father would have known, and that he would have some way of using the metal itself to provide the answers to the mystery of who had made the sphere.

"You said we were close to the shore?"

Haern glanced over. It was good to take his attention away from the metal, to give himself something else to focus on. "We aren't that far from the shore, and if all goes well, we should be able to reach Asador by following the shoreline."

"Your homeland is along the shore, isn't it?"

Haern nodded. "It is, but I don't know how far we are from it."

"Were you tempted to return when your people were here?"

"Not as tempted as I thought I would be. I want to see this through."

"What happens if they won't take us in?"

They had been through this before, but he understood Elise's concern. She was worried they'd need a different plan, but Haern had a strong sense they would have little difficulty getting the women accepted into the Binders.

"They will," he said.

And what they got to Asador, he didn't know quite what he would do. With everything else that needed, he couldn't stay there, and yet, he would need to track down someone who could Slide to carry him away, perhaps back to Elaeavn, or elsewhere. His plan when he got to Asador was to send word to Carth. Hopefully she would have some insight. If not, then Haern wasn't entirely sure.

"It's interesting," Elise said.

"What is?"

"Those explosives."

"They don't feel so interesting when they go off."

"It seems to me that they're only designed to trigger those who have control over the metal. The ones in the wagon only went off when you were using your control over the metal."

He'd believed there needed to be someone who triggered them, but maybe that wasn't the case at all. Maybe there *wasn't* someone nearby who was triggering these.

If they would explode without any influence, it made sense they would be triggered by someone who had some control over the metal.

"That wouldn't be Forgers, then."

Elise shook her head. "What makes you say that?"

"The Forgers have others who can use the metal."

And if it wasn't Forgers, then could it be someone who understood the metal well enough and was working against them?

The idea that others existed out there who were opposed to the Forgers appealed to him. His father had believed it had been up to him and Carth and had prevented others in the city from working with them to push back the threat of the Forgers, but if there were others, could they find them?

And if they found them, would they even be able to help?

"You don't think the Forgers would target their own people?"

"Not like this. These are poisoned." And even the poisoning was strange. He still wasn't certain how the spheres were made, only that they seemed to be created out of a single hunk of lorcith. It would be far too time-consuming for someone to place the nails in individually. More likely, the nails were drawn out of the spheres, which meant that the poison had to be on the surface of it.

He glanced down at his hands. He'd been holding one of the spheres.

What if the poison wasn't in the nails, but *on* the spheres?

Could that mean that there was poison on his hands?

He brought his hand up to his nose, sniffing. It didn't smell like anything other than earth, but there were plenty of odorless and tasteless poisons.

He needed to test it. It was the sort of thing Galen would encourage.

As he licked the tip of his fingers, Elise gasped. "What are you doing?"

"A test."

"What if you're wrong?"

Haern smiled at her. "I'm more concerned I might be right."

His lips began to feel numb. It worked onto his tongue, and then down his throat. Haern waited, worried that the poison might continue to set in, but the effect of it began to fade, retreating as if into nothing.

There was poison, no doubt about that, but it wasn't nearly as significant when he took it by mouth. Then again, that didn't surprise him. Galen had taught him that some poisons were far more dangerous when administered into the blood. When he had been pierced by the nails, the poison's effect had been far worse.

Haern sighed, leaning back. "It is poison, and I think

510 | D.K. HOLMBERG

it's on the surface of the sphere itself, not each of the nails."

"What does that help you with?"

"Nothing more than a basic understanding of what's taking place."

And he didn't have any idea what poison they used. What he did know was that he needed to be on the lookout for someone who knew both lorcith and poisons.

It was more than just the knowledge of lorcith. It was a knowledge of lorcith that was far greater than almost anyone he had encountered. If he could understand who that might have been, he thought that he might be able to track this down.

In the distance, the sounds of the ocean began to occasionally intrude. He pointed and Elise tipped her head to the side, listening. It was difficult over the creaking of the wagons and the occasional clump and whinny of the horses, but she nodded.

"I hear it."

"It means we're close to the water. We're heading in the right direction."

Haern was tempted to take to the air, to see if he could uncover anything more about where else they were heading, but he decided against it. There was a certain comfort in sitting next to Elise, riding atop the wagon, traveling with her, that was different than what he had while soaring through the air.

When doing that, he had another sort of comfort. That was one where he felt freedom, the power of the Great Watcher coursing through him, and a connection to his abilities—and his people. Sitting alongside her, traveling like this, he didn't feel as free, but he felt useful.

There was value in that, value in knowing they needed him.

Every so often, Elise would glance over at him, and Haern would smile at her. When she took his hand, he held hers, enjoying the proximity, the comfort, and the sense of purpose.

40

HAERN

Haern hovered. There was a distant sense of lorcith far below him, and he pushed that sense away, holding on to his position, while searching for evidence of lorcith elsewhere. So far, he hadn't encountered anything.

To his left, the ocean slammed against the shoreline, the steady lapping of waves sending a cascade of white froth along the shore. The wagons were quite a way inland, avoiding the shoreline, careful to stay to the more easily traveled ground. They had been heading upward over the last few days, the ground sloping gradually higher and higher, and he worried they would eventually get to a point where the horses—and the wagons— wouldn't be able to take them any further. Perhaps it wasn't the right strategy to follow the water, and yet, it was the only way he could think of to go.

There were no other signs of lorcith spheres.

Haern twisted in the air, looking down at the ground below him. As he did, he took in the sight of the wagons, snaking their way slowly forward. There was something reassuring about the onward movement, and though they didn't attempt to make rapid time, they were keeping a steady pace.

He had partly expected Galen and Rayen to return. They would've known where he was going, and with Lucy's ability to Slide, she should have been able to track him and the others down more easily, but they either hadn't tried to do so, or they were caught up with whatever it was they were doing.

Haern started to descend when movement in the north caught his attention.

Pushing his way forward, tracking along the coins, he put some distance between himself and the caravan of wagons. Even doing that left him a little uncomfortable. He didn't see anything.

That hadn't been his imagination. He was certain of that.

Haern frowned. He'd been through this before, and each time he'd nearly been surprised by an attack. Could there be someone up here again who might pose a danger to him? He didn't want to be caught off guard once more. He looked around, focusing on the ground, thinking that if he could catch something shimmering, the telltale sign of a Slide, maybe he would be able to detect what was taking place.

But there was nothing.

The landscape changed, getting rockier as he went higher and higher, and not far from him, it began to descend once again.

It was going to be difficult traveling this way by wagon. As the trail descended, it switched back and forth, a dangerous pathway along the rock. Haern stared for a moment, trying to gauge whether the wagons would be able to pass before deciding he thought they could.

Even if they could, it still wouldn't be an easy journey.

Maybe they would have to move inland and take a different pathway, but that would involve spending even more time. As much as he hated it, it was the safer option.

Haern turned back and felt the sudden draw of lorcith.

Without hesitating, he shot himself upward, streaking into the sky, holding on to his connection to the lorcith far down on the ground. It was a single coin, and he *pushed*, sending himself away, but at the same time, he *pushed* off on the surge of lorcith he detected.

The reaction saved him. He could feel lorcith streaking toward him, but as he *pushed* on it, it exploded far below him. He held the pressure as the explosion continued and waited until it passed.

When it was finished, Haern descended slowly at first, but then with increasing speed.

He dropped to the ground, looking around him.

There were fragments of lorcith scattered all over. Nails.

When he found the sphere, he made a slow circuit around it. The sphere had been flattened by the pressure of *pushing* on it. When the explosion had happened, Haern had shifted his focus from the coin to this sphere.

Why here?

As far as he could tell, there wasn't any connection. This was simply another place along the road that they were traveling. It wasn't busy, and it was unlikely that others with the ability to use lorcith would even come through here. Either they had chosen this spot on the chance that someone would—or they had known he was traveling through here.

Either way, he was troubled.

Haern took to the air, *pushing* off on the sphere and the remnants of the nails. He drew upon the nails, using them to help him travel. Once back in the air, Haern looked around, half expecting he would come across someone, prepared for an attack, but there was no sign of it.

Was he mistaken? He'd thought he'd seen movement, but maybe there hadn't been any.

Haern made his way back to the wagons and dropped back into the seat next to Elise.

"You found another one, didn't you?"

Haern nodded. "I don't really understand."

"It's almost as if they know you're there," Elise said.

Haern nodded. "That's my concern, too. How can anyone even know where we are?"

"What if they do know?" Elise paused, turning to look behind her. "What do you notice when you're attacked?"

"There's a sense of movement, but then I don't see anyone. The device comes toward me, drawn by my *pull* on lorcith, and then I detonate it."

Elise remained twisted so she could look at the caravan behind her. "I wonder if we're overlooking the possibility that someone with us could be responsible."

"No one coming with us from Dreshen would do this." Haern had a hard time thinking anyone among them would have betrayed them like that. They had all traveled together, working to get to safety.

Elise pressed her lips together in a tight frown. "No. I

don't think they would be responsible, but what if the women in the wagons weren't in danger?"

"We saw what happened to them."

"We *thought* we saw what happened to them. At least, we thought we knew why they were captured. What if we were wrong?"

The idea had some merit, but if there was someone working with them, then it would have to be someone who had abilities.

"What would we be looking for?" Elise asked.

"Probably someone who can Slide. Like I said, every time this happens, I feel as if there's someone there, but then they disappear."

"What if we test this?"

"How?"

"We make it seem as if you were going off again, and then you sneak back. Either that, or myself and some of the others can keep track while you're gone. We could keep an eye on the women in the other wagons." She twisted back to him. "It's not as though we know those women all that well. It's possible one of them might be working against us."

Elise signaled for a stop, and the wagons pulled up. It was late enough that it was reasonable to call it quits for the night. They made their camp, and the women fell into the pattern they had established of building a fire, preparing food, breaking out the casks of water. Haern decided to make his presence known. He walked through the camp, staying visible. If there was someone who was interested in harming him, he needed to draw her out.

Jayna appeared next to him as he slipped between a pair of wagons. "I understand we need to keep watch."

"If you're willing."

"Do you have anyone you suspect?"

"Not particularly. I wasn't even thinking it would be someone with us."

"The first time you were attacked was near the wagons, wasn't it?"

Haern had to think back to when he had first experienced the joy of outrunning the explosion from the lorcith spheres. It did seem like that was the first time. Since then, he had encountered others, and many of them were like this most recent one, no one there, nothing that would suggest there should be anyone around him, or anyone who would even know he was there.

"We need to understand why if it is someone here."

"By that, you mean you don't want to eliminate her," Jayna said.

Haern shook his head. "I didn't take you for that kind of violent type anyway."

"If someone's harming the people with me, I will do what is necessary."

Haern studied Jayna for a moment. "Thanks."

"You don't think that I would protect you?"

"I guess I hadn't considered it is much as I should have."

"You've been working with us, Haern, working to keep us safe, but it goes both ways. We don't have your abilities, but what we do have is strength in numbers. And you're one of our numbers. If someone is trying to hurt one of our people, well, I have no interest in allowing that."

Haern didn't know what to say. He chose to stay quiet. There really wasn't anything that he could say, anyway.

When they wandered by the wagons, Jayna glanced over at him. "Do you detect anything?"

He shook his head. "They're not storing it here."

"You think they're using this ability to quickly go and grab one."

"Maybe."

"And it only targets you."

"It does."

"That's interesting. It's almost as if someone thinks you're responsible for harming them."

"Which is why I have to wonder if it's someone on the wagon we rescued."

He wandered along the line of wagons, searching for a sense of lorcith, but he came up with nothing. If there was any lorcith there, Haern couldn't detect it.

When he was done, he rejoined Elise and the others at the campfire. He sat on the outer edge of the circle, Jayna on one side and Beatrice on the other. Both women had taken it upon themselves to keep an eye on him, which he found amusing but also reassuring. They were both quite capable, and every so often, Elise would glance in his direction, but it was the glance she shared with the other two women that made him understand.

They might be heading to Asador for protection, and to gain the help of the Binders, but what if that wasn't even necessary? These women were behaving more and more like how he remembered Carth behaving, and protecting themselves much like Carth and her people had.

The night passed uneventfully. Every so often, Haern would detect a sense of lorcith, but when it came to him, it was from his own stores, or from the trapped sphere he had stored in the back of the wagon.

When he settled in for the night in the back of one of the wagons, Elise joined him. They pulled the door closed, blocking it from the inside, and he looked at her, smiling to himself. "You're going to start tongues wagging."

She waved her hand. "They already wag. Why are you staying in the wagon tonight?"

"Until I have a better sense of who is doing this—if it is someone with us—I felt it was best to stay inside."

"You're okay with some company?"

"As long as it's you."

She frowned at him. "Who else would you accept?"

Haern laughed softly as she curled into him. "No one else."

They lay next to each other on the hard floor. He pulled a blanket over him and rested his head on his elbow. In the darkness within the wagon, he was able to make out Elise, but he doubted she would be able to see him very well. She rested her head on his chest, breathing in deeply.

"There was a boy I was fond of back in my village," she said after a while.

"Are you trying to make me jealous?"

She chuckled, a throaty sort of sound. "No. I remember thinking when I was younger how pretty he was. I remember running around the village, telling my parents how he and I would end up saying our vows before the sacred tree, and that we would one day have a family of our own." She fell silent, and as she did, she breathed heavily. It took Haern a moment to realize that she was weeping. "When everybody was lost, he was one of them. He and I weren't close. I mourn what we lost. What everyone in my village lost. And yet..."

"And yet what?"

"When I'm here, with you, or out there with them, realizing they need my help, I can't help but wonder whether this is what was meant for me." She started to pull away, but Hearn held her close. "It's awful, I know."

"You think you're awful because you're thankful we had an opportunity to meet?"

"I'm awful because I recognize that what I went through has changed me in a way I likely wouldn't have had I stayed in my village."

Haern rested silently, gathering his thoughts. "My mother used to tell me that she was a thief, but it took a war for her to realize she could be a leader." Haern smiled to himself. What he wouldn't give to know what his parents had been like back then. His mother, so confident now, so important for the rest of Elaeavn, and yet, to hear her talk about it, she had been nothing more than a thief. In his mind, she was much more than that, though he knew she didn't see herself in the same way. What would have become of her had she not needed to learn to lead? He wasn't sure if she would have grown into the same role, or if she had needed the prodding of the war in order to do so.

What of his father? If he hadn't been foreced to face the Forgers, maybe he would have remained behind.

Perhaps his parents might not have had the roles they had, but then again, Haern might have known his father better.

"I'm glad that we met," Elise whispered.

He smiled at her. "I'm glad we met, too." He leaned in, kissing her deeply on the lips.

She kissed back, and as he wrapped himself around her, he felt peace in a way he had not before.

41

HAERN

AN EXPLOSION AWOKE HAERN, LEAVING THE WAGON rocking softly.

He slipped on his pants, hurriedly sliding into his jacket, and scooted down the wagon until he reached the locked door. When he opened it, he looked around.

What had happened?

There was the sense of the explosion, and the air had an earthy odor, debris thrown up. From where he stood, he was limited in what he could determine.

Dropping a coin, he *pushed*, sending himself streaking into the air.

From up here, he could see what had happened. One of the wagons had exploded.

Haern dropped, readying a pair of knives, worried about what had taken place and whether anyone was in danger. When he landed, he set the knives to circling around him, ready for the possibility that he might need to *push* on them and protect himself, but there was no need.

There was nothing here.

As he made his way around the wagon, he saw no signs of anyone around it. Either they were not in it and therefore unharmed, or the explosion had completely obliterated them.

"What happened?"

Haern spun, almost *pushing* on his lorcith knives, but saw Jayna nearby. Beatrice was with her, and she shifted her shirt, pulling it back down. Elise ran up behind them, her eyes wide when she saw the wagon. She frowned a moment but then spun and turned off. Most likely she was going to organize the others once again. It didn't take long for her to realize what needed to be done, and to decide she had to be the one to do it.

"Did you hear it?"

"I didn't hear anything. I felt an explosion."

Haern frowned. He hadn't heard anything, either. The explosion had been powerful, and yet, there was no sign of fire, no sign of anything that would typically be associated with an explosion of this magnitude. Focusing on lorcith, he searched for it.

It was here.

"Gather those who are capable," Haern said.

"What happened?" Jayna asked.

"It's lorcith. A lot of it."

Haern collected the lorcith, drawing it to him, and forced it down in the center of the wagon.

As he did, he realized this was supposed to be their wagon. His and Elise's. It was the one they'd been traveling on throughout the entire day, but when it had come time to rest, Elise had guided him to a different one. That couldn't have been coincidence.

"I think they know we're suspicious," Haern whispered.

"Why?" Jayna asked.

"This was meant for me."

"No one would try to do this to you here."

Haern motioned to the pot. That was all that had survived the explosion. It had been resting near him on the top of the wagon, and he had left it there when they had gone off to survey the rest of the camp. "That was mine."

Surprisingly, the pot had survived, and it even had the twine still intact, wrapped around the lid. He sensed for the lorcith within and realized that it was missing.

Great Watcher!

Not only had the attack been meant for him, but they had used the sphere he'd brought back to the camp against him.

He should have been more careful.

"We need to interrogate everyone," Beatrice said.

"I don't think that's the right strategy," Haern said.

"If anyone could be involved, we need to question them."

"I think we need to approach this cautiously," Haern said. "If we can figure out who it is, in a way that doesn't reveal we're on to them, maybe we can determine where they're getting these lorcith explosives." As much as he wanted to know who was attacking him, he also wanted to know *how*. In his mind, that was just as important as anything else.

"I'll go and make sure everyone is unharmed," Beatrice said.

Jayna turned to him. "You should make it appear as if you're gone."

"You want the attacker to think I died in the explosion?"

"That might work, but no. I just want you to disappear. I think whoever did this will be more likely to speak freely if they think you aren't nearby."

Jayna had proven herself, and she deserved his faith.

He dropped a lorcith coin and then used it to *push* off into the sky.

How much sleep had he gotten? There were still quite a few hours left before morning, long enough that he knew he wouldn't be able to remain suspended in the air until dawn, but even then, he wasn't sure he could stay away from the rest of the caravan. If someone there was willing to attack him, he couldn't help but wonder what else they might be willing to do.

What motive might they have?

Regardless of what Jayna might think, having him there was useful. He could keep an eye on the others. Not only that, but his presence might unsettle whoever was responsible for the attacks.

Haern tried to think through what he knew about these different attacks. There had been the first when they had encountered the wagons. Then there was the attack when he and the others had gone after the wagons. That one had nearly killed him. He thought of each one, but there were no similarities between them, nothing that should explain what had taken place. Most of the women they'd rescued from the wagons would not have even been present.

Which left someone from Dreshen.

Could it be?

As much as he didn't like to think it, maybe it really was somebody who had come with them from the beginning.

Haern dropped to the ground and headed back toward the wagons, *pulling* on the lorcith that had exploded. He made his way toward the fire and found Elise there, trying to calm many of the other women. Some of them were crying, wailing, while others were sitting and rocking. All of the women who appeared completely distraught were ones they'd rescued from the wagon in the first place.

They couldn't have been responsible for it.

He looked at the other women, glancing from face to face, searching to see who didn't appear quite as troubled. The women who had come with them from Dreshen had been through quite a bit, and though many of them had seen much, an explosion like that would still be distressing.

Haern dropped the remains of the lorcith near the fire. He had pulled everything in the camp to the fire. When he was done, he made his way over to Elise.

She frowned at him.

"I think we've been wrong about the focus of the attack. I think it has to have been someone with us from the beginning," he whispered.

"No one with us has those abilities," Elise said.

Haern shook his head. "That we know of."

Elise stiffened and looked around, her gaze drifting

from woman to woman before turning back to Haern. "We will take care of this."

"We?"

She nodded. "This is something you don't need to be present for."

"Elise…"

She shook her head. "We will take care of this."

Haern walked away, standing just beyond the edge of the fire, watching. As he did, he focused on the sense of lorcith, trying to be prepared for anything. He watched all of the women at one time, paying close attention to any sign that someone might attempt to Slide.

Elise went over to Jayna and then Beatrice. They talked softly for a few moments. Haern couldn't shake the questions that filled him. What did he know about Jayna, anyway? She was a skilled fighter, and yet almost too skilled.

He shook away that question. It did them no good to be suspicious of her. She had gone with him willingly, fighting alongside him, captured like him. It wasn't Jayna.

He thought about some of the other women. What did he really know about them? He'd tried to get to know them during the journey, asking questions along the way, but he hadn't learned anything that would provide him with specific answers.

Perhaps that had been a mistake.

Haern continued to watch, and he was startled when Belarra started whimpering. As she did, he noticed shimmering around her.

"Elise!"

Without thinking too much of it, Haern sent a knife

streaking toward Belarra. It caught her, piercing her through the shoulder, and the shimmering faded.

Haern raced forward, and Jayna and Beatrice had Belarra pinned between them. Elise stood in front of her.

"Why?" she demanded.

"You can't understand. It was my assignment."

"Your what?"

"My assignment. I was told to remove him. It was how I would pay for my gift."

Haern continued toward her.

"What gift?" Elise asked.

"You don't understand."

"Help us understand," Jayna said, jerking on Belarra's arm with a little more force.

Belarra looked over at Haern, shaking her head. "I'm sorry. I didn't want to, but…"

She started to shimmer again, and Haern hurried forward, jamming the knife deeper into her shoulder. The sudden pain of it seemed to startle her, and her attempt to Slide faded.

"How?" His voice was soft, but anger filled him. He had been kind to Belarra, and he'd thought that kindness had mattered.

All this time, she had been attempting to harm him. Why wait until now?

"When we were in Dreshen, I was given a gift. There was a price to it, and…"

A gift. The way she described it reminded Haern of the Forgers, but the nature of the attack was not one that was typical for the Forgers.

Instead, this seemed to be something else.

If it wasn't Forgers, then it was someone else with the ability to manipulate metal.

Could it be the C'than? He didn't know as much about them, but seeing as how they had been responsible for attacking his father, and they would know he was the one who'd rescued him, it wouldn't be all that surprising to learn that the C'than had been responsible for this attack.

"Check the back of her head," he said softly.

Elise glanced at Haern, frowning. "Why?"

"Just do it."

He should've thought about it sooner. All this time, he'd seen Belarra touching the back of her head, and yet he had believed it was nothing more than a nervous tic. Not a tic at all, but the same technique that had been used on Lucy.

"What is that?" Jayna hissed.

Haern worked his way around so that he could see what Jayna saw. When he did, he realized there was an implant there, much like he had suspected. He didn't know much about what Lucy's implant had looked like, but the way this one grew into Belarra's skull, he suspected the mechanism was the same.

"This is how she was attacking me," Haern said. He turned to Belarra. "Where are you getting the lorcith spheres?"

"It doesn't matter."

Haern cocked his head to the side, studying her. "It very much matters. Where are you getting them?"

"There's a place where they're left for me. There are dozens of them."

"And the spheres in the wagon that exploded?"

"That was me. I placed them to make you think the men in the wagons were responsible."

It had worked. She had made him think that it was anyone but someone who was with them. How could he believe it was somebody who had been traveling with them? The idea that someone like that would betray them, that they would attack him, seemed almost impossible, and yet...

"Where?"

"Near Dreshen."

Haern frowned. Dreshen. Why would it be there?

They had met the false Binders in Dreshen, and there had been experiments with abilities. Had he made a mistake leaving so soon? Could there have been more there for him to discover?

He wasn't about to turn around and head back there, but they did raise questions for him.

"Who did this? Who gave you these spheres?"

"I don't know his name."

"What do you know him by?"

"He's known by one title only. The blacksmith."

Haern turned away, staring out into the darkness.

Elise came and joined him, standing next to him, slipping her arm into his. "What now?"

"We continue to Asador," he whispered.

"How much further do you think it is?"

He shrugged. "Not far now."

"What about this blacksmith?"

"It seems as if Galen and the others were looking for him, too."

"And?"

Haern turned to Elise, meeting her gaze. "And now we know where to find him. Somehow, we have to get word to him."

"Which means you're leaving us."

Haern stared at her for a moment. "That's not what it means. I have no intention of leaving."

"But what we discovered—"

"What we discovered doesn't change anything for me. Once we reach Asador, there will be a way to connect to Carth and her network. We'll get word. And hopefully, what we have discovered will matter."

He couldn't help but think that it would have to matter. Someone who had the ability to manipulate lorcith like this, and somebody who could place augmentations, either was with the C'than—what he thought was most likely—or they were somebody his people needed to know about. With weapons like this, they would be useful against the Forgers.

Could they use an ally like that?

Did they dare not try?

Elise squeezed his arm, and he looked down at her. "We know what happened now. We'll be safe the rest of the way to Asador."

Haern nodded. They would be safe the rest of the way to Asador, but once there, the real challenge would begin.

RYN

A STEADY TAPPING WOKE HER, AND RYN JOLTED UP, slamming her head into the wall of the closet. She swore under her breath, worried she'd already made too much noise.

Glancing over to where Dillon rested, she saw he was still deeply asleep. He breathed heavily, practically snoring, and if she awoke him, he wouldn't find it easy to get back to sleep. For what she thought would be necessary, she needed him to get all the rest he could, if only so he could help her when it came down to it. It was selfish, and regardless of that, she knew it was necessary.

The tapping returned, and Ryn listened, focusing on the sound, worried it might represent footsteps. She was thankful for her augmented senses, but while she would be able to hear the sound of others approaching, she worried that she wouldn't be able to escape very quickly if it came down to it. If it did, she would have to figure out how to get Dillon out of here, though he would be able to travel.

Getting to her feet, Ryn situated herself in front of the door. The tapping continued, a regular sound. When she heard it, she realized that it came from beneath her, deeper underground than where she was.

Strange.

Could there be a blacksmith here as well?

It was hard for her to believe there would be such deception in so many places, but she couldn't deny what she had heard.

Glancing back down to Dillon, she decided to let him sleep. As long as he didn't snore too loudly, he wouldn't draw any attention to himself, and she could sneak off, figure out what that tapping was, and return to him before anything happened.

Pulling the door open, she glanced down the hallway for a moment before stepping out. It was a narrow hall, and her brief sleep had given her enough respite that she felt regenerated, much more awake than she had in quite some time. She slipped off down the hall, following the steady tapping sound. When she reached the end of the hall, she paused, focusing on the source of the sound. She couldn't tell where it was coming from. Somewhere nearby, but where?

Ryn hesitated, looking around for anything that might tell her what it was. It wasn't the sound of footsteps. The regularity of it reminded her of the tapping she'd heard when she had first observed the sounds of the blacksmith in Dreshen.

There was a pause in the tapping, and when it came again, Ryn focused long enough to find the source before starting toward it. She reached a staircase leading down into the bowels of the earth. This staircase was incredibly narrow, barely wide enough for her to squeeze through, and she wound down it, every so often glancing behind her, looking for any sign of pursuit. There was no light, nothing that would help her find her way, and without her enhanced eyesight, she doubted she would have felt confident coming here.

She continued down the stairs, following as they twisted around. The tapping sound persisted, growing slightly louder as she went.

Finally, the stairs ended. Ryn hesitated at the bottom of the stairs, looking around, searching for anything and anyone who might be out here, but came across nothing.

It was little more than another hallway.

The tapping sound was louder now, closer.

Ryn searched for the source of the sound. It was here —at least on this level.

As she made her way, dark shadows were recessed along the walls. It took a moment to realize that those were doors, but they were narrow doors, much like the hall was narrow. Standing with her hand resting along the wall, she tried to hear any sounds on the other side but didn't detect anything.

The tapping wasn't coming from the door.

It came from further along the hall.

Ryn hurried, making her way along the hallway, listening as she went. The tapping persisted, growing louder. There was something else mixed within it, and had she not been this deep beneath the earth, focused on the sound of the tapping, she wasn't sure she would have recognized it.

Breathing.

Ryn was certain that was what she heard, but where was it coming from?

Near the end of the long hall, there was a door. She held her hand on it, focused on the sounds on the other side of the door, and they persisted.

What was it from?

She was convinced there was tapping on the other side of the door, but she was also convinced there was breathing.

This far beneath the earth, this place could only be one thing—a prison.

Ryn tested the handle, finding it locked.

Reaching into her pocket, she pulled out her knife and slipped it into the lock. As it often did, the knife changed, shifting a little, almost as if it took on the contours of the lock itself, and she turned it, carefully pushing the door open.

She stood there for a moment, looking inside, as her eyes adjusted. A bald man stood in one corner, his hand raised, a stone clutched in his palm, and...

He hurled it at her.

Ryn ducked, getting away from the stone, and reached for the door, prepared to pull it closed, but the man on the other side was quick. He grabbed it, prying it free from her fingers, and as she scrambled back, she stared at him.

"Dolan?"

The man hesitated. He held his arm cocked back, ready to throw something else—probably another rock.

Ryn didn't know many people in the Lexa palace, but when she had been here before, Dolan had been one of the most senior servants, a man the Great One had often visited with while having his morning tea. She'd always found it interesting that the Great One would visit with the servants as much as he did with his disciples, but Dolan was one he had seemed to favor.

"Emissary?" he whispered. "Could it be you?"

Ryn glanced over her shoulder before turning her attention back to Dolan. "It's me. What happened here?"

"Why are you here?"

"I came for help." Now that she said it, and having seen how much he seemed to struggle, she realized how foolish that had been. "I was in Dreshen looking into an attack that took place there when I was under attack myself."

"I've heard what happened in Dreshen."

Ryn frowned. "You've heard of it?"

Dolan nodded. "Word gets back to me."

"I was hoping to send word to the Great One."

"I'm afraid that won't be easy."

"What happened here?"

"Unfortunately, the palace is under attack."

"But I saw the Ai'thol on patrol out by the wall."

"You saw them, and they believe that they are still in service of the Ai'thol, but those within the palace have assumed a different type of control."

"We need to get word to the Great One."

"Unfortunately, my means of doing so is limited. He has gone silent."

It took a moment for that comment to register. What it meant was that Dolan had some way of communicating with the Great One.

More than that, it meant that he had gone silent here

along with his silence elsewhere. How long had she been in Dreshen? Probably two weeks, and in that time, she had continually expected the Great One to return, and yet he hadn't.

Could something have happened to him?

Ryn didn't want to think that way, but it was possible that it had.

"What happened here?"

Dolan looked past her. "I'm not the only one who was captured. Anyone who was viewed as loyal to the Great One was thrown in prison."

"How many are here?"

"A dozen. Perhaps more."

"What about the disciple?"

"Gone."

"Gone?"

Dolan nodded slowly. "He was killed when he refused to share what he knew about the Great One. He sacrificed himself."

"Why did they keep you alive?"

It was a harsh comment, but the same time, it was one that she needed to ask. It didn't make sense for them to have killed the disciple and kept the servants alive.

Not unless they knew that Dolan was something more than just a servant.

"I think they understood I have more information than I was sharing. They were thinking they could draw it out of me, but I refused. I will serve the Great One until my dying breath."

"I will as well."

"If you can get out of here, emissary, then you should do so. There are other places you can go that are still safe."

"Such as?"

"Nearby, I would suggest Morald. It would be a few days' travel, but…"

Ryn didn't know Morald well enough to know whether she would be able to find any safety there. It was possible that by the time she reached it, anyone who was loyal to the Great One would have met with the same fate as Dolan and those within Lexa.

Still, if the Great One didn't know about what had been taking place, then she needed to be responsible for ensuring he was informed.

Even if that meant she risked herself to do so.

She couldn't just leave, though. She couldn't abandon Dolan and the others here, not with what had taken place. They deserved more than that.

"Let me at least help you get out," she said.

"It's not safe," Dolan said.

"There has to be someplace you can hide."

"I don't know that there is."

Could she get them out of the palace? She could get them into the city, even if it meant asking Dillon to help. It would require they find another place to rest and recuperate, another place where Dillon could recover. It might be safe to remain in the city, but then again it might not be, and it was possible that doing this would drain him too much.

She wasn't about to leave servants of the Great One behind.

"Wait here," she said.

"Wait? Emissary—"

"I have some way of getting you to safety. Please. Wait here."

She hurried off, and when she reached the stairs, she slipped up them, watching the darkness for any signs of movement. There was nothing, and when she reached the hallway where she had left Dillon, she raced forward.

She paused at the door, listening for a moment.

He was still there, breathing heavily.

She hated that she would have to wake him for this and hoped he had gotten enough rest, but this was necessary—and important.

Pushing open the door, she found him sleeping. When she touched his shoulder, he awoke with a start, rolling over and then smiling at her. "Ryn. I feel—"

Ryn shook her head. "I need your help."

He sat up quickly, smacking his head on the lowest shelf before wincing and scooting out, rubbing where he had hit his head. "What is it?"

"I found cells deep below us."

"Cells?"

Ryn nodded. "A prison. One of the palace servants is held there."

"Why would they hold one of the palace servants?"

"Because of whatever is taking place. They killed the disciple, and they captured Dolan, a servant who has a relationship with the Great One."

"And you want me to transport him out?"

Ryn nodded.

"I don't know how hard that will be."

"We have to try."

"I can only take one—maybe two—at a time."

It would be slow, and it would mean he would make multiple trips. Hopefully he had the necessary strength. It all depended on how much rest he'd managed.

By the time they reached the bottom of the stairs, she found Dolan standing near her, waiting. He looked past Ryn, taking in the sight of Dillon, and suddenly lunged.

Ryn was so startled that she didn't know how to react. Dolan grabbed for Dillon, reaching for his neck, his hands wrapped around his throat.

"Dolan! What are you doing?"

The other man continued to squeeze, and Dillon started to fade.

Ryn grabbed for Dolan, putting herself between the two men, and pushed.

Surprisingly, she had more strength than she expected, and she forced them apart.

Dolan went staggering back, slamming into the nearby stone, and he looked over at Ryn, shaking his head. "What are you doing with him? I thought you were the Great One's emissary."

"I *am* the emissary. This man helped me."

"This man is with them. I saw—"

Dolan lunged forward again, and Ryn had to push herself forward, getting in the way. She prevented Dolan from grabbing Dillon, but she wasn't sure she was going to be able to keep them apart. If Dillon was going to help Dolan and the others escape, she needed the other man to recognize that Dillon wasn't going to harm him.

Turning to Dillon, she saw him rubbing his neck. "What's this about?"

"I don't know what he's talking about."

"Emissary, he was with them. I've seen him."

"You've seen him do what?"

"I've seen him with the others. He was with them when they brought us here."

"How long ago was that?"

"Not long. A week, maybe more."

It was difficult for her to know whether or not Dillon had been here. He could travel, which meant distances didn't limit him, but she had seen his weakness when it came to traveling. He couldn't fake the fatigue, and it made it difficult for her to believe that he had been here.

But then, there were the days he'd disappeared from Dreshen. The blacksmith hadn't known where he'd gone, and Dillon had claimed he was sick, but what if he wasn't? What if it was nothing more than an excuse?

She didn't know what to believe anymore.

Starting toward Dillon, she lowered her voice. "Why does he think this was you?"

Dillon looked past her, watching Dolan. "I don't know. I haven't been here before. I've been helping you, Ryn."

He had been helping, pushing himself to the point of exhaustion on her behalf.

That wasn't the kind of thing someone would do if they were trying to betray her.

"Could you be wrong?" she asked Dolan.

"I don't think so. I've seen this man before."

"But could you be wrong?"

Dolan glanced over to her. "Possibly."

"Possibly? You would attack him like this when you could possibly be wrong?"

"I've seen others with his eye color and his build. Look at him, emissary. He's with them."

"I vouch for him," she said.

Dolan blinked, turning his attention to Ryn. "You do?"

Ryn nodded. "I do. And he will get you out of here safely, but only if you don't continue to attack him."

She went to the first door, taking out her knife, slipping it in the lock, and twisting. She pulled it open. Inside was another dark-robed servant, and Dolan hurried in, slipping his arm under their shoulders, and guided them out.

Ryn went to the next door, doing the same. Behind it was an older woman, her hair frazzled, her clothing worn and tattered, and Dolan raced in, placing his arms underneath her, lifting her from the ground.

As she went to the next door, Dillon was there, leaning in and whispering in her ear. "Do you know all of these people?"

She shook her head. "I know only Dolan."

"Are you sure you can trust him?"

"Why?"

"What if they're here for a reason?"

Ryn paused. Dolan was whispering quietly to the woman, and the other man that they had rescued stood nearby. His jaw was clenched, his face lean. Despite his imprisonment, he still carried himself as if he didn't deserve to be there.

"I know what I heard up above."

"And you didn't investigate."

Ryn hesitated. He was right, and it was troubling she hadn't. She'd been so caught up in what she had experienced that she hadn't taken a moment to think things through. Maybe that was tied to her fatigue.

She knew the Great One visited with Dolan, but that didn't mean that the Great One trusted him any more than he did others. It was possible the Great One didn't trust Dolan and was visiting with him in order to try to help him understand the value that the Ai'thol offered the people of Lexa.

Could she be making a mistake?

Dolan turned to her. "Are you going to open any others?"

"Tell me what happened here."

"What do you mean?"

"Up above. You said the Great One was betrayed. What happened?"

Dolan glanced from the man to the woman. "I'm afraid I don't fully understand."

"That's my point. I don't understand. Can you tell me what happened? It doesn't make sense that you would be placed down here." The more she thought about it, the more she realized that was the case.

And… she realized something else.

She hadn't been forcing up her mental barriers, the barriers the Great One had trained her to hold.

In her exhaustion, she had forgotten about maintaining them.

She glanced over to Dillon, replacing her barriers. She had made a mistake. She should have kept them secured before.

There was no influence within her mind.

Breathing out in relief, she turned back to Dolan. "You haven't shared anything more with me."

"What is there to share with you, emissary? You've begun to doubt those of us who serve the Great One."

"I've begun to doubt everything."

What would the Great One say about that when he saw her next? Would he be disappointed that she'd begun to question? He'd wanted her to observe and detect, to find her own understanding of the world, but would he have wanted her to be so suspicious of everything?

She couldn't help but think he wouldn't have wanted that.

When she'd traveled with him, she'd observed, but she'd also believed everyone acted in the way the Great One believed. Then again, perhaps the Great One had known better.

Turning to Dillon, she whispered, "Wait for me."

"What are you going to do?"

"A test."

Ryn stepped forward, smiling at Dolan. "How many others are servants here?"

"Most of them."

"I have trouble understanding why they would imprison the servants here. It seems as if a place like this would be reserved for those with more potential to cause real harm."

"You don't believe servants can cause real harm?" Dolan asked.

"That's not it. It's just that I find it interesting you say they killed the disciple, but they left you alive." She should have questioned that more when Dolan had told her, but she had taken it on faith.

There would be no reason for attackers to have killed the disciple and left servants alive. None of it made good sense to her.

"How many attacked you?" Ryn asked.

"Emissary?"

"You would have known. I imagine you counted, keeping track on behalf of the Great One, especially if you serve as you say."

Dolan glanced at the woman before turning his attention back to her. "There were five or six we were able to find."

"I'm going to investigate. If all is as you say, then there's no reason for me to doubt you."

"Emissary, I assure you that—"

Ryn ignored him, turning to Dillon. "Can you place them back into one of the cells?" she whispered.

Dillon nodded. A wave of nausea rolled through her as he quickly traveled, grabbing Dolan and placing him on the other side of one of the doors. He returned and did the same with the woman and then the man, traveling far more quickly than he had before.

When he was done, he leaned forward, resting his hands on his thighs, breathing heavily. "That... that was hard work."

"I need you to be able to travel at least once more."

"I will, but I don't know that I can travel us throughout the palace."

"I don't need you to do that. Besides, I think we need to be seen."

"You want others to know you're here?"

"They need to know the emissary of the Great One is here."

It was dangerous, but at the same time, if she was with Dillon, there was the sense of safety his presence provided. He might not intend it, but he did offer her something she needed.

They made their way up the stairs, and she paused, glancing back into the darkness, waiting for the steady tapping to return. She didn't know if she was making a mistake or not, but she needed to find her own answers rather than rely upon Dolan and others to tell her.

They reached the hall where they had rested. Ryn paused. They could take another rest. If they did, she could allow Dillon to restore himself, to recover, but then she ran the risk of delaying things even more. As it was, she didn't know how much longer they could wait.

She hurried down the hallway, keeping Dillon near her. As she went, she grabbed for his hand. Perhaps it was better that she stayed with him, in contact with him, for the possibility they would have to travel.

As they headed up the stairs, she hesitated.

There was movement, but the sense of it was distant, not near enough to cause any danger.

She continued up the stairs. At the top of them, she paused. She straightened her spine, looking around, running her hands across the cloth of her cloak. She pushed back the hood, keeping the sleeves covering the bands of metal around her wrists that still throbbed, though less than before, and strode forward.

"I don't like this," Dillon said.

"We aren't in any danger."

"You don't know that."

"No. I was just trying to reassure you," she said.

Dillon shook his head. "You don't need to do that, either."

"I just thought—"

"I'll be ready if we need to transport out of here. Squeeze my hand if you think we do."

She nodded.

As they made their way along the hall, she heard voices.

This time, she headed toward them.

RYN

RYN WORRIED ABOUT WHAT SHE'D ENCOUNTER WHEN THEY reached the end of the hallway, and what type of people might be there. It was possible she would come across attackers much like those she'd found in Dreshen. If there were some like the blacksmith—or like Lorren—she needed to be careful, but she still felt as if she didn't have all the answers she needed. It would be better for her to observe this herself.

Three men made their way along the hall, each of them speaking softly. She didn't recognize any of them, though they wore the dark colors of the Ai'thol. One of them had a long scar along the side of his face. Two of them didn't have scars, and one had blondish hair while the other had black hair almost as dark as the night.

They stopped when they saw her.

"What is this?"

"I am Ryn Valeron, emissary of the Great One, Olandar Fahr."

She was careful to use the formal presentation of her

title and authority, wanting to ensure that they recognized her role. Would they even care?

"How are you here?"

She cocked her head to the side, fixing the lead man—the one with the scar of the Ai'thol—with as hard a glare as she could muster. Ryn wasn't sure she did enough to intimidate, but as the emissary of the Great One, she would be expected to have some authority.

"You question the emissary of the Great One?"

"I question your presence."

Ryn reached beneath her cloak, pulling out the sigil she wore on a necklace. She let it drop onto her chest. "And I would question what is taking place here."

The lead man hesitated. "Where did you get that?"

"Perhaps you didn't hear me," Ryn said again. Her heart was hammering. While Dillon might be able to transport them out of here, she didn't want him to need to do that. She needed answers, and the only way she would get them would be by staying here and seeing for herself what was taking place. Wasn't that what the Great One would expect of her?

Observe and detect.

What did she detect?

She took a moment to study the three men. While all three were dressed like the Ai'thol, only the lead man, the one with the scar, truly looked like one of the Ai'thol. He had the black jacket and pants, his silver belt looped around, and all he was missing was the dark cloak that would signify his presence within the Ai'thol. A badge on his chest indicated he was quite high ranking, high enough that he should recognize the Great One's emissary.

The other two were different. There was the man with the blond hair. He had a muscular build, larger than Dillon, but not quite as large as the blacksmith from Dreshen. He was tall, but the cut of his cloak was unusual. It swept off to the side, an angled appearance to it, and he wore a sword sheathed.

Her gaze swept over the sword, noting the curve to it. She'd seen swords like that before. Neelish. It indicated skill, which meant that if he were to attack, they would be in danger. The sellswords of Neeland were incredibly talented, and the Great One often spoke highly of them, remarking on how he'd hired them for their service.

That left the third man. With his dark hair, it was difficult to make out any features about him. It seemed almost as if darkness swirled around him.

Her breath caught. She had heard others described as having such an ability but hadn't expected to come across anyone from Ih. She'd thought that place destroyed, and the people from there gone. The dark cloak he wore took on a different meaning if that was the case.

Shadows.

Perhaps Dolan had been right.

Then again, it was possible the Ai'thol were trying to make inroads with Neeland and the remnants of Ih. Without knowing either way, she didn't feel comfortable making a decision and judging.

The Great One would be disappointed if she were to judge such a thing immediately, without taking the time to better understand.

"As I said, I am the emissary of the Great One, Olandar Fahr. I have come here on his behalf."

That wasn't entirely true, but she doubted the Great One would mind that she made such a claim.

"The Great One hasn't visited here in—"

"Nine months." Ryn took a step forward, keeping Dillon with her. "It's been nine months since the Great One's visit. I was here when he made the visit, and if you are aware of that visit, then perhaps you would recall my being here."

The other man held her gaze for a moment. She noticed how the corners of his eyes twitched. One hand drifted down to his side. He didn't appear to be armed, but that didn't reassure her.

"The Great One does not often take interest in Lexa."

"The Great One has interest in all his lands."

"I haven't seen that to be the case."

"Then perhaps you don't pay attention to the Great One." She smiled for a moment. "The Great One would argue otherwise. Seeing as how I've traveled with him extensively over the last year." She hesitated. "I believe there is a disciple stationed here. I would visit with him."

She tensed, ready to squeeze Dillon's hand, uncertain what would happen if they needed to escape. Would he be quick enough?

She had to think he would, and all they needed to do was get out of the palace, into the city, and then he could transport them somewhere else. They could stay ahead of any attack, though if she did that, if she abandoned Lexa, then the Great One would lose control of this place.

Perhaps it didn't matter. It wasn't her responsibility to

ensure each land remained under the control of the Great One. It was her responsibility to observe and detect.

"I'm afraid the disciple is unavailable at this moment," the man said.

"Why would that be? With a disciple present in Lexa, I would anticipate he should be readily available for the Great One's emissary at any given time."

"You will have to take that up with him."

"You will show me to him."

The Ai'thol hesitated, and as he did, nausea washed through her.

It wouldn't be Dillon.

That meant that it was someone else.

Ryn pushed.

The Ai'thol suddenly disappeared.

He could travel.

The Neelish sellsword started forward, and Ryn squeezed Dillon's hand.

With that, they transported.

They appeared in the entrance to the palace, and she glanced over at him.

"This is as far as I could take us. Something prevents me from going any further."

Ryn frowned.

There shouldn't be anything that restricted them from traveling any further, not unless someone was actively aware of the fact they were here.

Whatever limitations there were, they were inside.

Then again, they had walked in—not transported.

That mattered, though she wasn't sure quite how much.

As she looked around, she considered heading out the door. This was their opportunity to do it, but if she did that, there would be no coming back.

Looking up to the catwalk, she pointed. "Take us there."

"Ryn, I don't know how much more I can transport."

"You're going to have to do what you can. If it comes down to it…"

She didn't want to say much more. If it came down to it, there might not be much of a choice. With a Neelish sellsword, they ran the real risk of danger, the kind of danger she wasn't sure she was equipped to handle. Neither of them was a fighter, and while she could handle someone who attempted to travel toward her, pushing them away, she didn't think she could counter a fighter. It was better to run, stay alive, and be prepared to observe another time.

He squeezed her hand, and when he did, nausea rolled through her for a moment before fading. They stepped out on the narrow catwalk. She hurried along it, making her way toward where she remembered the disciple having been before. If Dolan was right—and if the disciple had been there and was killed—then she needed to know.

What was the likelihood that she would go from one place that was attacked to another?

Ryn hurried along the hallway. A set of wide double doors were at the end, and she paused long enough to test the door handle, finding it locked. Pulling her knife out of her pocket, she slipped it into the lock, waiting for it to shift, and then twisted. The door opened, and she stepped through to the other side.

The room was dark, and it took a moment for her eyes to adjust, focusing on what she could make out around her. It was an open chamber that she had visited when she had been here with the Great One before. She remembered how the disciple had offered this chamber to the Great One, but the Great One had chosen simpler quarters, wanting nothing more than to observe. It was typical of him. He didn't want to draw extra attention to himself, and she wasn't all that surprised by that.

This room was decorated with extensive furniture. The carpet alone was likely incredibly valuable, and the wardrobe near one wall had patterns worked into its face of different-colored woods that must have taken years to complete. A table near the center of the room cast a strange shadow, and Ryn made her way over to it, checking the lantern before igniting it and casting a soft glow around everything.

Dillon remained near the door, shifting his feet almost nervously. He glanced behind him before turning his attention back to Ryn.

"I don't like this," he said.

"We won't be here much longer," she said.

What she needed was evidence that something had happened to the disciple or that he'd gone elsewhere.

It looked to be an empty room. There was no sign of anything within it that would raise her suspicions, certainly nothing that would make her think something unfortunate had happened to the other man.

That being the case, she couldn't help but wonder if perhaps she was wrong.

What if the Ai'thol hadn't done anything to the disciple?

If that was the case, it meant Dolan was in the wrong, and it meant he belonged in the cell.

Ryn wandered around the inside of the room, looking at the wardrobe. On a whim, she pulled it open. Long cloaks hung within, the marker of the disciple's office. A necklace dangled down from a hook worked into one of the doors.

She glanced at that necklace. It was a sigil of the Great One, a marker of station, and it matched—or nearly so—the one she wore.

The disciple wouldn't have left that behind, would he?

She didn't think he would, which meant either something had happened, or...

She stepped away, closing the wardrobe.

"What were you hoping to find here?" Dillon asked.

"I'm not really sure."

"I think we'd better be moving."

As he said it, a wave of nausea began to work through her. Again, she pushed.

She had seen no swirling of colors, nothing to signify it came from Dillon, which suggested to her it was from the Ai'thol, or perhaps someone else. Either way, she needed to avoid it.

She glanced over to Dillon. "That wasn't you, was it?"

"What?"

Then it wasn't. Not that she had thought it was. If it had been him, she would have seen the swirling of colors around him, the signifier that he was preparing to travel.

Ryn waited, half expecting there would be another sense, but it didn't come again.

As she continued to look around her, she searched for signs of anything that would tell her what had happened to the disciple. There was nothing.

"Ryn?" Dillon said.

She turned away from the table where she'd been staring, looking at the lantern glowing on the surface, and frowned. "What is it?"

"Is it getting darker in here?"

"What?"

"It seems almost like it's darker."

It was a strange thing to say, and with a start, she lunged for Dillon, straining to reach him. If it were getting darker, that could only mean—

Dillon collapsed.

Ryn backed away, watching the man from Ih as he gradually approached. Now that she was aware of him, it was easy enough for her to make him out, but she hadn't noticed him before.

That was a powerful ability if he was able to overwhelm her enhanced eyesight.

"You are troublesome," he said.

"I am the emissary of the Great One, Olandar Fahr."

"So you said. It doesn't change the fact that you are troublesome." He started toward her. It seemed as if the shadows around him were swirling. There was power to those shadows, and it appeared almost as if they were alive, making their way toward her. The more she watched, the more certain she was that she needed to get away from him. With Dillon down, there wouldn't be any way for her to do so. She needed him to get up and help her.

Ryn looked around, searching for any way she might be able to get free, but the man blocked her way out. Not only that, but the way he used shadows seemed to bar her in. Though she wasn't sure, she worried he might be able to wrap them around her in a way that would prevent her from escaping.

She should have taken the opportunity to escape from the palace when she'd had it.

She scrambled back and bumped into the table. Slipping around it, she kept the man in front of her but doubted she'd be able to do so for much longer. He was stalking toward her, the shadows spreading around her, sweeping in. It wouldn't be much longer before he used them to practically embrace her, wrapping her in whatever strange power he had.

"When the Great One finds out—"

"The Great One will fail."

"You're with him, aren't you?"

"Who?"

"Him. Lareth."

The dark-haired man frowned. "If only you understood, but…" He shook his head, and Ryn staggered back another step, and then another, each time feeling as if she were retreating, but at the same time having nowhere else she could go.

All she could think about was how she wasn't a fighter. She was an observer. Her role was not to battle on behalf of the Great One. It was to witness everything he did, provide her view of it. That was all.

There were others who were supposed to be fighters on his behalf. Those fighters should be here.

And she had missed her opportunity. She could have rescued Dolan, but instead she had questioned him, placing him in the cell, and now she was going to end up captured by this dark man.

She slammed into the wardrobe.

When she did, a wave of nausea started to work up through her. Ryn prepared to push it away. When she did, the man surged toward her, darting forward. She tried to slip off to the side.

Nausea rolled through her, and he was there. Reaching her.

She fought, but callused hands grabbed her, and then nausea struck her again.

When it cleared, she blinked. She was outside, daylight breaking in the distance, the city of Lexa looming ahead of her. Within the middle of the city, she saw the palace.

Dillon held her hand, his callused fingers squeezing hers. She should have known that he had come for her, but all she had felt was the rolling nausea of someone preparing to travel to her.

Dillon leaned forward, breathing heavily. "That's about all I can do."

"Thank you."

"What happened?"

She shook her head. "I don't even know. I don't have any idea what he did, other than he was using shadows, controlling them as he wrapped them around me."

And had Dillon not traveled to her, she would have

been captured, subjected to whatever it was he'd intended to do to her.

"Give me a few moments to rest, and then we can go somewhere else."

As Ryn stared toward Lexa, she shook her head. "I don't think that we can."

"You saw what just happened."

"I did, and I know that if we go, whoever has taken control of the palace will maintain that hold."

"What do you intend to do?"

"I think we need to rescue Dolan and the others."

44

RYN

RYN SQUEEZED THE NECKLACE, GRIPPING THE SIGIL TIGHTLY. She held on to it, afraid to let go. Her hand made it warm, and she focused on her breathing, trying to slow it, keep it steady, though she felt as if she failed. As she squeezed on the locket, the sense of the Great One filled her.

If only he could find her.

He wouldn't have known she'd left Dreshen, and if he returned there, she wasn't worried about his safety, but she was worried he would wonder where she'd gone and why. If word got out that she'd gone off with Dillon, what kind of questions would the Great One ask?

And it didn't really matter. The Great One deserved to know she was unharmed, and yet, she wasn't entirely sure that was true. Now that she was sitting outside of Lexa, focusing on the city, staring at it as the sun continued to rise while listening to Dillon breathe heavily in his sleep, she was acutely aware of the pain throbbing in her arms and legs. She hadn't looked at where the metal pierced her skin since placing her cloak on, and she pulled up the sleeves, startled to see it seemed to be rewrapped more tightly around her wrists. It was almost as if the sacred metal were trying to pull itself into her body.

What would happen to her if it did?

Probably the same thing that had happened to her when the metal had been placed on the back of her head. That had absorbed within her the same way, a strange connection to it that seemed to be demanding she draw it in.

Other than an awareness of people traveling, Ryn didn't think she had any new abilities. That was useful enough and had been especially helpful while trying to escape the attack, allowing her the opportunity to push away those who might travel to her.

What if she had been pushing away the Great One?

She hadn't considered that before, but it was a real possibility. She might have pushed him away while trying to hold on to her connection.

This time, she wasn't going to wake Dillon up any sooner than necessary, determined to give him all the rest he needed in order to fully recover. The next step would be to get Dolan and the others out of the palace. It would take energy on his behalf, and when he was done, they would need to hurry and find safety in another way.

She still wasn't sure what they would do. Even when they managed to get to Dolan and the others, there was the possibility they would need to get them out of the palace, and with what she had determined with Dillon, it would involve an extra step, transporting them to the door and then them scurrying through it to transport once again.

Would they be fast enough?

She poured her concerns into the necklace, fearing what would need to happen.

Her mind continued to race, working through the various scenarios, uncertain whether she would succeed.

This was beyond her, wasn't it?

All she wanted to do was serve the Great One, to do as he'd asked, but this wasn't the kind of thing he'd ever asked of her.

Observe.

"Why would he place me in such a dangerous situation?" she whispered.

She wrapped her arms around her knees, looking around her. They were situated well outside of the city, in a gentle meadow dotted with flowers. Cows grazed nearby, penned in, but she saw no sign of the farmer who owned them. She was thankful for that, not sure what she would have done if she'd encountered the farmer. Would she have needed to continue traveling, moving further and further away from Lexa, or would she have been forced to fight?

That was not her way.

Thankfully, there'd been no sign of anyone else. Wind gusted from time to time, but the day was otherwise clear, the sunshine warm and comforting—almost too warm. It didn't entirely suit her mood.

She continued to squeeze the sigil. She wasn't sure why she did, only that she felt as if it connected her to the Great One in some way. It was probably nothing more than her imagination. If only he'd given her some way to call him, to summon him when she had the need—but if he had done that, she would probably have called him far more often than was necessary.

When she did find him, she was curious what he would do. She'd seen him angry a few times, but always for good reason, and always because he'd been disappointed by those serving him. It wouldn't be surprising for him to react in the same way now. Those who'd served him had disappointed him by losing control of the assets, and he would be angry.

Then again, perhaps something had happened to the Great One. There would have to be a reason for others to have been so willing to act out. They had to believe that they would get away with it, didn't they?

What if they'd heard something had happened to him?

She tried to work through the various reasons why his followers would have suddenly abandoned the Great One, and the one reason that made the most sense was they no longer had him to follow.

There was no one else who could take his place.

That seemed unlikely.

And while she wasn't a fighter, there were others who were.

Ryn sat upright.

Maybe that was the key. She had been thinking about how she would break into the palace, get to Dolan and the others, and find some way of sneaking them back out again, but that didn't solve the problem at all.

What she needed was to use those who still served the Great One.

And there were those people. She'd seen them around the outskirts of the palace. From what Dolan had said, there were those who didn't know about the attack, and they wouldn't have known what had taken place inside or what had happened to the disciple.

Ryn still had her sigil. It was the mark of the Great One.

She had hesitated to go to them before, concerned about their reaction, but perhaps that was what she needed to do.

She started working through things in her mind while Dillon slept, and as she did, she thought about everything she had seen in the city. It fit with what Dillon had said. There was an absence of life, but he was wrong about the source of it. It hadn't come from the Ai'thol. It had come from the fact that there was upheaval within the palace.

Was she capable of doing more?

She didn't know. In this case, if she took action, she'd be moving forward on the Great One's behalf. It was dangerous, but then again, doing nothing was dangerous, too.

The people in the city needed her to do something.

Ryn got to her feet. Strangely, the idea of taking action in this way felt exhilarating.

It was near nightfall when Dillon awoke. He sat up, rubbing the sleep from his eyes, looking up to the darkening sky before yawning and turning his attention to Ryn. "You let me sleep all day?"

"I've been thinking."

"About how to rescue the people inside the palace?"

She nodded. "Yes, but not the way we were initially planning it."

"How, then?"

"Dolan said there were only a half a dozen or so in the palace."

"And we know one of them is incredibly powerful."

"Probably all of them," Ryn said. "But I think they aren't acting with the rest of the Ai'thol."

"What do you mean?"

"I mean I need to go and be the emissary."

"You tried that, Ryn. When you were in the palace. You saw what happened."

"This is different. I think I need to be the emissary outside of the palace."

"What good will that do?"

She had given it a lot of thought, struggling to figure out what she could do and how it would make a difference, if at all. "I need to bring the Ai'thol together so they can act on behalf of the Great One again."

"Ryn—"

She turned to him. "You don't have to do this with me. I know how you feel about the Ai'thol, and I even know how you feel about the Great One. I thank you for everything you've done, but I don't think you'll be needed to break into the palace."

"That's it?"

"What more do you want me to say?"

"I didn't want you to just send me away."

"I'm not sending you away, Dillon. I'm giving you the option of leaving." He wasn't a part of this. That was another thing she'd realized while sitting there and thinking as the day stretched on. She'd asked for his help, and he'd given it willingly, saving her life and keeping her from danger, but at the same time, he was placing himself in danger for her.

There was no reason for that, since he didn't share her beliefs about the value of the work. He didn't view the Great One the same way she did. Still, he'd come along.

"I'm not leaving you like this."

"Dillon—"

He came toward her, grabbing her hands. "I want to help you see all sides, Ryn."

She stared at him, meeting his gaze for a moment. "Why?"

"Why am I helping you?"

She nodded. "There's nothing here for you. You don't have to do this."

"I know I don't have to, but I want to. I want to help you. And more than that, I think I can show you things your Great One cannot."

"I don't doubt the Great One."

"I'm not asking you to. I'm just asking you to do what you seem to have been doing anyway. Keep an open mind. Look around you and understand that perhaps everything you've experienced is not what it seemed to be."

She let out a heavy sigh. "What do you think I will observe that will change my mind?"

"Maybe nothing. You've seen the way your Great One's people work. These people once served him, and without his presence, they've taken it upon themselves to clamor for power. Does that not tell you something?"

"It tells me men search for power."

"And what about you?"

"I don't search for power."

"No? Then why have you stayed with him? Why have you served as his emissary?"

"Because he saved me," she said, turning away and looking at the city of Lexa. In the distance, lights flickered in windows. There was a sense of movement within the city, though much as Dillon had said, there wasn't the same sense of vibrancy here as she would have expected. Maybe it was nothing more than her imagination, but she couldn't help but feel as if there was something missing within the city.

"How did he save you?"

"I've already told you."

"Tell me again."

"Why?"

"Because you followed him."

"Why does that matter to you?"

Dillon took a deep breath. "Because I followed someone without considering whether I should."

"You did?"

Dillon nodded. "It was a while ago. There was a man who helped me. He offered me safety. A place to stay. Food to eat. I... I didn't have any of that. I felt vulnerable. He provided comfort." Dillon went silent, and he stared into the distance. "After a while, he started to ask me to use my ability on his behalf. At first, it was small things. He wanted me to take him places. Seeing as how he helped me, I willingly did that. He continued to train me, showing me how to work at the forge, honing my skill. He promised me that once I reached a certain level, I would find work anywhere as a blacksmith." Dillon grunted. "If only that were true. Most places have their own apprenticeships for blacksmiths. They don't like outsiders, though I'm not sure any place really likes outsiders."

"What else happened?"

"After he had me taking jobs for him, we started to break into places. It started small, reclaiming debts he said he was owed, but then it became larger and larger things. Eventually I realized I was being used. I ran."

"And you think the Great One is using me?"

"I don't know if he is or not. You seem to believe he's not, and maybe that's true, but then again, maybe it's not. It's possible he is using you."

"I didn't have any powers when he found me. That wasn't what he wanted me for. He brought me to safety. He gave me a place to stay. But he never asked anything of me."

"Hasn't he?"

"What do you think he's asked of me?"

"Obedience. Following him. Maybe he wants you to worship him."

Ryn smiled to herself. "That's not the kind of thing the Great One does."

"Perhaps not that you've seen, but others have a different experience."

"You keep making comments about that, but I don't think that's what the Great One wants."

"I hope it's not. I would hate for you to get caught up the same way I was caught up in things. I was used, and there are plenty of people in the world who would use others."

"How do I know you're not trying to use me?"

Dillon held her gaze for a long moment. "Unfortunately, you don't."

Ryn stared at him for a long moment, waiting for him to say something more, but he never did. Instead, he just stared at her, holding her gaze.

Could Dillon be using her? She didn't think so, but she couldn't say with certainty that he wasn't. What would he gain by using her? There wasn't anything she was capable of doing that would benefit him.

Other than her access to the Great One.

If he wanted to harm the Great One, then what better way to do it than to manipulate one of his emissaries?

"*Are* you using me?"

"I'm not, but that's a question you shouldn't have taken this long to ask. Others might be. Given your position, it wouldn't be surprising if they wanted to use you. Even the Great One might be doing so, though I know you like to think otherwise."

She remained silent for a while and took a deep breath. None of that changed what she needed to do. She had seen what had taken place inside the palace, and so if nothing else, she needed to act on that first. Once she did, then she could begin to figure out her next step. Somehow, she had to get word to the Great One.

"Then maybe it *is* time for you to go."

"That's not what I was getting at."

"Really? It seems to me it was. You've been trying to convince me I can't trust anyone, and you're right. How can I trust anyone when I don't know them? How can I trust you when I know you don't follow the Great One or what he's trying to accomplish?"

"I would think you could trust me more because you know I'm telling you the truth."

Ryn smiled at him. "Is it the truth?"

"Ryn—"

She stepped away from him. "I know what I need to do, Dillon. And I know what you need to do—which is return to Dreshen, return to the blacksmith, and continue with your training there."

"Just like that?"

"I think you'll find more like-minded people in Dreshen than you will here."

"What happens if they capture you?"

"They won't."

"You don't know that."

"I know what the Ai'thol will do. They will serve the Great One."

"You've seen they don't all serve the Great One."

"Some don't, but I think enough remain who do that we'll be able to rescue those trapped inside the palace."

There had to be a reason they hadn't drawn in the other Ai'thol. Either they couldn't, or they hadn't taken the time to do so yet.

If she waited, she ran the risk of the Ai'thol in the city being coopted and losing her opportunity. She needed to act now in order to rescue those within the palace. Any further delay would be a mistake.

"Thank you for everything you've done."

He took a step toward her, and she shook her head. "Don't. Please don't."

Ryn took a step back and started toward the city, keeping her attention on him. As she went, she kept waiting for him to come after her, and partly expected to feel a surge of nausea, something that would suggest he was going to travel toward her, but it never came.

As she neared the edge of the city, Dillon still at the periphery of her vision, she turned around, drew herself up, and prepared for the next step she would need to take.

She would serve as the emissary.

Only this time, it wouldn't be a matter of merely observing.

45

RYN

Approaching the city again left Ryn uncomfortable. She did so slowly, with trepidation, but at the same time, she couldn't help but feel a hint of excitement at doing so. She was acting on behalf of herself almost as much as the Great One. She needed information, and no longer would she be willing to sit back and wait to see what someone else might tell her. She would figure it out on her own.

It was late enough that the streets weren't all that busy, and she was thankful for that. She approached slowly, her gaze flickering around her as she went, searching for signs of danger. She was a woman—however young she might be—wandering alone in the city. That put her at risk, but she also carried with her the mark of the Great One. That would grant her safe passage.

At least, it *should* grant her safe passage.

Whatever was taking place here needed to be resolved, which meant she needed to be confident, approach the Ai'thol patrolling near the wall, and be prepared.

Once she did it, what would she do next?

Probably reinstill a sense of order within the palace. From there, she would decide what to do about Dreshen. If she couldn't get word to the Great One, then she might have to act on her own.

Weaving through the streets, she looked for anyone who might attempt to slow her, but she found no one. As she went, she half expected to come across the sense of traveling, that wave of nausea that would roll through her, indicating she was no longer safe, but while there was a distant sense of nausea, there was nothing acute.

That had to be good, didn't it?

She wasn't sure. All she knew was that she needed to reach the edge of the palace. From there she would head for the Ai'thol, looking for additional help.

It was strange making her way into the city like this. Stranger still was the fact that as she did, she couldn't shake what Dillon had said to her, the reminder that there was almost an absence of activity within the city.

That wasn't supposed to be the way the Ai'thol served. According to the Great One, the Ai'thol served in a way that meant safety and security, protection from the dangerous elements that existed out in the world. People like Lareth. People like the blacksmith. Lorren. The man from Ih who could use the shadows.

Ryn continued through the city, not stopping as she went. She kept her hood down, and as the palace came into view, she slowed. What she was doing was dangerous, and it was taking on a responsibility that was not meant to have been hers. At the same time, it was one she thought she needed to assume. She watched for signs of the Ai'thol, signs of anything here in the city, and realized that though she was here by herself, making her way through the city alone, she did not appear to be in any danger.

That surprised her.

It shouldn't surprise her. This was a place of the Great One, a place where he had his control, his influence, and where there should be no fear for those who lived within the borders.

She neared the wall. As she did, She counted three different Ai'thol, all of them patrolling steadily as they made their way around the palace.

The Great One's advice lingered in her mind. *Observe and report.*

What did she see?

Was there anything about the patrol that should worry her?

Not from what she detected. They were no different than the typical Ai'thol, and as she watched, she recognized steady movements.

Ryn started forward, and when she reached the nearest man, she studied his face. A scar on one side of his face indicated the blessing he'd taken. Not all of the Ai'thol had a blessing, but many did. Often, they viewed taking a blessing as the next step in their progression within the Ai'thol. It was a feeling that she'd shared. When she'd been given the opportunity to take a blessing, she had done so willingly—eagerly.

Perhaps too eagerly.

The Ai'thol glanced at her. His gaze didn't linger, quickly turning to look beyond her, as if she posed no threat.

And in that regard, he would be right. She wasn't a threat to him.

"You," she said, addressing the Ai'thol.

The man paused, turning toward her. One hand went to the hilt of his sword at his waist.

Ryn brought the pendant forward, flashing the marker of the Great One. "My name is Ryn Valeron, emissary of the Great One, Olandar Fahr."

His eyes widened slightly, and he dropped his hands to his waist, bowing deeply. "How may I serve, emissary?"

That was the response she had expected all along. It was the response she'd not yet gotten, which she should have worried about before now.

"How long have you been serving Lexa?"

"I have been stationed here for three months."

"And in that time, what have you observed?"

"Observed?"

"You have been paying attention on behalf of the Great One, have you not?"

Hearing those words come out of her mouth almost made her smile to herself. It was the kind of thing the Great One would have said.

"I serve in order to exalt the Great One," the man said.

"As well you should. He deserves to be exalted. I would ask what you've seen in Lexa over the months that you have served."

His gaze flickered over to the palace. When he hesitated, Ryn knew that she was on to something.

"There has been strange activity within the palace," he said. He practically flushed as he said it, and she wondered why that should be.

"What sort of strange activity?"

"Up until about a month ago, we would see the disciple make his visit known within the city. Once a week, he would parade through the city, but…"

"That stopped," Ryn said.

The Ai'thol nodded.

"What's your name?"

"Adam Morrin."

"I would have you gather as many of the Ai'thol as you can."

"Now?"

Ryn cocked her head, staring at him. "You would question the emissary?"

His gaze darted to the pendant before lifting to look her in the eyes. "Of course not, emissary."

He ran off, disappearing into the darkness.

Ryn waited. She could have suggested he meet her somewhere, but it was best for her to keep the palace in view. She focused on whether she could detect any sense of nausea rolling through her stomach but found none. She was careful to pay attention to the shadows as well.

She lost track of how long she had waited for Adam to return. When he did, there were a dozen Ai'thol with him. Most of them were in various states of dress, hurriedly pulling on jackets or pants, and one of them still buckling the sword around his waist. They stopped in front of her, standing in formation, and she nodded.

"Very good. The Great One will be pleased with your performance."

Relief swept across each of the men's faces.

"Many of you are probably wondering why I

THE COMING CHAOS | 577

summoned you here at this time of night." The men nodded, but no one spoke. It was a marker of just how well they would serve that they didn't. "I have come to Lexa because the disciple is missing."

With that, there did come a faint murmuring. Ryn decided to let it pass without comment. The men needed that opportunity.

"I have come to investigate."

"What do you need of us, emissary?"

This came from Adam. Either he was the most senior of the Ai'thol on patrol, or he had taken it upon himself to assume that role given that she had approached him. Either way, she decided it didn't matter. She would use him.

"What I need from you is to escort me into the palace."

"The emissary of the Great One would not need an escort," Adam said.

She cocked her head, staring at him. He looked down, refusing to meet her eyes.

"If the disciple is missing, there is danger. The Great One would be most displeased if something happened to his emissary as well."

She took a deep breath, drawing herself up as tall as she could, making certain the pendant hung for all to see. It was the only thing she had that marked her as belonging to the Great One, and she would use it.

"Of course, emissary. We will do whatever it takes."

She nodded, and they formed up around her, three in front, one on either side of her, and the rest lined up behind her. They waited for her to start forward, and they marched toward the palace.

A fluttering rolled through her chest, a nervousness she knew she shouldn't feel, but she couldn't help it. She was on edge. This was not the kind of thing she normally would do, but it was something she needed to do. They might run into trouble, and she wanted to be prepared for the possibility that they would face an attack. But she felt far safer now than she had when it had only been her and Dillon.

They reached the main entrance. The Ai'thol slowed, parting on either side of her to allow her to approach. Ryn took a deep breath, steadying herself, worried that if she weren't careful, the type of attack she might experience would be more than she could manage. She was safe. She was with other Ai'thol who served. They did so without question, joining her, following the leadership of the Great One.

Ryn nodded, and Adam strode forward.

Two others followed him, and they tested the door, but it was locked.

Adam glanced back at her, and she could see a question in his eyes.

What would she do?

She was the emissary of the Great One. She was supposed to be here.

Ryn pulled the knife out of her pocket, slipping it into the lock. As it often did, it seemed as if it wiggled, shifting, and took the shape of the lock. It was a useful knife for this purpose, though she had never tried using it for any other. As she twisted it, the door popped open.

Stepping back, Ryn slipped the knife back into her pocket.

The Ai'thol turned away from her, and they headed into the palace. It seemed as if they had a renewed purpose, a vigor to their step that hadn't been there before, and Ryn smiled to herself. They had wanted her to prove she belonged. The pendant was part of it, but her accessing the palace was another.

Standing inside the door, she looked around. There was no sense of movement, no nausea. There was nothing other than the smooth walls she'd seen when she'd been here before. Even then, she'd been under some duress, trying to hurry through, not only to figure out what was in here, but also because she was trying to escape.

"Check all the rooms," Ryn said.

"Yes, emissary," Adam said.

Most of the Ai'thol departed, but not all of them. Two stayed with her, and she remained in the entrance to the palace, waiting. The Ai'thol stood perfectly still. These were soldiers, men who'd trained to fight on behalf of the Great One. Both had the scars of their blessing, and with it, she knew they had some power of their own, though she wasn't sure what that might be. She found herself wondering whether she'd made a mistake with Dillon. Maybe she should have let him stay with her. But this was something of the Ai'thol, and he had proven that he had no interest in acting on their behalf.

Gradually, the others began to return, sharing their findings with her. There was no one.

When Adam returned, she met his eyes. "We must find the disciple."

"Of course, emissary."

"I believe there are cells several levels down. See who might be within them."

Adam frowned. "There are no cells within the palace."

She turned to the Ai'thol next to Adam. "What is your name?"

"Marcus Hamerschit."

"Marcus, I would like you to investigate the lower levels of the palace. If there is a staircase off a long and narrow hallway, I would like you to go down it and check to see if there is a long row of cells. If there are, break into each of the doors until you find who is held within. Oh, and Marcus, bring a lantern, as I suspect you'll find it is dark."

Marcus nodded and turned, Adam hurrying off with him.

"I need you to stand guard by the door to the disciple's room. The others need to ensure the safety of the palace. Are there any other Ai'thol within the city?"

One of the men nodded. He was shorter than the others, but his scar ran the entirety of his neck. It was a strange incision that suggested he'd been willing to take on a more dangerous type of blessing. "There's another regiment stationed on the far side of the city."

"Good. Go and gather them."

"For patrol?"

"Within the palace," Ryn said.

The man nodded, hurrying off. She started up the stairs, walking this time rather than traveling as she had with Dillon. When she reached the top of the stairs, heading down the hallway, she paused at the door leading into the disciple's rooms. All of the rooms had been searched, but she couldn't shake the sense that the man who controlled the shadows would have been able to hide from them. How long would he be able to do so?

She would have to be vigilant. With her enhanced eyesight, she should be able to notice anything that seemed unusual, and so she paused once inside the disciple's room. It looked no different than when she had been here only a few hours before, but her discomfort and unease were quite a bit less with the Ai'thol watching over her, ensuring her safety.

The two men who had followed her took up a position on either side of the door. Neither of them spoke.

Ryn headed into the room, turning the lantern up as brightly as she could, pushing back the darkness. She swept her gaze around, searching for any sign of unusual movement, anything that might suggest there was someone hiding here. Nothing came.

When she took a seat on the chair, Ryn let out a nervous sigh. Her heart finally slowed. Maybe she had been successful.

A knock on the door caught her attention and she turned to it. Dolan stood there, his hands clasped behind his back, his dark eyes shining with a question.

"Emissary. You have returned."

"You didn't think I would?"

"When you had your—friend?—place us back in the cells, we questioned whether you would return. It was difficult for us to know whether you had been influenced by them."

"Which is why you attacked him?"

"There was a man with them who looked just like him."

Ryn nodded. "I believe you, Dolan."

"What did you do with him?"

"I let him return to his people."

"Emissary?"

"I had no reason to restrain him."

"Even if he was responsible for what took place here?"

Ryn shook her head. "He wasn't." She looked around the room. "I am curious what happened with the disciple."

"I told you what they did to him."

"Yet you haven't told me why."

"Because he served."

Dolan took a step into the room, and she shook her head. Ryn wasn't sure who to trust, and until she had time to observe and decide, she was going to trust only those soldiers who were keeping guard at the door, and even then, she intended to do so with caution.

"What is your intention, emissary?"

"My intention is no different than it always has been. I intend to serve as the Great One requires."

"And how is that?"

Ryn looked down at her hands. She could feel the metal wrapped around, and though she no longer believed it was the sacred metal, it still behaved in a similar fashion. It had changed her, giving her an ability, and with that, she thought she could use it to find strength. It was possible she would develop other abilities, though she needed time to reflect upon what she had. More than that, she needed to get word to the Great One. She needed to decide what would happen with Dreshen.

First, though, she needed to ensure Lexa was secure.

"As his emissary, of course."

Dolan watched her for a long moment before bowing his head. "I am at your service, emissary."

Ryn stared straight ahead and smiled.

DANIEL

When Alistan had said he would show them why Carth had come to the city, Daniel thought that perhaps it would be something Alistan possessed, some item, perhaps even the Elder Stone itself. Daniel was not expecting Alistan to guide them from his home, back out into the darkness. He took a different way, meandering around the side of the home and along a narrow path. In the dark, Daniel could barely make out the garden growing on either side of the path, though he could smell it. The flowers had a fragrance that carried into the air, scents that were so different than what he was accustomed to in Elaeavn or anything he had known during his travels.

"Where are you taking us?" he asked.

Alistan glanced back. "You wanted to know why Carth remained in the city."

"From what you said, Carth was here because of this Collector."

"Oh, she was, but not at first. When she first came, she was looking for information. The longer she was here, the more she realized there was a connection to something more." They reached the gate, and Alistan paused with his hand at the door, looking over at them. "They were connected, you see."

He pushed the door open, heading back out into the city. Once through the gate, Rayen continued to push on shadows, sending them swirling around her, but as she did, he detected a certain resistance to her shadows. More and more of the buildings seemed to have the same stone that made it difficult for her to move past.

He paused in front of one, studying it. There was something strange about the stone, and he couldn't tell what that was. Was it simply that it was stone like this that he found unusual, or was it more about how the shadows failed around it?

"What is it?" Rayen asked, pausing next to him.

"Look at the way this is built," he said, motioning to the stone.

"I'm not sure what you're seeing," she said.

"It's not built out of blocks," he said. He looked up to Alistan who stood a couple of paces away, watching them. "How are these constructed?"

"An interesting question, and one that you will get an answer to, but first you need to come with me."

"Do you care to tell us where we're going?"

"Not until we get there."

Daniel didn't like blindly following the man, but at the same time, he didn't think he was going to harm them.

There was nothing about Alistan that suggested he was capable of hurting them, even if he attempted to.

"Lead on," Daniel said, waving his hand.

Alistan smiled at him and turned, heading back into the city. They made their way past more of the buildings constructed in the same manner, and Daniel couldn't help but look at them to see whether he could decipher anything from how they were built, but there was nothing.

Alistan paused at a small clearing. From here, the buildings changed, no longer constructed of the same stone. There was a space between those made of the stone and those that looked to be built out of wood. "We're leaving some of the oldest buildings in Keyall."

The wooden construction reminded him of the type of tavern they had first experienced when they had come to Keyall. As they continued, Daniel had to wonder where Alistan would lead them in the newer construction. He would've expected that if there was an Elder Stone, it would be located within the older part of the city. He passed a section that was crumbling, the buildings falling, and pieces of stone with massive holes inside them.

"What do you see?" Alistan asked, pausing in front of one of the ramshackle buildings.

Daniel studied the building, looking at it from each side. It gave him an opportunity to try to get a sense of how the building was constructed, the way that the walls were built. It seemed to be a single sheet of stone rather than blocks. Sections of it had crumbled, leaving a pile of the same black rock on the ground.

"It's an entire sheet of the same stone," Daniel said.

Alistan nodded. "That would be the key to how we build—or built—these buildings. We don't make them like that anymore. The technique in the construction has been lost for the most part. It's easier to build out of wood, though something has been lost, if you ask me."

"How did they move the stone?"

"That's a great question. Most of these other buildings are hundreds of years old, built long before anyone kept records." Alistan smiled. "I've searched for as much as I can about Keyall, trying to get a better understanding of how the people of this place managed to construct these buildings, but I haven't been able to come up with anything. Those who are native to this land have not shared if they know."

"You're not from Keyall?"

"They have welcomed me as if I were, but I am not of Keyall."

Perhaps this man wouldn't be able to help them find the Elder Stone if he wasn't a local.

"You haven't been able to uncover anything about how they moved the stone?" Rayen asked.

"There are theories. Some of the priests would like us to believe it was more of a mystical approach, though I know better. There are some—much like your friend— who have power and ability, and I have long suspected that it took people like that in order to move the stone into place and build the walls." Alistan turned and motioned to the rest of the city. "Keyall has been situated atop this rock for hundreds and hundreds of years. It was built as a fortification at first, though even then there were people who were native to this place."

Alistan started forward again, and Daniel expect him to continue on the street, but he surprised them by ducking into one of the buildings. As he followed, Daniel realized the building didn't have a roof—whatever protection from the elements had been there had long ago failed. Moonlight streamed in, faint slivers of silver casting shadows along the ground.

Daniel noticed one section that seemed to be reflecting the moonlight more brightly. He started toward it, when Rayen caught him by the wrist.

"I find all of this unusual," she said.

"Him or the fact that we are here?"

"Perhaps both. Carth never talked about a Collector."

"Maybe there's a reason behind that."

"I don't know. When it comes to Carth, if it were important, she would have shared."

Daniel started to step over the water when he paused.

There was something about it that drew him. He leaned over, staring at the way the moonlight reflected off its surface.

Not reflected.

The water itself seemed to have a faint glow to it.

His breath caught. It was a subtle bluish glow, and it reminded him of what he'd seen from the sacred crystals.

That couldn't be coincidence, could it?

He cupped his hands into the water, bringing it to his nose. Alistan had continued onward and was somewhere on the far side of the room, shuffling around.

"Do you see this?" he whispered. He glanced up to Rayen before flicking his gaze in Alistan's direction. He didn't want the other man to realize that they weren't there quite yet.

"The water or the moonlight reflecting off it?"

"The water where the moonlight *isn't* reflecting off it."

Rayen wrapped shadows around his hands. Even when doing that, the faint glowing persisted.

"It's the water," she whispered.

"I think so."

"What does that mean?"

Daniel frowned. "I don't know. The only thing that glows like that is the"—he glanced up, looking to see where Alistan had gone, but didn't see the other man —"crystals. They have a little bit brighter glow, but not so much that it would be all that different from this."

He'd never held one of the sacred crystals, but that didn't mean he couldn't recognize it.

He was tempted, and on a whim, he brought the water up to his mouth and tasted it.

It had a faintly coppery taste, almost slippery as well, and he brought his cupped hands to his mouth, drinking.

"Are you still with me?" Alistan called out.

Daniel headed toward him. "We're still here."

He hurried forward, reaching Alistan, and Rayen stayed with him. Every so often, he would look down and notice that his fingers were still glowing from where he had touched the water. He clasped his hands behind his back, not wanting Alistan to note he had come across the water. If he was right, then the *water* represented the Elder Stone, at least water like that. This couldn't be the only location for it, but the idea of water serving as an Elder Stone seemed right. There was something about

Keyall that suggested the city subsisted on water. It was situated in a difficult-to-reach location, with a deep-water harbor accessible by ship, and the people of the city that he had seen all looked to be tied to the sea, many of them fishermen or merchants or traders.

It made it more likely that the Elder Stone was tied to water.

"What do you want to show us?" he asked Alistan as he approached.

He brought them to a section of the rubble that had what appeared to be old stairs. "What do you see here?"

"I see stairs."

"What about the stairs?"

"Wherever they lead is gone," Daniel said.

Alistan circled the pile of debris. As he had suggested, it did look a bit like stairs, though whatever it framed was not visible anymore. The staircase stretched high overhead, quite stout, and not made of the same stone as much of the rest of the building.

"Indeed. Wherever they lead is gone. There are some who speculate that this was once an altar, though if it was, whatever they stood upon was gone."

"This was a temple?"

"The very first temple in Keyall," Alistan said. He continued to make his way around the stairs, smiling to himself. "For so many years I came here, trying to understand what it was about this place that brought people to it after all those years. You see, the original descendants of Keyall continued to come here. I never understood."

"It's the water," Daniel said.

Alistan turned to him, steepling his fingers together.

"You've been here for an evening, and already you identified that? That is faster than Carth managed in her time here."

"She didn't realize it was the water?"

"She did, but it took her quite a bit longer to recognize."

"What is it about the water?"

"You wanted to understand the power of Keyall, and that's why you came."

"That's not the entire reason I came, but it's part of it."

"Why, then, did you come?"

"We are looking for information about Elder Stones."

Alistan smiled. "You are much more like Carthenne than I realized."

"Did she come looking for Elder Stones?"

"I don't know if she understood what it was when she came. We looked into it together, and I helped her to see that the Elder Stones are a way to power. She didn't believe one existed in Keyall, and then she found it."

"The water."

Alistan nodded. "It seeps up from deep below us in this location, though there are other places where it's much more plentiful. That was where Carth found it. Swam in it, really."

"Carth swam in the water that represents the Elder Stone of Keyall?" Daniel asked.

"I suspect she didn't intend to, but it did give her an opportunity to have a better understanding of Keyall."

Daniel had to wonder what change Carth had experienced by having swum in one of the Elder Stones. Would she have been altered? Considering the way even experiencing the shadows had altered him, it was likely she had. He remembered the way she'd been able to use the wisdom stone in order to free Lareth, so there had to be something to it that would grant her some knowledge and increased ability.

Daniel considered Alistan for a moment. It was likely that he not only knew of the things Carth had done when she was here, but that he knew what Carth had gone through. She had dealt with someone called the Collector, and yet wasn't that also the time that she had dealt with Olandar Fahr?

"What do you know about a man Carth might've encountered when she was here?"

Alistan studied him for a moment. "What man might she have encountered?"

"He would have gone by the name Olandar Fahr?"

Alistan's eyes widened. "Tell me she isn't still chasing him."

"She's not still chasing him," Daniel said.

Alistan let out a relieved sigh. "That's good. It would be dangerous for Carth to try to confront him. He's one she should leave well enough alone."

"She's not chasing him so much as she's chasing the Ai'thol. And she's after knowledge he might already have."

Alistan studied him for a moment. "What sort of knowledge?"

"The knowledge of Elder Stones."

The other man frowned, and he began to pace around the ruins of this old temple. In the dark, he disappeared from time to time, blending into shadows. Daniel wondered how much of that was because of his connection to this place and how much of it was some ability he might have of his own. As he watched, Alistan reached the opening in the temple, and Daniel glanced over to Rayen before Sliding to him, following Alistan. Once out of the street, the other man made his way beyond the wooden buildings, outside of the city itself, continuing to meander along the cliff. Far below, the sound of waves crashing drifted to Daniel's ears, a reminder that the sea and its power were beneath them. Daniel kept waiting for Alistan to say something, anything, but the other man made his way silently.

Wind whipped around him, pulling at his hair and his cloak. Rayen took his hand, holding on, and he glanced over to see her watching him. There was a nervousness in her eyes, and he understood the reason behind it. Neither of them knew quite what Alistan was doing. Leading them outside of the city like this was almost a way of bringing them to danger, and yet, he didn't have that sense of Alistan.

In the distance, he caught sight of a wooden platform hanging off the edge of the cliff. Enormous ropes stretched from the platform to a small shed. It was here that Alistan went.

"Where are you taking us?" Daniel asked.

Alistan looked over at them. "Wait on the platform."

He frowned, but holding on to Rayen's hand, he made his way over to the platform, standing on it carefully, watching. Alistan headed inside the shed, and did something, and they began to descend. The other man hurried out from inside the shed, and when he appeared, he jumped onto the platform, alongside them.

"What is this?"

"This is where Carthenne was imprisoned long ago," he said.

"If you think that you can hold us in a prison—"

Alistan cut him off. "That's not my intention."

"Then what is your intention?"

"To show you to the Elder Stone."

DANIEL

IF DANIEL HAD NORMAL EYESIGHT, HE MIGHT HAVE panicked at this point. Darkness swallowed them, blacker than any night, and even with his enhanced eyesight, he didn't like crawling through the tunnel the way Alistan went. The other man seemed to make it through the tunnel almost as if there was no concern, and perhaps there was none to him.

Rayen stayed behind Daniel, and with the darkness around them, he wondered what she might be able to see, but he suspected most of this was comprised of the same stone as the rest of the city that prevented Rayen's abilities from working as they should.

They had been crawling through here for the better part of an hour, taking tunnel after tunnel, and through it all, Alistan told them to wait. He promised they would reach this Elder Stone soon, and yet the longer they went, the less certain Daniel was that he was telling them the truth. He had begun to wonder if this man might in fact be senile.

"The next part is the hardest," Alistan said.

"The next part?" Daniel's mouth was dry. Had he known they were going to take a climb like this, he might have brought water or other preparations, and he certainly would have been more ready than he was.

"The next part involves a little bit of faith, if you will."

Daniel frowned, glancing back at Rayen. "What sort of faith?"

"Well, in this case, the faith should be in Carthenne."

"Why?"

"Because she's the one who discovered this in the first place."

Daniel let out a tightly held breath and looked back at Rayen again. She was quiet, and he didn't blame her for the silence, but he would have liked her to be more vocal here. "You've been quiet."

"I don't like this," she whispered.

"The tunnel?"

"All of it. I have no access to the shadows in this place."

"Just remember that Carth went through it, too."

"If you think that will inspire me to move onward…"

Daniel shrugged. "I was just saying that if Carth can do it, then you certainly can."

"I am not Carthenne Rel," she said.

"No, but you are Rayen Shadow Born. I think that's more than enough."

Rayen was quiet for a moment before taking his hand and squeezing it. "For someone who was as foolish as you seemed to be when we first met, you often know the right thing to say."

"Are the two of you going to come? I know it's nice to

have the darkness, but I would be a little uncomfortable if you began to… well, you know."

Daniel held Rayen's eyes for a moment. He wasn't sure if she was even able to see him in the dark like this. The only reason he could was because of his enhanced eyesight, and she wouldn't have that advantage. Normally Rayen had as good or better vision as him in the darkness, but when it came to this place and the shadows, that advantage was diminished.

"Show us," Daniel said.

The man spun around and stepped forward.

And then disappeared.

"Alistan?"

The other man didn't answer, and Daniel frowned to himself. He wouldn't have any way of knowing how to get out of here without Alistan. Then again, they could simply Slide. It might be difficult hunched over as he was, but he suspected that he could just step forward in a Slide and return to Keyall before deciding what more they would need to do.

"He said we had to go by faith," Rayen said.

"I didn't expect that he meant we would simply have to disappear."

"Maybe there's something to where he's going," she said.

Daniel crawled forward, looking to see if he could uncover where Alistan might have vanished. He couldn't tell anything. That didn't mean anything to him, but it was possible there was a section within here where Alistan was able to hide.

Daniel crawled forward a step, and then another.

Then he was falling.

He spun around, trying to see if he could make out what had happened, trying to Slide, but he couldn't.

Then he splashed.

Daniel swung his arms, frantically trying to gain purchase, trying to understand where he was and what had happened. As he did, he realized there was a faint bluish glow all around him.

The Elder Stone.

"This is where you wanted to bring me?" He turned toward where Alistan swam nearby.

The other man smiled softly. "You might want to move out of the way."

Daniel started to swim toward him when Rayen splashed down next to him.

She gasped, beating at the water. As she surfaced, she turned toward him. "That was unexpected."

"He could have given us a warning," Daniel said.

"Had I given you a warning, would you have believed?"

"It's not a matter of faith."

"Perhaps not for you." Alistan swam toward a ledge, pulling himself up from it, and waited for Daniel and Rayen to join him. "This is the place that Carth found, and she might have been the first person in ages to have done so."

"This is your Elder Stone?"

"This is *Keyall's* Elder Stone. According to the myth, the elder of Keyall granted us this place as a way of shielding from outsiders."

"Keyall has quite a few traders. There isn't any shielding from outsiders."

"Now they do, but there was a time when trade with Keyall was uncommon."

"Why?" Daniel asked, trying to smooth some of the water out of his cloak. It would take a while to dry, and he didn't like being sopping wet like this. Rayen seemed less bothered than him, and after a moment, he realized that she seemed to be using the shadows to wring water off her. If only he had a similar ability.

"According to legend, the first people of Keyall came here to hide from something." Alistan made his way to the edge of the ledge, looking down at the water. "I haven't been able to determine what they were trying to escape from, only that whatever it was terrified the people. They spoke about it in vague terms, and even in the ancient writings, there isn't much I can uncover."

"Do you have any suspicions about what it is?"

He shrugged. "Some, but I am not sure. As I said, it's vague."

"How is it that you know so much about the Elder Stones?" Daniel asked.

"It has been my passion. I've searched for information about them for my entire life."

"And Carth knew this?"

"Carth understood that my passion was tied to the understanding rather than the possession."

"What's the difference?"

"The difference is that I did not seek knowledge of the Elder Stones in order to become powerful like Olandar Fahr. I sought knowledge so I could understand. There is a difference, and it's not inconsiderable."

Daniel shared a glance with Rayen. "We've been looking for knowledge about a fifth stone."

"Fifth?" Alistan asked before smiling. "Perhaps this isn't the best place for us to be talking about it. It is interesting, that is certain, and you have been given a great gift to have experienced the Elder Stone of Keyall, but maybe we should return to my home before it gets too late."

How would Daniel change now that he had plunged into the Elder Stone? He'd tasted it in the temple, but this seemed different. This was concentrated, surrounding him, and reminded him of what he had experienced when going to the chamber of shadows.

"Hold on," he said. He grabbed Rayen's hand, reached for Alistan, and Slid them back to the library. When they emerged, water dripped off him, and he glanced over to Alistan. "Sorry about that."

"What an ability!" Alistan said.

"I apologize for dripping all over your carpet."

"Carpet dries, but perhaps you would take off your cloak and hang it away from the table?"

Daniel looked over to perceive that he was standing close to the Tsatsun table where he had defeated Alistan. In the time they'd been gone, someone had come and reset the game board. Daniel reached forward and made a play on the other side of the board.

Pulling off his cloak, he hung it on a hook near the door. Rayen took one look at him and shook her head. Shadows streamed off her, working along his body. It felt almost as if there was pressure, and when she was done, his clothes were merely damp, not sopping wet.

"Carth would do it better," she said with a shrug, "but I don't have her potential with the flame. You're stuck with me using the shadows alone."

"Perhaps you wouldn't mind doing that with me?" Alistan said, moving to stand in front of Rayen.

She sent the shadows swirling around him, working along his arms and legs, squeezing the water out of him as well.

When she was done, he motioned for them to sit. He went to the table at the back, refilling his glass of wine, and took a seat. "Ah. Perhaps I should offer you some wine as well. How rude of me not to have done so."

"I'm fine," Daniel said.

Rayen shook her head. "I prefer ale."

Alistan tipped his glass toward them before taking a drink. "You might prefer ale, but there is something about wine that is simply exquisite. When it's made correctly, you get the flavor of where the grape was born. You can practically taste the soil."

He took a long drink, leaning forward to set the glass down.

"Now, I think that we need to have a conversation about the elders."

"Not the Elder Stones?"

"They are tied together, I suspect, and depending on which mythology you believe, you may take something from those conversations." He glanced from Rayen to Daniel. "What do you know about the elders?"

"Not much," Daniel said. "I know about the Elder Stones and have heard about the power they possess."

"The stones are merely a representation of the elders. According to legend, the elders of each land left an edge of their ability behind. In doing so, they enabled the people to know their power. Some know it more directly, such as the people of Keyall understanding the power here, but only if they follow the ancient teachings and worship in the temple. Others are more indirect, such as that of Ih or Lashasn."

"Lashasn?"

"Perhaps you know it by a different name, but it's a place of power and flame. It's the other half of Carth's homeland, and it is how she has become so powerful."

Daniel turned to look over at Rayen. He had thought that the other part of Carth's homeland was Nyaesh, where she'd trained with the A'ras.

"Lashasn is gone," Rayen said. "As is Ih."

"The lands may be gone, but the people are not. The power is not."

"For how much longer?" Rayen asked.

"You can't destroy the power of the elders," Alistan said.

"You can destroy the people. You can scatter them, and when that's done…"

Alistan frowned. "What happens when that is done?"

"The power begins to wane," Daniel said. That was what Rayen was getting at.

"Perhaps," he said.

"There's no perhaps. I've seen it."

"Or perhaps that power moves," Alistan said. He took another drink of his wine before setting the glass down.

"Lashasn may be gone, but the people are not. Those people took their power with them. How else do you think the A'ras exist? Ih might be lost, but they have reformed, calling themselves the Reshian. Shadows are not lost. Neither are flames. If Keyall were to disappear, the power of this place would move to wherever the descendants of this land go."

"You mentioned three of the Elder Stones," Daniel said.

"I have."

"How many of the Elder Stones do you know about?"

"I think the better question would be how many do *you* know about?"

"We know about the three that you mentioned, and there is another, the wisdom stone," Daniel said. He thought it was best he reveal that to Alistan, but he had no intention of sharing where to find the wisdom stone. That was something that needed to be kept a secret, at least for now, until he could decide how much he truly trusted Alistan.

"Ah. The wisdom stone is one of the more difficult ones to uncover. I know many have searched over the years, and many have claimed to have been touched by the gift of the wisdom stone, though the question has always remained how many were truly affected. It has been hidden, though if what I suspect is true, then it would be found at one of the great universities. Seeing as how Thyr is no more, that leaves Asador or Morchar or Dundas or Lorialn or..." He waved his hand, smiling. "As you see, there are plenty of possibilities." He cocked his head to the side, looking at them. "From the way you say it, I wonder if perhaps you have not already found it."

"Perhaps," Daniel said.

Alistan clapped his hands together. "I understand why you wouldn't share the location, but at least tell me if I'm correct in my theory."

"You are correct," Daniel said.

"Wonderful," he said. "I've been in Keyall so long I thought I would never learn."

"Can you tell us about the fifth stone?"

"There are more than five," Alistan said, frowning as he glanced from Daniel to Rayen.

"We don't think so," Daniel said.

"No? What of your homeland?"

"Everything we have learned about Elaeavn suggests that while there is power there, it doesn't represent an Elder Stone."

"No," Alistan said. "It must. Your people have such wonderful abilities."

"We do, but that doesn't mean that those abilities are representative of Elder Stones."

"What are they, then?"

How much should he reveal to Alistan? He didn't know the man well enough to trust him, and yet, there was something about him that he thought could be very helpful. It was more than just his knowledge. Daniel didn't know whether or not he really chased the Elder Stones for power. If he wasn't after them for the sake of power, then he was nothing more than a scholar, a care-taker like the librarians within Elaeavn.

"From what we can tell, what we thought were Elder

Stones in Elaeavn were something else. They are tied to the Great Watcher."

"Who is an elder," he said.

"We don't think so," Daniel said.

"What else could he be but an elder?" Alistan got to his feet, went over to one of the shelves, and returned with the book. He flipped through the pages before setting it down in front of Daniel. "Look through it. You will see what I mean."

Daniel paged through it, looking to see what it was that Alistan referred to, and as he did, he didn't come up with much of anything. "I can't read it."

"You can't read?" Alistan asked.

Daniel smiled. "I can read just fine, I just can't read *this*."

Alistan came around and looked over his shoulder. "Ah. I hadn't considered that you wouldn't be familiar with this language. It is an older language, but it should be widely known."

"Maybe widely known to you, but not everywhere."

"Perhaps not. Anyway, what this says is that there are various places of power, essentially touched by the gods, and what are the elders other than gods?"

"The Great Watcher is not an elder," Daniel said.

"Why would you believe that?"

"I didn't, at first. The more we've learned, the more I feel it's true. Whatever the Great Watcher might be, he sits outside of the elders."

"Outside of the elders?"

Daniel got up and went over to the Tsatsun board and grabbed five pieces. He carried them over to Alistan, placing the Stone in the center, and he began to arrange the other pieces around it. Without meaning to, he had grabbed five dissimilar pieces, pieces that could represent the elders, at least to whoever had created the game.

"We know of five elders, and each of them has some sort of power. They sit on what is called the Council of Elders."

"And this one?" Alistan asked, motioning to the middle piece. "What does the Stone represent?"

"As far as we can tell, the Stone represents the Great Watcher."

Alistan took the book back, leaning backward and studying them. "What gave you this idea?"

"It wasn't my idea. It was Carth's."

"And what gave her that idea?"

Daniel shook his head. "I don't exactly know. But we found something that suggests to us that it's right."

"What did you find?"

"Daniel—"

He shook his head. "I think we need to share with him as much as we can in order to better understand what we're dealing with, Rayen. I know we want to keep this to ourselves, but…"

But if Carth had wanted Alistan involved, wouldn't she have said something?

She would have known that he had knowledge and experience when it came to the Elder Stones. Why hadn't she mentioned him before?

"I think… I think we need to share with him what we know," Daniel said.

"It's dangerous."

"So is not knowing."

Rayen shrugged. "It's your choice. I'll go along with it."

"You think Carth would be upset?"

"I don't think you have to be worried about her so much as you have to be worried about them."

LUCY

Lucy walked along the shores of the C'than stronghold, looking out at the water. There was a strange energy here. The longer she was here, the more certain she was of what she detected. It came from more than just the sense of the power of the waves crashing along the shore. This was a different sense that filled her with unease.

Partly that had to do with what they planned. Or rather, what *she* planned. She didn't know if it was going to work, but the more she thought about what needed to happen, the more she understood she needed to play a part. In order to do so, she would have to use her ability on the Architect.

If she did so in the right way, she believed she would be able to draw him out, and more than that, she believed she would be able to draw out Olandar Fahr.

The sky continued to darken, the waves crashing against the shore. The longer she stared, the more certain she was that power was slamming repeatedly against the shore, and yet she wasn't sure if there was anything she could do about it.

The energy was almost overwhelming.

Lucy focused on that power, thinking about the waves, the chaos, and waited.

Carth was supposed to be here soon.

Thunder rumbled out in the distance, and she sat there, watching it, enjoying the way it moved toward her. There was power in that thunder, and power in the coming storm. She wondered if it might rain.

Darkness began to fall, and as she sat along the shoreline, she stared out at the waves, watching until it became obvious that the shadows were something beyond what she had believed at first.

They weren't related to the darkness of the coming storm at all. It was Carth and her power.

Getting to her feet, Lucy waited.

Whenever she had traveled with Carth, she had a sense that the other woman had other ways of transporting herself. She would have to in order to have been as prolific as she was over the years, to be able to move from place to place as easily as she had managed, and yet, Lucy had yet to see it. It was as if Carth had wanted to hide from anyone else whatever abilities she might possess.

Now that she was here and watching as the darkness rolled toward her, Lucy thought she understood. Carth *was* the shadows.

But she was also the flame. Because of that, she was able to do much more than anyone else. She was the chaos of the storm.

The shadows folded around her, and Lucy smiled to herself. "Are you going to reveal yourself?"

"I didn't expect you to be waiting and watching."

"What were you expecting?"

She turned around and found Carth standing across from her. The other woman was dressed in a dark cloak, though that might be only the shadows. Her hair was pulled back, and the darkness that swirled around her was testament to the power she possessed. A pair of swords was strapped to her sides.

"When Ras summoned me, I didn't expect anyone to be waiting for me."

"I've never seen you travel like that."

"Few have."

"Do you often come like that?"

"It takes considerable effort, so generally I don't. I know better than to use my connection to the shadows in such a way that would expend that much energy."

"How much energy does it take?"

"More than it once did." Carth glanced toward the tower. The shadows were swirling around her, and they mingled with the tower for a moment before retreating. "You brought others here."

She could detect that with little more than a touch of the shadows? She really was far more powerful than Lucy usually gave her credit for. She should remember that.

"I did. Ras offered to help a little bit, but that's not why I summoned you."

"You summoned me? I thought Ras was the one who called for my help."

"He called for you because of me. I've been tracking

the Architect, and I've come across a few things that are troublesome."

She told Carth about the attack in the town, the experiment she suspected was taking place, and then about the sense of the Architect, and her need to try to find where he was going. If they could collect the Architect, they might be able to get answers about the Ai'thol and Olandar Fahr.

"You risk yourself against a powerful man."

"You've done the same countless times."

"I have, and yet I'm not quite as defenseless."

"I wasn't defenseless. I managed to escape."

Lucy could practically feel the disappointment within Carth, and yet she didn't care. She wasn't going to do anything other than what she had done, and she'd needed to use that opportunity to try to track the Architect. Had she not, she might not have come up with another solution.

"It doesn't matter."

"It does. If we lose you, we lose a critical ally."

Lucy smiled. "I don't know that I'm all that critical."

"Then you haven't been paying attention. You have an important role to play in all of this, Lucy Elvraeth."

"Is that something you've Seen?"

"My time holding the wisdom stone may have given me some understanding, but it was fleeting. The stone itself is dangerous, and yet, I understand the value of it."

"That wasn't a no."

"Then no. It's nothing that I've Seen. It's recognizing what you've done. You're the one who's chasing down the danger of the C'than. Because of you, we understand just what has been taking place."

"But we don't. We know there must be others who have the knowledge we need, and until we have it, then we might not be able to stop anything."

"We are getting closer."

"What have you been doing?"

"I have been pursuing information."

"What kind of information?"

"The kind that suggests there is something more than what we understand taking place."

"Such as what?"

"Your friend Haern has been dealing with something. There was an attack. Whoever attacked used lorcith in ways I haven't seen before. From what I can tell from what Haern said, it's in a way he hasn't encountered before either."

"Haern wouldn't be the one to ask," Lucy said.

Carth watched her, saying nothing.

There was something about the quiet way she watched that suggested there was more than what Lucy knew.

"What is it?"

"It's nothing," Carth said.

"It's not nothing. You know something." Did it have anything to do with the reason Hearn had been muted when she'd tried Reading him?

"It's not what I know, it's what I've experienced. And what I've seen, along with what you are describing, suggests there has been more taking place than what we know. Someone else is active, someone beyond only Olandar Fahr."

"Why do I get the sense that troubles you?"

"It should trouble you. We don't know who this other person is, only that they have access to considerable power."

Lucy breathed out heavily, looking out toward the ocean. The darkness rolling toward the shore seemed to call to her, beckoning, and she stared outward, trying to focus her mind. It was difficult to do, and the more she stared, the more uncertain she was about what they might uncover. If this was only about Olandar Fahr, that was one thing. With everything they'd seen up to this point, she believed she could find Olandar Fahr, use the Architect to trap him, and yet if it was about something else, someone else, she wasn't entirely sure they would have enough knowledge to reach him.

"We know this other person has used the C'than," Lucy said.

"Possibly," Carth said.

"You don't know?"

"I'm not convinced it's the same, though it could be."

"And if it is?"

"Then I worry that even if we find them, they won't be the ally we think."

"Why not?"

Carth stared out over the water, and shadows stretched away from her. "I have been dealing with Olandar Fahr for a long time, and as long as I have been struggling against him, I have believed he was playing some game against me."

"Hasn't he?"

"I don't know. It's possible he has, but it's equally

possible there's something else taking place. Perhaps he has a different opponent than what we know."

"Who would that be?"

She shook her head. "Unfortunately, I don't have the answer to that, either." She turned back to Lucy. "What is it that you think we can do with the Architect?"

"I'd been thinking we'd be able to Push on him."

"You believe your control is enough that you'd be able to do that?"

"I don't know."

Carth watched her for a moment. "You don't know, but you wonder if it might be, and…" She cocked her head to the side, and shadows swirled. It was times like these when Lucy couldn't help but wonder if Carth were somehow Reading her. The other woman claimed she wasn't, but there was something in the way she looked at her, the analytic twist to her head, that suggested there was more going on than Lucy understood. "You called me back because you didn't want to risk this yourself."

"If I Push on the Architect, there's a chance he appears. I want to make sure we're strong enough to do this."

"Then we should do it."

"Who else would you suggest we find?"

"Beyond the Binders? I would suggest we find Daniel and Rayen."

"I haven't focused on Daniel in quite some time, and I don't even know where they might be."

Carth smiled tightly. "I might have some idea."

"Where?"

"I can help guide you to Rayen, but I don't know if I

will be able to connect you to her mind the same way. Do you think you can do the same with Daniel?"

"I used to be able to, but something changed."

"The shadows changed for him, Lucy."

"How is that possible?"

"It happened when he went in search of the Elder Stone."

Lucy couldn't imagine what it might be like for Daniel to suddenly have the ability of the shadows. And maybe he didn't, but she was aware that something had shifted, making it more difficult for her to find his mind. The more she focused on him, the harder it was for her to uncover anything. It was almost as if he were a blank to her.

"If we do this, then we must be prepared for the consequences," Carth said.

"What consequences?"

"The consequences that arise from drawing the Architect—and Olandar Fahr. The consequences that might arise if we are wrong."

"Why do you think we might be wrong?"

"Consider it something of an educated guess."

Carth stared at the distant shore, watching outward. The shadows drifted from her, and Lucy couldn't help but wonder if there might be something more to what Carth suggested. What was Carth keeping from her?

And maybe it was nothing. Carth was a strategist, first and foremost, so Lucy had to believe whatever it was the other woman discovered would be tied to strategy, though she had no idea what that might be.

"What of your help?" Carth asked.

"They aren't ready," Lucy said.

"You won't know if they're ready until you test them."

Lucy shook her head. "I'm unwilling to do that." There might be some of them who would be willing to fight, but none of them were fighters—not yet. In time, it was possible they might get to that point, but for now they were not. For now, all they had was the beginning of the knowledge Lucy had been teaching them.

It would take more time on her part to get them to that point, and even if she did spend more time, she wasn't convinced it would be enough to prepare them to where they could fight effectively.

There were some, like Eve, who might want to fight, and it might not matter how Lucy felt about it. They might choose to take action regardless of what choice she would have made for them. It was not her decision to make on their behalf.

But there were others, like Olivia, or Marcy, or countless others within the village, who were not ready. It was possible they would never be ready. They had to better understand the nature of the power they had been given, and until they did, there might not be anything they could do.

"It's not a choice you get to make on their behalf," Carth said.

"Is that how you feel about the Binders?"

"My experience with the Binders has shown me that some choose to fight. Some choose to help in other ways. Others to return to their lives. What has your experience been?"

Lucy squeezed her eyes shut but couldn't drown out

the waves in the distance. "All of them have chosen to stay."

"Just stay?"

"They want to better understand what abilities they might possess."

"Does that surprise you?"

"I suppose not. They want to know if there was any reason behind what was done to them, and if there's anything they might be able to do to master those abilities."

"And were you so different?"

"I was different in that I had abilities prior to anything happening."

"You did, but they weren't the same, were they?"

Lucy opened her eyes. "What are you asking of me?"

"I'm asking you to keep an open mind. It's the same as I asked the women I will help and have helped."

"All of them?"

"I've never forced anyone to serve," Carth said.

"You forced me."

"Did I?"

Lucy wanted to argue, but there was no real arguing to it. She hadn't been forced to serve, not really. She had chosen to do so. She had wanted to better understand her powers, and to know whether she had been controlled, Pushed along the way, and because of her time with Carth, she had a better understanding of what she had gone through. Because of Carth—and Ras, when she thought of it—she was free of any outside influence.

And it had made her stronger.

She was more than what she had ever been before. She

was no longer of Elaeavn, and yet, Lucy realized that was part of her struggle. She still felt as if she were without a place. With everything she'd gone through, she still didn't know what she might need to do. Was it only about staying with the C'than? Was it only about helping the women in the village? Or was it something more? She'd found the women within the village had been accepting of her serving the C'than, especially as they came to understand the C'than were not all involved the way they had believed.

"I suppose you didn't," she said.

Carth smiled at her. "I think we should gather the Binders, and then we will go after the rest of our help."

"Where would you have me Push him?"

"I have a feeling you won't have to Push him very hard at all."

"Why is that?"

"I have a sense that once you begin to influence his mind, you will find he's already making plans we can act upon."

Lucy frowned, watching Carth. "What aren't you telling me?"

"I have held nothing back from you."

"There's something. It has to do with the Architect, but I can't figure out what is that you think we need to better understand. Why aren't you telling me everything?"

"I'm not keeping anything from you, Lucy. Anything I might believe is nothing more than a theory. When it comes to playing the games I like to play, theories can be wrong, and it's not until you test them that you begin to uncover whether or not they are."

"And what theory is this?"

"You."

"Me?"

"Your experience with the Architect was unique. He used you, and yet from everything you've told me, he wasn't surprised by the augmentation you took on."

Lucy frowned, thinking about it. When she'd been exposed to the Architect, he hadn't been surprised. That was different than the rest of the Ai'thol, but at the same time, he had seemed to expect it. He had taken it in stride.

And hadn't he said he had been experimenting with something like that?

"Why does that matter?"

"It matters because it makes me question whether or not Olandar Fahr knows what the Architect was doing."

"The Architect works with Olandar Fahr."

"He does, but that doesn't mean he doesn't have his own plans. And with what we've encountered so far, I can't help but think that perhaps there is something we're overlooking. I have others looking into it, and yet so far they haven't uncovered anything."

"Which is why you want to find the Architect."

"The Architect can bring us toward Olandar Fahr. I believe that much, and it's possible he can do even more than that."

"You think the Architect can help you understand the other side."

She tipped her head, nodding. "I think if we begin to understand what the Architect's after, we might be able to learn what Olandar Fahr's after—and this other side."

LUCY

LUCY LOOKED AROUND. AS SHE STOOD ON THE EDGE OF THE shoreline, feeling the surge of energy around her, she thought that the other woman had to be right about this, though it involved finding something she wasn't sure if she could. It involved finding the Architect. She could feel his mind, the way that his thoughts were there, glittering through the back of her mind. The more she focused on him, the more certain she was that he was there, but it would take a stretch for her to reach him more easily.

The more that she focused on him, the more certain she was she knew where he was. And as Carth had suggested, it wasn't all that far from here.

"Are you ready?" Carth asked.

"I am, but what if this isn't right?"

"You are only influencing, not Pushing."

"And I don't know if that is even going to work," Lucy said.

Carth wanted her to influence, but the more Lucy thought about it, the more uncertain she was that influencing in the way Carth intended would even work. How could it when she didn't know whether the Architect would pay any attention to the pressure she exerted upon him?

Then again, what she needed to do was something subtle. She wasn't trying to force him to notice what she was doing. If he did, he would react. That was her greatest concern.

It had been Carth's idea. The more Lucy thought about it, the more she thought she understood the purpose behind it and the benefit to it.

The connection between her and the Architect went both ways. Not only did she have some way of reaching his mind, but Carth suspected that he had a way of reaching her mind. It was likely going to be subtle—unless Lucy Pushed just a little bit, enough for the Architect to know what she was doing.

And if he was aware of it, then they would fail.

What they needed to do was ensure he wasn't aware of what she was doing. It was the kind of influence she didn't know if she was capable of.

"Take a deep breath, and be ready for this," Carth said.

In the distance, the shoreline beckoned. "I don't understand why here."

"Because here is believable."

"You really want him to go where you think the other Elder Stone might be?"

"I want him to follow. Whether or not he does is a different story. If this fails, then we can try another approach. And yet, I don't think that it will."

Lucy breathed out. She focused on the Architect's

mind and began to let only a little bit of her connection seep out.

She took Carth's arm and borrowed from her mind. It was the image Carth gave her, that of a dense forest behind her, a place unlike any Lucy had ever visited, and with that image in her mind, she Slid.

When she emerged, the air was humid. There was energy here, though Lucy wasn't sure what that energy represented, or if there was any way to ensure it wasn't harmful to her. The only thing she knew was that she detected it. The longer she was here, the more certain she was that the energy was real, and that she was following the right path with Carth.

"This is where the remaining Elder Stone can be found?" Lucy asked.

"It's possible. I'm not entirely sure, though the more I learn about it, the more certain I am there is something here."

"What now?"

"Now you will continue to hold your connection."

"Between the Architect and me?"

Carth nodded.

She maintained that focus, that connection, and could feel the presence of his mind.

This time when she Slid, she emerged where she chose, not where he was choosing for her.

"What now?"

"Now we go for support."

"What sort of support?"

Carth grinned.

An image formed in Lucy's mind. It was the way Carth

communicated where she wanted Lucy to Slide, and it never ceased to surprise her how much control she had over what she presented to Lucy.

"Do you think you can reach it?"

"Why there?"

"Because I believe that Daniel and Rayen are there."

Lucy frowned, focusing on what she could detect of the vision. "I don't feel anything from Daniel Elvraeth."

"It's possible that you would not. And Rayen would be similarly closed to you, though for different reasons."

"And if they aren't there?"

"If they aren't there, we will look elsewhere."

"How long do you think we have?"

"Considering we are dealing with Olandar Fahr? Not long."

"What if we aren't dealing with Olandar Fahr?" She held Carth's gaze. "If it's like you said, and the Architect has made plans of his own, what if Olandar Fahr doesn't come?" And the more Lucy thought about it, the more likely she thought that was. The Architect was the type to make such plans, and more than that, he struck her as the kind of person who would use what he had uncovered, and perhaps abuse it.

"I think we will be pleasantly surprised."

"What do you know?"

"It's not what I know, but what I suspect."

Lucy focused on what Carth had shown her and Slid.

They emerged on a rocky shoreline, a sense of power all around her, though it was different than before.

She could feel that power, the same way she felt the power coming from the Elder Stone or the flame. There was something about it that resonated with her, and she knew with certainty there was an Elder Stone here, though not which one it was.

She turned her attention to Carth. "What place is this?"

"This is Keyall, and in Keyall, they have a unique defense against the shadows."

"Because of their Elder Stone."

"That's right."

"And that's why Daniel and Rayen have come here?"

Carth nodded.

"How would they have known about it?"

"Because Rayen knew about it. And there's a man here I have some experience with."

"I don't know how to take that."

Carth waved her hand. "Nothing like that. It's been a long time since I've had any thoughts about anything like that. In this case, he's someone who offered me help, and we have stayed in touch, though less so of late."

"What kind of help has he offered?"

"The kind I needed when I was in trouble."

"I can't imagine you ever being in trouble."

"You'd be surprised. And when it has to do with Olandar Fahr, the trouble is often much greater than you realize at first."

"You were in Keyall because of Olandar Fahr?"

"I was in Keyall because of someone else, but I left because of Olandar Fahr. It's a unique place, or at least I thought it was."

When she turned away, heading toward town, Lucy realized she didn't do so on the shadows. It was almost as if the shadows faded away, drifting from her, or perhaps she lost control over them.

Lucy stared, frowning to herself. What had she said? This place had some natural immunity to the shadows. She tested her ability to Slide and found that hadn't changed at all.

"We can just Slide wherever we need to go," she said.

"We can, but I would like to make sure that everything is as it should be here."

"What do you think would be different?"

"That's the problem. I don't know."

There had to be some reason Carth wanted to come here that was about more than just Daniel and Rayen. She might not be the same strategist as Carth, but she understood the other woman had plans upon plans, and many of them involved aspects of things Lucy didn't fully understand.

They reached a building. A tall wall surrounded it, and lights glowed from the upper floors. A pair of guards stood at the front gate. Carth simply stood in the middle of the street, watching them.

"Why does it seem like you are taunting them?" Lucy asked.

"I'm not taunting, but I am contemplating."

"Whether or not we should Slide?"

"Whether or not they are here."

"Do you want me to check?" She tried to focus on Daniel Elvraeth's thoughts but found it was difficult for her to do so. It had been that way for quite some time, and the longer she was here, the less certain she was that she was picking up on them at all. She knew him well enough that she thought she should be able to find him, but perhaps he was caught up in something that prevented him from sharing.

"You might not be able to determine anything here."

"Why is that?"

"It's the nature of the Elder Stone in Keyall. It gives some protection from the shadows, but it does something else that others have yet to see."

"And what is that?" Lucy looked around.

"This place is unique. It's a place of significant trade, and yet it has managed to stay out of the workings of the world for many years."

"Aren't there other places like that?"

"You would think so, but most places with ports the size of Keyall draw notice. In the case of Keyall, it's almost as if the city manages to defy notice. It's not so much that people aren't aware that it's here. It's just that even being aware that it's here doesn't really draw the same attention to it."

"You think the Elder Stone here prevents others from discovering its presence?"

Carth shrugged. For a moment, she seemed to glow slightly, not much, but enough for Lucy to make it out. It faded quickly.

The shadows did not occur. Lucy wondered if Carth was trying to use them and failing, or whether it was simply a matter of her not even attempting to do so. If she were somehow restricted from using them in this place, then it might be that she had no interest in doing so.

"I don't know if it's the Elder Stone, but it does have some influence."

"What are we waiting for?"

"A good question. We have done our part, and now I think it's time for us to see if we've succeeded in drawing out the Architect."

Carth held out her hand, and Lucy took it. An image formed within her mind, that of a room, shelves of books. And an older man dressed in a maroon robe. It was almost as if Lucy had been there, and she focused on it and Slid.

DANIEL

THE AIR SHIMMERED, AND DANIEL TURNED, SUDDENLY ON edge. He Slid, reaching for Rayen, and took a step back, grabbing her hand as he prepared to Slide away. She watched him, and shadows wrapped around her, spreading from her.

As the air shimmered, Daniel turned toward it, ready for the possibility he would have to fight. He grabbed for his sword, wishing he had his cloak, but he needn't have been concerned.

Lucy emerged from a Slide, Carth with her.

Carth took one look at Alistan, nodding at him. "You found him. Good. We need to go."

"What is this?" Daniel asked.

"Apparently, this is a battle, and I'm going to need your help," Carth said.

His heart started hammering. Rayen nodded, going to stand near Lucy and Carth.

"You can stay here if you'd like," Carth said to Alistan.

"Does this have to do with the Elder Stones?"

"It does."

"Then I will go."

Carth smiled. "I suspected you would." She grabbed Daniel's cloak from a hook on the wall, tossing it to him, and nodded. "Lucy will take us there."

They crowded together, Daniel taking Rayen's hand, and as Carth reached for his arm, she looked over at Rayen. "It's about time."

"What is?" Rayen said.

"You have been isolated long enough."

Rayen flushed.

Carth glanced at Daniel. "If you do anything to harm her, you understand what I will do to you."

Daniel nodded, avoiding Lucy's gaze.

They Slid.

Traveling with Lucy like this was nothing like when he Slid. Hers was power and speed, a jarring sensation that jerked them free of this space and transported them quickly. They emerged with a forest in the background—a forest Daniel recognized.

"Ceyaniah," he whispered.

Carth glanced over to him. "Where did you hear that word?"

"From the people."

"You reached Ceyaniah?"

Daniel nodded.

"How?"

"I Slid there."

Carth breathed out heavily. "I wish I had known this."

"Why?"

"This is the location for the fifth stone."

"It's not. We've been here. They don't have a stone."

"They may not have told you that they had a stone, but trust me, I have found there is one."

"How?"

"By following Olandar Fahr."

"He's here?"

"Not yet, but he will be, which is why—"

Carth didn't have a chance to finish. The air shimmered, the sense of Sliding occurring, and Daniel stared at it, counting a dozen, two dozen, even more, all appearing in front of them.

The Ai'thol.

"Are you going to be all right?" she asked.

"I think so," Daniel said.

Carth cocked an eye at him. "I wasn't talking to you. I was asking Alistan. You, on the other hand, will be needed."

"I will be fine, Carth. You understand the nature of my ability."

"Use it, then."

With that, Alistan disappeared.

It happened suddenly, rapidly, and so quickly that he was shocked at how quickly he managed to vanish. Were the situation any different, Daniel might have laughed. Here he had thought that Alistan didn't have any ability, but he was able to make himself basically invisible. That had to be tied to the Elder Stone from Keyall.

"What's going on here?" Daniel asked Carth.

"What's going on is that we need to stop them."

"How did you know they were going to be here?"

"We've been following Olandar Fahr."

"How?"

"She had help."

Daniel spun around and froze.

Rsiran Lareth was behind him.

"You were dead."

"Was I?"

"But Haern—"

"Haern is doing what he needs to do. I'm doing what I need to do."

Daniel frowned. "You forced Olandar Fahr into this?"

"He thought that he could hold me, and he did manage to do so for a little while, but…"

"It took me a while to realize Lareth was with him. When I did, I realized we had an opening."

"What now?"

"Now we need to stop this attack. They can't reach Ceyaniah," Carth said.

"Even if we stop this one, another one will come, won't it?"

"Perhaps, but I don't know how many people the Ai'thol have who know how to reach it."

Daniel glanced over to Rayen. "Are we ready?"

"For this? Always."

She grabbed her sword, unsheathing, and slipped forward on the shadows.

Daniel Slid, drawing himself after her, using her shadows as he did. He emerged, fighting alongside her, and Slid, cutting down two Ai'thol when he emerged. He felt something behind him, a strange sense that tickled the back of his mind, and he Slid again, twisting.

When he emerged from a Slide, following Rayen as she

632 | D.K. HOLMBERG

flowed on her shadows, he carved with his sword, cutting down another of the Ai'thol. The men died quietly. It was strange, but it seemed almost as if they had prepared for this. There might be several dozen Ai'thol, but even powered as they were, they weren't strong enough to stop them.

"This is a distraction," he said.

"What?" Rayen asked.

"A distraction. They're here as a sacrifice."

Daniel froze, looking around. If he knew one thing about Olandar Fahr, it was that he played with strategy. Everything he did had intention behind it and was designed to position himself for greater success.

One of the Ai'thol Slid toward him, emerging directly in front of him, and Daniel Slid forward on the shadows, carving with his sword as he went. When he emerged, he cut through the Ai'thol, and the man fell in a spray of blood. It was strange he could Slide on the shadows, and stranger still that it seemed he could have a physical presence when he emerged, using that to carve through the Ai'thol.

He turned his attention to Lareth. He was a blur, *pushing* and *pulling* on lorcith, sending it streaking through the Ai'thol, carving them up.

Carth was fighting much like Rayen had been, using shadows and sending explosions of heat, but all of this seemed wrong.

Another dozen Ai'thol appeared.

Another dozen followed.

"This isn't right," Daniel said.

"What isn't right?" Rayen asked.

"This. The attack. There's something off about it."

Turning his attention back to Lareth, he frowned. "What if he was played?"

"Lareth wouldn't have been played. He's been facing the Ai'thol for as long as Carth."

"Yet if he was traveling with Olandar Fahr, what if he wanted Lareth to think he was successful?"

It was the kind of strategy Daniel could see Olandar Fahr using. He could see him sacrificing his own people in order to position himself for success. How better to do that than to draw those with the strength to stop him away from where he actually intended to be?

"Alistan!"

"What is it?" Rayen asked, gliding on the shadows over to him. She wrapped two Ai'thol in the shadows, holding them until they collapsed.

"This is all part of his plan."

"Are you sure?"

"No, but…"

Rayen glanced from him to Carth before nodding. "What if you're right?"

"I'm afraid if I'm right, then we have already been delayed too much."

Alistan suddenly shimmered into view in front of them. It was startling, as if he shimmered into focus, similar to how someone shimmered when they were Sliding.

"What is it?"

"We need to find the fifth stone. That's where Olandar Fahr will actually be."

"Not here?" Alistan glanced to where Carth was fighting, looking to Lareth.

Daniel shook his head. "I don't think so. I think this is all a distraction."

"She has said he is the most skilled Tsatsun player she's ever met."

"This is just the kind of thing I could envision him doing."

Rayen kept them safe while they were talking. Every so often she would use her control over the shadows to knock back a couple of the Ai'thol, and there seemed to be a flood of them, one after the other. Even with that, there was no sense of urgency. The Ai'thol didn't try to get past them so much as they tried to distract them.

All of this felt wrong.

How was it that Carth didn't recognize it?

"Well, we do know the others, including the wisdom stone. We have Lashasn and Ih and Keyall. If there is a fifth stone that we don't know about, it would be helpful to know where the wisdom stone is."

"Why?"

"As you suggested," Alistan said. "The other pieces are spread in a circle. The last stone would be similar."

Daniel thought about what he knew from the maps, envisioning where Keyall would be, tracking along what he knew of Ih and Lashasn, adding in the wisdom stone. It wasn't a perfect circle, but at the same time, it did somewhat ring the land. The only space missing was...

He turned back to the forest.

Ceyaniah.

Could that be it?

Here they had thought they had found only the Council of Elders, but what if that was not the case?

What if the tree represented the Elder Stone?

And he'd been there already.

"We have to go to Ceyaniah," Daniel said.

"Are you sure?" Rayen asked.

"I think we have to. Otherwise, Olandar Fahr is going to succeed."

"If he's never been here before…"

"Just because he's never been there, that doesn't mean he won't be able to reach it. What happens if he's already discovered some way in? Look at what we were able to do."

"We were able to do it because you used a combined ability."

"And he can't? Let's just go look first."

"Where would you have us go?"

Daniel looked around at the ongoing fighting. They could disappear. He didn't feel as if they were needed here. Carth and Lareth alone could handle this. The others fighting them were powerful, but not nearly as powerful as the two of them.

If he were Olandar Fahr, and if he had reasoned out where the fifth Elder Stone would be located, how would he approach it?

From the water.

Daniel grabbed Alistan and Rayen and Slid.

He emerged near the shore. The forest rose behind him, impossibly dense, and at first he thought he was wrong. But then he turned.

A fleet of ships headed toward the shore.

There had to be two dozen ships, and several had already unloaded their passengers on the shore.

"You were right," Rayen said.

"I need to go get Carth."

"You need to get an army," Rayen said.

"Not an army," Alistan began, clasping his hands in front of him, staring at the ships. "But a way to redirect. In this, perhaps having Rel here would be beneficial."

"Do you want to stay here, or do you want to come with me?"

"I think that I need to stay," Alistan said.

"I was talking to Rayen."

"I'll stay. Someone has to keep an eye on him."

Daniel Slid.

When he emerged, back in the battle, he found Carth and Lareth along with Lucy confronting dozens of Ai'thol.

"It's a feint," he said, getting next to Carth.

"How do you know?"

"Because the real attack is along the shoreline."

Carth frowned, the corners of her eyes tightening for a moment before she shook her head. "Still playing games," she whispered.

"Ironic coming from you," Daniel said.

Rather than answering, Carth glided to Lucy and tapped on her arm, and they disappeared in a Slide.

Lareth looked over at him. "Where did they go?"

"Apparently the real battle is along the shore."

Lareth looked around him. "A sacrifice? All of this for a sacrifice?"

"I can help you."

"Go and join the others. I can take care of this."

Daniel looked around. There had to be forty or fifty Ai'thol still remaining.

"You can't do this on your own."

"They have captured me enough times. They made the mistake, though, of revealing how."

"How did they do it?"

"A metal I hadn't known about before. Now that I do…"

With that, Lareth shot into the air, hovering there.

He glanced down at Daniel. "It's easier if you go."

"Why?"

"I don't have to worry about hitting you."

Metal began to spin around Lareth, and Daniel Slid.

When he emerged along the shoreline, Carth and Lucy were on the shore, facing Ai'thol with far more skill than he expected. Soldiers from Ceyaniah appeared, heading toward them.

That wasn't his fight. They had that part of it, but there was something he could do. He would ensure that Olandar Fahr didn't reach the Elder Stone.

LUCY

THE SOUNDS AROUND HER WERE CHAOTIC, AND SHE TRIED to ignore them, knowing there wasn't anything she could do to fight. War wasn't Lucy's strength. There were others —like Carth and Rayen and Daniel, of all people. They were skilled fighters. As the battle progressed, Lucy understood she was not going to be a part of it.

Carth glided over to her on a slip of shadows. "It's time to go."

Lucy nodded, focusing on the Architect. He was nearby, she could feel him, and yet, she wasn't sure how close he had to be.

"Do you think we'll find Olandar Fahr?"

"I don't know. With as many Ai'thol as are appearing, I have to believe we will."

"Unless there's another reason."

"I don't know what the reason might be, unless…"

Carth pushed out with the shadows, her body starting to glow for a moment. She frowned, and her jaw clenched. It did that when she was thinking, planning, and

Lucy couldn't help but wonder what sort of plans Carth was coming up with now. And more than that, she couldn't help but wonder how they might involve her. Whatever Carth was doing, it could be dangerous.

The other woman nodded to her.

Lucy took Carth's hand, and they Slid.

They traveled toward a shoreline. When she emerged, she stepped free of the Slide, half expecting to be trapped or to feel the same pressure she had when dealing with the Architect before.

This time, there was no such pressure.

Ships were out on the sea, and there were a dozen or two people along the shoreline. All of them were Ai'thol, but not all of them had scars.

The Architect was there.

She hadn't seen him in months, but he looked much the same as then. Deep green eyes stared at her as he stalked along the coast, unmindful of the battle raging around them.

She nodded to him, and Carth ignored her. She had both swords in hand, and shadows were swirling around, striking at the Ai'thol. Suffocating them.

The way she attacked was brutal and deadly, and she brought them down quickly, carving the Ai'thol apart.

"Is he here?" Lucy asked.

She didn't feel as if she were trapped, but she worried something might happen that would hold her here. Having suffered under the Architect before, she didn't know if he'd be able to find some way to ensnare her.

"I don't see him," Carth said.

Lucy focused on the Architect.

He was a hundred yards away, standing along the shoreline. There were six others flanking him, all wearing dark cloaks, the style so different than the typical Ai'thol. None of them had the usual scar on their faces.

"Take them down," she said to Carth.

The other woman ignored her, and Lucy Slid over to her, shaking Carth, forcing her to pay attention. "I need to get the Architect, and you need to remove the people surrounding him."

Carth shook herself free, and she glanced along the shoreline, taking in the sight of the Architect. Shadows streamed away from her.

They reached some sort of resistance.

"Interesting," she said.

"You can't get to them?"

"No. But I can do this."

With that, Carth exploded forward in a mixture of her connection to the flame and the shadows. She jumped, gliding on the shadows through the air, and landed in front of them.

She brought her sword around, twisting, shadows swirling and thickening around her, and as Lucy watched, she could swear there was something pressing against Carth's shadows, but she couldn't make it out.

The more she watched, the more certain she was that whoever was fighting out there had incredible power. Carth tore through them, overwhelming their attempt at resisting her shadow magic, exploding with heat. Her entire body glowed each time she did, and then that glow retreated, backing away into the shadows.

She carved through them, her sword spinning, a spray of blood following her.

Three Ai'thol approached.

Lucy focused on their minds. She could feel their presence. There was resistance, and she forced her way through it. As she did, she Pushed.

It was a simple thing. A demand that they protect her.

They spun, marching down the shoreline, away from her, and into a different fray.

She had no qualms about using her power in that way, and none about using it against these people. What she was doing was necessary. She stormed forward, following the three soldiers who now defended her, and as they encountered more Ai'thol—some of them suddenly appearing, Sliding here—she Pushed on them.

It was a strange thing to be walking along the shore, with the sun shining overhead, the ships bobbing out on the waves, and feeling a chaos that came not from the water, as she was accustomed to, but from the violence all around her.

And it *was* chaotic.

It was difficult to tell if she was the only one fighting. Carth was tearing through some of the attackers in the distance, but there seemed to be something more taking place. As she watched, she thought that some of the Architect's men were fighting with other Ai'thol.

That couldn't be right. Could it be that she was Pushing on them?

It was hard for her to tell. She didn't have much control over Pushing, and yet it seemed as if they were acting on her behalf.

It was possible that was nothing more than her imagination, and so she continued to try to Push, gathering more and more soldiers toward her.

At a certain point, Lucy suspected she would reach the extent of her capability. The request was simple: *Protect her.* She wasn't trying to control them, and she wasn't attempting to direct how they did it, but with a strong enough Push, she didn't have to do any of those things. All she had to do was influence them in such a way that they would respond to her—and for her.

The five soldiers now in front of her reached Carth. She sent a quick Push, demanding they protect her as well.

They parted around Carth, hacking through the Ai'thol safeguarding the Architect, and Lucy focused on him.

She Pushed.

There was resistance, so she sent more and more power against him, straining to hold him here. She didn't have any way of preventing him from Sliding but realized she didn't have to do so completely on her own. Carth had her shadows swirling around the Architect.

It might not hold.

The resistance was there, and Lucy remembered what it had been like. It was the same resistance she had experienced when she had been trapped by the Architect the first time.

With that realization, there came a building pressure upon her.

She Pushed again.

This time, she attempted a Slide, but only within her mind.

She had no idea if it would even work. When she had attempted to do so before, it had seemed effective. She found resistance within the Architect's mind and continued to send more and more energy at him, trying to override anything he might do.

She reached through that resistance.

And then beyond.

The resistance was there, but with her connection to Sliding, she was able to Push beyond the barrier the Architect held. He could no longer avoid the power of her attempt to Push.

The request was as simple as it had been for the others.

You can't Slide.

She forced it with as much energy as she could, making the command tear through his mind.

And then she retreated.

She had no idea if it was even going to work, but she thought convincing him he couldn't Slide would hold him.

Something struck from behind her, and she spun around. A tall man with gray hair strode along the shoreline. He flickered as he went, Sliding with each step. Power swirled around him. She was unable to see anything but that power. It was almost as if he held the shadow and the flames and...

Olandar Fahr.

"Carth!"

The other woman glided toward her.

Lucy pointed, and Carth started toward him. Lucy spun her soldiers toward Olandar Fahr, sending one more Push to the Architect: *Sleep*.

Then she focused on Olandar Fahr.

Could they end this? After everything they'd gone through, everything they'd experienced, would they finally be able to stop him?

The soldiers ignored Carth and headed toward Olandar Fahr. Somehow, he used a surge of power that parted the soldiers on either side, sending them scattering.

He stopped directly in front of Carth. She tried to use shadows, but he managed to ignore them. There was an explosion of heat, but that didn't seem to faze Olandar Fahr, either. He was far too powerful for anything that Carth might throw at him.

"You won't reach the Elder Stone," Carth said.

Olandar Fahr grinned at her. "Do you think that's what I care about?"

"I know you're after power."

"I have power. Why would I need to chase even more?"

Carth held the shadows out in front of her. It occurred to Lucy she was using them as a barrier as much as anything else, as if she were nervous about what Olandar Fahr might attempt. "The same reason you've been chasing power for as long as I've known you."

"You can't begin to understand what I've been doing," he said.

"I might not, but there's one who does."

Olandar Fahr smiled tightly. "I will have him brought back to me."

"Are you so certain?"

"Do you think your small ability to influence someone else's mind matters to me?"

"It matters when it prevents you from using your soldiers against us," Carth said.

In the distance, others began to appear on the beach. They were strangely dressed, wrapped in silks, carrying spears, and they were moving with incredible speed, racing along the shoreline.

Lucy stared. She'd never seen anything like it, but with the way they moved, she could barely keep track.

An image floated into Lucy's mind, and she understood what Carth wanted of her. It came with resounding clarity.

Carth wanted her to take them away from here.

Why, though?

It was more than just wanting her to take Carth away. She wanted to bring the Architect away.

But they had Olandar Fahr.

As she watched, she realized they didn't have Olandar Fahr. Everything Carth was doing, all the power she was throwing at him, wasn't enough.

They had no way of stopping him. That was the point Carth was trying to make. Even though he stood in front of them, the first time she'd ever seen him, they wouldn't be strong enough.

Which meant that they had to find some other way.

If they could anticipate what he was doing, the way that he might attack next, then perhaps they might be able to stop him.

There was something else Lucy might be able to try.

She focused on Olandar Fahr, trying to Read him.

It was like ramming into a wall.

She'd never felt a mind so secured. She'd encountered others with an incredible ability to prevent her from reaching into their mind, but his was like nothing she had ever experienced.

Worse, she was aware of these others racing toward her.

She Slid, grabbing Carth, and Slid again, emerging briefly, grabbing the Architect, and then Slid again.

She emerged for a moment back near the battlefield, but the battle was over. There was no one there. Daniel and Rayen had gone somewhere else, and even Lareth had disappeared, going off to wherever he was traveling.

"Where to?" she asked Carth.

"The tower," she said.

Lucy nodded, and they Slid.

They emerged at the base of the tower, and Carth pushed open the door, heading inside, leaving Lucy to Slide the Architect. He remained unconscious, the Push enough to keep him sleeping. With him out, she used her ability to Read, rifling through his mind, but even now, there was resistance.

Once inside, she looked to Carth. "Where do we take him?"

"There is someplace inside here."

Ras appeared on the stairs, and he looked down at Carth. "I don't think this is wise."

"It might not be, but we can use him to get the answers we need."

"And what if he uses us to get the answers he needs?"

Carth frowned. "Do you feel that you are so incapable of protecting yourself from someone like him?"

"I don't know anything about him. It's possible he is far more capable than anyone we have ever encountered here."

"I'm sure you will manage well enough."

Another image appeared in Lucy's mind, and this one was here, but a place that she had never visited.

She Slid, carrying the Architect.

She emerged within the cell and released him.

Stone walls rose all around him, and there was a sense of energy here that came from the shadows, but also from something else. It was likely from some of the other Elder Stones, though she had no proof they had any power here. The walls were unadorned, and the entire place was cold, though she wondered if it were intentionally so. Most of the rest of the tower was warm. She backed away from the Architect, leaving him. In the time that they had been here, he had yet to move. She was prepared to Push on him if necessary, but there hadn't been the need.

It took a few moments before Carth got there, and once she did, she remained for a moment, looking around at everything within the cell. "This was supposed to hold Olandar Fahr," Carth said.

"Do you think it would?"

"I don't know. There was a time when I thought we would've been more evenly matched, but that wasn't the case today."

"Who are those others coming along the shoreline?"

"I don't know. I suspect they come from Ceyaniah, and

yet, unless I have an opportunity to ask Daniel and Rayen, it's possible we'll never know."

"What about the rest of the Ai'thol?"

"You had Pushed most of them."

Lucy nodded.

"Then they will do as you asked."

"I had them defend me. And you." She looked up from where the Architect lay on the ground, and met Carth's eyes.

"It's unlikely they will survive this," Carth said.

"Will it be worth it?"

"We won't know until he begins to share." Carth crouched down, staring at the Architect. "I imagine you have attempted to Read him?"

Lucy nodded. There was no point in denying it.

"And were you successful?"

She shook her head. "He blocked me from his mind."

"That's unfortunate, but not unexpected. We have other ways of obtaining information from people like him. He will share, whether or not he wants to."

Lucy shivered, and yet, after everything the Architect had done to her, he deserved to be questioned. He deserved to be the reason they found out what they needed to in order to stop Olandar Fahr. And he deserved whatever fate would befall him.

She hoped she was strong enough to see it through.

DANIEL

SHADOWS CAUGHT DANIEL'S ATTENTION, LINGERING NEAR the edge of the forest. When he emerged from the Slide, he found Rayen with Alistan just at the edge. "What are you doing?"

"I thought I saw someone coming in here."

Daniel looked through the trees, following the shadows. From here, he could trace the movement.

They would need to get to the tree first.

The Slide carried them through the forest and directly into the massive tree. The abruptness of it—and the energy required—was staggering. Daniel had grown accustomed to not feeling weakened by Sliding, and the fact that he did this time surprised him a little.

He took a deep breath, releasing Rayen and Alistan, and looked around the room. A lantern resting on the table glowed with a soft light.

"What is this place?" Alistan whispered.

"Apparently, this is the Council of Elders." Rayen made her way around the table, looking at each of the seats.

Without having their escorts here as they had the last time, there was more freedom for them to move about. "From what we understand, there are other places like this scattered throughout the world."

"Tables like this, or chambers like this?" Alistan asked.

"Perhaps both," Rayen said.

Alistan made his way toward the seats and the table, but the strange barrier prevented him from getting close. "Where are we?"

"Someplace inaccessible other than by Sliding," Daniel said.

"How did you find it?"

"With some difficulty."

He looked up, and Daniel followed the direction of his gaze. The tree opened up high overhead, creating a domed ceiling. There was nothing else in the chamber other than the table.

"Where are we?" he asked again.

"Inside of a tree," Daniel said. Alistan watched him, and Daniel shrugged. "Strange, I know."

"What else is strange is that these symbols match up with symbols I've seen for the elders," he said.

"What symbols?" Daniel asked.

Alistan motioned for Daniel to follow him, and when he did, he realized what the other man was pointing to. Each stool had a symbol worked into the top of the seat.

Daniel hadn't noticed that, but when he'd been here before, he'd been focused on the strangeness of the place. "Do you recognize them?"

"I don't, but I think I could find them."

"Back at your place," Daniel said.

Alistan nodded.

It felt as if they were going back and forth, and he still had not restored himself completely from the Slide here. He needed a little bit longer, and yet, within this place, his connection to the shadows seemed stronger than it had been in a while. Within Keyall, the shadows were gone, and the connection that he had to them, the strength they lent him, was missing.

Daniel sank down on one of the seats and breathed out.

"You should not be here."

He looked up, and Charlanna stood with her arms crossed in front of her, two of the men with spheres on either side of her. "Charlanna. We were just—"

"I know what you were just doing. We have just prevented another from trying to reach a place where they should not have been."

Another? Had they stopped Olandar Fahr?

What about Carth and Lucy?

Even if they had prevented Olandar Fahr from reaching this place, how long would they be able to do so? If he now knew that this was the location of the Elder Stone, it wouldn't be long before he returned, better prepared. And if he succeeded, what would happen?

That was the question, wasn't it? None of them knew what would take place. Olandar Fahr wanted access to the Elder Stones in order to utilize that power, but they didn't know what would happen if he succeeded. Would he be granted the power of the Great Watcher?

Charlanna took a step into the room and realized

Daniel was seated at the table. Her eyes widened slightly. "What are you doing?"

"I'm sorry. I was tired after reaching here. I know I shouldn't have presumed that I could sit."

"You should not have been able to."

"What?"

She approached him and stood just behind one of the other stools. "You should not have been able to sit."

"I don't understand."

She moved forward as if to take a seat and was rebuffed by the barrier in place around it.

"You should not be able to sit. What have you done to the table?"

"I didn't do anything." Daniel got up and glanced over to Rayen, who was moving forward, trying to get closer to the table and meeting with the same sort of resistance as Charlanna had.

"I can't either," Rayen said.

"Have you damaged the Council of Elders?" Charlanna asked.

Daniel stayed close to the seat, confused. What had happened? It didn't make any sense, but then again, he wasn't sure it was supposed to make sense to him. None of it had any reasonable explanation, and considering how old this table had to be, and the fact that it represented something he didn't fully understand, it was possible that he couldn't comprehend it.

"I didn't damage anything," he said.

He stepped away, and the seat he had taken began to lower.

It was a strange thing to observe. The seat slowly

descended, dropping silently into the ground as if being pulled under.

"What… what just happened?" he asked.

Charlanna's eyes went wide. "One of the Council has been chosen."

The Elder Stones Saga continues with book 5: The Depth of Deceit.

A dangerous plan might be the only way to defeat Olander Fahr.

With the threat of another attack, Haern must use his new abilities to make a dangerous gambit. Doing so requires he trust someone who has betrayed him once before, and count on others who still don't fully understand the nature of their abilities. If they succeed, they might finally be able to stop Olander Fahr before he manages to acquire another of the Elder Stones.

Daniel struggles to understand his connection to the shadows along with what it means that he can sit at the Council of Elders. When a new threat appears, his unique understanding of the shadows might be the key to survival.

Lucy continues her search to discover the longer game. With the Architect now imprisoned, she has access to someone who can guide her to where Olander Fahr might attack next, but they remain a step behind. A growing fear that someone has deceived her leads her in a new direction, but it's one that will require her to make a dangerous choice.

Isolated within the city of Lexa, Ryn must continue to serve the Great One, but a new challenge to her authority forces her to look for power in a different way.

Plans unfold, but for the first time, all begin to wonder if the one behind them is different than who they had believed. And if not Olander Fahr, who is the real threat?

The Lost Prophecy

The Threat of Madness

The Warrior Mage

Tower of the Gods

Twist of the Fibers

The Lost City

The Last Conclave

The Gift of Madness

The Great Betrayal

World of the Cloud Warrior Saga

The Cloud Warrior Saga

Chased by Fire

Bound by Fire

Changed by Fire

Fortress of Fire

Forged in Fire

Serpent of Fire

Servant of Fire

Born of Fire

Broken of Fire

Light of Fire

Cycle of Fire

The Endless War

Journey of Fire and Night

Darkness Rising